WHAT
THE
HAND

WHAT
THE
HAND

TODD STOCKWELL

ZFS PUBLISHING

Edited by Cheryl Redman

For Zoë

This is a work of fiction; the Bible is truth.

The Tyger

Tyger! Tyger! Burning bright
In the forest of the night,
What immortal hand or eye
Could frame thy fearful symmetry?

In what distant deeps or skies
Burnt the fires of thine eyes?
On what wings dare he aspire?
What the hand, dare seize the fire?

And what shoulder, & what art,
Could twist the sinews of thy heart?
And when thy heart began to beat,
What dread hand? & what dread feet?

What the hammer? What the chain?
In what furnace was thy brain?
What the anvil? what dread grasp
Dare its deadly terrors clasp?

When the stars threw down their spears,
And water'd Heaven with their tears,
Did he smile his work to see?
Did he who made the Lamb make thee?

Tyger! Tyger! burning bright
In the forests of the night,
What immortal hand or eye
Dare frame thy fearful symmetry?

– William Blake

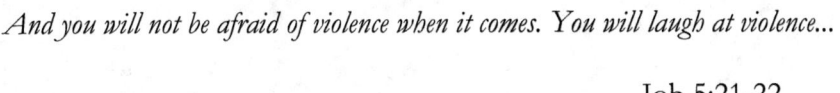

And you will not be afraid of violence when it comes. You will laugh at violence...

Job 5:21-22

1

I live in a shack on the outskirts of paradise, and I'm lucky to have it. It is stark, rectangular, made of a thin yet sturdy wood. Outside my window is a blue meadow surrounded by low hills of a bright orange grass, colors not seen on the old Earth. In the distance I can see the great houses of the meek and humble, and further still, the mansions and estates of the children, saints, and martyrs. And I am glad for them.

***

I have a new body. We all have new bodies. Had I known I'd be getting a new body, I probably would have eaten more junk food. There isn't any junk food here. We could have it if we wanted, I suppose, but nobody wants it now that we know what it actually tastes like. It tastes like poison, like antifreeze or drain cleaner might have tasted to us back then, back on the old Earth, where our bodies had been acclimated to the chemicals in these foods since birth to such an extent that most of us believed junk food tasted really, really good. So good, in fact, some people would get into their vehicles in the middle of the night, drive to an establishment that sold such food, order two cheeseburgers, french fries, a large soda, and some sort of cake or pie to boot.

Even if there were junk food here, it wouldn't affect the new bodies. Nothing affects the new bodies. There is no physical pain here; nor is there death. And there won't be any, not for a thousand years—992 to be exact.

***

The new bodies are pretty neat. They glow kind of like a light under the water or like an old casino sign.

***

I'm different than I was; it's not just the new body—I'm a different person, more childlike I suppose. Not like the selfish, spoiled, adult child I was on the old Earth. Christ said you have to be like a child to enter the Kingdom of Heaven. That might explain some of what I feel.

***

My immediate neighbors are folks like myself who made it into paradise by a spider hair. We had heard about Jesus and God and everything but chose to ignore it all, preferring to lie, and steal, and cheat, and cuss, and fornicate, and on and on. That is, until all the crap came down, and we suddenly found Jesus.

These neighbors live in shacks like mine. Well, not exactly like mine. Some people have painted or added little doodads here and there like they did on the old Earth. It didn't help then and it doesn't help now. A shack is a shack is a shack....

I thank the good Lord every day for my shack, my undeserved patch of paradise.

***

I hardly know anyone in my neighborhood. Like on the old Earth, nobody really wants to be friends with their neighbors here either. It would be like staring into a mirror all the time. Who the heck wants to do that?

Most of my friends didn't make it into paradise anyway. They are waiting out the thousand years with Satan in the pit. Then there will be a final judgment and one last chance at salvation. But there isn't a lot of hope for them. A person can't hang out with a guy like Satan for a thousand years without picking up more bad habits.

***

Yeah, there is a devil and Hell. There is Jesus and a new kingdom on a new Earth, and Heaven and angels, and all that other business in the Bible that nobody has to guess about, or argue about, or fight about, or kill each other over anymore.

***

Even though I live in this shack, I get to visit my daughter Sophie in her big house. All the children were given big houses when they arrived here. God figured they deserved them after living with adults who beat them, abused them, starved them, lied to them, or did any number of awful things to them.

I was pretty good to my daughter Sophie on the old Earth. I only cheated on her mother, broke up our family, lied to her all the time, and ignored her occasionally. Oh, and I was a big fat hypocrite, too.

Sophie lives in her big house with her mother, my ex-wife, Renee; I wasn't invited.

***

The best part of paradise is the time I get to spend with my daughter. It was also the best part of the old Earth. But you never would have known it.

***

I didn't get to see Sophie or her mother for a long time, not on the old Earth, not after the Rapture. Oh yeah, there was a Rapture—people disappearing all over the place and whatnot. I was playing catch with Sophie when she disappeared. It was just like it was written in the Book of Matthew: "Then shall two be in the field, the one shall be taken and the other left." I lobbed a ball, and it landed where Sophie had been standing not a second before. I knew right then what had happened, and I was happy for her, for both of them. The good people and the children got to go to Heaven early because God wanted to spare them the ugliness and the blood and gore and death and destruction, and every other horror that was to come with the seven year period of judgments known as the Tribulation.

Sophie was thirteen when she vanished from the old Earth, and then I didn't see her for all those years—except when I arrived in the New Kingdom she hadn't aged one bit. I nearly fainted from happiness. It would have killed me had I missed all that growing up. She is twenty-one and a young woman now.

***

The Rapture left behind a lot of death and destruction even before the Tribulation, pilotless planes careening toward the ground, cars crashing all over the place and whatnot. But later, after all the mayhem we'd seen, we joked about it anyway. We would sit around our cave chuckling like idiots at some of the Rapture stories we'd heard. Like the woman yelling at her husband as he drives down the road, only to realize nobody is listening or driving the car; or the guy on the operating table waking up with his stomach cut open and not a surgeon in sight; or the tandem skydiver suddenly realizing the instructor isn't there to pull the ripcord. Looking back, the stories weren't very funny at all. We just didn't have much to laugh about in those days.

***

I lived in a few different caves back then. Things were pretty awful on the old Earth. If you didn't live in a cave or suck up to the Antichrist, you'd be tortured in all manner of disgusting ways, until you either died or denounced your faith. I knew I'd cry like a baby before they even threatened to pull out a fingernail, so I decided to run for the hills at the first sign of real trouble, figuring I could hide until it was over.

***

Jesus said no one would know the exact time or day of his return, but the Mayans were fairly close. They predicted the world would end in 2012. They were wrong; 2012 came and went without a hitch. Still, it wasn't a bad guess when you consider the prediction was made some 5000 years before it all ended. They were into the occult; that's how they got close. They were also into cutting the hearts out of their live captives as a sacrifice to their gods. Those gods were actually demons messing around with their heads. These were the same demons who told them to make the calendar that ended in 2012.

***

Demons were always off with their predictions, and it was the same for anyone dabbling in the occult: Nostradamus, Edgar Casey, Jean Dixon, Mother Shipton, the Sumerians, the Egyptians, the Hopi Indians, and on and on. These mystics, soothsayers, seers, psychics, or whatever you want to call them, tapped into the future, but it was like looking through a drinking glass full of dirty water, so they were always getting the little things wrong, like dates and facts.

Nostradamus was better at it than most. Still, nobody knew what he was talking about half the time because he wrote down his predictions disguised as poetry. He had to be careful because, back in his day, some busybody might call you a witch, and the next thing you knew you were being burned alive, drowned, hanged, or some other nonsense just for even thinking you knew what was going to happen.

***

But you didn't have to predict things to be labeled a witch. Way back when on the old Earth, they might just burn you for being weird, or different, or stupid, or smart, or ugly, or pretty, or for no reason whatsoever.

***

A couple years back, I met a young woman, Isabel, once accused of being a witch. Isabel told me she had been burned alive at the stake in 1552. According to law, they were supposed to strangle people first before they burned them, but the audiences were always complaining about the lack of screaming, gore, and other good fun, so the executioners usually left out that somewhat critical step.

It was Isabel's husband who accused her of witchcraft. He did it because he wanted to marry a younger girl. Isabel herself had been forced to marry him when she was only fourteen. Her husband was forty-two when they were married. Forty-two was ancient back then. Lots of nice young girls were forced to marry ancient men in Isabel's time on the old Earth. That was when young girls first began throwing up on a regular basis—long before anorexia, bulimia, low self-esteem, and all that other madness had them doing it on purpose.

Since Isabel was an old woman in her early twenties, her husband wanted nothing to do with her anymore. He had his eye on the pretty thirteen-year-old daughter of the neighbor, another young girl who wanted nothing to do with him.

***

In my day on the old Earth, young girls and ancient men would get married all the time. They didn't have to marry; they married because they were foolish and insecure—the old men I mean.

***

Isabel's husband testified that he would wake up in the middle of the night to find his wife outside their cottage howling at the moon. Rather an obese fellow, he also testified she had placed a spell on him that made him eat everything in sight.

Nobody believed any of it—howling at the moon was merely a stereotypically evil trait even way back then, and Isabel's husband had been eating everything in sight since he was little, but Isabel's husband knew one of the guys on the tribunal, and the whole thing was a big gyp before it began.

Poor Isabel was dragged to the center of the town square, where they tried to get her to fly by beating her with sticks. Next, they took her to the weigh house because some genius in the church decided witches must be lighter than normal if they could fly, except nobody knew exactly what her normal weight should be—or anyone's, for that matter. So what did they do? They made something up.

By the end of the day Isabel found herself tied to a stake above a huge pile of wood. She passed out from fear or from the beating or both, but unfortunately her melting feet woke her up, and she suffered an agonizing death. What a world it was.

***

Most of the yahoos deciding who was and was not a witch worked for one church or another. And as much as God didn't like people messing around with the occult, these witch hunters were much more misguided, hypocritical, and evil than any of the people they were persecuting. That was when churches and religion in general began to get a bad rap.

***

Isabel had never howled at the moon or cast any spells. She wasn't even a very good cook and had absolutely nothing to do with her husband's huge appetite. She hadn't seen the future either. The only thing Isabel ever predicted was that her marriage would be miserable. She was right.

***

If you really want to know, the only place to find accurate predictions is the Bible. From Genesis to the Book of Revelation, there are over 10,000 predictions, and everything predicted has passed or will pass shortly. These aren't vague predictions like Nostradamus wrote. There are over 500 specific predictions in the Old Testament describing the coming Messiah alone, each fitting Jesus to a tee. The mathematical probability of even fifty of these predictions coming true is something like one in ten to the seventeenth power. That's a ten with seventeen zeros. To put that into some sort of context: you'd get better odds on shooting a three-pointer with a medicine ball from the moon.

***

And though there were all kinds of predictions from the Bible knocking everybody on the head in the last years, hardly anybody woke up. You couldn't turn on a television or radio without becoming depressed over some riot, war, storm, hurricane, tornado, earthquake, tsunami, fire, disease, or somebody starving to death or something. Jesus said these nightmarish events would be like the contractions of a woman giving birth: more intense and frequent as the delivery neared. He wasn't kidding.

***

No, most people, including myself, ignored all the signs. We mostly blamed it on nature, climate change, bad people, bad politics, bad luck, or some such thing. I guess nobody wanted to believe the end was near.

***

If you want to get technical, the end of the world never did or will occur, but the old Earth ended when Jesus returned. First, the Rapture came, taking with it about two billion people. Then, after more wars, the Antichrist solidified a one-world government, calling it the New World Order, offering peace and prosperity for a time. Except once he took power, he made it practically impossible to buy or sell anything without worshiping him as God and taking the Mark of the Beast—the once fabled 666 engraving or tattoo—which was actually a tiny computer chip embedded in the forearm and later in the forehead, after many changed their minds and dug it out of from under their own skin.

The New World Order originally wanted the chip to be placed in the forehead, predicting such behavior, but so many refused they went with the less invasive wrist procedure. That was until criminals began kidnapping people all over the place, lopping their arms off, and running over to ATMs with their newly acquired and grotesque swipe-cards. This unusual banking method was enough to sway the masses into receiving the head implant.

***

It was around that time I finally wised up and fled the city to live in a cave. Because, back when I was busy lying and cheating and stealing and fornicating and whatnot, a friend of mine, Charlie, who was always trying to convince me that Jesus was the only way out of my crappy life, told me about all of the stuff that was going to happen, and he also said this: "George, if one day lots and lots of people suddenly disappear and some maniac sets up a one-world government, do not, I repeat, do not take a mark or an implant or anything, even if it means starving or dying. Listen to me—do not take that mark—it will mean eternal damnation." Charlie's advice got me into this place.

***

It amazes me how so many people, familiar with the Bible, confronted with the Rapture, the New World Order, the Antichrist, and all the other predictions coming true, could have accepted the Mark of the Beast. I guess if some people are hungry enough, they will take on a future of eternal damnation in exchange for a meatball sandwich.

***

True, the New World Order did try and cover up the Rapture with a story of mass alien abductions, but it was pretty slim stuff, especially after the Antichrist began setting up shop.

The Antichrist was even mortally wounded like it was predicted in the Bible. Yep, some lonely, wannabe religious hero shot him right in the head with an exploding cartridge. It was all over the television, even—brain matter flying out the back of his head and everything. Three days later he was as good as new and more famous than the Beatles. Satan loves irony.

Yet, there they were, those who knew all about the predictions, anxiously waving their marks over the chip scanners to collect their pizzas, cheeseburgers, and all manner of cakes and pies, while I was on the run and could only dream of such goodies. So dream I did.

***

One of the Beatles, John Lennon, said the band was more popular than Jesus Christ. He was wrong. There were about a billion Christians and maybe one hundred million Beatles fans when he said it. He later apologized.

In 1980, a disturbed, attention-seeking young man, Mark Chapman, shot Lennon in the back outside his New York apartment. Chapman said he heard voices telling him to do it, but it was just demons messing around again.

***

Demons were always messing with people's heads. It was one of their favorite things to do, right up there with outright possession. They used to make a lot of crazy movies about possession: *The Exorcism of This One* and *The Haunting of That One*. People on the old Earth loved to see spinning heads, projectile vomit, contorting bodies, deep voices coming out of little girls, and all kinds of terrific junk like that. What most people didn't know was how real that stuff was. They found out after the Rapture when the demons were unleashed. That's why they stopped making all those exorcism movies; in fact, they stopped making horror movies altogether. Who would pay good money to see something they could watch from their own windows for nothing?

***

Besides, most of the movies made after the Rapture were about how great a one-world government would be, where everyone would live in harmony and peace and love, speak the same language, use the same money, wear the same clothes, drive the same cheapo cars, and have slumber parties or some such nonsense all the time.

And after the Antichrist took power, most of the movies were about him and how great he was, how we were all so lucky to have him as our leader. These movies were so boring they had to threaten people to go see them. If you didn't see at least one boring New World Order movie or one boring Antichrist movie a month, you'd be on some sort of list and men in black jumpsuits would drag you out of your house and beat the crap out of you. You could watch people getting the crap beat out of them all day long if you wanted.

***

But that was near the beginning of the Tribulation, before things really got interesting on the old Earth. By the grace of God, I missed the worst of it while hiding in caves. I made my first cave as comfortable as I could; it was roomier, at least, than the shack I have now. But it didn't last, as I was hounded and chased from cave to cave by the Minions of the Antichrist.

***

It was while hiding in my third cave that I met Danielle Knowles. We called her Danny. It was a deep cave and the safest one I'd found. I thought I was in love with Danny, except I didn't know anything about love.

I spotted her group with my binoculars one afternoon, peering out of my hole in the mountain. They were pillaging through the canyon below for food and searching for a cave of their own. They were the first people of any kind I'd seen in over a year, and I nearly broke a leg in my haste trying to get down the canyon to them.

***

Danny was eight years younger than me and looked like a 1940s movie starlet or at least a Suicide Girl. She had a nineteen-year-old son named Roger, with an IQ of 65, making him a target of the New World Order. The New World Order euthanized the cognitively challenged, the mentally ill, the very old, the feeble, and pretty much anyone who wasn't, in their opinion, genetically sound. That's why Danny took him and ran.

***

The Nazis did the same with their less desirables, except they were having so much fun, they expanded their program to include gypsies, homosexuals, criminals, communists, intellectuals, priests, Jehovah's Witnesses, Poles, Czechs, Russians, Jews, of course, and pretty much anyone else they felt like murdering. What a world it was.

***

Fortunately, The New World Order didn't get the chance to erase too many cognitively challenged people because most of them were taken in the Rapture, but Roger didn't make the cut because he was also a devil-worshiper and a psychopath.

***

I scared the bejeebers out of them when I emerged from the bushes with my scrappy beard, dirty clothes, and overall disheveled appearance. Joe Mellon, a retired police officer, almost shot me with his service revolver. He would have, too, except he was getting older and slower at drawing and firing, so I had plenty of time to duck behind a rock and yell out that I was a friendly. They didn't take long to convince because anyone with my appearance couldn't be of the New World Order, as the Minions of the Antichrist were well fed, cleanly shaved, and sharply dressed in their black jumpsuit uniforms.

Also in the party were Billy Sanchez, a line cook and ex-convict; two middle-aged sisters named Ida and Eva; a bulky, gay phone repairman, Howard Frost; and a twenty-four-year-old office clerk, who was in such shock after watching his wife raped and murdered that he forgot his own name. The sisters called him Speckle because of his large eyeglasses and small frame.

We became a tight little tribe for a while, until they were eventually picked off by Satan's Minions, or done in by demons and various disasters. Except for Roger, who took a few Minions down with him in a blaze of glory, as psychopaths are wont to do; and Danny, who left and became a martyr because she was braver and godlier than the rest of us; and me, of course, lucky me—I never did die. I got to see it all.

2

I've been here in paradise, or the New Kingdom, for nearly eight years, though it seems more like two. Time isn't like it used to be. You could be sitting around thinking about some little thing that happened or something stupid you did on the old Earth, and the next thing you know it's already a week later.

But you don't have to be too careful with thinking about things and losing time. People expect you to be late or even missing altogether, and they don't get offended at all or think you're some sort of flake like they would've on the old Earth.

***

Anyway, I should at least attempt to start somewhere near the beginning. My name is George Somerset, and I was born November twenty-second in the year 1967. That was exactly four years from the day President John Fitzgerald Kennedy was assassinated. On my birthday, the television would be filled with highlights of the president's life, the whole Kennedy clan running around Hyannis Port and the White House and whatnot. But mostly they'd run footage of the assassination. They'd play that over and over again. There'd be Kennedy, year after year, riding in that big open limousine with the First Lady, smiling and waving at everybody like he was just going to have another wonderful day at being the president and all.

I'd stand in front of the television in my footed pajamas, yelling loud as I could at the driver of that dang limo, "Speed that thing up, you dummy!" But sure as anything, that driver would continue crawling down the road without a care in the world, like he was going backwards practically.

The next thing you know, the president's brains are flying all over the place, and his poor wife is hanging over the trunk, trying to gather up her husband's scalp, all the brain matter and other gook, to put it back in his head, they figured, though nobody ever asked her.

***

They blamed it on a supposedly lone assassin named Lee Harvey Oswald. Oswald was mostly a patsy, as even he later figured out, another puppet of the Illuminati, who told him it was a good idea to shoot at the president. And since he was tired of everyone ignoring his ideas, ignoring all the things he said he did or said he was going to do, he listened.

***

The Illuminati were demons, more or less, and they'd been around for centuries. In my day they wore business suits and ran the world. There had always been demons on the old Earth, in many forms, beginning with Satan himself, slithering around Adam and Eve, tugging at their elbows, just like that one kid you knew who was always trying to get you to do something rotten.

Satan eventually brought down the rest of his buddies, other fallen angels, who mated with human women, creating the giants, the Illuminati, and the false gods: Zeus, Poseidon, Aphrodite, Isis, Athena, Hercules, Hades, Prometheus, Cupid, Venus, Mercury, and the other characters you read about in elementary school—they weren't just mythological figures. Who the heck could make those freaks up? Every culture passed their stories down. Sure, the stories had been exaggerated over time, but they actually walked the planet.

***

How do I know all this? I looked it up at the Hall of Knowledge. It's only a couple of miles from my shack. The Hall of Knowledge is more or less a giant library the size of ten or twelve Walmarts, and you can look up anything you feel like, anything at all. I found out where the Ark of the Covenant was stashed, why so many ships and planes were lost in the Bermuda Triangle, where Bigfoot was hiding the whole time with practically every hillbilly in America out looking for him, and how the universe was created. I even looked up how many sneakers I went through as a kid. And since the new bodies are a lot smarter than the old ones, you understand and remember most of it, no matter how dumb you were on the old Earth. Heck, you could probably learn quantum physics or something in a couple weeks.

***

Walmart was a giant store on the old Earth where you could buy pretty much anything. It was full of cheap products made in China. After they built a Walmart in your town, people wouldn't have to go into a bunch of smaller stores and buy quality products from people they knew whose families owned those smaller stores for generations. They could go to one place and spend a lot less money for their junk. Walmart was supposedly owned and managed by Christians. But the only good news they offered was that everyone in town could get a minimum wage job out of the deal if they wanted.

***

Yep, you can learn most anything at the Hall of Knowledge. The only thing you can't learn is how to be a better human being; that you have to do all by yourself—just like on the old Earth.

***

Anyway, I found out the Illuminati were bred from the favorite children of the fallen angels, the cream of the crop, stronger and smarter than their own brothers and sisters, or any five humans—some who could pick up a man and throw him like a Frisbee, and some who knew everything about everything. They knew about the planets and the stars, about space and time, about math and science, and they knew how to build things.

These demon offspring told the humans to worship them as gods. They made slaves of the humans and forced them to build statues and monuments in their images, so the humans could pray to them. Many of them were giants, some over ten feet tall, who caused havoc everywhere they went.

After some time, though, humans began to figure things out. They saw that these "gods" could be injured, that they grew old and died just like men. They eventually realized they weren't gods at all. Tired of them taking their women and pushing them around all the time, the humans rebelled. At first they killed a few in their sleep. Emboldened, they gathered in groups, attacking them head on. It was one of the bloodiest eras in history. Realizing their number was up, the false gods fought dirty and took as many humans with them as they could, but the sheer numbers eventually overwhelmed them. The false gods were on the run, hunted for centuries, until their numbers dwindled to just a handful of the stealthier ones, and the era of gods and giants became legend.

It was far from over, however. Hiding deep in the earth, these demon outcasts got together and figured out that a twelve foot guy with one big eye in the middle of his forehead, strolling to the corner store for a gallon of milk, might be somewhat of a target to the riled-up humans.

Thus, a new breed of Illuminati was born—demon offspring who could pass for humans. These were cold, robotic creatures, blending, mating, and working undiscovered among us. With their super intelligence, they acquired land, wealth, and power. The Illuminati formed and hid for centuries in the higher degrees and levels of Masonic clubs and other secret organizations, pushing their agendas on unsuspecting governments and corporations through manipulation and mayhem until they had enough power to control the world and pave the way for the Antichrist.

***

Lee Harvey Oswald was later killed by another Illuminati victim, a Dallas businessman with links to organized crime named Jack Ruby. He shot Oswald on television just like it was with the Antichrist, except it was in the stomach, in black and white, and too fuzzy to see the blood and guts and everything. Since Ruby had a lot more self-esteem than Oswald, and he wouldn't be talked into doing such a stupid thing like shooting someone on live television, the Illuminati had to threaten him with a Sicilian necktie.

***

A Sicilian necktie is a method of execution wherein the victim's throat is cut and the tongue pulled out through the slit. The Italian mob stole the idea from the Columbians, who came up with it in the late 1940s to send a message to political opponents. The message was this: don't mess with criminals or politicians.

***

The actual shooters in the JFK assassination were a professional hit team from France, hired and trained by the Illuminati. Just when the assassins began licking their chops, ready to collect all that money from the great job they'd completed, the Illuminati had them all whacked, too. You can't trust anybody!

***

I spend a lot of my time at the Hall of Knowledge, looking up the things that puzzled me when I was on the old Earth—things like disappearances, ghosts, dinosaurs, Heaven, Hell, creation, and all kinds of neat stuff. It's all there, anything you want to know.

Yes, I looked up Jimmy Hoffa. It turns out he wasn't killed by the mafia after all. No, aliens abducted him because he had a big head. Aliens were always abducting people with unusual features for this or that genetic experiment. That time they were looking for large brains, but when they cut open Hoffa's head they only found a thick skull, so they ended up tossing the whole mess.

Jimmy was pretty unlucky as far as alien abductions go—usually, they'd harvest some sperm or a few eggs, erase your memory, and drop you back on the highway naked or something.

They could easily get you back in your clothes, except most aliens are practical jokers. You wouldn't know it by looking at them, but aliens have a good sense of humor. They tend to be a bit mean spirited with their jokes, but, after all, they are related to the fallen angels.

It's true. Fallen angels and aliens share the same genes. Aliens didn't come from outer space, not originally anyway. When the outcast demons were making the new and improved Illuminati using their own DNA, they messed up quite a bit before they got what they wanted. These failed experiments made for all kinds of freaky humanoid creatures. Most of them were smothered or drowned, but some of them were pretty smart and useful, so they decided to keep them around. However, this became a problem because the creepy things mated and multiplied like cockroaches.

That is until one of the demons came up with an idea to build some rocket ships and send them off to other planets. For thousands of years, there were no aliens on the Earth. But once these deported space misfits became settled, and after some time, they began building their

16

own spacecraft, better machines—flying saucers and such. The aliens even figured out how to travel through wormholes, so they could pretty much go anywhere they pleased. After populating planets across the universe, they began their own genetic programs, spitting out aliens of every shape and size to use for their own creepy agendas, but mostly to do the bidding of Satan and the Illuminati.

***

Even though the Illuminati are genetic cousins of aliens, they have no sense of humor whatsoever. This is because the Illuminati were engineered to be utterly ruthless, coldblooded individuals, capable of anything, no matter how awful, especially if it moved them closer to one-world government. And they did their job well, pretty much running the show on the old Earth, causing pain, heartache, suffering, misery, and mayhem wherever they roamed. In any case, they didn't have a lot of time for practical jokes.

***

As far as Illuminati mayhem goes, The Kennedy assassination was relatively mild. It would barely crack their top 100, even as far as assassinations went. The last presidential assassination was a real doozy, however. It occurred on the old Earth after the first Jewish president, Arthur Joshua Friedman, was elected.

***

It took nearly 200 years for the United States to elect a Jewish president. Why did it take so long? For all its posturing of freedom and equality, like much of the western world, America was founded and ruled by white Protestants, who mostly believed that other races were inferior. And believed it or not, Jews were the most hated people of all time. They were more hated than Blacks or Latinos or Arabs or Asians or Indians or anybody else. It wasn't even close. No other people in history were despised, maligned, hounded, beaten, enslaved, persecuted, tortured, murdered, and exterminated to such a prolific and horrific extent.

***

Still, the Illuminati didn't assassinate President Friedman because he was Jewish. They had him killed because he wouldn't cooperate with their agenda. To dispose of the defiant President Friedman, the

Illuminati convinced another fellow who needed attention, the trusted White House gardener, Curtis Trout, to take a brand new red riding lawnmower onto the White House grounds. Trout was nicknamed Bigmouth by teammates on his high school swim team because he wouldn't shut up even in the water. The new lawnmower didn't actually work, though, because it was gutted and packed with an explosive device. What Bigmouth didn't know was that he wasn't smuggling in just any explosive device, but a small tactical nuclear bomb.

When Bigmouth set the twenty-minute timer, he assumed he would already be heading up the Washington Parkway toward Baltimore, safely on his way to his niece's sweet sixteen. The gardener had been molesting his niece since she was eleven and wanted to be there for her at the celebration.

He knew he would get caught eventually, but Bigmouth was looking forward to all the attention he would get from the media, the chance to tell his story over and over again, to go down in history, and whatever else he was daydreaming about as he turned onto the Parkway. But instead of achieving all that glory, he was vaporized along with 62,000 other people within a thirty-block radius of the White House.

***

The Illuminati looked to kill two birds with their nuclear assassination. Besides disposing of an uncooperative president, the Illuminati wanted to cripple the American economy to help usher in the one-world government. The destruction of the Capitol and the cleanup of the fallout would be another huge blow to America's finances, already depleted by poor management, terrorist attacks, unending wars, and recurring natural disasters.

***

The Illuminati made a big mistake when they helped Arthur Friedman get elected, and lots of people died because of it. They were also wrong about the sixteenth president, Abraham Lincoln. They were good with civil wars and all, but they didn't like old Abe messing around with the great institution of slavery. The Illuminati were all about slavery since they invented it a long time ago to mine for gold and other metals they needed to build spaceships for the aliens and otherwise control the planet. They also used slaves to help build the great pyramids.

***

I found that out at the Hall of Knowledge when I was trying to figure out how they managed to move those big pyramid stones since they weighed about two and a half tons apiece. The slaves, however, as most historians believed, were not there to move the stones, but only for the finish work and to get drinks and stuff. How did they move those great big stones? Magic—well, it would have looked like magic to the slaves and the other humans anyway, but it was actually an anti-gravity device developed by aliens.

***

As history would show, though the Illuminati convinced the actor John Wilkes Booth that his greatest performance would be on the balcony of the Ford Theater instead of the stage, slavery would not last, at least not in its very public form.

Yes, the Illuminati would lose this cherished invention of theirs as public policy; but not to worry, they were able to keep many of their other great inventions like war and murder, rape, abortion, torture, child abuse, human trafficking, prostitution, pornography, and on and on.

3

I spent my youth in the San Fernando Valley, a suburb of Los Angeles built on the backs of the aviation, military, and film industries. My father, an engineer, worked on various missile programs for Hughes Aircraft. My mother was a housewife and living saint.

***

Howard Hughes launched Hughes Aircraft in 1932 and would become the first American billionaire. The Bible states that it is "easier for a camel to pass through the eye of needle than for a rich man to get into Heaven." This is a bit of an exaggeration, but it was meant as a warning because it was pretty darn difficult to get into the New Kingdom if you died with lots of cash. Why? That kind of money kept most people separated from God. But the Bible doesn't say money is the root of all evil, it says: "Love of money is the root of all evil." So if you were at least willing to give it up at some point, you might have made it into paradise; otherwise, you were left open to vice, obsession, greed, paranoia, materialism, egotism, and especially demons. And the more obsessed with money you became, the worse it would get, until the demons were pretty much running your life.

Howard Hughes eventually went mad because he tried to hold onto his money without listening to the demons. The demons wanted him to participate by putting millions into the furtherance of one-world government. Since he refused, they tormented him with their voices until he went insane—so insane, he spent his last days in a dark room

20

wearing Kleenex boxes on his feet, counting piles of green peas, and pissing in jars.

Howard's demonic experience was a blessing in disguise, however. For his choice of insanity over capitulation to the Illuminati, he squeezed through the eye of the needle and landed in paradise. He now lives here in a place called Tent City, the only place in the New Kingdom where the dwellings are more humble than the shacks where I live. He lives there with most of the other rich people from the old Earth who did something or other good at the very last minute to escape the pit. And like the rest of us, he doesn't urinate at all anymore.

***

The Valley was a good enough place to grow up I guess. We spent most of our days running around with the other kids in the neighborhood. Back then, parents would let their kids out the door in the morning for school, or play, or to smoke cigarettes and knock each other in the head, and didn't much think about them till dinner time. Parents didn't worry that some maniac or pervert might steal their children off the streets.

But that all changed in the late seventies when kids began disappearing all over the place. Hardly any of these kids were taken by aliens. Aliens couldn't take anybody who didn't open themselves up to demons in some way. Since kids were mostly innocent and protected by guardian angels and all, demons and aliens usually left them alone.

On the other hand, child-raping, murdering psychos were grabbing children left and right. These sick individuals had been around a long time. They just hadn't received a lot of heat or press because, for centuries, unwanted, orphaned, and runaway children were viewed as disposable, so they had plenty to choose from. I mean way back when, you could send a kid to work for fifteen hours in a dark mine or some other awful place, beat the crap out of them, lock them in a closet for the night without food, and hardly anyone gave a gosh. Who had time to worry about a few missing or murdered throwaways?

Much later, laws were enacted specifically to protect children from maniacs and awful parents. These laws helped people to view children in a more protective light. Orphans and runaways were harder to come by, so when these scumbags began crawling out of their holes in droves to kidnap and otherwise harm any kid they could get their hands on, the public took notice.

***

In 1979, a six-year-old boy named Etan Patz left his New York apartment to catch the school bus. He was never seen on the old Earth again. To help in the search for the missing boy, his photo was placed on a milk carton. By the mid-1980s, you could hardly find a milk carton without some poor kid's picture on it. One minute you're all set to have a great day running all over the place with your friends or whatever, pouring milk on your Captain Crunch, and the next thing you know, you're staring at some kidnapped kid who might have been tortured and murdered and only God knew what else.

It was enough to give any parent a permanent panic disorder. Most parents just stopped letting their children out by themselves altogether. And by the early nineties it was pretty rare to see a little kid walking around alone. The sounds of children at play in the streets of the old Earth were all but muted, their childhoods stolen by a handful of murderous and perverted creeps.

***

Of all the outrages that went on during man's reign on the old Earth, the abuse, molestation, kidnapping, and murder of children was the saddest and most horrible. It got so bad God almost cut free will to intervene again, just like he did when He wasted everyone in the Great Flood. But instead, Jesus or one of His angels would jump into a kid's body right before they were to be molested, punched, choked, tortured, or otherwise harmed, to endure the suffering for them. That's why many of these poor kids, if they were found alive, couldn't seem to remember much when interviewed by detectives or psychologists.

***

Yeah, there was a big flood that wiped out most of the planet. Even some of the most skeptical Bible-hating scientists agreed on that one. Yes, there was a Noah, and he built an ark and stuffed the whole thing with animals. Yes, it rained for forty days and forty nights. The darn thing was sitting right there on top of Mount Ararat in Turkey the whole time. Nobody could find the ark because it was so high and covered in ice and snow most of the time. Besides, the Illuminati told the Turkish government to keep everyone the heck away from it so the truth of its existence wouldn't attract any more believers. Yes, I read about it at the Hall of Knowledge.

***

Most of that missing kid stuff, thank the good Lord, was after my childhood. In my day every kid in the neighborhood gathered on the streets in front of their homes to play football, hide and seek, ditch, catch, ride skateboards, stand around, throw sticks, or whatever else they could figure out to keep from dying of boredom.

What a hassle that was for us, too, because we didn't have all that high-tech gaming junk, the internet, iPods, iPads, or cell phones and whatnot. If you wanted to make a phone call, you had to walk all the way to the kitchen. If you wanted to listen to music, you had to mess with a big old record player or tune it in on the radio. If you wanted to know something that wasn't taught in school, you had to go to a public library and check out a book with a little card in it and a date stamped on it. And if you didn't return the book by that date, they'd fine you a nickel a day or something, and that was just about your whole allowance. And so you wouldn't have any money for practically a month, but your dad would spank the crap out of you anyway for being irresponsible, when you were just trying to finish the stupid book and you forgot because you were just a dumb kid.

***

For the most part, the Valley was rows of same-like houses with same-like families. The moms stayed home while the dads went off to work. My mother was the sweetest lady on the planet and my life saver; my father was pragmatic and hard, and he yelled and whipped us an awful lot.

***

I have two older brothers, Gerry and Geoff, and a younger sister, Gina. Parents were always giving their children names with the same first letter in those days. I guess it made it easier for them to yell at us or get everybody moving in the same direction. And the names were always called in the same order, from oldest to youngest, so we couldn't tell who was in the most trouble: "Gerry, Geoff, George, Gina, get in here," or "Gerry, Geoff, George, Gina, take the trash cans to the curb," or "Gerry, Geoff, George, Gina, who broke the mustard jar?" and on and on.

***

Every weekend we were dragged to the local Catholic parish for services and catechism classes. Church was an hour of torture, but catechism was worse because it seemed to take over most of our Saturday, the rest of which was spent pulling a never-ending crop of weeds or doing some other made-up chore in our backyard.

That yard was only about 1100 square feet, but somehow it was never quite finished, at least not to my dad's satisfaction. I don't know how he came up with so many projects in that tiny backyard. I guess it was because he spent most of his childhood doing chores on a farm in Nebraska, so he figured we needed to work even if there was nothing to do.

***

I don't know why I dreaded church so much as a kid. I'm not sure if it was the hard pews, the kneeling, the old priest who always seemed to be yelling at us when he was only reading, my mom pinching us for squirming, my father smacking us on the back of our heads for fidgeting, or just the heaviness of the place. It felt ancient or something, like the very first pope himself might show up at any minute. Or perhaps it was the overwhelming presence of my own guilty conscience. Whatever it was, I couldn't wait to get out of there every Sunday. And, unfortunately, I stopped going to church as soon as my parents stopped forcing me to go.

***

I was pathetically skinny growing up. I barely had any chest at all. I should have been bigger, though, because I could sure eat. It seemed like I was famished all the time, even though I stuffed my face all day long. I could eat three chickens at one sitting when I was only about eight. My mom couldn't understand where I put it all. I would sneak into the kitchen after everyone went to bed and eat a bowl or two of cereal, and more if I had had to fight my brothers for the leftovers at dinner because I would always lose.

I would lose because my brothers were much bigger, but also because I was a horrible fighter to begin with. My father wasn't the type of guy who would teach you neat junk like fighting or pay to have

24

you sent to karate school or someplace. Some of the kids in my elementary school already knew karate and kung fu and boxing, and all kinds of cool stuff like that. This one kid, Tory, would smack other kids around every day with his karate. One day at recess, I beat him to the drinking fountain, and he karate-chopped me in the neck and then kicked my feet out from under me in about a second flat, knocking me on my butt. It hurt like heck, but it was pretty impressive how smooth and fast he dropped me. He was only nine years old.

***

I attracted lots of bullies growing up. It was mostly my fault. The most attention I got from my brothers was when they were pushing me around, so I learned to pester them until they came after me. But it didn't stop with them. I became a smart aleck to anyone and everyone, not having the good sense to pick and choose with any caution those I verbally slighted. And the more annoyed someone became with me, the more I word-punched, until they whined, walked away, or smacked me.

I didn't learn my lesson until I was a sophomore in high school. I guess I hadn't been beaten hard enough till then. It all started when I was placed at the same table as Susan Shaker in second period Home Economics. She was a junior and the snotty girlfriend of a particularly large and nasty senior named Bret McNeil.

***

Mostly only girls took Home Economics back then, but this class was full of males, me included, because of the unusually attractive teacher, Mrs. Enderbiden, who was Swedish or Danish or something, and always wearing these fantastically tight skirts and sweaters. She was pretty much the main topic of conversation among the boys for all three years of high school.

***

Anyway, I don't remember exactly what I said to McNeil's girlfriend to set her off. I just remember she bugged the crap out of me because she kept referring to Bret as her fiancé, which was completely ridiculous because she was only a year older than me and neither of them even had a job or anything, but it was just the sort of pretentious thing she would always say anyway. She'd say stuff like, "My fiancé is taking me to Bob's Big Boy tonight," or "My fiancé and I just love the strawberry milkshakes at Bob's Big Boy," and on and on.

I must have said something stupid because she turned to me with the coldest stare I'd ever seen on a girl. "My fiancé is going to beat the living tar out of you after school today." The way she said it, so matter of fact, already scared the living tar out of me. Always on the ready with some clever retort, for once, I had practically nothing to say. All I could manage was, "Huh?"

"You heard me," was all she said, and she turned her back to me.

***

I don't think I was ever that afraid in my whole life, not even when I was hiding, flat on my belly, deadly silent, watching the flashlights of the Minions of the Antichrist bouncing off the walls of our cave.

***

I stared at the large clock till the end of that period, and again during each of the four remaining periods, begging the hands to slow down, listening to the seconds tick, each louder than the loudest droning lecture, louder than the loudest classroom racket.

Too soon, the last bell of the day rang. I was shaking, but for some reason I didn't freeze, nor did I seek help from a teacher, which would have been the smart thing to do. No, I picked up my books and shuffled out of that classroom and down the hall like a condemned man escorted by invisible guards.

I couldn't bring myself to look up as I walked, but I could sense something different around me. The movement in the hall was abnormal. It didn't flow with the usual rush of students anxious to escape the dullness of public education. I lifted my head slightly. They were congregating, waiting against the walls in their little cliques, whispering and pointing. And just as I realized it was all for me, I ran into a wall of a boy. Bret McNeil, at least a foot taller and three times my width, blocked my path. I looked up at him because I had little choice, except maybe to continue staring at the floor.

This kid was central casting for bully. He had blonde, scraggly hair with hints of red throughout, a deeply pocked and freckled face. His nose was extra sharp, his long chin seemed to pull his bottom teeth away from his upper lip in such a way that he always looked to be

26

grimacing in pain. His small eyes stared hard at me, popping from their sockets like loose contact lenses. "You messin' with my girlfriend?" McNeil snarled.

The pockets of students moved in around us. I couldn't drop a pencil in that hallway on any other day without being spotted and hollered at by some overly vigilant teacher, but, of course, none were anywhere to be found as I was about to die a bloody death not five feet from one of their classrooms.

I had nothing to say at that moment; I couldn't have spoken if I had. I looked down. He pushed me. "You hear me?" he shouted, even more fired up now because of the crowd and my inability to respond.

"No," I finally said, barely audible.

"What did you say, you little punk?" and he pushed me again.

I was forced back a few steps, but I just kept staring at the ground. "No," I said a little louder.

"Look at me!"

I didn't want to look at him; he was scary up close—heck, even far away. But he grabbed my chin, lifting my face till I was looking straight up his dirty nose. "That's my girlfriend, scrub. You don't mess with my girlfriend!"

I was about to plead for my life when, out of the corner of my eye, I spotted something that changed everything. There was Susan Shaker, front row to the coming slaughter, grinning from ear to ear like she'd just won a first class trip to Fiji for her and her dumb boyfriend.

I'm not sure why, but seeing the look on her face took the fear right out of me. I wasn't afraid at all any longer; in fact, I was angry, so I did what I always did when I was angry or cornered. I opened my big fat mouth. "I thought she was your fiancée?" I said, stretching out the word fiancée as long as I could to get the full effect.

Of course, it was a big mistake. The crowd broke out laughing. I glanced up enough to finally view the surrounding horde. They were having a lot of fun at our expense, and for about a half a second I was actually enjoying myself, too, until I looked back up into the now red face of Bret McNeil and realized he had no choice but to give me the beating of my life. And so he did.

***

Bret didn't knock me unconscious or anything, but he pummeled me to the ground, giving me a black eye and a bunch of other bruises. I made only a halfhearted attempt at fighting back because I knew I would get it worse if I resisted. After a while, figuring I was done, he left me to nurse my wounds.

**

Kids back then, even big dumb jocks like McNeil, had a lot more scruples when it came to fighting. I mean a kid might beat you up and all, but he wouldn't keep kicking you in the head or something once he knew you were beat. I don't know how many videos I have seen where some kid was already unconscious, yet the kicks and the punches and the bottles, and everything else kept coming without mercy. Nobody died from a fight when I was a kid, but in the years before the Rapture, kids were often seriously injured, brain-damaged or paralyzed—even killed—in stupid fights over nothing. There was no longer any sense of fairness or sportsmanship, or whatever you want to call it. The old Earth had become a violent free-for-all even on the playgrounds.

**

I didn't hate Bret McNeil or Susan Shaker after he kicked my butt on her orders. In fact, in just a few days, I felt no animosity toward them whatsoever. But that was the way it was with me. I don't know why, but I just couldn't hold a grudge. Maybe that's why God didn't hold my botched life against me.

I actually felt sorry for them in a way because they weren't very likable people. It seemed they only had each other. He was a football player, but none of the other football players wanted to hang out with him. And she was so nasty to be around that everyone avoided her like the cafeteria meatloaf. I never said one word to them after the pummeling, but they continued, until they graduated, to scowl at me when I passed them in the hallways.

**

I also realized they had done me a favor, teaching me to choose my words more carefully, saving me from an unknown number of beatings and retaliations.

**

28

Bret and Susan actually did get married right out of high school, or so I heard. I wonder if they stayed together. Perhaps I'll go and visit them to ask them about it—I mean if they made it here. I hope they did. Honestly.

***

That was the weird thing about first coming to the New Kingdom. You might have gone out of your way to find somebody you hardly knew or didn't even like on the old Earth, just to ask them about something stupid. Or to look for some complete stranger you read about to confirm some fact or story, like you were all the sudden some kind of reporter or investigator or something. But no one was in any kind of rush to see all the people they were close to on the old Earth when they arrived. I mean I saw my daughter straight away, but it took me three months to visit my poor mother and father, and over a year to visit my siblings. I guess I was too busy working through my own junk and just plain feeling guilty.

***

Even if I had died and gone straight to Heaven, I wouldn't have seen everyone right away. People on the old Earth often assumed that once you got to Heaven you'd be greeted by all these dead relatives like some kind of big ghostly family reunion. Or they'd all show up to welcome you and teach you the ropes like they have it all figured out or something—aunts and uncles and cousins and everyone hugging you, escorting you around and whatnot. I barely knew any of them when I was alive. What the heck would you say to everyone after just having had the shock of your life, realizing you're dead and all?

***

All in all, I suppose my childhood was pretty normal; at least I wasn't abused or anything like that. It sure didn't account for all the trouble I got into later. I pretty much acted like a delinquent jackass until I left the San Fernando Valley to join the Army at twenty-three, and even after that.

***

I finally did learn how to fight, though. The Army taught me hand-to-hand combat, and even how to kill a man. Then they sent me to Fort Sill in Oklahoma to drink beer.

29

4

It took me twenty years to leave the San Fernando Valley and as many to get back. It was during my divorce from Renee that I decided to go live somewhere cheap and familiar, so I was living in an apartment near the house where I grew up when the tactical nuclear bomb took a big chunk out of Washington and killed the Jewish president.

***

Everyone assumed it was another Islamic terrorist attack, as was the intention of the Illuminati. And because the bomb was small enough and so effective, and there was no trace of evidence left to say otherwise, everyone continued to believe it.

The Illuminati plan was to get the American people all juiced up, patriotic, and on the offense again, just like we'd been after Islamic terrorists brought down both towers of the World Trade Center, put a hole in the Pentagon, and destroyed three passenger jets, causing the gruesome deaths of some 3000 men, women, and children going about their business. They wanted us to support another attack on a guilty or not-so-guilty country.

A fourth plane, United Airlines Flight 93, missed its intended target after a group of gutsy passengers stormed the hijacked cockpit with hot coffee and a snack cart, saving the White House and any number of its inhabitants. Still, the hijackers were able to place the plane into an irreversible nosedive, crashing it into a strip mine in Pennsylvania. There were no survivors.

I read something strange about Flight 93 at the Hall of Knowledge. Two of the hijackers, who just minutes earlier had stabbed a female flight attendant and slit the throats of the two pilots, were steering the doomed plane and daydreaming about the seventy-two virgins they were promised and a bunch of other nonsense driving them to commit horrible acts of homicidal madness and destruction in the name of their god, when they heard the loud banging of the snack cart on the cockpit door as it was being pummeled open by the ` determined passengers.

Once they realized they would never make it to the White House, the hijackers sent the plane diving toward the Earth. They were able to yell, "Allah is the greatest!" a few times before being drenched in hot coffee.

After that, writhing in pain from the hot liquid pouring down their faces, they screamed incoherently. The passengers tried to pull the plane out of the nosedive, all the while praying aloud. Everyone was disintegrated along with the plane when it hit the ground.

The next thing the passengers knew, they were standing with Christ in Heaven. They said they hadn't felt a thing. The hijackers weren't as fortunate. But that isn't the strange part. The strange part was the last words of the hijacker sitting in the copilot seat.

He said this: "Sweet Jesus!"

***

The Illuminati plan to get Americans hyped up over the nuclear attack on the Capitol worked like a charm. Americans wanted revenge. This time it was decided that it would be a good idea to help Israel bomb Iran back into the Stone Age. I was all for it. I had been duped along with everyone else, although I found out later the Iranian attack was justified anyway. Not for any specific terrorist act, but because the Iranian leader was another Illuminati puppet who was getting ready to annihilate Israel.

This nut was told by demons that he needed to build a nuclear weapon and launch it at Jerusalem in order to usher in Armageddon, just so a character called the Twelfth Imam could establish an Islamic paradise.

What the demons knew that the Iranian leader did not know was that Armageddon was going to come anyway, and the Twelfth Imam was just another dead guy who couldn't come back even if he wanted to. And he didn't want to.

How do I know? No, I didn't read about it at the Hall of Knowledge; I asked him. The guy once known as the Twelfth Imam lives eight shacks down from me. He was just an ordinary kid when he was on the old Earth, and he told me the whole thing was a big misunderstanding, which the demons then exploited to make him the spearhead of a fanatical sect of Islam:

"It all began when I became lost in the mountains near my home in ancient Persia while on a hunting trip with my father," he said. "For some reason, my father was embarrassed and told everyone that Allah took me. I wandered around the wilderness for a few days until a caravan heading to Assyria picked me up. I had no choice but to go with them or die in the mountains. After what my father said, people were making up all kinds of stupid stories, like the one about me hiding in the caves until my return centuries later to save the Muslim people. How ridiculous is that? I was only eight years old. How could I survive in cave for week, let alone hundreds of years, even if someone could live that long? What a lot of goat poop!"

***

If Armageddon was going to happen with or without the nutty Iranian leader anyway, why did demons bother to put all these crazy ideas about the Twelfth Imam into the Iranian leader's head? They were messing around again.

***

The American-supported attack on Iran by Israel opened up a huge can of worms in that region, paving the way for one of the great miracles predicted in the Old Testament by the prophet Ezekiel. The prophecy described an attack on Israel by a coalition of forces from Russia, Iran, Turkey, and Sudan. This attack would be so overwhelming that the destruction of Israel would seem like the only possible outcome. However, God would intervene with "fire from the sky" and help Israel destroy the invading armies before they could do any damage.

Israel had been worried about Iran's nuclear program for many years. Iran's alliance with Russia was a major factor in the Israeli government's hesitation in doing something about it. But the rhetoric from the knuckleheaded Iranian leader, who had already asked for the destruction of Israel, had been heating up. Together with the confirmation that Iran was then ready with a functioning warhead, the U.S. clamoring for some form of payback was enough to get the attack off the ground. In six hours of sorties, Israeli Bombers with laser guided missiles and American cluster bombs decimated Iran's nuclear facilities.

Three months later, Iran and its cohorts were on the offensive, with the Russian Air Force and the Turkish Navy backing them. All seemed lost for the tiny nation of Israel. Neither the U.S. nor any other ally had time to react. Minutes from annihilation, Israel felt it had little choice but to implement the Samson Option, which would launch enough nuclear weapons to basically disintegrate not only their attackers, but all of the surrounding area, including Israel itself.

***

The Samson Option was named after the Biblical Samson, who was granted superhuman strength by God, the source of which was embedded in his long hair. Samson's strength was taken from him when his backstabbing girlfriend, Delilah, had his hair shaved while he was sleeping. This enabled his longtime Philistine enemies to capture him. The Philistines tied him to giant pillars in their temple to sacrifice him to one of their demon gods. The problem was they waited too long and some of his hair had grown back. Still, he wasn't strong enough to break his bonds, so he prayed about it, and God returned his strength and then some, except the Philistines were too many and they had spears and bows. Samson decided if he was going to die anyway, he might as well do God a favor and take down some Philistines with him. So he destroyed the pillars along with the temple, killing himself and most of the hated Philistines.

***

I looked up Philistines at the Hall of Knowledge. They were a particularly nasty group of devil-worshipers, full of giants and other demon offspring. They were all about causing mayhem and havoc and waging war on the Jews, and God despised them for it.

God despised anyone who messed with the Jews. This is what the enemies of Israel never understood. The Jewish people had been through enough. God promised that once Israel became a nation again, it would never be taken. God protected the Jewish state with a vengeance. Nations whose polices were against Israel were cursed and would not prosper. Those who waged war against the tiny country, no matter how superior their forces, would be soundly defeated. In war after war, battle after battle, against overwhelming odds, Israel crushed its attackers.

***

The idea behind the Samson Option was developed by the new Jewish state from their centuries of persecution—especially the Holocaust, where too many went quietly to the trains, camps, and ovens because they didn't want to believe what was happening. They vowed never to go down again without a fight. And they never did.

***

As it turned out, Israel did not resort to the Samson Option, but they came very close. The news and the media would later downplay the whole event, calling it a freak accident of nature. But however they spun it, the incident was an undeniable and complete miracle. This was how one of the few reliable news sources of the time put it:

Seconds from their targets, hundreds of Russian, Iranian, Turkish, and Sudanese Jets and bombers filled the skies, while navies from Turkey and Sudan advanced from the Mediterranean and Red Seas, the Israeli finger ready on the Samson trigger. But from the clouds, there clapped a great thunder, and rips of lightning struck the morning sky from every direction. Fire rained down and red hailstones big as boulders followed, crushing, burning, and exploding the threatening forces in the air and on the sea, until none were left to fight.

***

Practically the whole world watched this event on live television—another Biblical prediction slapping everyone in the face. How come those witnessing the miracle didn't turn to Christ? How come I didn't run to the nearest church to confess my sins and proclaim my faith? Stupidity, of course.

***

Besides, all that crazy stuff was going on while my own world was falling apart, and being a self-centered moron, I was oddly excited about the whole nuclear hit on the Capitol, the one-sided battle in the Middle East, and all the other madness going on everywhere. I'd sit around my ugly apartment in Tarzana, drinking beer all day, watching the world go down the toilet on cable news. It sure made my problems seem less important. I mean, I didn't want anybody dead or anything, but if it had to happen it was excellent timing.

Things had been going bad for me for some time. I'd lost my company, our home was in foreclosure, Renee had kicked me out and filed for divorce, and I'd broken my poor daughter's heart.

It all began with the stupid business. You see, I had been a loan originator for a short time on the old Earth, when a partner and I decided to open our own mortgage brokerage. We made a small fortune giving out horrible loans to unsuspecting and greedy borrowers.

Our favorite type of loan went by several names: *The Option Arm*, *The Pick a Pay*; or, for those in the know, *The Neg. Am* loan. Neg. Am. was short for negative amortization, which meant borrowers lost equity each month making payments that were less than the interest owed. The idea was to lure them in with a lower payment and a low starting interest rate. It worked. Everyone wanted in on the fun. Home prices soared and so did the demand for these awful loans. I even convinced myself I was doing borrowers a big favor by getting them into the house of their dreams they couldn't afford.

The truth was, we would get at least four points on every loan because the bankers were excited about the huge interest rates they'd be getting once the initial teaser rate expired. And we would charge another two points because the borrowers were just as excited as the banks, but over those initial low payments. That meant we made $18,000 on every $300,000 loan. Whole plate of mackerel! Was I making some cake or what? And I spent it, too, on clothes, food, cars, gambling, drugs, booze, strippers, lions and tigers and bears, oh my!

But the end would come swiftly for the mortgage boom and for me. Just when the banks were licking their chops, ready for all those fat interest payments, they got whacked, too! When their $1500 dollar mortgage payments became $3500, guess what? The borrowers couldn't pay back the banks.

And guess what else? Exactly. The Illuminati had planned the whole mess: the loosening of restrictions on the financial markets, the drop in interest rates, the push to get unqualified borrowers gobbling up home loans, the slicing and dicing and selling of the loans to hedge funds—and it didn't take much convincing. They just pushed for a few changes in the rules and then let greed take its natural course. The borrowers lost, the mortgage companies lost, the small banks, the homeowners, the taxpayers, the country lost. Who won? Wall Street, the insiders, the huge bankers, the foreign bankers, the world's elite, the Illuminati.

***

The Illuminati plan was to collapse the American dollar. They had been pushing for a North American Union similar to what they had achieved in Europe, but Americans were much more stubborn and prideful about their dirt than the Europeans, and it was taking too much time.

They'd already gotten presidents Bill Clinton and George W. Bush to ignore our sovereignty by selling companies and jobs to the highest foreign bidders, and by ridiculous free trade agreements that benefitted every other country but the United States, and by border security that couldn't measure up to the security at a drive-in movie theater.

Next, the Illuminati got President Barack Obama to step in with massive bailouts to the same banks and firms that caused the whole mess, ensuring their continued power. This paved the way for the eventual collapse of the dollar, the North American Union, and a replacement currency called the Amero.

***

Obama was basically a socialist, globalist, and one-world government pusher. He spent trillions on bigger government, rewarded people on the dole, tried to nationalize the auto industry and healthcare, taxed the heck out of everyone, deferred policy-making to the United Nations, and kissed the behinds of the international community.

Later, however, Barack had a change of heart, because he asked forgiveness for his part in ushering in the New World Order and turned to Jesus. That change of heart got him into the suburbs of the New Kingdom. I've seen his place: a four bedroom with white shutters and a well-manicured lawn on a quiet street.

***

Most of the streets are quiet in the New Kingdom. People are polite

36

and helpful to their neighbors, but they don't bother each other with needless chat. They are much more introspective than they were on the old Earth, always reflecting on this or that aspect of their former lives.

Wise men throughout history espoused the virtues of silence, producing such wonderful lines as "Silence is golden," "Be seen and not heard," "Men of few words are the best men," "Never miss a good chance to shut up," "When you have nothing to say, say nothing," "Till human voices wake us and we drown," just to mention a few. But in the end, these great words were lost amongst the noise, wisdom virtually ignored by people on the old Earth who worshiped the gossiper, blowhard, or fast talker, as if silence itself was the enemy.

Perhaps it was. Maybe people didn't want to listen to the nonsense floating around in their own heads, voices reminding them of their failings, or their past.

Floating around somewhere in my head was the knowledge of the inevitability of my mortgage company's demise. I filtered out that noise, listening only to the voices of my pride and greed telling me the whole mortgage debacle was a temporary calamity, and so I drained our savings and maxed out our personal credit cards to keep the business going.

But it was doomed. The banks had decided to stop lending months before—except they never bothered to tell the lowly brokerages about it.

Still, Renee was a good sport about the whole thing. She never would have left me over money, not even financial ruin. She left me because I turned my back on her, because I betrayed her, because I was already gone.

***

The divorce rate in the United States was already over sixty percent when we split. By the time the Antichrist took over it was closer to eighty percent. This statistic gave the New World Order an excuse to abolish the institution of marriage altogether. The Antichrist didn't like marriage, and he especially didn't like families—not that there were any real families left after the children were taken in the Rapture.

The reason the divorce rate was so high even before the New World Order was because, for most people, divorce was easier than staying together. In the past divorce was the harder thing to do because it went against people's ethics. Back in the day, people considered marriage a moral and religious commitment, and they would stick to it for the most part, come what may. But ethics, long the target of the Illuminati, who were out to destroy the family, morality, compassion, goodwill, honesty, and on and on, had nearly become a thing of the past.

***

I had discarded my business and personal ethics. I was losing any sense of morality through booze, drugs, and other vices. I was dishonest. I had wrecked my family. I had some compassion left, but mostly for myself, as I let my daughter's heart break.

***

That's the thing people didn't quite grasp about divorce—the extent of the devastation children went through. Parents would say stuff like, "We were fighting in front of the kids all the time," or "It was better for them after the divorce." And family therapists and marriage counselors would all agree, as if they had some special insight into the mind of a child.

I mean there were always exceptions—like if a father was a complete lunatic or something, beating the crap out of everyone and whatnot, or, as in my case, cheating on his spouse, abandoning his family physically and emotionally—of course then it would make sense for a wife to run for the hills, but eighty percent wasn't about exceptions. Divorce had become the norm. The Illuminati had been pushing their bogus psychology on unsuspecting families and academia for decades, making it easy for everyone to destroy their children's sense of security and well-being.

***

The human family on the old Earth was God's creation, the parent-child relationship a model of our relationship to Him. Just as nothing is more devastating than separation from God, the family unit was everything to a child. Children were told over and over again by those they trusted that everything would be all right. We told Sophie the same thing. But it wasn't all right, and it never would be.

Some children cried, some misbehaved, some pouted or threw tantrums, some lashed out, and some remained silent and unreachable.

But to some extent they would internalize the utter hopelessness they felt and would never be quite the same.

***

I ignored it, but I saw it then as clear as I see it now—the change in my little girl. Sophie was pretending, pretending all the time—pretending for us because we kept asking her to. But her eyes could not pretend, however hard she tried. They were green and large and light on the outside, but further back, back where the soul was supposed to break the curtain, it could not, for she was hurt and lost and in the dark.

5

By the time I received final confirmation of my divorce, I had been living in the Valley apartment for close to a year. I visited Sophie or had her staying with me on a regular basis and without much restriction. But Renee had asked for and received a more concrete schedule in the divorce, and eventually my visitation rights were reduced to one night a week and every other weekend. It was more stable for Sophie, but it was tearing me up inside, and I stopped trying. I quit looking for a job, spent what little money I had on drugs and alcohol, and hung around my apartment using and wallowing in self-pity, at least when my daughter wasn't around.

Sophie was twelve by then, and she had my number. No matter how sober I was while she was with me, she knew something was different. She told her mom she was uncomfortable around me and didn't want to spend the night anymore. I didn't blame her at all—me and my crummy and dirty apartment, jobless, tired from all the partying in between, offering her bits and pieces of myself. How pathetic I was. But I felt abandoned and played the victim anyway. It was then that I really gave up. I let the demons in, and we had a long party until the earthquake hit.

***

The Great Los Angeles Earthquake was one more addition to the many natural disasters on the planet, steadily increasing in frequency and power since such things were recorded. These were more of the "birth pangs" described by Jesus in the Book of Matthew, created by the ugly energy of man and allowed by God to encourage repentance.

***

I was watching television late one night in bed, trying to come off a two-day coke binge so I could visit my daughter the next evening in a somewhat respectable state, when I was awakened by a loud roar and a shaking that became more violent with every second.

Then there was a terrific jolt that catapulted me into the ceiling. When I landed, my bed fell through the ceiling below, along with the whole cruddy apartment building. Had I not been on the top floor, I might have been crushed like the twenty-seven people who died at the Tarzana Gateway Apartments that night, some so smashed they had to be scooped up with shovels.

***

A few days later, I would go back to sift through the wreckage for my things while they dealt with the carnage. Morbidly enough, after I gathered what little was salvageable, I hung around to watch the gruesome abstersion, but worse, this childhood rhyme popped into my head:

> *Fatty and Skinny went to bed*
> *Fatty rolled over and Skinny was dead.*
> *Fatty called the doctor, and the doctor said,*
> *What's that pancake doing in bed?*

***

The earthquake had a magnitude of 9.3, making it the second largest quake in recorded history. It had the power of 24,000 Hiroshimas, devastating Los Angeles and killing some 167,000 people. The city would never be fully rebuilt. The immediate aftermath caused fires, flooding, food and water shortages, looting, and mayhem of all kinds—another Saturday night in the Los Angeles area.

Actually, there hadn't been a regular Saturday night in Los Angeles for some time. Martial law had been declared and a midnight curfew imposed soon after the president's assassination and destruction of the Capitol caused the economy to tank, and severe rioting broke out across the country.

Because most of the regular Army was off fighting in other countries, a new army called the American Security Force was formed.

The ASF was already in place when the earthquake hit, out in patrols enforcing the midnight curfew with orders to shoot on sight anyone who dared break it.

Ironically, the ASF was largely a foreign army, another brainchild of the Illuminati, already in the works well before the assassination and rioting occurred. The Illuminati had slowly dismantled the state police and militias, infusing the ASF with anyone they could sign up coming over the borders, believing foreigners would have fewer qualms about killing American citizens in the streets. They were right.

On the night of the earthquake, groups of these ASF soldiers, who had only previously broken the boredom by getting a rare shot off at a curfew breaker, not only had the excitement of the earthquake, but now, because of it, confused and frightened targets presented themselves all over the place. Some of their group leaders had the common sense to forego the shooting order in light of the situation, overriding the moans and groans of their trigger-happy cadets, but others took full advantage of the disaster, firing on the funny, screaming people in their pajamas, nightgowns, and underwear.

***

Somehow, buried underneath my ceiling and all manner of debris, I survived relatively unscathed. With one thought in mind, I picked myself out the rubble. I needed to get to my daughter.

With my car buried somewhere in the apartment garage, I had to reach the house on foot. This wasn't the best part of town before the earthquake, and despite the curfew, there were already groups of thugs rummaging through the mess, looking for food, valuables, and victims to molest. So I decided I better have some kind of weapon for the journey. I could still see my bed through the maze of dust and drywall, and I was hoping I could get under it to where I kept an aluminum softball bat. I was just pulling away a piece of drywall when someone kicked me in the back. I looked up to find a couple of rough characters ready to pounce. "I don't have anything on me!" I pleaded. "Can't you see I'm in my underwear, pal?"

***

While the hooligan who kicked me pondered that, I dove under the bed, flailing desperately for my bat. He and his buddy, hooligan #2, grabbed a leg and pulled as I managed to get my hands on the silver beauty. I came out swinging, whipping it into #1's ankle. He fell over, and I was then able to stand while I turned 180 degrees, leveling the bat at #2's head, inflicting a blow that sent his ear an inch into his skull. I then beat #1, who was busy nursing his ankle, probably to death.

***

Except it didn't happen anything at all like that, like I was suddenly Buford Pusser. I read the actual account at the Hall of Knowledge. I completely fabricated the whole thing. I mean I did hit the first guy in the ankle, but that was about it. The second guy tripped and fell on some debris while I was flailing at him with the bat. I swung at him a few times after he was on the ground but only managed to hit him once in the shoulder. Still, I wasn't lying about it. I was simply delusional. I mean I actually remember beating those guys severely; such was my inebriated and panicked state. I really thought it happened that way. I even asked God's forgiveness for possibly killing them.

***

The only reason I bring it up now is to make the point that I would have done anything to get to Sophie that night. I was on a mission and nothing was going to stop me. I was willing to kill or be killed to get to my little girl. The old Earth saying, "Love makes the world go around," is true. I looked it up. It made me willing to kill, and it made me, a middle-aged man with a coke habit, run seven miles through the burning and chaotic neighbors around Los Angeles, all the way to my ex-wife's house. Along the route, I heard gunshots that may or may not have been directed toward me. I did not notice and I did not care. I was going to get to my daughter. I loved her enough to die for her but not enough to live for her. Love is an interesting thing.

***

It turned out there hadn't been much to worry about. Like most of the drywall and pinewood homes in the area, my ex-wife's house held up pretty well, and Sophie and Renee were fine. Furniture tossed about the house, the floors covered with broken dishes, glasses, and other items flung from shelves and cabinets, but all in all it was a pretty fair earthquake to my family, considering the damage, injury, and loss of life elsewhere in the city.

***

Yes, I begged my wife's forgiveness, again. And since my wife was a generous and good person, and scared to death with everything going on in the world, and because she knew how much Sophie wanted things the way they were, and because she needed help around the house with the earthquake mess and all, she let me slither back into their lives.

And for a while things were good. But I'd already let the demons in, and it was only a matter of time before I messed things up again.

***

Those were the last days I would spend with Sophie on the old Earth. I took the same job I'd had during college, driving a taxi. I worked from five o'clock in the evening until the midnight curfew, watched television till one or two a.m., slept till a quarter to eight, took Sophie to school, picked her up, watched movies, played video games, or kicked a soccer ball around the yard with her. We even had some laughs again.

***

Living with Renee and Sophie again was wonderful, but I was down about everything else in my life. I couldn't get over myself, over losing our home and my business. I couldn't let the good be enough. I was weak and tired, and the demons and the cocaine kept calling. And so, eventually, Renee caught me and kicked me to the curb. I loved my daughter with everything I was. Let it be said—I loved my daughter not enough.

***

Besides the Great Earthquake, quite a few huge natural disasters hit the planet around the same time, causing untold numbers of casualties. An abnormal monsoon season caused massive flooding across Asia, wiping out a few hundred thousand people, and no less than fifteen good sized hurricanes along the Gulf and East coasts killed at least as many more. One hurricane decimated the City of Houston and another completely flooded Long Island and lower Manhattan. Then there were the volcanic eruptions in Iceland, Japan, and the Philippines, more wars breaking out everywhere, new famines not only in Africa but India and China as well, and strange and unstoppable diseases spreading sickness over large population centers in third world countries. Every week a calamity was reported somewhere. It should have gotten everyone's attention. The due date was nearing, while most of us continued our nonsensical journeys.

And when the pressure mounted, and the world felt like it would boil over like some great disregarded stew, there came a sudden break in the fun. Yeah, just like that, nothing happened for about five months. It was a weird calm. I think that's what finally woke up the last holdouts to make the cut. But even those of us who didn't wake up couldn't deny the feeling something big was about to happen.

And something big did happen. First, a star appeared out of nowhere, large and bright as two full moons. My daughter told me it was God's star. I told her, of course it was. And it was, but I had no idea at the time.

Then, a few days later, they disappeared——some people who you thought were good and decent people, some people who you thought were Christians and some people you knew were not, and other people, too. People you might never have expected.

I knew what happened. A lot of us did. And I knew why I was left behind. Most of my life had been spent taking the easy way out, doing the things that made me feel good, no matter who got hurt. I had turned my back on God a long time ago. I couldn't remember the last time I had been in a church, read a Bible, or even said a lousy prayer.

***

I had a lot of time to think about my life after they were gone, pondering where it all went wrong. Looking back, all I could see was a blur of lies, immorality, vice, greed, gluttony, vandalism, theft, and all manner of nonsense.

I didn't even remember exactly when or why I became a loser. It seemed I'd always had this lack of character. I remembered stealing dimes from my elementary school cafeteria where I was the milk monitor in the first grade. I was caught by a freckle-faced girl. She yelled for the cafeteria lady, except I was able to calm her down and talk my way out of it somehow. At six years old I was already an accomplished liar.

***

My father couldn't stomach a liar. Late one night when I was ten, I crept into the kitchen and ate a cake donut with pink frosting and white

45

coconut flakes. I took it out of a box of half a dozen or so my dad had been saving for breakfast.

The next morning I heard him shouting our names: "Gerry, Geoff, George, Gina..." Lining us up like Marine recruits, he began his interrogation, quickly eliminating Gina after deciding she was too small to reach the donuts, which had been sitting on top of the refrigerator. None of us said a word. I was too scared to confess, and, of course, Gerry and Geoff didn't have any idea what the heck he was talking about. So my father said we better figure out who stole the donut and sent us to our bedroom to work it out amongst ourselves.

Gerry and Geoff went at each other right away because they thought I was too young or chicken to be involved, but I joined in anyway because that's what the best liars do. Then we all had a heart attack because my father opened the door real fast, hollering at us some more. "Did you figure it out? What's taking you so long?"

Nobody said anything because they didn't know anything, except for me, and I wasn't going to say anything. So my father decided to bring us back into the den one at time to give us a whipping if we didn't tell him who did it, because this cake donut had suddenly become the missing Hope Diamond or something.

Now, any guilty party with courage or a conscience would have confessed right then and there. But I had neither, so I let my brothers suffer, meanwhile acting quite indignant about the whole mess. Heck, I probably would have blamed it on my kid sister if I thought anyone would have bought it.

***

My father's theory of punishing everyone, guilty or not, was also quite popular during the Spanish Inquisition, but it wasn't very effective for getting at the truth. It did, however, garner lots of bogus confessions. Not too many people can have their fingernails pulled off, their eyes gouged out, or their testicles crushed without admitting something, even if it never actually happened.

***

Nonbelievers loved using the Spanish Inquisition as an example to attack Christianity. How could a loving God cause such cruelty, they would ask? Answer: He didn't. That stuff had nothing to do with

Christianity. It was all about power, greed, fear, and just plain meanness. It was also about demons whispering in people's ears.

People on the old Earth loved their free will as long as they didn't have to think about it too much, or as long as they could blame God when it didn't work in their favor. The truth was that free will was God's greatest gift. What would be the point of anything without it? Everything would be meaningless. We would be nothing more than a bunch of robots. God, of course, understood this when He created us. But what most people didn't understand about free will is that you can't have it both ways. You can't do whatever you want to do, but then have someone stop you from messing it up all the time. That's not free will.

Another thing people didn't like or understand about free will is this: people who lie, steal, torture, maim, kill, and are otherwise knuckleheads get to have it, too.

Still, God didn't leave us sitting around with our free will like unsupervised children in a fudge factory. He gave us abundance and the knowhow to find food, shelter, and to create prosperity. He spoke through to us through prophets, offered guidance and laws so we could function together, helped us to fend off demons and all manner of enemies, sent angels and visions, even performed miracles.

But it didn't matter. Once the problems were solved, the battles fought, the thirst quenched, the bellies full, most people forgot about Him. They forgot about the guidance, the help, and all the visions and miracles because they lacked faith. Such is the nature of man with a choice.

So people separated themselves from God; they become self-righteous or unrighteous or cold or lukewarm or oblivious or great or stupid—it was their choice, their free will.

We were all once the chosen people, God's children, created out of pure love. But most of us decided it wasn't enough; we decided we'd rather be selfish, lie, steal, overindulge, and commit all manner of vicious acts against whomever.

So, how many burning bushes could he appear in? How many Red Seas did you want Him to part? How much water turned to wine? How many blind men made to see? How many brought back from the dead? He was already stretching free will to the limit as it was.

Finally, He just said the heck with it, and came up with a plan so no one could say He didn't know how hard it was to live as a human, to suffer as a human, to experience loss, and to avoid sin. He had Himself and His son born in the flesh as one person, planted that flesh in the middle of what was arguably the most ruthless empire in history, and then He told everyone who He was. All the while knowing full well this would get Him spit upon, beaten, whipped, and nailed to two pieces of wood until He bled to death; knowing full well He would be tortured to death; knowing full well He would have to watch His own son die. And He did it all to give us the greatest gift of all—the gift of forgiveness, love, salvation, free will, and eternal life.

God didn't ask us to start a bunch of religions and torture or murder everybody who wouldn't accept a particular doctrine. He didn't ask us to travel the world, beating and otherwise forcing so-called heathens into becoming Christians. He didn't ask us to start a bunch of pointless wars on His behalf. He didn't ask us to strap on bombs and blow each other to kingdom come. He didn't ask us to tell other people they were going to Hell. He didn't ask us to start a television show to solicit money from the faithful. He didn't expect us to be perfect. He only asked that we accept His gift. What could be easier than that?

And yet, few of us could manage even this. I know I didn't manage it very well. Still, at the last second, He gave me another shot. God is pretty generous that way. Everybody gets lots and lots of shots.

***

I love this one, too. Some atheist or God hater would inevitably say this when discussing Christianity: "Well, I didn't ask to be born." As if the gift of life were somehow worthless. And these were always the people most involved in the worldly goings-on, so caught up in life they never bothered to seek and wonder what it was all about.

***

I'm one to talk. No one was more involved in the nonsense of the old Earth. I guess the only difference between an atheist and myself was that the truth was somewhere inside, gnawing at me all the time, and I chose to ignore it—which is much, much worse.

***

My oldest brother, Gerry, went into the den first, ready to give a false confession just to end the whole mess. My father, however, had his ace in the hole, which was the pink frosting, a detail he had not yet disclosed. Gerry, bless his heart, could not win. If he admitted the theft without the crucial frosting detail, he would be whipped for lying; if he didn't confess or finger one of us, he would be whipped anyway. Soon he was back in the bedroom crying and rubbing his behind. Geoff was next, and he came back shortly with the same result. Finally, it was my turn. I was blubbering and shaking long before I got to the den. I was a pretty frail kid and nothing scared me more than the thought of a whipping from my father.

***

As little as ten years later, this kind of bare ass whipping with a heavy belt could have been persecuted as a felony, but back then it was all part of good parenting and memory building.

***

My father hadn't uttered a syllable before I began confessing. I told him about the color and the cake, and even reminded him about the little white coconut flakes, and I winced and I waited for my beating. It didn't happen.

My father had something else in mind. I don't know where he came up with this stuff, but it was brilliant. His punishment was worse than any whipping, for it caused not only pain, but humiliation and excommunication. Like King Solomon himself, my father pointed a finger at me, passing his bold judgment without expression. "George," he said, "you will have to tell your brothers what you've done."

***

Next, my brothers beat the crap out of me.

6

It was good my brothers knocked me silly now and again. If they hadn't, I probably would have turned out much worse. As it was, I began to rack up an unimpressive record of delinquent behavior. Now I wasn't exactly a known criminal, or even an unknown one, but for no good reason I was always involved in lies, thieving, scams, and run-ins with law enforcement. I stole money from my parents and neighbors. I was suspended for vandalism in the sixth grade. My first arrest came in the ninth grade when undercover cops nabbed my buddy Larry and me after we went streaking through an X-rated movie theater.

***

Two vice detectives sat munching on popcorn, keeping an eye out for wankers and other perverts, when Larry and I ran naked in front of the screen. One of the officers choked on his popcorn before they hurtled four rows of seats and bolted out the door after us. We were trying to put our clothes back on when they tackled us in the parking lot like we'd just mugged their mothers.

We weren't weirdos or anything, but we felt like it, standing there mostly naked trying to explain ourselves to the detectives. What we were guilty of was being stupid enough to listen to Larry's older brother, who had beguiled us with stories from the sixties about orgies and streaking and whatnot. And since we didn't know any girls or even how to talk to them, and it would've been easier to talk ourselves out of a pimple than a girl into an orgy, we thought streaking through a porno theater might offer the requisite thrills.

My father picked me up from the jail with a disgusted look. When I got home he called me a pervert and grounded me for two months. He'd stopped whipping me the year before.

***

I would have preferred a whipping to my father calling me a pervert any day. Of all the things a kid would not want to be called by his dad, pervert had to be the top of the list.

***

My father died of cancer soon after I turned twenty. Before he died, he went to a doctor to see about a dark growth on his leg. The doctor told him it was melanoma, a form of cancer, which had traveled to his lymph nodes. The doctor also told him he had two years to live. Two years later—almost to the day—he died.

***

Doctors were always telling people they were going to die on the old Earth, although there was lots of evidence that doing so would become a self-fulfilling prophecy. Hope kept many people alive, but some doctors didn't believe in anything they couldn't learn in medical school or read about in a medical journal. Doctors spent lots of time and hard work getting their degrees and their medical licenses, so most of them hated being wrong.

***

A year before my father died, he had to quit working at Hughes Aircraft because the cancer was eating his lungs alive. He had been working there twenty-nine years and was just a year from retirement and his full pension. What did old Howard's company do to reward him for all those years of service? They gave him a third of his pension. Not only did he never get to enjoy any of his retirement after all that work, he went to the grave with the knowledge that his wife would have to struggle after he was gone. For a man like my father, that was much worse than any pain and death sentence combined.

***

It wasn't Howard's fault. He was up in Heaven biding his time while his tent was being prepared in the New Kingdom. Besides, he had given up the reins of his company to a board of directors with no soul long before he died.

***

My father hated his job at Hughes Aircraft and always talked about quitting and starting his own mail order business. He even drew up logos for the new company. I never did find out what he was planning to distribute through the mail. Maybe his plan never got that far. Anyway, he had a family to support, and he would never have taken such a risk. That was the difference between my generation and his. If we didn't like something we'd just quit—everyone be dammed.

So my father continued on, leading his life of loud desperation, and I know, in a way, I hated him for it; such was the degree of my selfishness. I must have wished him dead a hundred times because of the whippings and the constant yelling, and because I thought he didn't like me. But when he was dying, I cried like a baby. The big man was down, wasted on morphine, unable even to wipe the drool from his own mouth.

***

I'd always believed I was a complete disappointment to my father. But when I asked him about it after I finally got around to seeing him here, he said I was only a minor disappointment. Of course, he never got to see what an upstanding citizen I became. Had he known my complete history on the old Earth, he surely would have downgraded his assessment.

***

No, he had no idea what happened to me after he died. People on the old Earth were always saying stuff like, "This person or other is up there looking down on you," or "So and so is with you," or "That family member is watching you," like all your dead relatives had nothing better to do but spy on you. It wasn't like that at all. They were in Heaven, for goodness' sake. Why the heck would they want to pay attention to all the nonsense on the old Earth even if they could? It would be like going to an amusement park to watch television.

***

Now ghosts were a different story. They were lurking all over the old Earth. That was about the third thing I looked up at the Hall of Knowledge. There were about two million TV shows dealing with ghosts or ghost hunting. I must have seen half of them. And they were all the same. Some ghost hunter or psychic would be knocking around an old house, or castle, or insane asylum, or someplace or other, in the middle of the night, loaded down with cameras, microphones, infrared lights, all manner of ghost-chasing gadgets, trying to get evidence of the existence of one of these things. Invariably, they would film an orb of light or a shadow, or record some static that sounded like human voices or children laughing, or some other barely audible noise. Still, it must have impressed the heck out of a lot of people because these shows got huge ratings.

I was pretty impressed myself. I just couldn't understand where these disembodied souls fit into Christianity and Heaven and Hell and everything, but I went to the Hall of Knowledge to find out. And that's exactly what they were: disembodied souls. I read all about it in this book titled, *The Ghosts of the old Earth.*

It turns out people didn't lose their free will just because they were dead. All that stuff about going toward the light was true, but the light was still a choice. Borderline souls, people like me, who didn't exactly live exemplary lives, might fear the light, or just decide they weren't quite ready, so they would just hang around the old Earth in their spirit form clinging to places they once knew.

The problem was that the spirit realm was full of dead demons and such. These evil characters were always fishing for lost souls hanging around, so they could jump in and possess them. When one of these "paranormal investigators" heard an angry voice saying, "Get out," that wasn't the voice of a human soul, but that of the possessing demon trying to get rid of the ghost hunter, just so they wouldn't bring in some wacky medium who might try and guide the poor soul to the light.

Unfortunately, a lot of these lost souls were children. The reason being, although all children had angels to guide them toward the light after they died, they didn't lose their free will. And some of these were the type of kid who would shoot spit wads at you all during class or stab you in the neck with a pencil or something, so a kid like that might just be mischievous enough to run from their guiding angel at the last second. They'd find some place familiar, and there they would hang as ghosts until they were ready for the light.

These souls would eventually make it into Heaven with or without mediums to show them the way. Mediums and the like were completely unnecessary. That's exactly why the Bible warned people to stay away from occult activities, because the useless medium and the ghost hunter would be just as likely to have a demon jump in and possess them as would a lost soul.

***

There were a few other arrests beside the one outside the porno theater, for stupid junk mostly, fighting in a bar and showing a fake ID to a police officer. I won't bore everyone with all the details of those, but the last time I was arrested was for bookmaking. I was taking sports bets from other students at the local college (where I was studying who knows what) to supplement my student loans and pay for my nightly bar ventures. The campus police got wind of it and sent a bunch of vice cops from the LAPD to my mom's house where I was freeloading. Fortunately, she wasn't home at the time, but I was put in jail for the night and expelled from school, and I broke the poor woman's heart. Had my dad been alive, he would have beaten the living crap out of me; my mom just kicked me out of the house.

***

People who grew up later on the old Earth wouldn't have believed that the police would raid a house with guns drawn over a gambling complaint. Because by the mid-1990s, every Tom, Dick, and Harry with a computer could bet on any sport on the planet or play any casino game for real money from the comfort of their living rooms.

Gambling and other vices like prostitution and drugs were becoming the norm on the old Earth. This was all part of the Illuminati plan. The destruction of every great civilization began with the loosening of morality. And the modern world would be no different.

Youth would always mock the moral gauges of their elders in America and elsewhere. Every generation was the same in that regard—it was just a matter of degree. There had always been vice and immorality on the old Earth—such was the nature of man—but there was also a level of shame to keep things in check. With each passing generation, that level would diminish as the Illuminati broke down the family and the Church. Even when I was growing up, there was very

54

little shame, but near the end, it became obscene.

Way back when, a guy like me who wanted to do something creepy like visit a prostitute, blow the family grocery money at a casino, or get high or stupid drunk or something would have to sneak around and lie about it. But just before the Rapture it became a free-for-all. Parents would smoke weed and do other drugs with their kids, married couples would hang out in strip clubs to get lap dances together, families would go to casinos, teachers would sleep with their students, a mother would put her daughter on the pill, a father would take his son to a prostitute and get himself one at the same time, and on and on.

A kid hardly had a chance. They couldn't turn on a television, open a magazine, or listen to a song without being bombarded by images of sex, orgies, drug use, violence, and all manner of immorality.

Any sense of morality and any convictions related to Christian mores had been slowly dismantled by the Illuminati. In America, the last real bastion of the Christian Church, this was accomplished under the auspices of free speech and separation of church and state.

***

America had largely been successful because it was founded on, and because Americans lived, for the most part, by Judeo-Christian principles. God had been on America's side since its inception, but with each passing generation, more and more Americans were rejecting God, and American society was losing the battle with immorality. As goes America, so goes the world, was the theory. And it was correct. The Illuminati plan was right on schedule. The new Roman Empire had arrived and was ripening for the fall.

***

And I was but another happy and willing citizen of Rome. Hail, Caesar!

***

After my mom kicked me out of the house because of the bookmaking incident, I moved in with two of my friends who shared a condominium a few miles away. I missed seeing my mom all the time, but otherwise nothing much changed for me, except that I switched freeloading addresses and had nobody to make eggs or do my laundry.

Eventually, my friends got sick of supporting me, so I got a job at a place called the Price Club, which was basically a giant warehouse converted into a super grocery and department store, where people and families could buy anything en masse. If you needed cereal, for instance, you wouldn't get a normal box, you'd get a box the size of a small safe. How people poured their cereal into an average size bowl, I still don't know. If you wanted ketchup, you didn't buy a normal bottle, you bought five or six giant bottles in one big old package— enough to start your own baseball stadium concession.

I worked in the television and electronics department. This was before the age of the personal computer and all the other high-tech junk, when an electronics department looked more like a garage sale, consisting of televisions weighing as much as a four-cylinder car; refrigerators, washers and dryers; clock radios, stereos you might put in your room and stereos you might put on your shoulder to annoy everyone.

Did I know anything about the televisions or stereos, or any electronic device for that matter? Only what I read in the little pamphlets provided by the manufacturers, most of which I couldn't understand. And I read very little. I spent most of my time at the Price Club hiding in a cubbyhole behind the big screen television and refrigerator boxes, avoiding customers and recovering from hangovers.

***

But I shouldn't disparage my days at the Price Club. This is where I met Charlie. And though he never knew it on the old Earth, he saved my life and probably my soul. Charlie also worked in the electronics department, except he actually took his job seriously. Since he worked during the week and I worked mostly weekends, we didn't run into each other an awful lot, until one day when I took a shift for a weekday guy who wanted to see Poison, Warrant, Ratt, or another lame hair band, somehow big enough to play on a Tuesday night at the Forum. This guy wanted to get there early to drink six or eight beers, chug a pint of whiskey, and smoke a bag of weed with his buddies so he would be good and plastered because that's the only way anybody could stand one of these bands.

Anyway, the trade left me working with this Charlie guy, whom I had never talked to before but only saw as he was leaving or coming, and might have said "ay" or "what's up?" or some other Neanderthal greeting considered cool at the time because you got to avoid actual communication. When I went into the break room to eat my hot dog, pizza, rolled-up cheese and meat burrito-looking thing, or whatever they gave me for free that day, he was reading a book titled *The Late Great Planet Earth*, by Hal Lindsey.

Hal Lindsey was this guy who used to be a big sinner like everyone else but found Jesus and turned his life around, becoming a great pastor, writer, and teacher of prophecy. He was one of the first to take a hard look at the books of the Bible and interpret their prophetic meaning within the context of current events.

Now I'd never heard of this book, but for some reason, I thought the title was interesting, so when we got back to our department I asked him about it. He seemed surprised and hesitated for a few seconds. "It's about the end of the world," he said.

"That's what I thought—science fiction or something," I said.

"No, it's about the real end of the world."

I laughed a little at that. This was well before there was a book a day written about 2012 and the Apocalypse. "How could it be about the real end of the world? Last I checked we're still here," I said.

"It's about the future, the things that will happen shortly."

"Like what? Like nuclear war or something?"

"Yeah, but there's a lot more to it," he said, and he began telling me about Israel and Russia, and the Antichrist, and the Mark of the Beast, and all kinds of crazy stuff I hadn't heard before.

"Well, how does he know?" I said.

"It's all in the Bible."

Now having had a short attention span in both church and catechism, I didn't know jack about the Bible. "Really?" I said. "I never knew that."

"Well, it's all there," he said, and he went on to explain some of the prophecies along with their interpretations.

***

We ended up talking for the rest of the shift, and though I didn't know what he was saying half the time, I was pretty darn riveted. We became friends after that, at least at work—we didn't exactly hang in the same circles.

And he was different. Nobody I knew talked like him; nobody I knew ever said practically anything worthwhile, except my mom and my father when he was alive, and maybe a teacher or an employer here and there. But I never had a real conversation with any of my friends until I met Charlie. He also got me reading the Bible and other books about Christianity, which got me interested in reading about history and politics and all kinds of stuff. I even ended up going to Charlie's church a few times. And I believed everything he told me and everything I learned there. It made sense to me for some reason. But I didn't become born-again or anything. I was nowhere close to giving up the trappings of the world. Come what may, I was going to have it my way. And so I did; and so it came.

Charlie and I drifted apart after some time, and I would never see him again on the old Earth. Instead of building a relationship of substance with a Christian, I wasted my days with my fellow miscreants, chasing money and girls, smoking weed, and watching endless hours of television.

***

Until one day when all that fine programming was interrupted by an important announcement: *U.S. Marine and Army forces have launched their attack on Iraq in response to the invasion of Kuwait by the Iraqi Army led by dictator Saddam Hussein.*

That was the first time in my life I knew exactly what I wanted to do. I don't know if it was because my dad was a soldier and his dad was a soldier and his dad was a soldier, but I knew I wanted to be a soldier, and not only that, I wanted to fight in a war. The next day I went down to the recruiting office and signed up. Everyone thought I was crazy.

***

I didn't believe them till three months later when I was still in boot camp, standing at attention with a shaved head being screamed at by a particularly vicious drill sergeant, the war long over.

***

Combat ground operations in the first Gulf War: 100 hours. George Somerset's impulsive Army stint: 3 years, 4 months, 17 days.

58

7

The day I read about ghosts was the same day I read about guardian angels and the lost city of Atlantis and I don't remember what else. That's how it is at the Hall of Knowledge. You'll be reading about one thing, leading you to another thing, which will lead you to something else, and the next thing you know the place is closing for the night.

***

I found out that every kid on the planet had a guardian angel, but not his own. One of these magnificent creatures could handle about two or three hundred kids all by themselves. That's how fast they are, but only because they are able to move in and out of the spiritual and physical realms like it's nothing. They are about two feet taller than the average human, without an ounce of fat, and with big old wings like in all the pictures. I didn't need to look up that part. They're flying all over the place around here.

***

And I didn't know archeologists on the old Earth had already found the once fabled city of Atlantis buried under the ocean using deep-ground radar and digital mapping, and they'd been excavating the site when the Antichrist shut the whole operation down because he didn't want them finding anything incriminating about him.

Atlantis was one of the many ancient civilizations that tried to do things without God in their lives. As far as pagan civilizations go, they were actually quite successful. They had been given advanced technologies by aliens and demons and the like, which allowed them to flourish and live pretty great lives, for a while anyway. But, like all godless peoples, they were doomed. Why? Without God, sooner or later, greed and immorality overshadow other pursuits. Without God, bad people and knuckleheads eventually run everything into the ground.

***

What happened to Atlantis? It was already destroying itself from the inside when a big tsunami turned their great island into a giant fish tank prop.

***

I get carried away with anything having to do with history. I once taught history and spent half my life on the old Earth reading books about history or watching it on television. It was one of few things on the old Earth that offered me contentment. That's probably why I spend so much time at the Hall of Knowledge. And I guess it's a lot easier than thinking about my own history.

***

I was pretty surprised the first time I went to the Hall of Knowledge. Considering all the other futuristic junk in the New Kingdom, I was expecting more of a high-tech facility with voice-activated computers and such, all the information right at your fingertips and whatnot. But the place is actually pretty old school as far as libraries go. I mean don't get me wrong, the building itself would put to shame any modern construction on the old Earth. Still, the place is classic looking, made of a smooth gold and white marble that looks as if it was carved from a single stone. Out front, atop a football-field wide staircase, sit four Romanesque columns, each the size of a small New York apartment building. Inside, the ceilings have been painted by Michelangelo himself, depicting hundreds of epic historical scenes, which include the Crucifixion, Moses reading the *Ten Commandments*, and the Battle of Armageddon, to name a few. There are rows and rows of two-story wooden bookcases, too many to count, on them all the books of the world worth reading, and all the books of Heaven, perfectly restored and categorized. These mountains of shelves are separated by a low wall of filing cabinets, not unlike cabinets in an old Earth library. There are also a bunch of librarians to help you find the section or book you want, so you don't have to spend all your time digging. And there are couches long as buses, big soft chairs, and huge desks with hard wooden chairs scattered about, where you can read comfortably or study and take notes if you'd rather.

***

All the libraries on the old Earth were closed after the Antichrist took over. He didn't want people reading certain things and asking a lot of dumb questions like: "Are you the Antichrist?" or "Why should we follow you when we know it will end badly for us?" No, he didn't want anyone thinking logically about him, or anything really, so books were burned by the truckload.

***

God doesn't worry about people reading anything or asking questions. He has nothing to hide. The truth is here for the taking. And you can't help yourself anyway. You'll read something, leading

you to questions about this or that, so you'll look up something else, leading to more questions, until you know all kinds of things you never knew before, and all that extra knowledge leads to even more questions.

Like after reading about Atlantis, I began wondering about all those ancient societies and empires like the Samarians, the Mesopotamians, the Mayans, the Egyptians, the Romans and whatnot. I wanted to know why God, being all-seeing and all- knowing, would bother with these fallible cultures when He knew they were doomed to begin with.

I also couldn't understand why God, who could see the whole future, would create a society with enough horrible people to destroy themselves or other nations, or why He would bother to make an angel who would eventually rebel and attempt to corrupt the whole world.

Even on the old Earth, I believed God had a plan, and I somehow knew it to be true. But that didn't mean I didn't have questions. I could have just written it all off as free will, but that would have been too simple an explanation. People needed faith on the old Earth, but here I had the Hall of Knowledge at my disposal, so I began to dig for answers.

Why couldn't Satan just be a bad angel with free will who rebelled and didn't help corrupt the rest of the world so badly that God had to intervene and toss a bunch of people into Hell? And why was there a Hell at all? I mean isn't an eternity of burning overkill for certain misbehaviors and rejection of God? Couldn't they just be given a hundred years of hard labor or something?

Now some answers are easy to find, but some—some are a bit more complicated. You can't just walk up and pull a big book off a shelf titled *The Answer to All Your Questions*. I mean you have books on aliens, ghosts, the Napoleonic Wars, the joys of sailing, and everything else you can think of. The "what" is the easy part; the "why" is a whole different animal. So after several hours spent banging my head against the wall, I decided to break down and ask one of the librarians.

The closest librarian was a black man standing on a ladder thirty feet in the air. He had an armful of books, so I waited while he replaced them carefully on the great shelves. When he finished he looked down at me and smiled wide as one of the thick books he'd just replaced.

Librarians on the old Earth hardly ever smiled. I think it was part of their training or in their contracts to be as intimidating as possible, just so you wouldn't bother them about stupid stuff.

"Can I help you, sir?" he said.

"I was just wondering if you could help me find something."

"Of course, sir, that's why I'm here," he added rather gleefully, shooting down the ladder as if it were a greased pole.

"That was pretty slick."

"Lots of practice—the new bodies don't hurt, either. So what can I help you with?"

"Well, I have some questions," I said, feeling a little awkward about the whole thing.

"Questions—everybody has questions. What kind of questions?" he asked.

I hesitated. "I don't know, like about Satan and Hell, and other things."

"Big things." He was being playful. "'Did he who made the Lamb make thee?'"

"I don't understand."

"You're not the first to ask these questions," he said.

"I'm not?"

"No…hardly. People have been asking those questions since they could form sentences. That was William Blake."

"So I should get his book?"

He chuckled. "It's from a poem."

"So, I should get the poem?" I said.

"Follow me," he said, and he led me to one of the many study tables where he sat me down and took the seat across from me. "What's your name?"

"I'm George, and you?"

"James—James Franklin, born 1927 on the old Earth."

"You're quite a bit older than I am."

"None the wiser, but I might know a book for you. It's called *To Kill a Mockingbird.*"

"I've seen that movie. I think we read that book, too, in junior high or something." Now I was remembering. "It's about a lawyer in the South?"

"Yes, he defends a 'brother' falsely accused of raping a white woman," James said.

"That's the book with the answers?" I didn't see any connection.

"That's the book with the key," he said.

"Where do I find it?"

"I could show you, but I don't think it would help," James said, and he leaned in. "You have to know what you're looking for."

"What am I looking for?"

"A needle in a haystack—or, in this case, a diamond in a barrel of diamonds. It's something the lawyer, Atticus Finch, says to his daughter."

"What did he say?"

"He said, 'You can't understand someone until you consider things from his point of view, until you get into his skin and walk around.'"

I pondered what those words might have to do with my questions. "I think I get it—like those bumper stickers: *What would Jesus do?*"

"I'm not exactly sure what that is, but I think you're on the right track," James said.

"I wonder—so I need to put myself in His shoes. I don't know—I don't believe I can come close to thinking like Him," I said.

"Well, you might be surprised."

"I doubt it. In fact, I'm probably one of the least qualified up here."

"You wouldn't be here if He wasn't already inside you."

"I sure didn't get any of His common sense."

He laughed. "Maybe not, but you have His DNA, and common sense you can actually learn."

"I don't know."

"I do—just give it a shot."

"I guess I could," I said.

"Of course you can. You have all the time in the world."

***

So I found myself a comfortable chair and took the librarian's advice. I asked my questions and tried to answer them wearing God's big shoes. I thought about nothing else all day. I left the library in the early evening thinking about it. I walked home to my shack thinking about it. I lay in bed thinking about it. I woke thinking about it. I thought about it for days and days, and after some time, I began to get the answers. Now, maybe I wasn't wearing His shoes, but perhaps I managed to pull on a pair of His slippers.

***

I'm this all-powerful being; I can do anything I want. I can create the most complex thing imaginable with just my will. I can give and take life. I created Heaven and the universe. I can do and have anything I want, and I can look into the future and see all the results.

So, what do I want? I want to eat the best foods in the world, I want to have the most beautiful women in the world, I want to live in the biggest mansion you've ever seen, and I want to have a bunch of servants catering to my every whim.

Nope, that's just me, the numbskull. I'm thinking more like a human, so back to God. What would God do? Even if He wanted junk like that, He would be able to look into the future—and what would He see? He would see a fat, bored, unsatisfied king, tired of having everything He wants.

Now a lesser being, an immoral being, might be satisfied with an eternity of

64

sloth and debauchery, but fortunately for us, God is a much more advanced and honorable being. So God would ask himself: "What is most important to me and who I am?"

So I ask. And the answer I decide must be my truth because that is the only answer I could possibly have. So who am I, and what is my truth? My truth is what is most important to me. My daughter is most important to me—my love for her. But I'm back in my shoes again. Still, love has to be the most important thing. So my truth is love. And I am my truth; therefore, I am love. How do I be and do love? How do I express love? I give love. But how do I give love? I give of myself.

And so I decide I will make a creature, another like myself, who can feel, give, even be love. So I begin to think up creatures to love and be love. I begin to imagine such creatures, so many different kinds. And I see their beauty and the love they can give and receive, and I see their wonderful futures in a perfect world.

But these creatures are missing something. They have love—what could they be missing? Of course, they are missing truth. But what is truth besides love? Love is my truth, but do they have truth if they only have my love? I chose my truth. If I really love them, they must choose their own truth. And so I imagine them with the ability to choose their truth.

Now what do I see in their future? I see horrors that were once unimaginable to me because they are not of my exact nature, and these creatures have the ability to choose their own nature. I see murder and rape and torture, all manner of mayhem, such death and destruction and ugliness that so sickens me, I can't even think of creating anything with a choice for many, many years.

But after a time, I began to think back on some of the other creatures with choice I had imagined: the animals, so majestic and loving, and the angels who loved and protected the humans, and the humans who made families out of love and loved me for my gift.

I remember those humans' futures, their good deeds, peacefulness, generosity, growth, compassion, love. And I especially remember all the children, with their laughter, their innocence, and their unconditional love.

I am in a pickle. Because I have so much love to give, and I have imagined these wonderful creatures with a choice, these angels and humans so much like myself—especially the humans who would be made in my image. But unless I act, none of them will ever exist, none of them will laugh, none of them will do great things, none of them will love. There will be no love and no truth.

So I begin to imagine them again. But every time I imagine them together, every time I see their futures together, no matter how I spin it, I see horror and death *again. I see good people and even innocent children suffering beyond reason or belief.*

I see this because bad people and dark angels will corrupt, and even the most seemingly insignificant, infinitesimal, act of corruption or sin will eventually snowball into grotesque suffering.

In some of the imagined scenarios, it takes eons; in some, millions of years; in some, thousands of years; and in some, merely centuries, but the ugliness always happens.

I realize that the bad creatures and the good creatures can't live together. So I imagine them in separate worlds, and I see one beautiful world and one ugly world. But I see I am at square one again because I have placed them in dichotomic cocoons, and there is no truth in those antipodes.

It is then that I realize another great truth: that without the bad, without the evil, there can be no real goodness. There is no skirting this dilemma, no perfect answer, no perfect world.

I now know my gift of love is also a gift of great suffering, not only for the creatures, but also for me because I will have to let them suffer, when I would rather suffer for them. But I also know that, like me, the best of the good creatures will gladly suffer for the bad ones, and they will be even more beautiful for it. So I discover yet another great truth: there is more good than evil in suffering. It is better to create.

***

So I am left to choose the scenario. I don't want to choose the one which lasts eons. Even though there is more good than evil in still suffering, I don't want to prolong it. But I also don't want to choose the one which lasts mere centuries because I want to give my gift to many, many creatures, and I want to include all the creatures I imagined. So I settle on millions of years.

***

I begin to create. I don't leave anyone or anything out. I create the universe, and the stars, and all the planets where they will dwell. And I make Heaven for the angels and Earth for the humans. I create microorganisms, plants, bugs, reptiles, dinosaurs, animals, mammals, even Cro-Magnons, and so many more. I create angels and humans, male and female.

Some of the creatures I imagined can't live together all the time because they will eat or overwhelm each other, so I give them each their time on the Earth and their time in Heaven, and I give many of the creatures souls so they can always exist because it would be cruel not to.

***

Now I am a just and moral God. And I know that like the other futures, the future of this scenario is doomed. So being a just and moral God, I can't let it go on until the souls of the good people are corrupted by the souls of the evil and separated from me. Because the nature of evil is to eventually suck the goodness and the love from even the best of man and angel.

***

And this is what Hell is. It is not simply a fiery pit of anguish and suffering; it is the result of separation from God. I did not create Hell to punish everyone who separates from God. I did not create Hell at all. The greed and jealousy, the debauchery and violence, the ugliness—it only grows stronger and more powerful as angels and humans evolve in its filth. Hell is the inevitability of the Godless and the wicked.

This was the future I always saw, the future I dreaded—this Hell that is always created when the souls of the evil are left unchecked. The demonic cajole, parley, and fight until they box all the souls into a cavernous, fiery, dark hole of pain and madness without relief. This was the future I had to accept in order to create.

But I realize that at some point I will have to step in and stop this future, so the good aren't sucked into the world of the evil, because that would be unjust, and it would destroy the futures of the good as well.

***

I also realize I am in an even bigger pickle because I will have to suspend free will to stop Hell from occurring too soon for everyone, and this would be an untruth. But that's when I realize yet another great truth: justice is also truth. It would not be justice to let the good be destroyed with the bad. I am the only one strong enough to provide this justice.

***

Some days later, I decided to walk back to the Hall of Knowledge to thank James the librarian. It was another perfect day in paradise. I felt closer to God than I ever had before. By trying to understand God, I was stronger somehow. I looked up at the sky directly into the light of the sun for a long time. I did not squint or even blink, and my new eyes did not hurt at all, while the whole of the sky became an intense bright light.

That's when I felt His presence. He was telling me something— that paradise wasn't the end, that I was still changing, that I could be better. It made me smile, and I thought about all I had learned already.

And while I walked, lost in thought, I found myself trying to think like Him again, but something was different, and I began to fill His big shoes, it seemed, for the first time. And that's when a voice enveloped me. It said this:

Because I am stronger, I must do one more thing. This will be the greatest truth and my greatest gift. I am scared of this truth because I will suffer more than anyone, and I must watch my own Son suffer. But this is something I have to do. I will send the Christ.

8

There were still nearly six billion people left on the planet after the Rapture, but I might as well have been alone. Sophie and Renee were gone. Gerry, Geoff, Gina and my mother were gone. My father had been dead a long time. And any friends worth having were gone.

***

After it happened I stared for a long time at the spot where Sophie last stood. I heard the screams and the explosions and crashing vehicles, but I could not move. I heard the sound of a large plane getting closer, and I wished it would land on top of me, crushing my sorry body as flat as those poor souls in the earthquake. I pictured my white tennis shoes sticking out from the wreckage like the ruby red slippers of the Wicked Witch of the East.

***

It was not to be. But the plane came close, and it hit with such force it knocked me off my feet. Then a huge explosion of fire rolled across the suburbs like napalm in the jungle. I heard the frightening sound of ripping metal, and screams so horrible I heard them for days. It was enough to snap me out of my self-loathing, and I ran to do something completely out of character, which was to see if I could help.

***

The rest of that day is still a blur. There were people on fire that could be put out and people who died while I stood by helpless. There were body parts in bushes and trees and body parts I pulled from underneath debris, thinking incorrectly they were attached to someone. There were people screaming and people crying. There were dead people and living people, and I felt like neither.

***

The fire trucks and the ambulances and the police cars came, and they took the wounded and the dead away. Nobody talked about the missing people; nobody talked much at all.

***

When there was nothing left to do, I went to Renee's house, though I knew in my heart she was gone, too. I had to be near where they once were. When I opened the door, Sophie's dog Wiley, a light brown Dachshund, greeted me excitedly as he never had before.

The dog must have sensed something amiss and was just happy for familiar company. I picked up the dog and took him to Sophie's room, now a museum of a young girl's dreams for the old Earth. I sat on Sophie's bed, cradling Wiley as if he were my little girl, crying for myself and all I'd destroyed.

***

Adolf Hitler had a Dachshund. I saw the little guy in some home movies of the dictator at his mountain residence in Berchtesgaden. I remember feeling sorry for that dog. In the film the dog is seen wagging his tail, jumping all over the place, licking the Fuhrer like any other master, and not the inhuman, diabolical, mass-murderer of men, women and children he was.

***

I did not turn on the television that evening but heard the strange loud humming noises outside. I was too grieved to care what it was. However, the next morning, when I turned on the news, over and over again they showed the pictures of the early evening sky filled with hundreds of large triangular craft. Even through the television, I could hear the loud humming of the colorful space ships clearly as if they were still right outside my house.

Then the president held a press conference to tell the world that one of the alien cultures we were in contact with had betrayed us and kidnapped millions of people.

The whole thing was a big setup, which had begun many months before the Rapture when the president showed up on television with a couple of real live ETs and proceeded to disclose a relationship between the U.S. government and creatures from outer space going back to the 1930s.

Now there are about 800 different species of ETs of all colors, shapes and sizes. But, wisely, the president chose a species that was fairly humanoid-looking. Their skin was ashen, their eyes dark and cat-like, but otherwise they didn't make you want to throw up or anything.

He went on to say how great and friendly and cooperative and helpful these things supposedly were, and how the government had kept it a secret because they didn't want to alarm everyone and freak out religious people. And how they meant us no harm, and how they just wanted to give us all these great new technologies so life on Earth would be wonderful for everyone, and a bunch of other nonsense.

But now the president was saying that with the help of the "good" aliens, the government wouldn't rest until all the missing people were returned safely. This was complete baloney, of course, because they were all in Heaven. It was all part of the Illuminati plan to prevent the Rapture from converting a bunch of people into Christians. Still, lots of people bought it, mostly because it was easier to face than the reality of being left behind.

***

Since so many politicians, including the vice president, the secretary of state, and most of the senate were destroyed during the nuclear assassination the year before, this president had been in office less than a year and was a relatively unknown congressman from the state of New Mexico named Whitey Newton.

And it was no coincidence his district included the city of Roswell, the notorious birthplace of government conspiracy regarding UFOs. Whitey Newton had been cavorting with aliens since the 1980s. Those aliens had been in the area since the 1930s, long before rumors of a crashed flying saucer and recovered bodies began to surface around the Roswell Military Base. Newton was working for the CIA when he was sent to Roswell by the Illuminati to coordinate policy between the U.S. government and the visitors from outer space.

***

The Roswell Incident, as the purported crash was known, was easily covered up at the time, but the conspiracy theories never went away. I found out the real story of Roswell at the Hall of Knowledge.

***

In 1947, a cowboy happened upon the wreckage of an alien spacecraft once manned by a species known to ufologists as the Grays because of their unique coloring, roughly the shade of dolphin skin. The Grays were four feet tall with huge heads and giant black eyes. For years they had been allowed by the government to operate their genetic experiments on humans and animals in exchange for advanced weapons information.

The wreckage the cowboy discovered was that of a small saucer, which had been snatching various bovines for dissection when a bull that was not properly hypnotized got loose on board and began kicking and butting the crap out of the Grays inside the tiny spaceship.

The pilot tried to keep the thing airborne, while the other Grays, the bewildered bull, broken instruments, and pliant alien metal flew about the ship. He managed to get the saucer level, but he couldn't avoid the crash altogether. The ship skidded across the desert floor, bouncing off sand, brush, cacti, and any number of desert varmints. All the while, their big heads banged about the cabin as the bull knocked them around, until the saucer broke in half, and the little Grays were thrown hundreds of feet.

Now it was those big alien heads that saved the pilot and scientist Grays for the moment, but the other two crewmen died before they hit the sand from all the bouncing around and the butting and kicking of the bull and whatnot. Somehow the bull survived and sniffed his way back to his herd.

The cowboy never saw the injured and dead aliens, but dutifully reported the wreckage to the local authorities, who informed the nearby Army base commander. The base commander was not privy to the government/alien relationship, and as soon as he returned from the crash site, he eagerly told the local press that wreckage of a flying disk had been found. He thought he'd made the discovery of the century. The only discovery he'd made was that talking about flying saucers earned one an ass-chewing and a sure demotion.

And while the base commander was having the riot act read to him by a four-star general, a special operations unit guided by the Illuminati was already busy sealing off the area and creating the infamous weather balloon cover story. This fantasy of a veteran Army officer mistaking a weather balloon for a flying saucer would be like a ship captain mistaking a battleship for a floating tin can. Yet everyone, including the press and local law enforcement, happily swallowed the ridiculous yarn.

***

The hand of Illuminati was everywhere, and there was no need for elaborate or even intelligent cover stories: balloons, kites, lightning, swamp gas, stars, airplane lights and blimps all worked surprisingly well on the tiny human brains.

***

Once the crash site was sealed off, the Illuminati-controlled special operations unit, along with a select group of grunts from the Army base, began to search through and gather the debris. What these soldiers didn't know was that they would later be sworn to secrecy with threats of immediate and great bodily damage, as well as future harm to their loved ones.

One of the grunts, a young Baptist from Oklahoma, Gordon Allen Smilko, would suffer a worse fate. Private Smilko was the unlucky soldier who happened upon the two live Grays lying in agony a mere fifteen feet apart. At first he thought he was looking at two children, but as he came closer it quickly became clear to him that they were no humans. Still, Smilko wasn't afraid—partially because of his strong faith and partially because the special operations guys were fairly close by and seemed to know what they were doing.

The injured Grays, who could adequately understand and mimic almost any language, called for help. When the private reached the scientist Gray, a purple liquid seeped from his mouth as he gurgled over and over again the phrase that would also be the alien's last words: "The big cow is waking up."

Figuring the alien in front of him was finished, Smilko hurried over to the other Gray, who was obviously in a lot of pain. That one, the pilot, was asking for his foot, which was lying just out of his reach and covered in purple blood. Hesitantly, the sickened grunt edged the severed foot closer to the creature with the butt of his rifle. Then he fired off a shot to alert the other searchers.

The Gray pilot abruptly snatched his severed foot and secured it under his armpit. Satisfied that help was on the way, he began to converse with the private. "Are you in charge?" asked the alien, who was wincing and groaning and difficult to understand, what with his foot being gone and all.

Private Smilko couldn't believe how calm the creature was, considering the extreme nature of his wounds. "Maybe you shouldn't be talking right now, little man….Stay still; help is coming."

"Please answer me, sir. Are you in charge?" said the strange pilot.

"No, little fellow," Private Smilko replied. "Are you a Martian?"

"What is a Martian?" said the pilot.

"You know, little man, men from Mars."

"No one can live on Mars anymore. I am from a planet called Quevis," said the pilot.

"What you doing here?" said Smilko.

"I cannot tell you that," the pilot said flatly.

The grunt, not liking what he was looking at one bit, rubbed his chin and thought for moment. "Well, are you a good or evil thing?" he asked.

"What is evil?"

"You know—bad stuff!"

"Bad stuff? Like what?"

"Satan stuff, like stealin', rapin', and killin'. I heard you kidnap people," said Smilko.

"What is Satan?" asked the pilot.

"You know, Lucifer, the devil, the destroyer, the dark prince, the ruler of all that is unholy!" Smilko fired back.

The pilot seemed to be thinking on it.

"The fallen angel," added Smilko.

Now the pilot was sure he understood and managed a smile. "Apollyon, yes, Apollyon!" he said.

***

Apollyon was just another name for Satan or Lucifer. He was also known in Greek mythology as the God Apollo. Apollyon was one of God's favorites, an extraordinarily beautiful and intelligent creature, an angel among angels.

But Apollyon had his faults. He needed constant attention and was never satisfied. He didn't like having someone around who was better than him. He thought he could do a better job running the universe. He was a cancer in Heaven, always complaining about everything.

He also liked to make dramatic speeches, shouting and waving his arms around to rile up the other angels. Many were foolish enough to listen and began to tag along and complain right along with the power-hungry angel.

***

On the old Earth, this same behavior of yelling and weird gestures while trying to control everyone was seen in many infamous world leaders: Hitler, Stalin, Napoleon, Mussolini, and Castro come to mind. This was because they'd allowed Apollyon to tell their brains what to do. Satan knew that people became easily mesmerized and convinced of things by yelling and weird gestures and such because it had worked for him.

***

God, who didn't like what was going on with Apollyon one bit, didn't do much but shake his head and watch because he had already decided in favor of free will. So Apollyon and his horde were able to hatch a plan to take over Heaven and an all-out war ensued, which, of course, they lost, and God kicked them out of Heaven and on to the more physical realm of the planets as punishment.

Later, God decided to make another creature more like himself. That's when Adam and Eve were created. They were given their own little Heaven, a paradise on the Earth, until Satan corrupted the two of them. Satan wanted to corrupt all of mankind, figuring if he gathered up enough souls for the pit, he might be able to beat God at his own game. He was wrong.

Satan did, however, get many humans to turn to the dark side because humans were extremely susceptible to the power of persuasion. Satan was a heck of a salesman, and a good salesman on the old Earth could easily get someone to buy all manner of garbage, including bridges they didn't own, swamp land, and defective automobiles called lemons.

Once Adam and Eve crossed that line, there was no getting back their innocence. All sales in paradise are final. They gave themselves to an Earth lorded over by Satan himself. Adam and Eve had to choose between God and Satan. They eventually chose God and turned their lives around, but by then, they and their children and their children's children knew sin—having the "knowledge of good and evil"—and so were constantly in flux between sin, confession, guilt, self-loathing, heartache, and all manner of inner conflict.

***

But what did having the "knowledge of good and evil" mean, exactly? People on the old Earth were often perplexed by this, and by the whole story of Adam and Eve, for that matter. Why was this snake talking to them? Why would God have a forbidden apple tree of such importance sitting right there for the taking? How could two people populate the entire planet, and on and on?

What people needed to remember was that the stories in the Old Testament had to be passed down orally for generations before there were written languages. The stories were repeated mostly in the evenings in front of the community fire where children were present. So, they were told for dramatic effect, but also with lots of censorship to spare the children, and they were told in terms that could be understood by relatively primitive cultures.

So what was missing in the story of Adam and Eve? Answer: the sex and the science. Remember, Adam and Eve were "created in the image of God," which meant they carried God's DNA. As long as they only procreated with each other, their children would carry this pure DNA.

But God didn't stop with Adam and Eve. If you read the Bible carefully, you can pick up the clues. Cain, who killed his brother Abel, and was supposed to be one of only four people populating the planet, suddenly finds a wife. Where the heck did she come from? Well, God was creating all kinds of people back then.

As it was, these storytellers had their hands full remembering all the details they had to keep straight. Were they supposed to tell the story of Jim and Nancy, Bob and Alice, Ricky and Shirley, and everyone else?

No. It wouldn't have been possible. So they just told the story of the first two humans God created, with the direct bloodline (through Noah, Abraham, Daniel, and on and on) down to Jesus, fulfilling prophecy while proving Christ to be flesh and blood.

And they didn't know how to explain DNA, so they did the best they could. And they also decided to leave out all the sex because, frankly, it was embarrassing, especially with children listening. Satan was described as a snake because he stole Eve away from her husband. Sex was the apple that spread Satan's corrupted DNA, the "knowledge of good and evil."

There is an obscure passage in the Book of Genesis that many Biblical scholars chose to ignore, simply because it confused the heck out of them or made them uncomfortable. It is this: "The Nephilim were on the Earth in those days, and also afterward, when the sons of God came in to the daughters of men, and they bore children to them..."

Nephilim in Hebrew means "to fall." The Nephilim were Satan and his crew, the fallen angels, who came to Earth to cause all manner of trouble. When they saw how beautiful God's women were, they talked them into the sack, fusing their DNA with human DNA, forever tainting the genetic lines of mankind.

***

Without the Hall of Knowledge, I wouldn't have known about any of this, nor would I have known about the conversation between the lowly private and the pilot from outer space.

***

Private Smilko was beginning to put the pieces together, deciding he was right about this thing being a demon. "Apollyon from the Bible?" said the private.

"Yes, the great god!" said the pilot.

"There ain't but one God," said the private, and now he was pretty angry with the little pilot.

"Where I come from, there are many gods."

"I knew you was a demon!" cried the private.

"I am me."

***

The pilot began to spit up the purple blood. Private Smilko sat next to him, lifting up his body gently, and cradling the little alien in his relatively huge Oklahoman lap.

***

The low voices of the Illuminati's special operations unit could be heard. They were close.

***

Private Smilko took out his pocket Bible, laid it on the pilot's stomach and petted the creature's big head. "Don't you worry, little buddy, help is coming."

"I think you should go," said the pilot.

"Why?" said Smilko.

"It's dangerous."

"You think they might hurt me?"

"They *are* going to hurt you."

"Why would they hurt me?"

"You have seen me; you have talked to me," said the pilot, his eyes barely open.

"You rest, little guy—I'll be all right," said Smilko.

'Please go—they'll kill you," said the pilot as he tried to get up.

"Stay still…you'll make it worse."

"Go!" said the pilot.

"You don't sound much like a demon," said Smilko.

***

Later, Private Smilko's interrogators asked him what the alien had told him. When he informed them that the pilot had been warning him, they didn't believe him and punched and kicked him to death. Then they burned his body.

Gordon Allen Smilko was buried with military honors. His parents had been told he died while saving some fellow soldiers after a truck crash. When Smilko returned for the last man, the truck exploded, they said, and the brave private was blown to pieces. "He was a hero," they added. It was the only thing they told his parents that was true.

***

Smilko is doing fine. He got himself a big house in paradise.

***

As for the alien pilot: for his attempt at saving Smilko, God gave him a soul and a planet to live on with other kindly aliens.

***

Private Smilko wasn't the only hero to die from knowing too much about aliens or other strange goings-on. There were many who had crossed paths with the Illuminati and their nefarious agendas. The Hall of Knowledge is full of the stories of their untimely deaths and disappearances. Most of them were treated as martyrs and live in mansions in the New Kingdom.

Some of those martyrs were alien abductees who were returned. The hypnosis that was supposed to make them forget the traumatic event had always been a work in progress, so most of the abductees remembered bits and pieces, suffering all manner of psychological effects, including night terrors, anxiety, depression, and psychosis. Still, this helped the Illuminati to marginalize them as nutcases. But some remembered way too much and later died under mysterious circumstances, like bizarre car accidents and sudden illnesses, methods favored by the Illuminati.

***

One of the first documented alien abductions was the case of Betty and Barney Hill. They were on their way home to Portsmouth, New Hampshire, after a short vacation to Canada, when some aliens nabbed them in order to extract DNA from their bodily fluids.

The Hills were cruising along, minding their own business, when a giant glowing ball began tailing them down the highway. They weren't sure what it was, so Barney stopped the car and got out to have a look. As the light moved closer, he could see that it was some sort of spacecraft. He could also make out at least five humanoid-looking creatures peering at him through a large window in the craft. He became frightened, jumped back in the car, and sped away. That was the last thing they remembered, except they couldn't figure out why it had taken them so long to get home. At least two hours were missing. Then Betty began to have nightmares about boarding a spacecraft and being examined by strange beings. Later, under hypnosis, they would both tell the same story about the abduction.

Now a lot of people thought Barney Hill made the whole thing up. It was easier to believe he was lying than some flying saucer story. However, a little common sense should have prevailed in Barney's case. The last thing a black man married to a white woman in 1963 would ever do is draw attention to himself with some cockamamie story about being abducted by aliens. They went to Canada in the first place just so they could walk around together for a few days without being bothered by ignorant Americans.

Another reason people were more inclined to believe that old Barney had made the story up was because people were always lying about this or that anyway on the old Earth. Heck, I used to lie about five or six times a day for no reason whatsoever.

9

After the Rapture, the spaceships, and the alien kidnapping story, the world was pretty aghast for a couple of days. That was about the attention span of most people at the time for monumental earth- shattering events, what with cell phones, headphones, Bluetooth contraptions, iPods, iPads, laptops, and all manner of devices permanently attached to everyone like they were on their own personal mission to Mars.

Also, the people left behind, like myself, were more self-centered and self-absorbed than those sitting in Heaven. And so the world became a much uglier place. There was more violence and chaos than ever before.

**

In America, the middle class had been all but wiped out. The dollar became worthless and the Euro became the world's reserve currency. People were out of work and hungry. The U.S. Army joined with the American Security Force to quell the madness in the streets.

Desperate, the American government looked to the United Nations, which had taken over the European Union, having turned those countries around when they were falling apart. The United Nations urged the United States to open its borders to the south and merge with Canada to the north. Within a few months, a deal was brokered, and Whitey Newton became the first president of the North American Union. Newton's first and last executive order was the minting of a new currency, the Amero. His new position would last less than six months.

***

All of this was by Illuminati design. A new figure in world politics had been emerging for some time. He was the head of the U.N. when the Rapture occurred, and it wasn't long before he seized power over Europe and aimed his sights on North America. His name was Victor Julius Talley. His number was 666 because he was the human vessel of the 666th angel created by God. That angel was a demon, whose name was Lucifer, also known as Apollyon, Satan, and the Destroyer. Victor Talley was the Antichrist.

Even before morphing into the Antichrist, Talley was Illuminati, a devil worshiper, supernaturally intelligent, charming and charismatic, and a con man of the highest order. He was fluent in sixteen languages, gathering enormous crowds wherever he spoke. I had to force myself to turn off the television when he came on because although I already believed him to be the Antichrist, I'd find myself mesmerized, agreeing with his points, buying into his bull-crap along with everyone else.

People were looking for a savior. They were tired of the violence and the chaos, and especially the poor economy. Victor Talley offered solutions. He joined with the aliens, who provided new farming technologies and energy sources. He created goodwill, prosperity, and peace wherever he reigned—for a time.

Talley even became a great friend to Israel and a hero to the world when he solved the impossibly stalemated Middle East crisis seemingly overnight.

That, too, impressed me. Palestine and the surrounding Arab countries, in fact much of the world, had this insane hatred for the Jewish people going back centuries. Their very presence in the region caused all manner of violent conflict. Governments and politicians had been trying to fix the problem, without success, even before Israel became a nation. After that, the situation became a political nightmare, an impossible stalemate brought on by blind hatred, interrupted only by needless and futile acts of aggression and terror. Israel would offer peace, making concession after concession, giving away land until they had very little of it left. But the Palestinian and Arab leaders would settle for nothing less than the complete dismantling of Israel.

Still, most of world continued to blame Israel for the problem. War after war was fought, treaty after treaty made and broken, and no one, it seemed, could solve the problem until the Antichrist brokered a peace.

Before Victor Talley, the United Nations' main function seemed to be to mess with Israel, passing resolution after resolution condemning the small country, while completely ignoring severe human rights violations in other areas of the world. The U.N. general assembly passed an average of twenty resolutions a year against Israel, ten times more than all other countries combined.

Equally partisan, the world media sided with Arabs and Muslims even at the cost of reason and common sense, at the same time spitting venom toward Israel at every opportunity. I mean a Muslim could strap on a bomb and blow up a bus full of women and children, or saw the head off some poor guy with a dull sword, place the footage on the Internet, and the media would barely take notice. But if Israeli soldiers so much as fired rubber bullets at Arab rioters, they'd give the incident prime coverage.

Later, at the Hall of Knowledge, I found out that the supernatural had fueled much of the policy and vitriol aimed at Jews and the Jewish State. It was never about race or religion. It wasn't even about politics or land. Six million Jews were slaughtered while the people of Germany let it happen with barely a breath of protest. How could so many remain idle while a race of people were being annihilated? It wasn't exactly what one would call normal behavior. Satan and the Illuminati had pulled the strings and the puppets of the world gladly followed.

***

Nobody even cared about that splinter of barren land next to the Mediterranean Sea until the Jews began settling en masse. So why was it the focus of so much of the world's troubles? The whole country is 260 miles long and 70 miles wide, for Heaven's sake. Arabs controlled Egypt, Saudi Arabia, Syria, Iraq, Lebanon, Jordon, Yemen—hundreds of thousands of square miles. The landmass of Saudi Arabia alone could contain over a hundred Israels, yet the world continued to blame them over the plight of the Palestinians, robbed of their land by greedy Jews.

There was never any such thing as a Palestinian until all the nonsense began. There were only Jews, Arabs, and Muslims. They lived side by side in an area known as Palestine, which was an area ruled by the British. Because the land was so desolate (God said that no one would be able to grow on it until the Jewish people returned, which is exactly what happened) nobody had tried to make a nation of it since the Jews ruled it 2000 years before.

Figuring the Jewish people for the bigger claim, the British assigned the whole area to be Jewish Palestine. Word got out, and Jews from all over the world began to return to their homeland and another Bible prophecy was fulfilled.

And wouldn't you know it—things began to grow again, the area thrived. That's when local Arabs finally took an interest. They wanted the newly flourishing land for themselves and began pouring into Jewish Palestine in droves. Did the Jews throw them out? No, they welcomed them.

Then, under pressure from neighboring Arab countries, the British divided the area again with seventy-five percent to be deemed Arab Palestine, leaving only twenty-five percent now to the Jews. This was yet another strange decision involving the fate of the region.

But the Jews didn't complain. They accepted this unreasonable proposal, even allowing the Arabs and Muslims living in their twenty-five percent to remain as friends and neighbors. And many did.

Still, none of this created the mythical country of Palestine. The Arabs took their seventy-five percent and most of that land became the country of Jordan.

But the Arabs and Muslims weren't satisfied. I guess they figured there must be something great over there in that twenty-five percent if they accepted the offer without a fight. Anyway, sensing weakness and opportunity, they attacked like rabid dogs, massacring Jews on both sides of the dividing lines.

After lying down throughout the Holocaust, the Jewish people had had enough. They fought back with a vengeance, driving off the hostile Arabs and the pro-Arab Brits.

Finally, the British also had enough, giving the matter to the U.N., who then made another incredible, satanically-influenced decision. They now decided to divide up the Jews' remaining twenty-five percent, handing another twelve percent of Jewish Palestine over to the Arabs who already had seventy-five percent of the whole enchilada.

Once again, the Jews accepted the compromise. But finally, in 1948, they declared their own Jewish State. Immediately, seven neighboring Arab armies attacked.

Warned of the attack on Israel and the intended annihilation of its Jewish citizens, those Arabs, living peacefully in Israel, fled town in a hurry without bothering to pack. They figured they'd be moving back shortly after the slaughter, and to claim their Jewish friends' and neighbors' property as well.

Lo and behold, the expected annihilation didn't happen. The little nation was surrounded, outgunned and outmanned, yet the Arabs were soundly defeated.

God had promised that once the Jews returned and established their own nation again, they would never be forced to leave it again. And they never were.

What happened to all the disappointed Arabs who had left to wait out Israel's predicted defeat during the first attack? They hung around the area that would later become Palestine, complaining about how they were forced out of their homes by the Jews.

Why? Because their Arab brothers wanted nothing to do with them. Instead of inviting them in to settle or offering them a little bit of land from their massive countries for their own nation, the neighboring Arab states thought it better to use them as pawns, portraying them as victims robbed of their land by the evil Jews, and the Middle East Crisis was born.

***

The reestablishment of Israel also started the Biblical prophetic clock. Although Jesus said no one would know the exact moment of His return, He gave a pretty startling prediction regarding the generation living during the reestablishment of the Jewish Nation. He said, "...that generation would not pass" before His return. Latest that put it was maybe 2048, give or take 10 years, and of course He came back much earlier. It couldn't have been any clearer. "Hello," He was saying, "I'm coming very soon, George. Wake the heck up, Buddy!"

***

I was a slow learner. I was already too late for the Rapture and now this Antichrist guy was starting to take over the world, and still, I was just beginning to embrace Christianity.

I knew what was coming from what Charlie had told me, but I wanted to know more, so I picked up every Christian book I could find concerning the end-times, which wasn't easy. The day after the Rapture, the Illuminati-run government had stripped all the bookstores and libraries of prophetic books. Still, after hitting up a dozen bookstores, I was able to purchase a few that had been missed.

It was amazing how right these modern day "prophets" had been regarding the events that were to come. They had the Rapture, Antichrist, and one-world government business nailed. If they were right about the rest of what they were writing, I remember thinking at the time, things were about to get scary real fast.

***

If I had it to do over again, I would have stood in the middle of Times Square, preaching the Word of God until they carted me off for torture and murder. But, though I was reading the Bible and praying more, my faith was still pretty weak, and I was nowhere close to becoming a martyr.

I mean for a long time after Sophie disappeared, I thought I wanted to die. I was numb enough to risk injury trying to help after the plane wreck, but that wasn't the real me. I had always looked out for number one, and that hadn't changed. So after the numbness wore off, my survival instincts kicked in, and I realized I was as scared of dying as I had always been, and so began planning my escape.

I soon discovered there were a whole lot of websites and books dedicated to sticking round after an apocalypse. The first thing I wanted to know was where the best place to hide would be. There were many choices, mostly in other countries, but that wouldn't do. I was going to stay where I was until the last possible moment, so I needed someplace drivable, preferably in California, as I thought it would also be more difficult to get out of the state once the crap hit the fan. I was right, but it would be much worse than I thought. After the Mark of the Beast was imposed, it became difficult to leave even the city.

I eventually settled on an area of lava pits in Northern California just below the Sierra Mountain Range and close to fresh water. The place was teeming with wildlife and had plenty of caves. I drove up a few times until I found the right cave, deep enough for hiding but with a view of the valley and road below.

I used to watch this television show about a guy who would walk into the wilderness or desert someplace, wearing practically nothing but his underwear and carrying only a pocketknife and a length of rope. He'd stay out there for about a week eating plants and bugs, and the occasional fish or rabbit, at least until he'd manage to trap a pig or something. So I figured with some knowledge of the wilderness, guns and plenty of ammunition, a ton of food, sleeping bags and blankets, a generator, traps and fishing poles, firewood, flashlights and batteries, a stove, and a bunch of other junk, I might be able to survive.

I mean I wasn't completely ignorant of the outdoors. I had been a Boy Scout and had gone on my share of bivouacs in the Army. Still, I wasn't about to go unprepared. I read and researched, and gathered everything I would possibly need. And twice a month, I made the long drive north to stash more goods in my new hideout. Eventually, I decided I was ready, and so I waited.

***

According to my books on Christian prophecy and what I remembered from my conversations with Charlie, the Antichrist was going to solidify his power by forming a world government and religion. Then he would require everyone to have some sort of mark on their body if they wanted to participate in the economy—and by participate I mean eat. The mark would require the bearer to denounce God and pledge devotion to the Antichrist. Weak Christian or not, that path, I knew, was a one-way ticket to the pit. On that one I had heard Charlie loud and clear. *"Even if it means death, never take a mark to buy or sell."*

***

After the North American Union was formed, things moved surprisingly fast. Victor Talley was adding a country a day to his European Union, which they were now calling the New World Order. He had already annexed most of Europe, Africa, Australia, and the Middle East, and the only real holdouts were in Asia and the North American Union. The pressure on those countries was relentless. Everything the Antichrist touched turned to milk and honey. All the countries under the flag of the New World Order were peaceful and booming, but everywhere else: unrest, unemployment, food shortages, and the like. Canada, Mexico, and the U.S legislative branches all urged President Newton to give in, and it wasn't long before the dire economic situation left him little choice.

***

At first, Talley set himself up as the democratic president of the New World Order. Under him was a senate made up mostly of former leaders of the countries he'd annexed. Talley worked with these guys to establish one currency, one huge army, and a central government located in Iraq. There, a city called New Babel was built practically overnight. New Babel rivaled the city of New York in size, but with purely modern construction and an obscene opulence.

How did they build it so fast? The aliens helped them.

***

The revival of Babylon was predicted in the Bible. Babylon was the largest and most advanced empire of the ancient world, but full of demons, giants, and miscreants of every kind. Such mayhem and depravity existed that it put to shame the worst days of Rome.

An arrogant king named Nimrod, who would eventually become possessed by demons, once ruled the Babylonian empire. By brute force, he had conquered the known world and created the first one-world government. Nimrod, a direct descendent of Noah, then rejected God in favor of worshiping the fallen angels and their legends. The seat of his empire was the great city of Babel, built to honor those false gods.

The Bible story was that the Babylonians became full of pride and decided to build a tower up to Heaven in order that they might be on the same footing as God. Again, what the storytellers couldn't relate with and didn't pass along was the science and technology involved in the construction of the so-called Tower of Babel. The Tower of Babel wasn't a tower at all, and even the original Greek translations of the Bible suggest a "gateway for gods" rather than a tower. But the storytellers couldn't fathom a means by which Heaven could be reached without building straight up to the clouds.

Well, what was it then? It was an attempt at building a stargate, a portal used to transcend space and time to travel the universe. The Illuminati provided Nimrod and his architects with the blueprints and materials, and the Babylonians were off and running.

God, however, had other plans. He could never allow such a pathway that would expose humans to even more demon and alien activity, so he confused the languages, preventing the Babylonians from communicating effectively enough to finish the stargate. It worked. So well, in fact, it broke up the whole of civilization into what would eventually become the modern world with its many borders, cultures, and languages.

***

That is, until the Antichrist began bringing everyone back together. The countries of Eastern Asia, mostly controlled by China, were the largest holdouts. China was a beast unto itself, a vast communist empire that at the time of the Antichrist controlled Japan, North and South Korea, Malaysia, Singapore, Taiwan, Cambodia, Vietnam, Thailand, and Indonesia. China also had the largest army ever seen, and a nuclear arsenal large enough to wipe out the rest of the world a thousand times over. They weren't about to succumb to any one-world government unless it was to be run by them. Their resistance would eventually lead to a great battle in a Middle Eastern valley known as Armageddon.

***

As soon as the Antichrist set up shop in New Babel, he dismantled the Senate of the New World Order. Those few Senators who wouldn't go quietly began to resign or die under mysterious circumstances. Soon, the New World Order president became the New World Order supreme leader.

***

In a large room in the city of London, a wall of computers had been gathering information about every individual on the planet since the early 1980s. These computers, nicknamed the Beast, were doing essentially the same thing that a fictional computer of the same name was supposed to have been doing since the 1970s. The fictional computer was from a novel about the end of the world.

In the novel, the Beast was three stories tall because that's how big the author thought a computer would have to be to store that much information. But this was a great exaggeration even by 1970s computer standards. By 1980, just one of the real Beast computers, about the size of an average door, could handle the job. Still, more were added to speed up the information gathering.

The real Beast was owned by a company called Vester. This Illuminati-run company had supposedly set up the computers to gather customer information for marketing purposes. The information was sold to other companies for this reason, but the genuine work of Vester had always been preparation.

***

My name and Social Security number were entered into the Beast when I applied for credit cards on my first day of college.

***

Credit card companies on the old Earth would routinely set up little booths on college campuses, where they would hand out credit cards like condoms to unsuspecting students. These credit cards had interest rates and limits that would shame a Mafia loan shark. American Express offered students a card with unlimited funds. Several banks offered students Visa Cards with interest rates over twenty-five percent.

***

I accepted an American Express Card, three Visa Cards, and a MasterCard for good measure. By the time I turned twenty, I carried $42,000 in credit card debt, which I couldn't pay, so I didn't. My credit was ruined for seven years. The Beast duly noted that I was a bad risk.

The Beast not only tracked each purchase I made with the credit cards, debit cards, and checks I used, but also my movements. The Beast knew what I ate, what I wore, where I traveled, the movies I watched, the bands I went to see, the gifts I bought, what my hobbies were, the schools I went to, where I worked, how much I made, the Internet sites I searched, and on and on. The Beast knew me better than I knew myself.

The Beast knew something else about me, too. The Beast knew I would run.

10

There is, of course, something humbling about cave life. Staring for hours at the visiting rodents and crawling things softens the ego as one begins to realize the smallness of life. This was the beginning of my salvation, as I would have to change, to be reborn before I could enter the kingdom of God.

***

Before Danny and her party happened upon me, I spent my days staring at creatures, praying, and gathering food. I also read quite a bit and listened to the radio, but infrequently, as I was limited on gas and batteries.

***

I had stashed away about fifty books on various subjects, including a Bible my mom had given me because she was worried about my soul. She was right to be worried. The Bible would have helped me to avoid a lot of anguish had I bothered to open it with any frequency before the Rapture.

***

The Bible is eternity, life, and the true bread on the table. The answers to all needs, problems, worries, heartache, and anguish are in the Book. You have only to pick it up with an open heart. Even the birds were content, "...fed and housed," the Bible teaches, "yet so much more precious is a man or woman to God."

Reading the Bible with an open mind and heart—not for an hour here and there, or a few consecutive days—but embracing it; letting it become the start and the end of each day; honoring its greatness and importance, even for a time, feeds like nothing else, so when you become distracted, when you leave it, you never forget its nourishment and long for it consciously and subconsciously.

***

Did I begin each day with the Bible? Did I embrace it? Did I honor its importance? Did I read it with an open heart? Not really. Even after the Rapture and all I'd seen, I was like most people on the old Earth with their heads on the ground. If they had nothing, they were thinking about how to get something; if they had everything, they were thinking about how to get more. But something and everything was usually close by, wasting away on a shelf, in a drawer, in a box in the garage, or in the corner of a cave.

So like most, I read the Bible when I was hungry, troubled, depressed, or lonely. After I read and prayed, the food would come, the fear would go, I'd feel better. But once satisfied, I would ignore the Book for a time. Still, God never held it against me. God was a good guy like that.

***

I had a calendar where I marked the days in my first cave. On the 127th day, the Minions of the Antichrist found my SUV. It wasn't the first encounter I'd had with the men in the black jumpsuits. These men could not be reasoned with. These men had no compassion. These men were brutal and relentless. If I didn't do something soon, they would find me.

Now there were only three of them, so I probably could have picked them off with my rifle before they reached the cave, but I knew if had, the New World Order would send a small army to look for them. It was time to leave.

I was already prepared for this possibility—a cycle that would repeat itself often—and I had a large backpack ready. I would have to come back for the bulk of my supplies later. I threw on the pack, stuffed a pistol in my belt, grabbed my rifle and headed up the mountain to find a new home.

***

The Minions were the Antichrist's version of Heinrich Himmler's SS, the infamous Nazi paramilitary organization responsible for beatings, torture, and the mass murder of millions. Like the SS, the Minions were handpicked for their brutality. And like the SS, the Minions would drag people out of their houses in the middle of the night to beat or cart them away, often never to be seen again.

***

Many times, I had stood by and watched as the Minions harassed my neighbors. Each time, I vowed afterwards to jump in, but I never did. I knew it would mean at least a severe beating and possibly death, and I was afraid.

Late one night, before I left my home to live in that first cave, I awoke to the sound of Wiley barking and the Minions pounding on my front door. *It was my turn.* I knew exactly what they wanted. I had been to all their stupid movies, listened to Victor Tally's redundant speeches, checked in at the local New World Order office, received my new identification card, accepted my ration slips, had even been assigned a surgery date. Except the date came and went, and I hadn't shown up.

I kicked myself for not leaving the city when I had had the chance. Back then I wasn't sure exactly what the Mark would consist of, but I figured I would leave as soon as they began the requirement.

This was a mistake. Months before they began the implant surgeries, they locked the city down with roadblocks. When the implants were announced, I tested the roads leading out of the city and ran into checkpoints every time. Without special travel papers, no one was allowed to leave.

My only hope was the four-wheel drive on my SUV and getting out through the hills and mountains bordering the highways leading out of the county. Each day, I ventured out to find a path, but even the dirt roads had checkpoints, and traveling cross-country inevitably led to dead ends.

***

Now it was too late; now they were at my door. I should have locked Wiley in another room, but he was a sweet dog, harmless to strangers, so I merely pushed him aside and opened the door quickly before they had a chance to break it down.

There were four of the cold men in black jumpsuits, their wrists bearing the Mark of the Beast. Immediately one of them grabbed me by the collar and shoved me against the wall. Wiley, bless his heart, went after his ankle, and another Minion shot him dead.

"No!" I shouted, and I fought against the Minion to reach my dog, till the others grabbed me and threw me down. Wiley was my last link to Sophie, and I had become quite attached, even reliant on, the little fellow. I began to sob. "Why did you have to shoot him?" I asked.

"Shut up! The mutt had it coming," said the Minion who shot him.

***

That was basically the same thing my grandmother told my father after the old man who lived next door shot his dog when he was a boy. Each time my father's dog got loose she would run over to the neighbor's backyard to bark at the rabbits in their cages. The old man was an ornery son-of-a-gun. One day he became fed up and shot the dog with a twenty-two rifle. My father heard the shot and ran over to find his dog lying wounded in front of the rabbit cage. He carried her back to his house and asked his mom to call a doctor. "She's a goner, and we can't spare anything for a doctor," she said.

My father cried and cradled the dog on the porch while she succumbed to the wound. "Stop crying," said his mom. "She had it coming anyway."

My father never got another dog, and he wouldn't touch any of the dogs we had in the house growing up. He didn't want to become attached, and now I understood why.

***

I was embarrassed because I couldn't stop crying. And like my grandmother, one of the Minions urged me to stop, except he used a baton to my stomach to do it.

As soon as I could breathe again, they brought me into the living room, sat me in a chair, and the tallest one slapped me a couple times. He was Hispanic, spoke with a slight accent, obviously the leader of the bunch. "I am Captain Guerra. We just wanted to ask you a few questions, Mr. Somerset."

***

Except for his height and sadistic nature, the SS wouldn't have had much to do with Captain Guerra, unless it was to cart him off to the gas chambers. The SS only took pureblooded Aryans. The Antichrist, on the other hand, was an equal opportunity employer. Race was never an issue. Anyone with a soul would do.

***

"Why didn't you report for surgery?" continued the captain.

I had prepared for this moment. "I was sick. I had an infection," I answered.

He slapped me again. Apparently, I hadn't prepared well enough. "Don't lie to me, Somerset. You were supposed to show up with a clearance. It's in your notice!" Captain Guerra said.

"I was too ill to come down."

"Where is the clearance then?" said Guerra.

"I only got the medicine. I didn't know I would still be sick."

Again, he slapped me. "You're lying. What kind of infection?"

"I'm not lying." Of course I was lying, but I had scored some pills from a doctor two weeks earlier after feigning a urinary tract infection. He wrote me a prescription for antibiotics. "I had a respiratory infection…in my lungs—I couldn't get out of bed."

"Where is the bottle?"

"It's in the bathroom in the master bedroom—in the medicine cabinet."

"Check it, Carter," ordered the captain, and the husky one who shot my dog took off down the hallway. Captain Guerra stared at me with a vicious smirk on his face. "He better find it."

In a moment Carter was back with the empty bottle. I had lied to the pharmacist that I didn't want my live-in girlfriend finding out about the urinary infection and asked him not to label it that way. The bottle Carter brought back read only: *For Infection.*

The captain looked at it for a long time before he set the bottle down on my coffee table. He seemed to calm down. He told the other two to search the whole house. "You got anything to drink?" he said.

"Yeah, what do you want? I think I got some juice left….I got water."

"You got juice?"

***

Fruit and fruit juices were a rare commodity, as were most fresh goods during the early days of the New World Order in America, before the Antichrist began working his magic by providing an abundance of goods to the masses bearing the Mark of the Beast. This would also serve to wear down the holdouts, surrounded by plenty yet forced to scrape by until they complied. Before all that, it was tough to find even essentials, but my former drug dealer had turned to dealing in black market goods, and I was able to obtain certain hard-to-find items for a price.

***

"A little apple juice…I'll get it." I started to get up.

Guerra put his hand out to block me and turned to the husky one again. "Get me some juice, Carter."

Guerra, pulling up a chair, sat across from me as close as he could get. I could hear his men rummaging through the house. Guerra was smirking and staring again. Carter came back with the juice and the captain spoke, "We know you're a runner."

"A runner?" I knew exactly what he was talking about.

"Don't play dumb," said Guerra, and he slapped me again.

"You mean I want to leave town somehow. I don't have anywhere to go even if I could."

"We know everything, Georgie. We know about the camping supplies and the survival gear. We know about the food and the bottled water. We know about the guns. We know about the Christian books and the Internet searches: *best places to live off the land.* You're not very slick, Georgie."

Just then the two Minions ransacking the house returned and one of them interrupted, "We found nothing."

"We got a mountain man here boys—a real Daniel Boone," said Guerra. Carter and the other men laughed. "Where are the goods, Georgie?"

"I don't know what you're talking about."

The captain stopped smiling and stood. "Stand up, Georgie," he said. I did. He was an inch from my face. "Don't be stupid, Georgie— I could take you down to headquarters and beat it out of you."

***

I knew something was up then. I was wondering why Guerra wasn't already beating the crap out of me. I never heard a Minion tell anybody they were going to be beaten at a later time, unless they were already beating them up while informing them it was to get worse. And the slapping thing was odd, too. These Minion guys weren't big on slapping. They were much more into punching. No, something wasn't right. I wouldn't find out why until later, but these guys, I knew, weren't going to hurt me that day, so I stopped being so afraid. Still, I decided to cooperate as much as I could to buy some time; besides, I was tired of being slapped.

"I don't want any trouble."

"Of course you don't, not this kind. Where is the stuff?"

"You mean the camping gear?"

"All of it—the gear, the food stores, the weapons," said Guerra.

"It's not here anymore," I said.

"Where is it?"

"I tried for a long time to get out of the city, but I couldn't, so I ended up eating the food and selling everything else."

"Do you know what the penalty is for selling weapons?"

I knew it was death. "This was a long time ago, before all those laws came out," I said.

***

The founding fathers had guaranteed Americans the right to bear arms. They wanted individuals to be able to protect themselves, not only from individuals who might cause harm, but also from tyrannical governments like the New World Order. Slowly, beginning with semi-automatic weapons, the Illuminati-controlled government banned ownership of other firearms. By the time the NWO took over, hundreds of millions of weapons had been confiscated and destroyed, and it was illegal for the average citizen to own a firearm of any kind. When resistance to the dictatorship did finally break out, the small bands of poorly armed patriots were easily wiped out.

***

"Who did you sell them to?" Guerra said.

"Different people…strangers…like I said, it was a long time ago."

Captain Guerra paced about the room for a moment like he didn't know what to do unless he was punching someone. I knew if it were up to him, I'd have been beaten to a bloody pulp already and probably dead.

He pulled out a small envelope from his front pocket. "You have a date with the surgeon in a week and a half. If you miss it, you will know the real me," Guerra said, and with that, he led his men out the door.

***

I cried some more for Wiley, my last living connection to Sophie, and buried him in the backyard on the exact spot where she disappeared.

***

I couldn't sleep that night. I sat on the couch, staring at the date on the appointment card. It wasn't enough time. Over and over, I had tested the perimeter of the city without success. I didn't know what to do. I couldn't face the prospect of torture. I knew I couldn't hold up. I heard the horror stories from some of the victims who'd caved. I wouldn't have lasted five minutes before I'd have cut my own wrist open and shoved the chip in myself. I stayed up most of the night praying for a solution.

***

Microchip technology had been around and improving rapidly since the late 1950s. By the time the Beast was feeding the tiny machines, some were as small as a grain of rice and some contained billions of transistors.

My father designed microchips for the guidance systems of missiles at Hughes Aircraft in the 1970s. These microchips told the missiles where to go. In 2003, during the Iraq war, micro-chipped missiles were synced with precision laser beams guided by satellites. These new "smart bombs" were used in the opening attack on Bagdad.

The president at the time, George W. Bush, used the term shock-and-awe to describe the attack, which was seen live on cable news all over the world. There were lots of flashes, bangs, explosions, buildings collapsing and whatnot, and it *was* pretty awesome and shocking. But the real shocker was the war lasting another eight years, producing some 200,000 civilian and military casualties.

So, with all the smart weaponry, why did the war last so long? The Bush Administration got so carried away with the shock-and-awe part they forgot the rest of the plan. Instead of locking the place down and declaring martial law, they let everyone run around like grad night. Looters, criminals, radicals, insurgents, terrorists, and other knuckleheads had a field day, until it became too late to rein in the chaos.

This kind of madness would never have happened during World War II. After the defeat of Germany, martial law was declared, curfews were enforced, and looters, resisters, and knuckleheads were shot on sight. What do you know? It worked. Germany was mostly under control in a matter of weeks, and the rebuilding could begin without thousands more needlessly being killed.

***

The same microchip technology, which fed information to the smart bombs, was then used to create implants first placed in dogs and cats as homing devices. But the manufacturers had broader plans. Various government agencies, corporations, and banks had been pushing for their use in humans for years. Their argument was that the chips would eliminate security problems, prevent bank fraud, and make it easy to track missing persons, criminals, and terrorists. The public wanted no part of it—not until things got really bad.

After economies around the globe began to tank, before the Antichrist took full control, crime had been getting out of control. Muggings, robberies, kidnappings, and even murders occurred in places once relatively crime-free, on a regular basis and in broad daylight. Criminals were especially interested in credit and debit cards. Most crooks would steal the card numbers from restaurants, retail stores, and trash bins, or by computer hacking, but the more violent ones kidnapped and forced their victims to give up the PIN codes or make withdrawals by beating and torturing them, or threatening family members. The government insisted the implants would solve the crime problem, so they began accepting volunteers. And because people were afraid, many did.

***

Soon after the Antichrist moved the government to New Babel, he brought the London computers there, linking them to a microchip manufacturing plant that began making the implantable chips in mass quantities. The Beast was growing.

***

Not only was it the number of the Antichrist, 666 also represented the eighteen numbers laid out in three sequences of six, which were imprinted on the microchips and were the key to the information on the implants. The 666 microchip was a whole different animal compared to the volunteer implants of the previous decade, which were basically small credit cards inserted beneath the skin. This chip would contain a person's whole life. It would also come with strings.

Before the surgeries, the patients were brought to a special room. These rooms were called churches because they contained altars with statues of the Antichrist. The patient would have to kneel, denounce Jesus Christ, and worship the Antichrist as God. After the surgery, their wrists would be placed in a machine to stamp them with a tattoo. The tattoo looked like an old Roman coin. It was a black circle with a picture of Talley and the clear but staggered numbers 666. This was exactly what John saw in the vision he wrote about in Revelation. There would be no more pretenses.

***

Some of my neighbors on the old Earth had already received the implants and the tattoos. Like guilty children, they seemed nervous, and for some reason, wanted to talk to those in the neighborhood, including me, who didn't yet have the Mark. I didn't trust them.

In less than two weeks, it would be my turn to accept the Mark or die a horrible death. I don't know when I finally fell asleep, but it was late. Even so, I woke up early, tired but too anxious and scared to go back to sleep. Staring up at the ceiling, I repeated my prayers from the night before.

After I got out of bed, I went to the backyard and stood at Wiley's grave. That's when I remembered something: another dead dog, this one stiff and floating in our pool. It was at the old house over the hill where we lived when I owned the mortgage company. I had completely forgotten the incident or pushed it out of my mind somehow.

We had only had the dog for a week or something. He was a stray little ratty dog with so much hair you couldn't see his face. He snored and made funny wheezing noises. Sophie and Renee found it at the park. Sophie begged me to keep it. I told her no. I didn't want to deal with it. We were set to take the dog to the pound that weekend. I was the only one home. I let the dog out to pee. It was an accident.

But it wasn't an accident. I was seeing it clearly for the first time. I had forgotten about the dog. It was a hot day, but I didn't think to fill his water because I was going to be right back to let him in the house. Except I was distracted by a phone call.

It was my partner in the mortgage company and other criminal enterprises, Justin Lister. I was working from home that day. Justin had called me up for one of our infamous lunches, which always began in a dark bar with a crap load of drinks and ended up at a racetrack, casino, strip club, or some other soul degenerating location. So I left. I left the poor dehydrated dog to find a drink in the swimming pool.

I was trashed by the time I came home to find the dog floating in the pool. I buried him quickly. I even blamed it on Renee because she wouldn't let me throw him in the pool to teach the dog to swim when they first brought him home. Then I made myself forget.

***

But that morning in the backyard, standing over Wiley's grave, it all came back. Now I understood why I had cried over a nameless dog I barely knew. I felt the guilt and the shame again. I lived the poor dog's hot afternoon over and over in my mind, and I cried again. I cried for his suffering. I cried for my little girl who was heartbroken. I cried for the consequences of all my lies. I cried until I couldn't cry anymore.

***

Then I remembered something else I'd forgotten, as clearly as if it had happened the day before—an incident which occurred about five months prior. I was waiting in one of the long lines to get into a market with mostly empty shelves, when I recognized one of my former employees, a loan processor named Mary Hammond. I spotted her coming out of the market with a small bag. She had been an efficient processor, kind and quite attractive. Now she was still very pretty but much thinner than I remembered, and tired looking, as most of us were in those days. "Mary," I said as she passed by.

"George?" she said, and her expression changed quickly from wonder to near indifference.

I thought I knew why. I had left my employees under awful circumstances. They were let go without pay when the company folded because we were broke. "Yeah, it's me. Wow, it's great to see you!"

She didn't say anything. I stepped out of line, grabbed her by the elbow, and led her away from the crowd. "Let go, you're going to lose your place," she said.

I pointed to her nearly empty bag. "It doesn't look like I'll miss very much."

She pulled her elbow from my grip. "I have to go."

"Sorry. Look, I apologize for all that business with the company. There was nothing left, Mary."

"Maybe you and Justin spent it all on your big houses, and your cars, and your booze." This wasn't the pushover I remembered.

"I'm sorry. I really am. I was an idiot. I have some extra food and things at the house. I want you to have it."

"I don't want it. You can share it with your creepy friend."

"Are you talking about Justin?"

"Yeah, your partner." she said.

"I haven't seen him in years."

"Why does he have my records? Why is he harassing me?"

"What are you talking about?" I had no clue.

"I think you know what I'm talking about. Always thick as thieves, you two."

"I haven't seen him. I swear, Mary. What is going on?"

She didn't answer. She ran off mumbling after that, something about us leaving her alone. I was dumbfounded.

***

But the morning after Wiley was shot, after I prayed most of the night asking for a solution, I finally understood. And his name was all I could think about the rest of the day: *Justin Lister.*

What else would he be doing? He was the greatest salesman I ever met. He could sell Irish to a leprechaun. He taught me every sales trick in the book. Moreover, he was an opportunist. There was only one place to find opportunity then. He would have sold himself to the New World Order. Now I understood why I hadn't been hauled in and beaten to death by the Minions. Good old Justin. I had my answer. The Lord does work in mysterious ways.

11

For better or worse, and mostly worse, Justin Lister had been my friend. It wasn't that he was awful and I was good, but that we were both awful, and more awful when we were together.

***

Now I drove the same route I once commuted daily, to the building that housed our old company. I hadn't seen Justin in a long time, but we didn't separate on horrible terms. I never blamed him for the company failing. His spending was out of control; he'd pushed for expansion when we weren't stable; hired a mediocre manager to do his job because he wanted to play golf most days; partied most nights, so he was only half there when he was at work; and a bunch of other mistakes that sped up the company's demise, but I was complicit in all of it; moreover, I was a partner in all of it.

Besides, we made tons of money just like he said we would. We just spent it like drunken sailors with three months to live. And none of it would have mattered anyway. Once the housing market collapsed and the banks stopped lending, we were too big not to fail.

***

"Too big to fail" was a term made popular after the Obama Administration bailed out the banks and Wall Street firms responsible for the housing collapse. Where did the term come from? The companies needing the bailouts made it up. Eventually, they would all come to realize that no one except God was too big to fail.

***

I didn't blame Justin for wrecking my family, either. I did that all on my own. I just couldn't hang out with him anymore because he had become like a mirror to me, a reminder of all I had destroyed.

***

I passed our old offices, now abandoned, having been damaged beyond repair in the Great Earthquake. I was heading downtown to where two new buildings contained the headquarters of the New World Order. I wasn't nervous. I would be very nervous, in fact terrified, the next time I saw him, but this time I was quite calm. We had been through so much together, and in that respect, we would always be brothers of a sort.

Once I'd figured out Justin was working for the New World Order, he was easy enough to find. The New World Order was no longer shy about what they were doing or who was working for them, so it was a simple matter of pulling up the employee directory on their website. Justin didn't know I was coming. I knew the lines were monitored and thought it better not to phone first.

I parked away from the building and walked the four blocks. Beyond the cold stares of the security guards in the lobby, I wasn't bothered, so I found the directory and proceeded to his department on the eighteenth floor. His title was Compliance Minister, which was ironic because compliance was the last thing Justin was interested in during his lending career.

The elevator opened to a varnished cherry wall, emblazoned in gold letters that read *New World Order Compliance Ministry*. I skirted the wall, walking past a series of smaller offices till I came to an open door at the end of the corridor. A secretary sat at a small desk near the door, and she began to ask me something, but I told her I was an old friend and moved past her. I could hear the loud, familiar voice, so I stood in the doorway and waited. Justin Lister was always on the phone. It used to drive me crazy. It was weird seeing him again; it brought back all the memories, good and bad.

***

My shaky career path brought me to the offices of Mercury Mortgage, where Justin hired and trained me to be a loan officer and salesman. Before that I had been a bookmaker, soldier, cab driver, high school teacher, and real estate investor of sorts.

***

The Army taught me discipline—which I mostly ignored—but, more importantly, it gave me an education. We had so much down time at the base, and there wasn't much to do that was productive, except to take the college courses offered at the Base Education Center by the University of Oklahoma. After I was discharged, I took the credits I'd earned and the money from the G.I. Bill and applied to the Political Science program on their main campus.

I rented a cheap, one room apartment in Oklahoma City, drove a taxi most of the night, and went to classes four days a week. I finished my Bachelor's degree in two years and stuck around two more to get a teaching credential.

I stopped driving a taxi after I got my first teaching job. It was at a Catholic school in Oklahoma. I taught U.S. History, and things were good. The students seemed to like me. They didn't talk too much or throw stuff at me when I was writing on the chalkboard or anything. But I had already been away for a long time, so after two years, I moved back to Los Angeles, where the only teaching jobs available at the time were at predominately black schools in the inner city.

For the most part, the students at Douglas High didn't have any fathers at home. Most had friends and relatives who had been murdered, sometimes right in front of them. Also, this was high school, but a lot of the students were reading at elementary school levels. Many of them hated school anyway and had little respect for anybody because nobody in their lives except maybe their mothers ever did anything decent for them. And they hated authority because their fathers or some policeman would show up occasionally just to lecture them, hassle them, molest them, or smack them around. These kids were also hungry much of the time and rarely had any money unless they stole it or otherwise broke the law to get it. And they were often afraid to walk the streets of their own neighborhoods.

All this caused them to be shell shocked or otherwise preoccupied. They couldn't focus on school for the most part, and they especially didn't like any know-it-all white man telling them about other white guys like George Washington, Theodore Roosevelt, Winston

Churchill, or even Abraham Lincoln, who to them, were about as relevant and exciting as a badminton match.

I really tried to be a good teacher the first couple of years, but they wore me out eventually, and the whole thing is mostly a blur now because I became the walking dead for the next few years, going through the motions, putting the Cs on the F papers to fill the quotas, dumbing down the curriculum, fudging the attendance, and acting like I gave a crap.

That is, until the last three years when I completely gave up, strolling into class just before the bell rang, popping in a movie, sleeping at my desk, and heading out the door again even before some of the students.

***

I might have lasted till retirement that way, but I became disgusted with myself, so one day I stood up and began teaching again. The students actually listened for a little while—they must have been in shock or something.

It turns out I had a fire in me. The problem with the fire was that it wasn't passion. The fire was anger. And when the students sidled back into their old ways, I began ranting and yelling at them. I was going mad. I was that teacher, the crazy one I knew from my own high school.

Then I lost it completely. It was a Friday, the last period of the day nearly over. I graded papers while the students milled around waiting for the bell to ring. I looked up and spotted a student hanging around the computers in the back of the room acting cagey. I asked him what he was up to, and he ignored me. I asked him again, and he said, "Nothing," and went back to his seat. I went over there anyway to discover he'd opened three or four hot sauce packets and squirted them all over the computers and keyboards.

Seven years of pent-up rage exploded in me at that moment. I grabbed the kid by his jacket collar, dragged him across the room, and tossed him about six feet out of the door of my classroom. He rolled on the concrete, scraping his arm.

His dad, who hadn't seen a high school since his own expulsion, suddenly became the concerned parent, showing up at the principal's office every other day to demand my firing, while threatening to file suit against the district.

***

I wasn't fired. The principal was a drinking buddy of mine, and he managed to calm the guy down. I had to apologize to the student, but that was no big deal—I was sorry about the whole thing anyway.

But I was done. I finished out the semester and told them I wouldn't be back. I knew that if I stuck around something else bad was going to happen. My teaching career was over.

***

By that time, Renee and I had been married six years. She took my quitting pretty well. She was good like that. She didn't worry too much about what I did, as long as I was happy. She made her own money, and I had money saved and some retirement to cash in if it came to that.

***

Gerry, my oldest brother, was always involved in some scheme or entrepreneurial venture. Always legitimate stuff, but schemes nonetheless. He still lived in the Los Angeles area, and knowing I was out of work, he called me up one day to ask me if I wanted in on his latest venture. At the time, a wave of real estate speculation swept the country. His idea seemed sound, to buy a few distressed houses, fix them up, and resell them at a profit. I thought, what the heck, and off we went. It was hard work, but we bought in at the right time because six months later, just after we finished the first house, there was a huge housing boom.

***

This was the beginning of the Illuminati plan to collapse America's housing market. Once the short term interest-only loans adjusted to the much higher fixed rates, people began borrowing on their own equity to make the house payments. It was unsustainable. The collapse was inevitable.

***

While Gerry and I worked on the houses, I attended a real estate licensing course at night to help with the resale of the properties. We ended up finishing five houses and making a killing off them without paying commissions.

My brother had guessed the boom wouldn't last, but at that time it still had a few years left. He decided to move on to another venture. He had always handled the construction end, so I didn't feel confident going on without him.

I had some money, but it wouldn't last forever. I needed a new career. I didn't like the idea of driving people around to look at houses, so I decided to try my hand at the only other thing my real estate license was good for: lending.

***

I met Justin Lister when I walked into the offices of Mercury Mortgage in response to a newspaper ad he had placed looking for loan officers. He had come from Florida, where his former partners in another mortgage company ousted him for being a complete maniac. He'd convinced the owners of Mercury they needed a lead calling division to acquire more secondary market loans. These were loans that regular banks wouldn't touch because they were too risky. Justin told them they would make a fortune in rebate and up front charges on these types of loans. They were being sold.

***

My interview with Justin Lister was the easiest interview I'd ever had. I hardly said a word. He talked and talked, and he didn't ask me one question he didn't already know the answer to. He asked questions like, "If I told you that you were going to make $100,000 in your first year here, what would you say?" And I answered something like, "That would be great!" And he said, "Wrong, you should have said you were going to make twice that."

And he talked some more. I didn't remember but a fraction of what he said by the time it was over. But I had the job, and I had a date and time to report for training as a loan officer. I had been sold.

***

Turns out, he didn't care what I said. He didn't care about my work history or my degree. He didn't even care that I had a real estate license. As long as I wasn't a complete moron, he was just looking for another body to fill his training course. The job itself would weed out the undesirables.

109

***

My vision of a loan officer was of wearing a suit and tie, escorting a client into a corner office at some quiet bank, showing them to a comfortable chair in front of an elegant wooden desk, sitting them down to discuss the bank's various loan products.

This was not to be. What Justin had in mind for us was a boiler room. He had been given one large room full of dozens of tiny desks with phones. The room was attached to a private office at the far end of the bottom floor of Mercury Mortgage. Justin occupied the private office, which had a window into the boiler room, where he could gaze out to ensure we were constantly dialing.

After all, lead calling was a numbers game. One hundred phone calls meant thirty contacts, which meant ten packages sent to prospective clients, which meant three returns, which meant one deal. The training had been in three parts: *Product Knowledge*—all about crappy loans; *Applications and Qualifications*—all about applying for and receiving crappy loans; and *Lead Management*—all about selling crappy loans.

***

Most of the loans we sold were refinance loans, meaning someone would take their perfectly good loan and turn it into one of our lousy ones. Why did they do it? Because we told them it was a good idea, and because they would get a big check and lower their monthly payments. They could even pay off all their credit cards with one of our loans.

This was great—for about three years anyway. What did these borrowers end up with after three years? They owed more money on their house at a much higher interest rate, leaving them an ungodly mortgage payment. And they had spent the big check, so they were forced to max out their credit cards again to pay for it all.

You're welcome. Thank you for your business.

***

The *Lead Management* portion of the training consisted of a segment titled *Handling Objections*. This was training in how to respond to someone having legitimate concerns about the loan you were trying to sell and asking legitimate questions about those concerns. We'd all sit around the boiler room firing questions and comments at each other, practicing the patented rebuttals Justin had provided. It went something like this:

Prospect: Isn't it bad to pay only interest?

Loan Rep: Even with a conventional loan, you'd be paying mostly interest during the first few years. With the market rising the way it is, you'll be increasing your equity anyway. Take advantage of the lower payments now and we can refinance you again in a couple of years.

Prospect: How much will this loan cost me?

Loan Rep: Cost? I'm going to save you on your monthly payments and put a big fat check in your pocket.

Prospect: I'm not interested.

Loan Rep: What is it that you're not interested in? A lower interest rate? Lower monthly payments? Paying off your high interest credit cards? The big fat check I'm going to put in your pocket?

Prospect: My credit is horrible right now.

Loan Rep: As long as you have a job, I can get you a loan.

Prospect: I'm out of work.

Loan Rep: Then we definitely need to talk. Right now you need to lower your monthly payments. I have the perfect loan. I can get you a hundred percent financing. You won't need to show any income. It's our no income, no asset loan. We call it the NINJA because it's perfect for a smart yet limited investor like you.

…And on and on.

***

Justin's *Handling Objections* training was flagrantly dishonest. I was a natural. I excelled. In fact, I excelled in all the Loan Officer Training courses.

Like lead calling, Loan Officer Training was a numbers game. Forty hires meant thirty would show up for training. Thirty trainees meant twenty would finish. Twenty on the phone meant ten would last a month. Ten trainees sticking it out meant five successful loan officers. Five successful loan officers meant one killer.

I was a killer. A killer had to be fanatically persistent. A good loan officer made 100 to 150 calls a day. I made 250. This was tedious work. Perhaps the long hours in my backyard growing up, pulling the never-ending crop of weeds for my father, had prepared me. A killer had to love rejection. My father and my drill sergeant instilled that quality in me. Finally, a killer had to believe his own lies. That was easy. That was all me.

***

I made close to $40,000 in my first three months as a loan officer, and I was just getting started. My fourth month was looking to be my biggest yet. Justin Lister took me under his wing. This meant that he took me to happy hour with him—every night of the week. I told him I needed to be back at the office making phone calls. He told me not to worry about it. He told me he had bigger plans for us. My work suffered.

***

Justin laid it all out for me over a dozen vodka tonics. He wasn't planning on managing his division for much longer. Why should the owners of Mercury Mortgage make all the real money off his know-how? I thought we were making great money. He called it chicken feed. He said we should be making ten times what we were being paid. He was going to start his own mortgage brokerage. He needed a partner. He needed a backer. He'd been spending all his money suing his former partners. He was going to get millions out of the case, he said. He knew I had money from my real estate investments and the

recent loans I'd closed. He also needed someone with a broker's license. Since I already had my real estate license, he told me, I only needed to pass a simple test. I was being sold again.

***

Justin and I were different in many ways, but when it came to self-destruction, we were little less than twins separated at birth. We shook hands and celebrated our new partnership with more drinks and a few lines of cocaine. I called my wife and told her I would be working late again. It was the beginning of an ugly friendship and the beginning of the end of my marriage.

12

Nothing much had changed about him, except he was sitting at a bigger desk in a bigger office, and he bore the Mark. After he hung up the phone, he took a large gulp of coffee from an oversized Miami Hurricanes mug.

"Put that down. Coffee is for closers," I said.

He looked up, startled, but only for a second, and laughed.

"Oh my God, George Somerset! And you remember that!" Justin said.

The coffee line was from the movie, *Glengarry Glen Ross*, about a struggling sales office, which had been required viewing in Justin's loan officer training course. "Of course, I remember everything you taught me, though I'd like to forget most of it," I half joked.

I walked toward his desk. He met me halfway, giving me an awkward, still friendly hug. "Man, I knew I would see you again, but I didn't know when. You don't hate me anymore?"

"I never hated you. I never even blamed you...my life was so messed up...I needed a break...and Renee..."

He just smiled and closed the door. "Sit down, sit down. It's good to see you, pal."

We both sat. "It's good to see you, too." And it was. It was good to see any familiar face since the Rapture.

"I'm sorry about Renee and Sophie."

I knew where this would lead. Motioning to his mug, I tried to change the subject. "Still following the Hurricanes?"

"Always," he said. "Too bad they lost most of their best players because of those damn aliens."

It was no use, and I couldn't ignore it; the alien cover-up upset me too much. "Yeah, those damn rogue aliens. You're not buying any of that nonsense, are you?" I said.

His look told me I had crossed a line. He glanced at my wrist from across his desk and punched the button on his intercom. "Kelly, can you prep surgery for me?"

"What?" the receptionist said over the intercom.

He was laughing now. I wasn't. "Hilarious," I said.

He became serious again. "Never mind, Kelly....What are you doing, George?"

"I need your help."

"I've been helping you. Why do you think you haven't been dragged downtown? We know all about you."

"You know all about me?" I said.

"We know you're preparing to run. Do you know what happens to runners? Why do you want to run, George?"

"You know why."

"I don't know. I really don't."

"Why are you here, Justin?"

"This is my job."

"What? Harassing people like poor Mary Hammond?" I said.

"Harassing her? I was trying to help the stupid woman!"

"She was just another close for you."

He smiled and shook his head. "I know you think I'm a jerk, but I've helped a lot of my friends."

"Your job is to get people to volunteer for the surgery. She is just a number to you. Just like getting people into a bad loan."

"I like Mary. She's making a big mistake...just like you are!"

"So, you kill two birds with one stone. You hit on her like you did before at our office and make your quota at the same time."

"So what? I was being nice to her."

"You mean you want to sleep with her and take her soul," I said.

He scoffed at me. "Take her soul. What are you talking about? You believe all that nonsense? You're blowing it, George. What are you going to do? Are you going to starve? Get your head kicked in? Go to prison? They'll break you."

"Better than eternal damnation."

He laughed. "Have you talked to God personally? Have you seen the devil? Millions of people are going about their business, and they've got food on their tables and a roof over their heads. It's not so bad out there if you play ball."

"It won't last."

"How do you know?"

"I read the Bible...I read the prophets...."

"Hocus pocus—for every one of your books, I can show you fifty others that say differently."

"You can't sell me, Justin."

"Then why are you here?"

"I need your help."

"I told you—I've already been helping you. I can't do anything else for you. You've got to get the surgery, my friend. You don't want to miss another appointment."

"I'm not taking the Mark."

"Don't be stupid."

"I'm not taking the Mark, Justin."

"I can't help you if you don't help yourself. Isn't that what the Bible says?"

"Please don't quote the Bible—it's not one of your rebuttal lists. Just help me. I need travel papers."

Justin smiled and shook his head. Then he put his hands over his face and didn't move for some time. Finally, he put his hands down. "I can't."

"I need your help."

"Do you know what happens to me if they find out?"

"Aren't you the Compliance Minister? How many of you have offices this nice? You've got some juice around here."

"I still bleed the same."

"You can pull it off."

"You don't know what you're asking, George."

"You owe me."

"I owe you?" he asked without conviction.

"You spent everything you earned on yourself. I put all the money I had into the business, and I lost everything. I believed in you. I put you before my own family, and I lost them for it."

He looked angry, but he didn't say anything for a long time. He softened his expression and shook his head some more. "You're killing me," he said finally.

I smiled. Now I knew that he could help me, that he *would* help me.

"No, you know I can *really* be killed for this. This isn't going to be easy. You're a known potential runner," he said.

"You can sell it," I said. He got up then and walked around his desk. I stood and we hugged, and it felt for a moment like before it all went to crap.

"Come with me, Justin. It's not too late for any of us."

He put his marked wrist in my face. "What, cut off my own arm? Don't be ridiculous."

***

Among the other goodies, the chip under his skin contained a homing device connected to a satellite, which could pinpoint its exact location at all times. Running with the implant was not an option.

***

"I'll cut it off for you," I said, again only half joking. "It says in the Bible, 'Whatever makes you sin, cut it off'. You know all this stuff— you were raised more Christian than I was. Baptist, wasn't it?" He didn't answer; he seemed to be contemplating. I took another shot. "Turn back, Justin—you have nothing to lose."

"You can't sell me, either."

"I know," I said. He had that look on his face. He was back in work mode. It was pointless.

"Give me a few days. I think I can get you some papers."

"You never took no for an answer before."

"The papers won't guarantee anything," he added.

116

"I know you'll do your best—thanks, friend," I said, and turned to leave.

"Wait," he said and he looked at me for a moment. Then he laughed a little. "If you do make it—tell the big guy what I did for you."

I looked back at him. He wasn't laughing anymore; he wasn't even smiling. "I will, Justin. I will."

***

A few days later, true to his word, I received Justin's package. I had my travel papers and an appointment with a doctor he knew for the following day. The papers were good for the weekend. I wouldn't be reported missing till the following Monday. After that, I would be a hunted man.

***

I packed the SUV with a weekend's worth of clothing and snacks, just as I had always planned so as not to draw suspicion at the checkpoint. My cover story about driving up to San Francisco to bring back my aunt, whose home had been destroyed in World War III, was Justin's idea. The story would be believable, he said, because lots of people were driving up to various crippled cities to gather displaced relatives and friends back to the Los Angeles area.

***

World War III was not so much a world war as it was a series of rebellions by different countries against the establishment of the New World Order. It was the Antichrist's idea to call it World War III to give his victory over the rebellions some prestige and credibility. But it was God who had been the real victor. If He hadn't intervened to prevent most of the nuclear missiles from being launched, the initial strikes, the fallout, and all other residual effects would have destroyed much of the world's population. Since God was all about giving people lots and lots of chances, this wouldn't do at all.

God also encouraged the aliens, with their advanced technologies, to clean up the fallout and nuclear waste floating around from the bombs that did fall. What they used was essentially a giant vacuum cleaner, which sucked up all the bad air, cleaned it, and spit it out again. The aliens were made to believe they would be helping the Antichrist. The Antichrist couldn't have cared less about the environment, but he was on board with the cleanup anyway. He didn't want a bunch of radiation-poisoned people turning to Christ at the last second. He took all the credit for saving the world.

***

Twenty-six cities across the globe had been hit by nuclear weapons during World War III. Besides San Francisco, New Orleans and Denver were the other American cities destroyed. And worldwide, the New World Order could add Vancouver, Mexico City, Paris, and Madrid to the list. The rebels got the worst of it, however, losing— among others—Moscow, Saint Petersburg, Tokyo, Cairo, Manila, Johannesburg, Lima, Rio de Janeiro, Delhi, Karachi, Istanbul, Tehran, and Damascus.

***

I read about the city of Damascus at the Hall of Knowledge. It was once the capitol of Syria. It had been conquered many times but never destroyed. It was the oldest continuously inhabited city in the world. Syria was known for its hatred of Israel. The prophet Isaiah had predicted that the city would end up a "heap of ruins" in the last days. He was right. It was the first city destroyed in World War III.

***

Driving out of the city toward the checkpoint, I was freaking out. It wasn't my San Francisco cover story I was worried about, but getting out of the city without the Mark. I didn't know until Justin informed me, but no one without the Mark was allowed a travel pass. He said my only chance was the letter he provided stating that my body had rejected the implant the first time, so I had been rescheduled for the surgery. The story was that my travel papers were issued before my body rejected the implant.

To make it believable, I had to have my wrist cut and stitched by a doctor Justin bribed. The final touch was a henna tattoo mimicking the partial and broken row of sixes across a coin-like image of the Antichrist tattooed on all the Mark-bearers.

Still, even with all the subterfuge, Justin said my chances were less than fifty percent. The checkpoint Minions were under strict orders not to let anyone through without the Mark.

***

One mile from the checkpoint, the traffic turned bumper to bumper, fanning out to four separate exits, barricaded and manned by armed Minions in black jumpsuits. I closed my eyes and prayed, then moved the SUV toward the checkpoint farthest right.

The cars ahead were moving at a fair pace. At the checkpoints drivers would stop, rolling down their windows to hold their marked wrists out for the Minion's portable scanners. A Minion would then examine the driver's travel permit before circling the vehicle to scan the marks of any passengers. Meanwhile, other Minions would search for contraband and stowaways.

At the farthest checkpoint, a commotion broke out, and I could see someone being pulled from the back of a small van. Several Minions surrounded the vehicle, dragged everyone out, and shot each one of them by the side of the road. What a world it was.

***

During World War II, Nazis were always shooting people at checkpoints. It was one of their favorite things to do—right up there with gassing Jews.

***

I surprised myself by not going into a deeper panic; instead, the incident was oddly calming. I kept thinking it wasn't such a bad way to go, all things considered. It sure beat the heck out of being dragged downtown to be beaten and tortured, and who knew what else.

Now it was my turn. I rolled down the window, showed my sewn wrist to the clean-cut Minion, offering him the medical papers and the letter. "My body rejected the implant. I'm rescheduled in a couple weeks," I said, perhaps in a manner too rehearsed.

The Minion opened the folded papers, examining them for a moment. "Pull the vehicle over to the side," he commanded.

I moved the vehicle to the shoulder, watching through my side mirror as the Minion showed my papers to a lanky fellow with a lieutenant's bar on his sleeve. I realized he was in charge after he began yelling at a group of Minions who were standing around. The next thing I knew, my vehicle was surrounded. Three of them dragged me out and threw me to the ground. "What the Hell are you guys doing? I've got my permit!" I pleaded, attempting to rise.

A Minion stepped on my back with a heavy boot, flattening me again. "Stay down!" he said.

"Hey man, what did I do?" I said.

"Shut up!"

I turned my head sideways so that my mouth wasn't in the gravel any longer, and watched, with one eye, the lanky Minion with the red bar saunter over to where I lay, surrounded by his chuckling, gun-wielding subordinates. He stared down at me for a long while before he spoke. "Shoot him," was all he said.

I heard the chamber of a rifle being pulled back, and I closed both eyes and prayed. That's when I heard a familiar, high pitched voice I couldn't quite place. "Let that man up...What in the world!" shouted the voice.

That was my line, I thought, and I opened an eye to see the Minion with the rifle pointed at my head looking in the opposite direction.

"I know him. That's Mr. Somerset! Let him up!" said the one with the high voice.

He must have had some authority because two Minions immediately pulled me to my feet to meet my savior, whose red hair and light, freckled face could not be mistaken. It was Kevin Shockley, or Major Shockley now, from the rank on his shoulders, the skinny computer whiz who often cleaned my clock in chess back at Douglas High in Los Angeles, where I taught a lifetime ago.

Shockley's parents had both carried the albino gene, a tough inheritance for any adolescent, but for a black kid in an all-black school, it was a nightmare. He'd beg me for a game almost every day during lunch just to avoid the students in the general population, who picked on him mercilessly because of his unusual appearance.

"Mr. Somerset. Do you remember saying that all the time? *What in the World*—I loved that!"

Of course I remembered. I used the phrase in class often, mostly as a buffer to my foul mouth. "Shockley—my gosh—yes I do. Wow, look at you!" I had never been so glad to see anyone.

Shockley was in the black jumpsuit bearing a purple leaf on each shoulder and strapped with two holstered pistols like General Patton, but he looked like the same nerdy kid to me. He turned to his subordinates grinning. "This is my old teacher—he's all right—let him be."

The lieutenant who ordered me shot spoke up, "This man doesn't have the Mark, sir."

"Let me see those papers." All the sudden he sounded like a major and not the scared kid I once knew. He took the papers from the lieutenant, looked at them for a moment, grabbing my wrist at the same time to look at the sew job and forged tattoo. "Well, can't you see he's had to have it removed? There's an official letter here from the Compliance Ministry, and you were about to shoot the man!"

The lieutenant only shrugged, apparently content with the possibility of shooting an innocent person.

Shockley pulled me aside. "You know I'm doing you a favor here?"

"I know, Major," I said.

"You saved my ass back in high school," he said.

"You look like you can take care of yourself."

He smiled. "They will find you, and it won't be pretty."

"Probably," I said. "But I have to try."

"You were always a little crazy, Mr. Somerset."

I wanted to tell him, to warn him about what was coming, but I was afraid he might change his mind. "Thanks," was all I said.

"Get out of here, Mr. Somerset."

I casually saluted my old student and turned away. I felt sorry for him, but I saw only the scared student hiding in my classroom, not the murderer he had become. I jumped in my SUV and pulled out slowly, my back cringing—half expecting a bullet, until the highway opened up, and I was finally away from Los Angeles, and for the last time.

13

So I began my days as a caveman, eating the goods I had stored, hunting and fishing and stealing where I could. I read and I prayed, listening to the New World Order propaganda and the occasional pirated reports on the radio, alone for over a year, until Danny and her group happened upon me.

They all looked unhealthy and so afraid when they arrived. As dirty and scary as I must have looked to them, I conveyed something they admired, something they did not yet possess but would soon share. Be it only a cave—I was a man with a home.

None of them said very much while they scarfed down the food I gave them. It was one of the sisters, Ida, who spoke first, and I don't think she stopped talking for three days running. Ida told the stories of how they escaped their various towns and met on the road one at a time like characters in the Wizard of Oz.

***

Except for Roger, they had come from the Christian faith in some manner before drifting away for various reasons. Ida and her sister Eva were raised as Methodists. Eva was hardcore until her divorce, and Ida went to church sporadically, until she was in her thirties and gave it up altogether. Ida, who never married, took in Eva after she left her husband.

Eventually, they moved to Las Vegas where they worked at different casinos dealing blackjack. Vegas had been relatively easy to escape from, she said, because the Antichrist had less than a platoon of Minions stationed throughout the city.

***

I read later that the Antichrist had purposely kept the pressure off Las Vegas so people could continue to gamble, drink gallons of alcohol, ingest all manner of drugs, frequent strip clubs, visit prostitutes, and on and on.

***

After they left Vegas, the sisters headed to the ocean because they figured they could catch a boat to another country that wasn't yet occupied by the NWO. They ran out of gas soon after they crossed into California. Since all open gas stations were manned by groups of Minions, the sisters were forced to proceed on foot.

They lost about twenty pounds apiece before they reached the Salinas Valley, where they happened upon the scarecrow, Speckle, sitting in a pear orchard mumbling incoherently. Speckle wore black glasses with thick lenses that made his eyes bigger and more intense than they already were. He had what the soldiers who fought in World War II labeled the thousand-yard stare. This was the vacant, unfocused gaze of a soldier who had seen, too much, the horrors of war. They managed to gather that the skinny man had recently witnessed the rape and murder of his wife at the hands of some Minions outside a convenience store, where the two of them had gone to purchase goods for their escape. What a world it was. The sisters felt sorry for him and invited him on their trek. He couldn't remember his name and the sisters often had to remind him to walk and eat.

***

Three days later, after venturing off the road to look for water, they found Howard Frost camping a few hundred feet from the highway. A former phone repairman, Howard was over six feet tall, wide as an offensive lineman but gentle as all get out. Nonetheless, the thirty-eight-year-old "Cowardly Lion" of the bunch comforted the sisters, as they felt protected just having the big man around. He'd lived near the area and pointed them toward some caves he'd once ventured to as a Boy Scout, keeping them off the main roads during their long hike.

Howard, a homosexual, wrestled constantly with his Christian faith. Feeling completely alone and utterly defeated by his mid-twenties,

Howard decided to reject God completely, at least in his own mind. But God never rejected him, never left his side, never let him completely fall.

What Howard didn't understand was that he was just another human being and a sinner like everyone else. And that God didn't expect him to be perfect, but only to accept His gift and His love.

***

Sticking to the theme—all who were left to happen upon were a tin man, a little girl and her dog, and a wizard to take them home. The once heartless Billy Sanchez, a tattooed line cook and ex-con, would satisfy the former.

Billy's parents had abandoned him early on. His father, Hector Sanchez, raised more by Hispanic gangs than his own parents, was a lifer convicted of murdering a police officer who pulled him over for an expired registration. Hector thought the law had finally caught up to him for any one of his many crimes, so he shot the officer in the face as soon as the poor fellow reached his window. Billy's Polish mother was already a heroin addict when she met Hector. By the time Billy was born, his father was in prison, and his mother's habit was too debilitating to properly care for the baby, suffering the withdrawals of her addiction himself.

So Billy grew up in several foster homes, one of which was run by a particularly nasty husband and wife duo fond of beating the boy with the end of a severed lamp cord and stuffing him in a linen closet for much of the day.

Billy channeled his suffering into the anger that already festered in his genes, bullying and beating the crap out of any kid he could get his hands on. His violent exploits landed him in Juvenile Hall, where by age thirteen he began a series of institutional incarcerations that, at twenty-two, earned him a five-year stint in San Quentin for beating up an employee at a movie theater who had made the mistake of asking him for a ticket he didn't have.

Billy had reached the big time. But the former bully was just another pretty young conquest to the hardened and sex-starved animals prowling the penitentiary. Billy knew he was in trouble when two of these monsters cornered him on his way into the cellblock from the exercise yard. A passing guard interrupted the assault, but the message was clear: *They were going to get him.*

That night, fretting in his cell, Billy did something he'd never done before. He asked God to help him. The very next morning, he was called into the cellblock Supervisor's office. The Supervisor informed him he could be moved to minimum security, but he would have to take a job. There were two openings: the prison library and the Christian chapel. Either would keep him a safe distance from his new friends, but Billy knew the job meant for him.

A year and a half later, Billy would be released for good behavior. Before that, a prison Bible scholar who also worked in the chapel mentored him. The scholar was serving a twenty-five year term for armed bank robbery. He had been a devout Christian for a dozen years before Billy walked into the chapel.

His new mentor, worried about the instant fervor in the way Billy seemed to embrace Christianity, encouraged the boy but cautioned him over the excess zeal that might cause him to crash once the reality of Christian living set in. It wasn't, he told Billy, a life full of constant miracles and daily enlightenment, but a hard road of self-discovery and inner change, often beset by difficult tests of faith, and most difficult of all, the tedium of devout living.

But Billy, prone to extremes and addictions, ignored the advice, and upon his release ventured to the nearest corner to preach the Good News. But this was not a living, and it wasn't a life for most Christians, let alone a relative newcomer. Just as his mentor had feared, Billy crashed and burned, slipping back into his old ways, until he was further from God than when he'd begun.

***

This was something shaky Christians, those who "planted their seed on rocky soil," often failed to consider. The faith might grow for a while, but it would eventually wither, and each time it dissipated or went away it became even more difficult to retrieve.

***

Still, God did not forget the little beaten boy, stuffed in a closet. Three years later, his cellblock Bible study paid off in a big way when Billy began to recognize the signs he'd studied in Revelation and immediately saw the Antichrist for the slime-bag he was. He found some heart, grabbed his Bible and a backpack full of goods, and hit the road.

***

Our Dorothy, a not-so-little girl, and her feeble-minded son lived in a tiny house on a hill in San Francisco. Danielle Knowles had never been to Kansas, but she was raised in the Midwest by strict Baptist parents who preached so little love and so much fire and brimstone that she felt she needed to escape the flames, and Iowa, when she was barely sixteen.

Upon leaving her Iowan family, she hitchhiked to the West Coast where she became the lead singer of a punk rock band called the Dirks. The name was derived from a combination of jerk and another word. The band never went anywhere except to lead her into a life of drugs and years of meandering. After a failed marriage and an abortion, she gave birth to her son Roger out of wedlock. Roger was both the joy and frustration of her troubled life.

***

As an infant and toddler, Roger seemed a perfect and even angelic child, but it soon became clear to Danny that something wasn't quite right with the boy. He was too quiet and unresponsive much of the time. The doctors told her Roger was suffering from mild retardation. Devastated at first, she came to realize she loved Roger even more for his affliction, and they made a happy world together until he hit the fourth grade.

At that point, Roger began to change drastically. Frustrated with learning, socializing, and the constant teasing from other kids, he began a long, slow rebellion of delinquency, ditching school, shoplifting, and vandalism, all culminating when at fourteen he attacked and choked a fellow student nearly unconscious after an argument in the cafeteria over a grilled cheese sandwich.

Roger went through a year of therapy and seemed to settle down after that, but sometime during his first year of high school he picked up a book on Satanism, began wearing black and drawing endless pentagrams on his folders and notebooks. Danny was worried, but Roger's counselor suggested it was a phase, and she let it slide. After all, she'd been a rebellious child herself and had moved past it.

Soon after, Roger began hanging around a group of students known as Goths because of their dark clothing, music, hair, and eye-makeup. The Goths considered themselves outcasts and rebels, but none of them were fixated on Satanism like Roger. Still, his feeble brain surmised they were just like him, and besides, they were the only kids who would let him hang out with them. But it wasn't because he looked Goth or otherwise fit in with them in any way. It was because one of the Goth girls who knew him from junior high school felt sorry for him and talked the other Goths into putting up with him. This wasn't too hard because Roger didn't know what his new friends were talking about much of the time and kept his mouth shut, so they never realized he had a handicap, or that he was a burgeoning psychopath with little or no moral compass.

Another Goth girl, Sheila, who wasn't all that bright herself, even took a shining to Roger, believing him to be the strong, silent type and not simply an imbecile. They were soon holding hands and playing boyfriend and girlfriend in their naïve way.

***

The book on Satanism Roger found at the library was called the *Satanic Bible*. Anton LaVey, the crafty founder of the Church of Satan, wrote the vile book. LaVey preached a watered-down version of Satanism to the general public, but in secret he was a full-blown devil worshiper who conducted all sorts of wacky rituals to honor his dark deity. Coincidentally, he once lived and taught his unholy ways in an old Victorian house just a few blocks from Danny and Roger's home in San Francisco.

***

Roger couldn't really understand and never even read much of the *Satanic Bible*. He picked it up at bookstore on his way home from school after he was drawn to the pentagram on the book's cover. Roger did, however, focus on certain lines in LaVey's book that appealed to his challenged mind. One of these quotes was, "Blessed are the destroyers of false hope, for they are the true Messiahs—Cursed are the god adorers, for they shall be shorn sheep!" He couldn't understand the quote, and he had to look up the words "adorers" and "shorn," but for some reason he loved the phrase, "Blessed are the destroyers" and the words "Cursed" and "god" in the same sentence.

***

A deathbed witness to Anton LaVey's last words said he cried out, "Oh God, oh God…there is something very wrong," and proceeded to ask for forgiveness. I'm not sure what happened after that. I suppose I could look it up. I do know there was one quote of his I did agree with. He once said, "It's too bad that stupidity isn't painful."

***

One day after school, Roger and Sheila went out and bought a Ouija Board. The *Ouija Board* was manufactured and distributed by a company called Parker Brothers. Parker Brothers considered the Ouija Board to be to a family board game. Parker Brothers produced other family board games like *Monopoly*, where the object was to buy up as many properties as one could in order to bankrupt family and friends; and *Risk*, where the object was to build massive armies in order to rule the world by destroying the armies of family and friends.

***

The first time Roger and Sheila played with the Ouija Board nothing much happened. They just asked a bunch of silly questions about their love life and their future together, either of them forcing the disk to answer the way they wanted. They soon grew tired and left the board to make out, play video games, or whatever else they did to amuse themselves. Weeks later, however, after Roger had been reading more of LaVey's book, the game took an exciting turn for the young couple.

***

Roger and Sheila were talking about Sheila's stepfather, who used to beat her mercilessly with a drum stick before—drunk and stoned one night after a late show—he drove his rock band's van off a cliff, killing everyone in the fiery crash.

Roger said he hoped Bobby was in Hell and asked Sheila, pointing to the Ouija board, if she wanted to find out. They pulled the game out of the box, placed their fingers lightly on the disk, and began asking questions:

Shelia: We are looking for a piece of garbage named Bobby Norris. Can somebody help us find this loser?

Nothing happened for a long time, and Roger and Sheila were ready to make out and play video games again when the disk seemed to move by itself.

Ouija: YES

Roger and Sheila looked at each other in amazement and pushed on:

Sheila: Who are you?

Again, the disc moved on its own.

Ouija: A... F...R...I...E...N...D

Sheila: Do you know Bobby?

Ouija: E...V...E...R...Y...B...O...D...Y

***

Most kids would have been scared out of their minds by this point, but Roger and Sheila couldn't stop grinning at each other. They both believed this was the most exciting and wonderful thing that had ever happened to them.

Sheila: Where is Bobby?

Ouija: B...U...R...N

Now they were freaking out with excitement.

Sheila: In Hell?

Ouija: H...E...L...L

***

After that, the Ouija board was all they could talk about. They spent hours conversing with the stranger about other dead people, black magic, the future, and on and on. Later, they brought the other Goths over to join in the fun, but it never worked the same with everyone around, so they usually ended up smoking marijuana, drinking Danny's vodka, or snorting lines of methamphetamine and whatever else they could get their hands on.

***

Roger and Sheila never made the connection, but things began to spiral out of control soon after they met the stranger on the Ouija board. Danny, working all day and attending night school, couldn't be there to supervise much of the time. The pair began ditching school frequently to drink or take drugs, and to communicate with their new friend.

129

But there was more. They were acting strangely irritated and angry. They fought with each other over stupid things that normally made them laugh. Eventually, they broke up, which devastated Roger, who sought comfort through the stranger on the board.

***

Then, two months after their breakup, Sheila took one too many of her mom's oxycodone, overdosed, and went into a coma. A few days later, she was dead.

***

Distraught over Sheila's death, Roger began speaking more frantically to the stranger. Eventually, he revealed himself to be a demon named Cresil. Although Cresil didn't mention it to Roger, he was known in his own circles as the demon of laziness. This is because he preferred lying around the caverns of the underworld chewing on bugs and whatnot, waiting for humans to come to him, rather than actively seeking lost souls like the other demons. Cresil talked the dimwitted Roger into praying to his master Lucifer for guidance. The devil was happy to oblige and so began Roger's slow decent into madness.

***

Danny had her hands full with Roger, but the rest of her life had been steadily improving. Although she had been a waitress by day, making just enough to take care of the both of them and pay the rent, she managed to put herself through a court reporting course at night and had recently been hired by the state with a starting salary of $56,500, which was twice as much as she had ever made in any one year during her entire working life. Danny was ecstatic. She could finally afford to get Roger the help he needed. But then something happened. Two billion people mysteriously disappeared.

***

Next door to Danny and Roger, there lived a sixty-six-year-old retired policeman named Joe Mellon and his wife Aubrey. The Mellons befriended Danny and Roger almost as soon as the pair moved into their neighborhood of thirty-nine years. Over time, they had grown quite close—Joe and Aubrey acting as surrogate parents to Danny and surrogate grandparents to the misguided Roger.

It was Joe who had suggested court reporting for Danny, even bringing her to the courthouse to watch the breakneck typists in action. He loved Danny and Roger. The boy didn't get along with many people, but he seemed to genuinely like the old man, and Joe was happy to mentor the lost Roger, much as it was an uphill battle, and as taken aback as he was by the boy's satanic leanings. Besides, he couldn't get enough of Danny, who reminded him of his own daughter Teresa. Teresa had been stabbed to death during a mugging in downtown San Francisco when she was just thirty-one.

***

The murderer of Joe and Aubrey's daughter was an illegal alien named Sergio Nunez. Sergio Nunez came across the Mexico border into the United States when he was nineteen. He traveled with a small group of hardworking immigrants intent on making a better life for themselves and their families.

Sergio's only intent was to continue with the criminal activity and mayhem he had enjoyed so much back in Mexico. And so, by the time Nunez stabbed Teresa five times outside her apartment one night as a bonus for stealing her purse, he had already been arrested four times for various crimes, including robbery, assault with a deadly weapon, battery, and rape.

Although Nunez finally landed in prison for the murder of Joe's daughter, he'd never spent more than a week in jail for any of the other crimes he'd committed in America. This was because San Francisco was a *Sanctuary City*, which meant if you were an American citizen and you stole a pack of chewing gum from a convenience store, you would be more likely to do jail time than an illegal immigrant like Nunez who had been arrested after beating and raping his young girlfriend.

***

So why did San Francisco and so many other American cities adopt the insane policies of a *Sanctuary City*? Because if an illegal alien were to be sent to prison or deported, they wouldn't be able to vote for the politicians who created the *Sanctuary City* in the first place.

***

On the day of the Rapture, Joe and Aubrey were sitting on the couch. He loved Aubrey dearly, and his only complaint was that she was always trying to drag him to church. Since his daughter's murder, Joe didn't care much for church, religion, or God, for that matter.

Even so, almost as soon as he observed the popcorn fall onto the carpet from the missing hand of his absent wife, Joe knew what had happened. Some of his wife's rants about the end of the world must have sunk in. His first instinct was to go next door and check on his adopted family.

***

Danny was busy doing laundry, while Roger listened to loud music in his room, when Joe stormed into their house with barely a knock. Neither had a clue about what had happened. Joe told Danny about his wife's disappearance and his assumption about the Rapture. They turned on the news to watch the reports of the missing flooding the airwaves. The light of her dysfunctional Baptist upbringing kicked in, and Danny was immediately on the same page as Joe. She dug through her belongings in the boxes she had retrieved from her parents' farm shortly after their deaths and found her old Bible. As soon as she opened it, she was filled with a sense of peace.

***

While on the old Earth, Danny would never understand her parents' lack of affection, but she finally understood the importance of their religious teachings. Now she felt only grateful to know what she knew, letting go a lifetime of pent-up angst.

***

And she began to impart to Joe all the knowledge her parents had given her, filling in the details about the Rapture, the Antichrist, the Mark of the Beast, and the Second Coming.

They watched the news together for a week straight. The flying saucers, the media and government explanations—none of it influenced Danny or Joe one bit. So they began, just as I had, to formulate an escape plan for the three of them, setting out on weekend forays to reconnoiter the surrounding wilderness for a likely hideout.

They, too, had decided to wait for the New World Order to require the Mark before actually leaving the city, but a certain NWO policy had prompted her to a more expedient departure, and she began her search for a safer dwelling in earnest.

132

***

Depopulation had always been on the Illuminati agenda because smaller populations were easier to control, but now with the economic crisis in full swing, they were able to persuade the masses to reevaluate certain unethical solutions such as euthanasia. Following the Nazi model, the NWO began to isolate the sick and very elderly, as well as the insane, mentally challenged, and feeble-minded.

***

Danny received a letter from the NWO's Department of Human Services requiring her son Roger to report for a medical evaluation. She knew exactly what that meant, and she vowed she would never let Roger be taken from her.

***

Although she and Joe hadn't been completely satisfied with any of the hideouts they'd thus far scouted, they both agreed to settle on something that coming weekend. This time they would fill her van with supplies, leave them at whatever hideout they chose, and return one last time to settle their affairs.

However, this was not to be—they would never see their homes, their neighborhood, or even the city again. San Francisco would be leveled during their last reconnaissance.

***

The tornado that hit their city was a nuclear bomb. World War III had begun. Fortunately, they were far enough away from the blast and the fallout, and could only watch, in horror, the brilliant and devastating light.

***

Many months later, Danny, Roger, and Joe were moving again. Their hideout had been too close to civilization. They'd spotted Minions nearly every day and were always afraid. In the middle of the night, they packed their hidden van and slowly pulled onto the highway, driving north until they ran out of gas. Then they gathered what they could carry and ventured on to a trail in the woods, where they would meet the giant, gentle man; the vacant-eyed shell of a man; the kindly, talkative sisters; the once heartless ex-con; and eventually,

133

the man in the cave, hiding behind layers of curtains, but offering food and a temporary home.

14

In the years before the Rapture, except for the time I spent with Sophie and Renee, I had, for the most part, become a loner. I preferred it that way because I was in hiding, not from the world, but from my paranoid perception of its reflective and judgmental nature. But being a loner in the regular world and being an absolutely isolated cave dweller are two completely different existences. I had essentially placed myself in solitary confinement, and I was slowly going mad.

***

By the time Danny's party came along, I was having regular and disturbing conversations with myself. The only thing separating me from complete madness was my awareness of the insanity of the conversations, but even that was growing thin. And so, when my new friends arrived, I was immediately grateful for the company, and within a few days, the curtain of madness lifted, and I was again my relatively normal self.

But that first night, sitting across a low fire, listening intently to their experiences on the road, I was clinging to sanity and shocked at being in the company of human beings. I could not keep my eyes off Danny, who seemed more relaxed and in charge than any of the others. She spoke of nuclear destruction, starving on the road, and hiding for their lives from the Minions as if it were another day at work. She was beautiful, tough and smart, and soon I decided I was falling in love with her.

***

Danny, of course, was not my first crush, just my last. I thought I loved quite a few girls during my days on the old Earth, but I knew nothing about romantic love, until I looked it up at the Hall of Knowledge. What did I find out? There was no such thing.

***

People on the old Earth were always saying stuff like, "I'm crazy about her," or "I'm madly in love with him." There was madness and there was love, but they had nothing whatsoever to do with each other. Real love was about unselfishness, compassion, and genuine affection. What people on the old Earth referred to as romantic love was the exact opposite: it was about ego, lust, selfishness, and jealousy.

***

All told, I was a hopeless romantic on the old Earth, bringing misery to myself and most of the girls I met as well. My first crush was a kewpie doll looking thing in second grade named Lilly, whom I pined over for about two weeks, which was about a century and a half to a seven-year-old. In the fifth grade, it was the blonde and striking Claire Grant. She looked like a miniature Grace Kelly, and her name even sounded like it belonged to a movie star. Since I wasn't yet smart enough to keep my mouth shut about my feelings toward girls, I told Claire I liked her. Well, I didn't tell her—I had one of my friends do it. And she was gracious and pretty nice about it, too, or so I thought, smiling and ignoring me and all. What I didn't know was that most of the other boys at the elementary school had already professed their devotions to her, so I was hurt when she began holding hands with a popular sixth grader, one of these guys already shaving or something.

***

That little bit of pain didn't stop me from confessing my adoration again. No, it was the next vixen that shut me up like a snitch in a trunk. Now I know it doesn't mean anything, but Tracey Shawn had red hair, and she was the first girl I liked with noticeable breasts, which scared me for some reason. She sat across from me in sixth period math during my first semester of junior high school. I made her laugh with my smart-alecky comments about the teacher and some of the students, and I guess she thought I was sort of cool because of that.

Since she had gone to a different elementary school, she had no idea who I was. Junior high school was great that way, a chance to reinvent oneself, or so I thought. After I told her I liked her, we began hanging out after school outside the classroom, holding hands and pecking at each other. Our relationship lasted four days.

That fourth day, I saw her at lunch talking to Tory Zane, the same kid who had karate-chopped me and knocked me on my behind at the drinking fountain back in the fourth grade. I learned later that he liked her and told her the complete and embarrassing history of my years at West Hills Elementary, just so he could put a wrench in our relationship. Tory told her about all the times I got my butt kicked, and about the time I cried in class over a grade, and the time my dad shaved my head, so I ditched school because I was too embarrassed to show up, and the time I had diarrhea and didn't quite make it out of class, and on and on.

It worked. That very afternoon, she made this humiliating and heart wrenching breakup announcement in front of the whole class: "I don't hang out with crybaby losers who crap their pants." I didn't even blame her.

***

I was afraid to talk to a girl for a long time after that. But that silence was probably the reason I landed my first date, or it might just have been that Hope Picas was unusually aggressive for a fourteen-year-old.

Hope was popular and used to attention, so I guess it bothered her that I never said a word. She sat next to me in art class, refusing to leave me alone until I spoke to her, and then wouldn't stop bugging me until I agreed to take her to the movies.

My mom dropped me off at the theater where Hope met me on a Saturday afternoon. I took her to a couple of seats at the back corner of the theater because that was where I'd seen older couples sitting before. It was kind of awkward because the movie had been out for a while and the theater was pretty much empty. But Hope didn't seem to mind, so there we sat with better seats everywhere. She was sort of leaning on me, eating a big barrel of popcorn and sucking on a giant soda, while I fidgeted in my seat, too nervous to eat or drink even.

***

Food and drink portions had steadily grown to obscene dimensions on the old Earth, especially in America, where the obesity rate was staggering. A few people were even too large to fit through their own front doors and had to have walls removed just so they could be taken to hospitals. Even giant toddlers and huge little kids were seen everywhere. They were cute and all because you wanted to squeeze their cheeks, but the poor things were ridiculously unhealthy.

The problem was that most food and drink products were crammed with fat and sugar by manufacturing companies so people would become addicted to the bad food. It turns out the Illuminati had been behind the whole thing. They figured obese people would be less likely to rebel against their drive for one-world government and would be first in line to accept the Mark of the Beast, so they could continue eating their pizzas and cheeseburgers and whatnot. They were right.

It was also an Illuminati idea to give junk food big names like *Jumbo Dog*, *Grande Burrito*, *Big Sip*, *Mega-Fries*, *Monster Burger*, and the like. This fooled people into thinking they were getting some kind of great deal. Americans loved a bargain even if it caused obesity, diabetes, clogged arteries, high cholesterol, heart attacks, and early death.

When doctors and other health advocates began complaining about the obesity levels and the practices of the large food companies pushing the crappy food, the Illuminati changed their strategy. They had their scientists come up with chemicals that mirrored sugars and fats but weren't full of calories. The next thing you knew, everything was diet this and low calorie that, slim this and skinny that, and on and on.

So everybody became thin again? Nope. The Illuminati had pulled another fast one. The chemicals in these diet products were more addictive than real fats and sugars, so even though they were lower in calories, they boosted craving levels so the people using these products would eat twice as much food, bringing them right back to where they were before they went on the stupid diet.

But the real genius of the Illuminati plan was that even skinny people began using these addictive low calorie products, and so they began adding excess fat as well. And as an added bonus, these FDA approved chemicals caused digestion problems, infections, cancer, immune disorders, and all manner of previously unknown syndromes.

***

Hope Picas was making me more nervous because she wasn't watching the movie while she worked on her jumbo popcorn. She was looking at me. And I was more than a little annoyed because the movie was starting to get good. But there she was, staring at me and chomping on that big popcorn during all the best parts. Finally, she said what was on her mind: "Are you gonna kiss me or what?"

I looked over and even in the dark I could see she had little pieces of popcorn stuck to the butter on her lips. And still, I got up the nerve to kiss her, except she was way ahead of me, moving her lips and tongue all over my mouth and cheeks and nose and everywhere else. I wasn't enjoying any of it because I had butter and salvia and tiny chunks of popcorn all over my face, and all I could think about was washing my face the whole time and maybe finishing the movie.

***

She called me the next day, but I was so uncomfortable and embarrassed about the whole thing I could barely speak. I think she got the message because a couple days later I saw her at school making out with this big, tough Italian kid who was the only kid who owned a leather jacket not made of plastic. Plus, he greased his hair back like this supposedly cool TV guy, Fonzie, who also wore a leather jacket on a show they called *Happy Days* because everyone was so happy it was still the 1950s, instead of later when everything went to crap. And the Italian kid didn't even get laughed at or anything because he was so big and scary and all.

***

I didn't have a date or kiss a girl for about four years after that. My friends were already having sex or something close to it, or lying about it at least, but I was already seventeen and a senior, and the prom was coming and all I had managed was to follow a few sophomore girls around the school, trying to gather enough courage to ask them out.

The worst part about it was the constant questions and comments from my parents: *"Did you get your tickets for the prom yet? Who are you taking? What about that girl from junior high? I'll ask so and so if her daughter is available. You're such a good-looking boy. Both your brothers went to the prom…why don't you want to go?"* And on and on. It was hopeless, though, so I just told myself and anybody who would listen that I didn't want to go because I hated everybody in my class anyway. I don't think they bought it.

**

After the prom and hearing about everybody's wonderful experiences with the cheesy suits and bad food, I was completely depressed and determined to change things in the romance department. To accomplish this, my adolescent brain told me I needed experience. My solution was to find a prostitute. So I stole eighty bucks from the gas station where I worked and headed to the only place I was sure I'd find one: the infamous corner of Hollywood and Vine, known worldwide through movies and television as the mecca of streetwalking in America.

**

The next thing you know, I'm driving up and down Hollywood Boulevard near the Vine Street intersection, unable to spot a single woman who didn't appear to be homeless, let alone the smorgasbord of tall, beautiful young women I had pictured.

I used the family station wagon for this adventure, which was way past its prime, having been handed to me by my brother Geoff, who got it from our older brother Gerry, who got it from my father, in such bad shape it could only be started by crawling underneath and applying a screwdriver to the starter motor. This monstrosity had once been green with wood panels, but was then painted bright yellow because that was the cheapest paint available at the time, so I was lucky not to have been spotted and pulled over after all the illegal U-turns I made that day in the great banana.

**

No, I couldn't find prostitute one. I even branched out to both ends of the long iconic boulevard, but it made no difference. The truth was, there hadn't been a prostitute on Hollywood or Vine for nearly twenty years because if a dumb teenager knew its reputation so did the police, who shut it down long before it ever became legend or myth.

I finally gave up and headed home, only I got lost and ended up on Sunset Boulevard, which hadn't yet become a legend for such things but was well on its way.

They weren't exactly beauty queens or remotely anything from my unrealistic fantasies—but there they were, at least ten or fifteen prostitutes, walking and sitting and smoking and waving, so that even a dumb teenager could tell what they were up to.

***

Jesus befriended and saved the prostitute Mary Magdalene, who had embraced His teachings. He didn't approve of prostitution or anything; He just preferred to hang around genuine people, especially known sinners open to change, as opposed to pompous, self-righteous, religious types like the Pharisees and such.

Later, some misguided writers and filmmakers speculated that Jesus and Mary Magdalene were more than friends, even suggesting they had been married and had children together, or some such nonsense. I don't know, maybe He had something a little more important to do than dating, like saving mankind.

One of these movies, based on a bestselling book, was about a world famous American code breaker who is called to investigate some crazy murder at the Louvre Museum in France. I guess because there weren't any homicide detectives available that day. This dead body is lying right under the Mona Lisa, and it turns out the famous Di Vinci painting of a smirking woman is hiding the secret that Mary Magdalene had Christ's children and this murdered guy knew all about it.

The code breaker is chased around Paris and everywhere else by this big bald albino guy who is murdering everyone and beating himself because he is so pious and all, and of course he can't be caught because he doesn't stick out like a sore thumb or anything. It turns out this albino guy is a member of a secret society within the Catholic Church that has vowed to protect the even bigger secret of Christ's marriage and family.

So let me get this straight. After knowing Christ personally, embracing His teachings, witnessing His miracles, death, and resurrection, the apostles are so blown away they spend the rest of their lives traveling the known world to spread His teachings; suffering through ostracism, exile, prison and torture; often dying horrible deaths—experiences which are documented—yet the whole time, they fail to mention to anyone that Jesus had been hiding a wife and kids and a Labrador retriever.

The only thing remotely true about this movie was the existence of a secret society that had infiltrated the Catholic Church and a lot of other institutions. It was the same secret society that fabricated the whole story about Christ's supposed family in the first place. What was that secret society? You guessed it.

***

I honed in on a brunette walking slowly past one of the many motels lining the Sunset Strip. I was nervous as heck, but my hormones won out, so I pulled over and rolled down the window anyway. She immediately approached the vehicle, leaning in to have a look at me. She was older than I first thought, about thirty-five but still pretty, and she talked to me in a sweet voice that didn't seem phony or anything, though I was gullible. "You're a cutie-pie—what can I do for you, honey?"

I don't know what I expected, but for some reason I wasn't expecting any questions, so I said the first thing that came to mind, "I want a date." I must have heard someone call it that in a movie or something, and it seemed to work, anyway.

"Sure, sweetie—how much you got?"

"How much does it cost?" Even back then, I instinctively knew that one doesn't show all their cards in a sales negotiation.

"What do you want to do?"

"Everything," I answered, having absolutely no idea what everything was.

She just looked at me for a bit. Finally she said, "Sixty bucks."

"Ok." That was the limit of my negotiation skills.

She jumped in the station wagon, the same vehicle that had dropped us at school and Boy Scouts, had taken us to dinner, movies, parks and zoos, and on so many family vacations. "My room is up the street," she said.

***

The room was a ghastly brown, from the worn carpet to the thickly painted, pine-wood ceiling, and it smelled of disinfectant, perfume, stale cigarette smoke, and who knew what else. But I didn't care because I was too busy worrying about what was about to happen.

She told me to take off my clothes, so I did. Then she unzipped and pulled her skirt away. She was wearing full-length panty hose, except she still had her blouse on for some reason. I didn't say anything, though it was kind of weird, like I accidently walked in on an aunt or the neighbor lady getting ready to go out for dinner or something.

The situation had me nervous and flaccid, and really just wanting to get the heck out of there by that point. But she knew what she was doing, I guess, and she got me to relax, and we didn't do everything or much at all even, but I suppose we accomplished what I set out to do.

***

The experience didn't exactly turn me into Casanova, or even Woody Allen, not by a long shot; in fact, I was more nervous and messed up about sex than ever. It would have been better had I waited till I was married. It was an ideal far too often ignored, which led to failed relationships, broken marriages, shattered families, heartbroken and damaged children, abortion, and all manner of personal angst.

***

I was responsible for two abortions during my short reign of romantic terror on the old Earth—two beautiful children whom I sentenced to a violent death. They are here now, living with people who love and care for them, and they do not know me.

***

No, my adventure in Hollywood didn't land me any girlfriends or even one girlfriend. On the contrary, it sent me on a two-year cold streak broken only by frequent masturbation. But things began to change about the time I turned nineteen. In those two years, I had grown taller, a little wider, and somehow less dorky. Girls began to notice. And I noticed them noticing me.

***

It was shortly thereafter that my friends and I applied for and received the birth certificates of some children who would have been twenty-one had they not died when they were still very little. With these we were able to acquire the fake IDs that opened up to us the world of bars and nightclubs two years before our time, carrying their good names through our drunken debauchery. Those years are mostly a blur.

Still, I somehow managed to have a couple of girlfriends.

Carla, a haunting beauty, looked like a grown woman, but acted like she was about fourteen. Her scumbag stepfather had drugged and raped her when she was twelve, and I never understood at the time just how destroyed she had been. After he was released from prison, he began calling her with death threats. I guess assault, rape, and ruining her life hadn't been enough for him. One minute Carla would be ranting and raving, and the next, she'd be curled up in my arms whimpering like a kicked puppy. The whole thing was too much for me, and I broke up with her for some German girl who was only in town for two weeks. I was a real prince.

Then I met this funny, Christian girl, Kimberly, who worked at some office where I was a temp. I even went to church with her a bunch of times. I have no idea what she saw in me, except she was recently divorced and temporarily out of her mind when we met. Her ex-husband worked in the film industry, traveling and cheating on her all over the place; otherwise, she would never have gotten divorced, let alone hooked up with somebody like myself. We dated for a long time, but all the while I had one foot out the door—I preferred being a clown, and besides, I knew she was too nice for me.

Years later, she called me out of the blue. She was acting kind of strange, reminiscing about the past and everything. I was a little embarrassed because Renee was nearby, and I got off the phone in a hurry. I found out later she had inoperable breast cancer at the time she called and was dead within six months. She was only thirty-three. All she wanted to do was talk a little bit.

***

Anyway, they had been better off without me. I went back to my couch and my childishness. Until one day, when one of my couch-providing friends suggested a trip to Hawaii. I said yes. I guess I thought I needed a vacation from lying around all day. We scraped and borrowed, managing enough for a cheap package vacation with a couple hundred bucks to spare for food and beer. What I didn't know was the price of that trip would be marriage and divorce.

***

Her name was Lanie Spencer, and I remember holding her close in a cool pool on the high roof of a hotel somewhere in Honolulu, and how, for a long time, that was the best day of my whole life. She lived in England, except she wasn't pasty like most Brits. She was tall, exotic, dark skinned, the result of a South African mixed bloodline. She carried herself like a ballerina. When we met, she was only seventeen, except she had lied, telling me she was nineteen. I believed her because the average high school girl from England had eight times the sense and sophistication of any ten college coeds in America, at least the ones I knew.

***

My stomach hurt, so I thought I was in love. After the trip, we wrote letters and ran up phone bills until I scraped up enough money to visit her at her home outside London. A year later, she came to the States, and we got married because we were madly in love and not because we were a couple of dumb kids or anything.

But within a short time, working a terrible job at a two-bit auto insurance office, living in a dingy apartment, going nowhere, I began to realize I was just a dumb kid after all, and I didn't want any responsibility. I kept sending her back and forth, while I tried to get my life together. But I sent her home one too many times, and she met some guy with a good job and a nice place, and she divorced me and crushed me, even though I didn't want her around.

I drifted in a stupor of pain and self-pity I thought would never end after that. But she made me want something more out of life, want to make something of myself, so I could get married and have a family someday. And I did, sort of.

***

I met Sophie's mother at a nightclub. Looking back, I guess I met most of the girls I knew at nightclubs or bars. Why? Unless they made the first move, I pretty much had to be drunk just to talk to a girl.

I was leaning against a bar somewhere with one of my friends, trying to look uninterested, like there was some great purpose to our being there besides groveling over women. Renee was standing in front of the bar with a group of her friends. She had the biggest mane of curly hair and the prettiest eyes you ever saw.

They were laughing and ordering these drinks, which were all the rage at the time because they had these stupid and supposedly sexy

145

names. Renee shouted out her order, which I won't repeat. I thought the whole sexy drink name thing was pretty silly, so I rolled my eyes at her just when she happened to look my way. She stormed right over to tell me that no one rolled their eyes at her. I apologized, though I didn't know then that the girls who laughed about stupid sexy drink names were the least casual about sex.

And she *was* a good girl, Catholic, but not the fake kind like I was. She was tough and opinionated, she didn't take my crap, and I loved that about her. We began dating and kissing an awful lot. I kissed Renee more than any girl I ever met. It was enough to kiss her, and I started thinking I could marry this girl. I even began throwing the word love around again. So we got engaged.

Now everything should have been peachy-keen after that, with us being in love and all. Because that's how love was supposed to work on the old Earth, and there were plenty of great examples of beautiful romantic relationships leading to perfect marriages, only I can't think of any.

But, of course, it didn't work out that way. Why not? Well, I can't speak for the rest of the old Earth, but in our case, she was hardheaded and I was still a child, so between her pride and my immaturity, we fought like a couple of blind cats trying to escape a dog kennel.

So why did we stay together? Was it our mutual adoration, our starry-eyed romance, our deep undying love? No, neither of us wanted to admit defeat.

***

I told you there was no such thing as romantic love and how I read all about it at the Hall of Knowledge. But don't get me wrong—love was everything. God was love and God created out of love. It's just that love and what we used to call romantic love have nothing whatsoever to do with each other.

So what was the point of all those crazy feelings people on the old Earth associated with love? There was none. God wanted men and women to be attracted to each other so they could create life, give that life a family, and experience the same love God knew for us. Except, as usual, we got away from God and messed the whole thing up.

***

God could have just zapped babies and children into existence, but He wanted to give His gift of creation to us. Since men were physically stronger and more motivated to hunt and fish and all the other crap that bored the heck out of most women, and because women were more nurturing and all, He decided to let females conceive and carry life.

After God gave men and women the means to create life, He needed to motivate them, otherwise the men would just stand around grunting, and the women would be inclined to beat the hairy numbskulls off with sticks. There would be too few births, and mankind would have been gone within a generation. So God gave them libidos, making the act pleasurable so people would "go forth and multiply" and such.

But, as with most good and pleasurable things, man decided they wanted more—to take God's gift, something intimate and beautiful, to gobble it up like so many cheeseburgers, to twist it and run it into the ground. The things they came up with were filthy and humiliating, frankly. So much so, that even the participants were embarrassed by their acts, until the last days when they wore their immorality like the proud parents of abomination they'd become.

God saw it coming, of course, but that was the quandary of free will again. Why should He let the dirtbags ruin something so beautiful for the people who respected the gift, who grew close, built a relationship, cherished one another, became intimate, and made a family together?

There was an order to things. God had shown the way, but, once again, man ignored His teachings, inventing an amalgamation of love, stolen and rewritten from God's words, a fatal blend of love, attraction, passion, friendship, sex, lust, debauchery, gluttony, jealousy, and ego. It would begin innocently enough, with attraction and the simple act of courtship. Until the sin of jealousy kicked in, turning courtship to rivalry; then ego made it a competition, gluttony a sport, debauchery a game. The idea became to woo as many women as possible. Men became princes, poets, preeners, crooners, cads, cavorters, rascals, rogues, romantics, and other liars. So effective were their sad exploits, they were passed down the centuries through song, poem, literature and film, and believed by almost everyone.

It excited people's egos to think they were wanted desperately by someone, and in turn, their own desperate need to be wanted made them pretend to want someone back. This nonsense became the thing we call romantic love, and it made everyone act like a bunch of idiots. Even children succumbed to the madness of romantic love, and by the time they were ready to be married, they had absolutely no idea what they were doing. So what did they do? They got married anyway. And whom did they marry? Why the best liars, of course.

Love is love. It is the same love between a man and a woman as it is between God and man, between parent and child, between friends, man and man, woman and woman, man and dog, between a woman and a bunch of stray cats. It varies in intensity, based on intimacy and a strong connection, but it is the same love. It was only when corrupt passions came into the mix that things became confused. Whether heterosexual, homosexual, bisexual, asexual, or whatever else, we all had our inclinations, propensities, hang-ups, eccentricities, or outright fetishes when it came to sex. None of it had anything to do with love—it was sin, plain and simple. It was only in the relationships where love existed.

The best relationships, the best marriages were built on the building blocks of love: God, family, respect, compassion, and friendship. Without those, marriage was nothing more than a pack of lies, a sham, a manmade ideal as worthless and fragile as the paper that supposedly bound it.

***

And Renee and I were no different. I lied to her and she lied to herself. And it was fun and games until Sophie came along. And it was then that God expected us to get over ourselves, to get over our selfishness, to become a family for our daughter, and to put the child first, just as Jesus had put us first. Renee, for the most part, did just that, while I hemmed and hawed and ruined my daughter's life with good and not-so-good intentions.

***

The great romantic, William Shakespeare, once wrote, "Love is not love that alters when it alteration finds, or bends with the remover to be removed." And he would have been exactly right, except he wasn't talking about real love. No, he was just another liar, like me, promoting the myth of romantic love. So I let our love be altered and bent until it was unrecognizable, a meaningless venture of delusions destined for divorce.

***

And that's where I was headed again after meeting Danny—from one kind of insanity to another; insanity brought on by isolation to that of romantic love.

15

One of my favorite movies on the old Earth was *Jeremiah Johnson*. It starred the actor Robert Redford as an ex-soldier who leaves the trappings of civilization to live in the majestic Rocky Mountains, which once spanned eight American States. He survives bears, hostile Indians, starvation, and freezing weather, living off the land by his courage and wit.

How much courage and wit had to do with my survival is up for debate. The hand of God and my books on survival had more to do with it than anything. Still, I did imagine myself a mountain man for a time, anxious to show my new guests the skills I had acquired during my many months in the wilderness.

And my new guests were quite the captive audience, but only because they wanted to survive and because there wasn't much else to do.

***

I gave them a tour of my latest cave, showing them how I kept the supplies buried in case the Minions showed up. I learned my lesson after the Minions discovered my first cave and destroyed my possessions. After that, I had to sneak down into one of local towns and steal to replenish the essentials. Of course, I knew one of the Ten Commandments is "Thou shalt not steal," and though I was trying to be a better Christian, I was still much more interested in my own survival. Not that keeping that particular commandment was high on God's priority list during this juncture in history. I kept it to a minimum anyway, not out of adherence to God's laws, but because it inevitably resulted in parties of Minions scouring the mountain searching for perpetrators. There had already been too many close calls.

***

Next, I led my new friends around to the traps I'd set to show them how they were constructed. Two of the traps had snared rabbits that morning, while another held a captive squirrel. They were quite impressed with that, or at least very hungry.

At any rate, we gathered up the catch and took it back to the cave, where I clubbed the rabbits and drowned the squirrel in a manner of minutes. Then I showed them how to properly dress and cook the varmints.

I watched my guests, especially the women, for their reactions during all of this. Ida and Eva seemed pretty aghast, but Danny never even flinched. The men were also a bit taken aback by the whole thing, except for Roger who was transfixed and frothing at the mouth like I had just taken ribs out of the refrigerator, slathered them with sauce, and thrown them on the grill.

But none of their reactions mattered much. They were too hungry in the end to care how the food got to their mouths. And within a week, they would be clubbing, skinning, and cooking cute, furry creatures themselves with about as much emotion as it once took to make fajitas in their own kitchens.

***

God hadn't created us to be a bunch of wimps. He knew we had to be tough to survive on the old Earth. And though of late, for the most part, we had cushioned ourselves in the luxuries of the modern world, we were instinctively survivors, and left to our own resources, we had the capacity to tackle great hardship. Still, we had limitations. Only by faith and the grace of God could men endure such great suffering.

***

If the Book of Revelation was our Tribulation playbook, the Book of Job was our survival guide. Job was no allegorical figure but flesh and blood, his story real. Job was righteous in the eyes of the Lord, his faith unmatched among men. But even the most righteous men were

151

imperfect in God's eyes, and Job, because of his great faith, was made an example.

Satan had been causing havoc all over the Earth to those who had turned from God, and he was bragging that he could turn any man from God if given the chance. Well, God knew better, of course, but talk was cheap, so He allowed Satan to do his worst and picked the best man for the job (I know).

Job never knew what hit him. Satan had a local band of miscreants raid his estates, murder his servants, and destroy his livestock. Then he sent a great wind to collapse his house, killing his sons and daughters. While Job grieved, Satan struck again, afflicting him with painful boils from head to toe.

Job, having lost nearly everything, miserable and heartbroken, questioned God, but he never lost faith. Even though he didn't understand it one bit, he continued to trust that God knew what he was doing. And for this, he was rewarded with many more children and twice the riches.

***

So why did Job have to suffer? Why did any of us? I already figured out there was more goodness than evil in suffering, that it made the faithful stronger. But why did one man suffer while others seem to cruise through life? I was curious and looked up the answer at the Hall of Knowledge.

***

There was some truth to the expression, "Only the good die young." If you were already destined for Heaven, God would more often than not leave you to fate, and Satan wouldn't bother protecting you either because to him you were a lost cause. But if you were a sinner with a shot at redemption, God would offer you protection but also challenges, to give you time and opportunity to turn things around, while Satan might protect you and feed you goodies to keep your pit opportunities available. So, if you were a sinner and life was going along too smoothly, and it continued that way, it usually meant there was little hope, that you were set in your ways, and unredeemable. Therefore, why would God or Satan waste their time? God already knew your unfortunate destiny, and Satan already had you in his grip.

None of us is blameless. The righteous were made to suffer to bring them even closer to God, to make them more glorious in God's eyes, to show other men the power of faith. The rebellious were made to suffer to put the fear of God in them, and hopefully, bring them back to the fold. But the unrighteous, the completely lost, the names unwritten in the Book of Life, their lives were left to chance and might also perish without suffering.

***

Yeah, there's a big old Book of Life. Yes, it has all the names of the people going to Heaven written in it. It's sitting right there in the middle of the Hall of Knowledge. It's behind some pretty thick glass. It must weigh 300 pounds. No, you can't look inside it yet, not for a thousand years, not until the final judgment, not while there are people to be saved.

***

For some odd reason, skeptics and Bible scoffers would have a field day with this. They'd ask rhetorically, "How is it free will if the names are already in the book, our destiny predetermined?"

This thinking is really stupid, but I'll explain it anyway in simple terms. There was once a very popular movie about a boy who gets into what is arguably the ugliest sports car ever built, except this one has been converted into a time machine, so who cares. The boy travels to the future where he finds a sports almanac, which is then stolen by his nemesis. The nemesis guy also steals the car, taking the almanac to the past to hand it to his younger self in order to make a fortune gambling because the book lists the final scores to all future sporting matches.

So the rhetorical questions I have that should explain things for the naysayers and God-haters are these: did the existence of the sports almanac stop any of the sporting matches from being played? Did its existence change the outcome of any of those matches?

And one more question: would the almanac have any meaning if the matches had never been played?

***

We weren't the only ones in the throes of a Job experience. There were groups such as ours all across the planet, made up of the stubborn remnants of the material world—people with enough good in them to

153

deserve yet another chance, but not enough good sense to have taken it earlier.

***

I did wonder about the possibility that we had been brought together for some purpose. I looked around at my new guests for similarities that might validate my speculations. I could not find any. But I was looking in the wrong place. I was trying to find the faults we shared that might have led us to our purgatory in the mountains, when I should have been looking for the good in us.

***

It doesn't matter. I could know all the things I didn't know about them already. I could read their biographies at the Hall of Knowledge. I could find out where they went to school and what grades they received. I could find out how their parents treated them. I could look up their places of employment and the people they dated. I could know their habits and their hobbies. I could know their good deeds, and I could know their sins. I could find out exactly why we were there together. None of it matters. It only matters that we *were* there together, went through it together, and I knew them as they were then.

***

I missed waking up to the voices of the sisters after they were gone, but I can't say I wasn't more than a little perturbed at the incessant chatting and gossiping from dawn to sleep. If at all possible, Ida was the more talkative, but they fed off each other, nonetheless, and Eva could certainly hold her own.

Both sisters looked after us, happily cooking, catering, even cleaning up our messes—Eva giving us a smirk and a sideways, scolding eye to say you should know better, but we love you anyway. I was closer to Ida in the beginning because she wasn't as serious as Eva, and I could get away with teasing her. This made her laugh, and I liked that about her. Plus, she could be funny herself, with her thin yet accurate observations of others, so I hung around the cooking area quite often, listening to their nonsense and giving Ida a bad time.

***

Beyond the chatter, the mothering, and a few other sisterly quirks,

I would find out that Eva wasn't much like her sister after all. It happened late one morning while I sat cleaning fish by the river. Eva walked past me along the bank with a bundle of clothes for washing. Seeing her only from behind and mistaking her for Ida, I threw a handful of guts in her direction. She knew straight away it had been meant for Ida because we didn't have that kind of relationship.

She stopped and gave me the stink eye. "I'm not Ida."

Still, I laughed. "Sorry, Eva."

The laughing annoyed her even more, and she stomped off down river.

I dropped the fish, catching up to her as she placed the bundle of laundry on a large rock at the edge of the water. "Hey, wait a minute," I said, "I'm really sorry. You know I wouldn't have thrown that at you."

She looked at me without saying anything for some time. When she did speak, it was like she was someone else entirely. Gone was the gossipy lilt that accompanied her sister in their duet of blather. She spoke solemnly. "That's just it. Why does everyone like Ida so much and not me?"

***

This was exactly why God's job was so tough on the old Earth, I thought. No matter the circumstance, people would essentially remain the same. Billions had disappeared, nuclear bombs had demolished cities, Satan ruled the world while his Minions hunted us, the earth shook on a daily basis, and the coming judgments of the Tribulation were a certainty. Yet, bless her heart, here she was, concerning herself with social matters, as if we were on a high school campus or someplace and not hiding from the end of the world.

***

But I shouldn't have excluded myself from those examining thoughts. I wished nothing more than to be the big man on campus, with Danny as my sweetheart. Besides, I was wrong about Eva. In fact, I would come to find she was quantum leaps ahead of me in substance and heart.

***

"It's not like that, Eva. You're just different. She's bubbly, easier to joke with is all," I said.

"I know I'm not funny like her. I try to be, but I'm just not."

"I'm full of fish. Give me a second." I washed my bloody, smelly hands in the river and sat her down next to me on the same rock where her laundry rested.

Before all the madness in the world, I would have kept it light. And though I would never completely escape my tendencies toward avoidance on the old Earth, at least with some reflection, it was easier in those dark times to be direct. "Why do you do it?" I said.

"Do what?"

I paused but I said it. "Pretend to be like her."

She bawled then. I mean she really bawled. Tears poured down her face until I was worried I might have to get her sister or Danny. "Eva...hey...it's all right...really...I didn't mean anything," I said, placing a smelly hand on her shoulder without thinking. But she didn't seem to care. She just kept crying away.

I started to get up. "I'll get Ida," I said.

But she pulled me back down. She seemed to calm down after that. Still, I braced myself for the usual angry reaction to my attempts at consoling women. It was not to be.

"You're right. It's not me. I'm not at all like her. I just don't remember who I am anymore," she said. "I wasn't always like this. It was just easier."

"Easier?" I said.

"I wanted to forget...and I went to live with my sister. She was so happy. She had so many friends. I wanted to fit in with them."

"What did you want to forget?"

She wiped the last tears from her face. "I know we seem like we've been attached at the hip since birth, but we lived apart for most of our lives...in another state...."

"No...can't be...I don't believe it...in a *whole* other state. It must have been a border state, where you could still hold hands or something."

She smiled and punched me in the arm. "You're not funny."

I grinned like a proud four-year-old. "Sorry. Continue."

"I was saying...I had a family. We lived in a little town called Quartzsite. And yes, it was a border town, but not to Idaho where my sister lived," she said, smiling and hitting me in the arm again.

I just smiled back.

"It's in Arizona," she continued, "It's a hot, hot place. In the summer it'd be like 115 on a good day. My husband and me—Lee was his name—we lived there for eight years. Lee wasn't a horrible man, but he drank an awful lot."

"That'll put a chink in things."

"It did. Believe it or not, I was a Bible thumper. Not just the church-going kind—but a diehard, door to door, Bible pusher."

"No kidding?" I said, and picturing her knocking on doors to preach made me laugh a little for some reason.

"Stop. We had three boys together…." she paused and the tears came again.

She had never mentioned them, and the way she stopped, I already knew something bad must have happened to them before the Rapture. I felt like an idiot for laughing before. I put a fishy arm around her. "I'm sorry, Eva."

She leaned into me and pushed her words through the pain, "They were beautiful boys….I named them after the Gospels…Matthew, Mark, Luke…"

"Good names," I said.

"They were all a year apart. I pushed them out…one, two, three…." Eva smiled then, but just briefly. "Five, six, and seven years old….Lee wasn't a horrible man, but the drinking….He worked hard. He was a contractor…a good one….I don't know what we were doing in that awful place…Hell on Earth…."

Except for the light rush of the river, it was fairly quiet. I thought it odd because morning in the forest always brought with it the steady jingle of birds and other small wildlife. Perhaps it was later than I realized; perhaps they had stopped to listen to Eva's sad tale.

She continued. "I prayed for the man every day. I begged him to change his ways, to quit drinking, to go to church with me. He went to prison for what he did; I would have left him regardless….Maybe I nagged him too much….Maybe I prayed too much….Maybe I thought I was better than everyone else."

Eva abruptly stopped crying. I thought she might have run out of tears. She had a blank look about her, staring at something or nothing in the distance.

"What happened to your boys?"

She closed her eyes and tilted her head up until she felt the heat of the sun on her face, filtered through one end of the forest. "The sun...I despise the sun...I would rather be in dark rooms, gaggling with other women about nothing. I could stay in the cave all day, cooking and cleaning...sleeping...hiding."

"They're okay now, Eva. You'll be with them soon," I said.

"I don't know, George...I'm afraid...my faith....I can't get it back."

"It's not gone...." I sure liked propping up everyone else's faith, while mine danced precariously on a tightrope of apathy.

"That stupid man...that stupid, stupid man," she said.

"Tell me, Eva...."

"He wasn't supposed to go anywhere....It was his day off. I didn't let him take the boys without me. He drank beer from the moment he got up. I shouldn't have left them alone, but I was out...spreading the Word," she added abruptly, with not a little sarcasm, and directed at herself. "But Lee took them anyway....All the sudden he had to fix the toilet....Been bugging him about it for months, but all the sudden it can't wait. He said he thought he was gonna be just a minute—that's why he didn't bother even to roll down the window a crack, or bring them into the hardware store with him. He said it wasn't even that hot."

The tears came hard again. "I'm sorry, Eva."

"Only five, six, and seven...five, six, and seven...." she repeated, the painful chant.

"All of them?"

She didn't speak.

"Don't think about it, Eva. God took the boys quicker than you think. He didn't let them suffer." This was before I knew it was true, how the angels or Jesus would jump in to suffer for the little ones, but I said it anyway.

"Are you sure?" It was the first time she sounded hopeful.

I heard chirping and other sounds besides the water start up, or maybe I'd only imagined the silence. "I'm sure, Eva. I'm sure."

I held her awhile and stayed to help her with the washing. We talked about the future, about seeing our children again. I carried my fish; she carried her clothes, and we walked back together. Halfway to the camp, Eva stopped and gave me a wide smile.

It made me smile. "What?" I asked.

"You smell," she said.

I laughed. "See, you are funny."

16

Eva and I were close after that, but whatever amount of time I spent with her or her sister, or even Danny, for that matter, was nothing compared to the time I spent with the boys. I couldn't do without women, and I certainly didn't want to, but it had always been easier for me to be with men, especially if we were involved together in an ordeal or adventure of some sort.

***

I mentioned before that man was built for hardship and suffering, but men, as opposed to most women, actually needed it. It's true. Why did Thoreau write, "The mass of men lead lives of quiet desperation...."? Not simply because the daily tedium of the forced grind initiates such a state in men, but because they long for something bigger, something monumental, a great adventure, a tragedy even, but maybe most of all, and terrible as it might be, war.

***

Some liberal thinkers would whine about war even when the cause was just. And true, war was bloody, horrible, frightening, sad, heartbreaking, and more often than not, pointless. But these whiners were often the guys who refused to fight in the first place. The average man, the average soldier, would rather be nowhere else than fighting side by side with and for his brothers in arms, leaving the causes and the blood on the hands of the tyrants and politicians.

***

These same liberals would invariably blame God for war, which was odd, considering most of them didn't believe in God. God never wanted war. He wasn't up in Heaven like some insane child, moving people around like toy soldiers on a giant, ersatz battlefield. So why did He create men whose nature was to embrace it? Why, to fight the devil, of course.

*****

The Illuminati understood this, and that it would be problematic for the Antichrist's push toward one-world government, and actually developed an insidious program to slowly feminize men and subsequent generations so they would be less likely to fight back. No kidding, I couldn't make this stuff up.

Now Howard might have argued with me about this because he considered himself to be a man's man. And I didn't disagree. He could be as tough as any of us. But I wasn't referring to gay men. Gay men fought bravely and died just the same as heterosexuals. And many relished the opportunity to fight as well. Besides, there were also plenty of women who wanted to fight, and throughout history had proved themselves on battlefields.

No, the Illuminati agenda on this one was much more realistic than trying to make men gay. Their goal was to take the warrior out of men. They implemented their agenda by getting psychologists and the like to promote the coddling of boys to sickening levels, urging mothers and fathers to pamper them on par with their female siblings, to stilt competitiveness, to offer constant and unwarranted praise, and to end even mild physical punishment.

Next, the Illuminati set out to emasculate men in the work place and in their own households. Much of this was achieved on the back end of the women's movement, which began in earnest to right the wrongs of employment inequality and abuse in the family. While this was being achieved, the Illuminati saw an opportunity to implement their plans with media and peer-driven campaigns, attacking mothers and homemakers as somehow inferior to women who had chosen to forgo marriage or focus solely on their careers.

In time, their efforts served to breakdown the traditional family structure. It was part of man's nature to lead his family—not in an abusive or tyrannical manner, but as breadwinner, guide, loving husband, and father figure to his children. Most women picked their mates and married on the basis of such traits.

The women's movement was important to help protect women from violence and inequality, but after it was hijacked by the Illuminati, it served to distort gender roles to dysfunctional extremes, placing families in chaos. Men began to feel worthless and weak, women unprotected and insecure, and children confused. The divorce rate skyrocketed.

The old Earth even had a term to describe the ideal "product" of their emasculation agenda: metrosexual. This was a type of man who cared more about hair products and skinny jeans than family or adventure. Man was evolving from warrior into wimp. A metrosexual wouldn't be caught dead on a battlefield.

***

Regardless of their efforts, the Illuminati had little effect on our "band of brothers" in this area. Whether the metrosexuals had been raptured or whether they were out waving their marked wrists about, buying turtlenecks and whatnot, was of little concern, except to note there were none among us.

No, we were always out wandering the mountain, hunting, scouting, searching for Minions, looking for trouble, or at least a minor adventure to serve our masculinity. Each morning, we'd gather our weapons and supplies, bid farewell to the women, and march out of camp as proudly as any soldier off to battle. Danny and the sisters would make fun of our misplaced bravado. But it didn't faze us, not one bit; such was the disconnection of our masculine world.

***

Speckle also remained behind, always close to the sisters, staring off into space, lost somewhere to a reality where the horror of his wife's rape and murder remained hidden from his own consciousness.

***

The band played on without him, and I had my friendships with all of them, even Roger, who existed in realms I sometimes couldn't fathom. Perhaps Howard was my favorite because he and I were closest in age. With Joe being in his late sixties and Billy having just turned thirty, Howard and I landed somewhere between Joe's fatherly advice and trying to mentor the headstrong Billy and the wayward Roger. Together, we were like some weird family on an extended, generational camping trip gone terribly wrong.

***

Regardless of our positions in the "family," Howard and I conversed with each other the most often because he liked to debate things, as did I. But the rare thing about him was that he could debate without becoming emotional or angry. Billy and Joe couldn't understand how we could be slinging such vitriolic verbiage at each other one moment and laughing with each other the next. Billy would have beaten the crap out of me and Joe might never have spoken to me again had I taken such tones with them.

But Howard didn't mind at all; in fact, he relished it as I did. I could attack one of his viewpoints, or say something stupid or hypocritical about homosexuals, and he'd fight back, but we would always leave smiling.

***

Homosexuals on the old Earth sometimes hated Christians for this very reason. They assumed, and often with good reason, that Christians looked down on them as freaks of nature or sexual deviants destined for Hell. But they were sorely mistaken. Those spewing condemnations upon them were hardly Christians, but religious fanatics, not unlike the Pharisees, rebuked for sitting in judgment of Christ: "…first take the log out of your own eye, and then you will see clearly to take the speck out of your brother's eye," and the like.

***

Howard knew and understood me. He knew how much time I spent pointing out my own faults. When I gave him my opinion, he knew it wasn't in the spirit of self-righteousness but of mutual understanding, and he never became angry.

That was the thing that bothered me about some of the liberals I knew on the old Earth. I wasn't all that conservative, even in my later years, but try and pick on one of their political or social positions and they seemed to take it personally, all reason eventually tossed out the window in favor of gross exaggeration and outright name calling.

Howard was different. He may have aligned himself with liberals, for he possessed the great compassion, peacefulness, and insight they sometimes pretended, but he was real, and good, and undefined by any agenda.

***

Still, in the end, it didn't matter if you were conservative or liberal, democratic or republican, right wing, left wing, socialist, communist, anarchist, or apolitical. The Illuminati ran the show on the old Earth and we had all played our parts.

***

Often, while Howard and I debated, Joe would shake his head as if we were his incorrigible sons, and after we'd worn ourselves out, he'd impart a few short but impactful words on the subject that usually derailed one or both of our arguments.

Joe Mellon was a smart man, and he offered the hard experience of a thirty-year police veteran, and more importantly, the wisdom and advice of a man of years.

He was also an expert fisherman. But he didn't let on right away. In fact, when I set out to teach everyone how to fish, he watched with amusement, not saying a word, as I sat by the river for an hour before I pulled one scrawny trout. Not until then did he take over, fixing a proper bait, skipping across rocks like a much younger man to a deep and still pool of water, dropping the hook and line carefully, letting it drift just so. Within minutes, his line tugged, and he landed a trout that made my fish look like a carnival prize. He had a good laugh at my expense. They all did.

I didn't care. Time and again, in the lakes and streams, he worked his magic. Without his great fishing abilities, we surely would have had to risk more pilfering or starved to death.

***

Those extra raids would have fallen on Billy's shoulders. Though he was sometimes the loose cannon, Billy was a darn good thief, and while one of us stood watch, he'd slide in and out of the houses of the locals with bags of stolen goods like a buff and tattooed Pink Panther. I warned him of the dangers, but he was fearless and eager for the raids. He would have gone every night, had we not held him back. He, too, saved our lives.

164

***

"We merry men, we band of brothers," we roamed the mountains, hunting and gathering, preparing for battle as real men should. And when threat of battle came one late afternoon from a platoon of Minions armed with automatic weapons surging up from the valley below, what did we do? We ran, of course.

***

It was actually Roger who spotted them. For once, he was looking in the right direction. We were—all of us boys—resting and talking nonsense on the mountainside after a long hike—ironically enough— to search an alternate escape route for just such an invasion. It wouldn't help us that day. The Minions had been spotted too late.

***

Joe had us laughing after informing Billy he would be arresting him for burglary just as soon as we finished fighting the Battle of Armageddon and things got back to normal, when Roger spoke up in an unusually peppy voice.

"I'm gonna have some fun today," he said.

I ignored him because he was prone to non sequiturs, strange utterances which could lead to even stranger conversations I preferred to avoid. But, fortunately, Billy took the bait. "Why's that, Roger?" he said.

"I'm going to kill some Minions."

Joe looked over at Roger, who was staring intently down the valley. "Maybe some other day, Roger," he said.

"You guys are pussies."

"Yes, we're pussies, Roger. And not particularly fond of slow torture, either," I said.

"Plus we need to get back so the girls don't get mad at us," said Joe, and he laughed at his own add-on to Roger's deprecating remark.

I laughed, too. "Yeah, let's go, Roger," I said.

But Roger just kept staring down into the valley. Billy grabbed his arm to steer him back to camp. "I'll kill them myself, then," said Roger.

That's when Billy looked down. "Oh, man!" he said.

"What?" I said, and I moved to where they were standing to peer

165

over the edge. There must have been a hundred of them, spaced about ten feet apart and spread across the valley, carrying assault weapons, moving methodically up the mountain. "Why didn't you say something, you idiot?"

"I did," said Roger.

Joe was looking by then. "Move," he said, grabbing Roger roughly by his shirt collar and spinning him around toward the direction of the cave.

***

We ran until Joe lost steam and slowed to a fast walk. It didn't matter; none of us would have lasted much longer at that pace. We were only about a half mile from the cave, most of it uphill, and even walking, by the time we arrived, we were too out of breath to tell the girls about the Minions. We just pointed back toward the direction we had come. It was enough. The girls began to pack the camp.

***

"How many, Joe?" asked Danny.

Joe was busy throwing up. "Plenty," I said.

Eva and Ida began stuffing the daypacks with bottles of water and food.

By this time Joe had recovered. "Don't bother—there's no time— everything in the hole!" he said.

I had to agree. We had two contingency plans: hide or run. There were too many of them, and they were too close. There was no time to cover our tracks. They would have caught us on the trails.

We would bury and cover all traces of the camp, then head to the back of the cave where we could each borrow in one of the many small crevices. It would be risky if they found the cave, but still better than running because they would surely track us.

The hole we had dug was under a thicket of trees about seventy-five yards from the cave. Fortunately, in preparation for just such an event, most of the supplies were already there, so, even with little help from the exhausted men, the girls made short work of getting the rest of our things hidden.

After covering and camouflaging the hole, we carefully swept away our tracks with fir branches as we moved backwards toward the mouth of the cave. Once inside, because the floor of the cave was rocky and we moved in single file, Billy, holding up the rear and shining a flashlight, easily wiped away the few traces of our movements, and we made our way quickly to the back.

Nobody was looking forward to the crevices, which were thin, deep, and pitch black. And though we had periodically swept them out, there was no way to clean every orifice, so the possibility of being joined by rat, snake, or spider was very real. Also, there would be no comforting one another—each crevice just big enough to accommodate one person.

We were, however, familiar with the experience, as we had drilled periodically, spending ten minutes at a time in our own crevice, which Joe had assigned. Roger, the wild card, was placed furthest to the rear of the cave because we couldn't risk him opening his mouth or jumping out to confront a searching Minion. The rest of us were spread out, with Billy and I armed, positioned nearest to the entrance to take out any Minions if discovered, giving the others a possible chance at escape.

Unfortunately, the plan wouldn't be very effective with so many Minions combing the mountain. Our only hope was that the cave and crevices were dark and deep enough to keep us hidden. And that Roger could keep still long enough as not to give us away.

***

As a boy I'd read a story by Edgar Allen Poe, about this Italian guy who gets revenge on an old friend by getting him drunk and walling him up in his wine cellar. After sobering up, the poor man finds himself chained within a catacomb, while brick by brick his would-be murderer seals him into the upright tomb. He begs the man to release him, but his assailant shows no pity, even tossing in a lighted torch before placing the last brick, as if to prolong his victim's anticipation of death by forcing him to view the flickering fire, a reminder of his own fading light. In a way, I never got over the story. I could think of nothing more horrible than being buried alive. During our rehearsals, I would imagine spending my last bullet to no avail, the remaining Minions, also without mercy, laughing as they shoved rocks and dirt into my hiding place, leaving me to suffocate or slowly die of thirst in the darkness.

***

But that day we could hear the noises of the Minions moving closer to the camp, and all I could think about was getting to my dark hovel before they found the cave.

***

Billy and I signaled to each other that everyone was secure, but before I could turn around, Roger began mumbling about something. "Roger, you gotta be quiet for a bit. I'll let you know when it's safe," I said.

"I want out of here," he said, this time loud and clear.

"Be quiet, Roger!" came Danny's firm voice from out of her crevice. "We've been over this!"

"There is something in here, Mom!" he said.

I heard a Minion calling out orders somewhere in the distance outside the cave. "Shut up, Roger—they're close!" I said.

"It's crawling on me."

"Shut up!" said Billy.

Joe poked out of his hole. "What the Hell's going on?" he said.

"Please, Roger!" said Danny.

"Shut that kid up," said Howard.

"Everyone quiet." I said, and I hurried over to Roger's crevice, shining a small flashlight inside. Roger had already scooted toward the front where I could see him fairly easily. He was on his belly, squirming back and forth.

"Get it off me!" he said.

"I can't see anything," I said.

"It's on my back."

"Come out a little more then." I still couldn't see anything. "Where?"

"Get it off me!" This time he practically screamed.

"I'll shoot you if you yell again, Roger!" said Billy.

"Go to your spot, Billy," I said.

"He's gonna get us all killed!" said Billy.

"Go!" I said. With that he grumbled and walked away. "Where, Roger?"

"Under my shirt." This time, when he squirmed a little to one side, I spotted something moving toward his neck.

"Stay still," I said.

"What is it?" said Danny.

I lifted his shirt slowly, prepared to knock it away with the flashlight. But when I lifted the shirt further it bolted from under his collar and onto his neck where it paused. I recognized it right away, and though it looked menacing enough with its fangs and stiff brown fur, I was relieved.

I told Roger to stay still again and placed my hand against his neck, easing my fingers underneath the creature's legs. It took a couple of quick steps onto the back of my hand, which I lowered gently to the floor of the cave, and with a shake the thing sidled away.

***

What was it? It was a killing machine, of bugs and the occasional lizard anyway. It was also capable of eating its own kind. We had encountered them many times on the mountain. It was a California Brown Tarantula, a bit disconcerting in appearance and known to deliver a painful bite when cornered, but unaggressive and otherwise harmless to humans.

***

Still, I wasn't going to say the word spider. Everyone was already on edge. "Just a deer mouse," I said, knowing the girls were familiar with the cute little rodent that made its home on the mountain, venturing through our camp on occasion to scrounge for food. "He's gone. Slide back." Roger complied, and once he was out of sight, I turned off my flashlight and hurried toward my spot. There wouldn't be enough time to cover my tracks.

I hadn't gone two steps before I heard voices. They were closer than I thought, but I could still make it because my crevice, though toward the front, was a good sixty feet from the mouth of the cave, just past a curve in the tunnel where it was still quite dark.

***

"Search the cave." I heard the order just as I stuck my foot in the same crack I'd always used to lift myself high enough to reach the opening.

Sitting directly across from Billy's spot, my hole was about eight feet off the ground and about four feet deep, but with very little wriggle room.

I set my pistol on the ledge of the crevice, except this time, instead of pulling myself up carefully and sliding in slowly and sideways, I jumped off the crack with one foot and dove in head first on my belly, turning sideways and parallel with the opening only after I hit the back wall, and not lightly, with my skull.

From this position, I could only see the upper half of the opposite wall, just above Billy's spot, but I only had to lift my head slightly and peer over the fold of rock to view the floor of the cave. I would see their lights when they came, and I could pick them off if I scooted far enough over the fold. I pulled my weapon into my body and with that I felt oddly comfortable in my rocky cradle.

***

The feeling wouldn't last. I could hear footsteps on the gravelly floor of the cave moving slowly. I began to sweat and shiver at the same time. I should have had the pistol in front of me, ready to fire, but I couldn't make myself move and continued gripping it with numbing force tightly to my chest. Then I heard more voices.

"There's nothing in here," said someone who sounded Middle Eastern, though I wasn't positive. He said it like he was trying to sound bored, but I could hear his nervousness.

"I know, Hodi, but the Sergeant said to check it thoroughly," said another male voice, this accent purely New York.

"What are we looking for, rats?" said the nervous one called Hodi.

I was still terrified, but Hodi's nervousness and there only being two of them helped calm me some. Sliding the pistol away from my body, I placed a shaky finger on the trigger.

"Look, the sooner we check it out, the sooner we get out of here. I don't want to get shot for something stupid," said New York.

***

The Minions didn't mess around with discipline. There were no hearings or court-martials. If you screwed up enough or disobeyed orders, you'd more likely than not be shot where you stood. Like the California Tarantula, the Minions, too, would eat their own kind.

"Okay, okay, but there's nothing here," said Hodi.

"Look at all these holes. We need to check them," said New York.

I braced myself. I could see their flashlights bouncing off the cave walls. I prayed Billy wouldn't panic and come out shooting.

"Are you kidding me? There are too many to check," said Hodi. "I'm getting hungry."

"Well, let's check the biggest ones."

"What if there's a snake?"

"Enough, Hodi! Let's get it done!"

I tried to steady the pistol, but I was shaking too badly, so I laid it on the rock face, still pointing out but with my finger off the trigger, afraid it would accidentally fire. I could tell they were moving from hole to hole. The light came and went, Hodi complaining more with each failed search, until I could hear him just below my crevice. I saw the top of his head bounce briefly by the opening in front of me. But then he kept moving.

"Did you even look in there?" said New York.

"Yeah, I looked."

"I'm serious, Hodi."

"You know…I'm getting a little tired of you calling the shots. Who the Hell put you in charge of me? I don't recall the ceremony where you were awarded the boss of Hodi badge. See this chevron? It's the same one you got. It means I'm a corporal and you're a corporal. You are not the sergeant. You are not the captain. You are not the king cave hunter! Got it, General? Now, I will go back and check that stinking hole, but then I'm going to get me some of that dog food they're calling chili down there."

"Fine, numbskull—but if we get in trouble for this, I'm gonna beat you to death before they shoot us!" I could hear Hodi laughing. "You think I'm joking—I'm going to check the back of the cave," said New York.

Now I figured we were done. New York would find them if I didn't do something quick. I had no choice. As soon as Hodi poked his head up, I would put a bullet in him and then chase down New York, if Billy didn't get to him first.

***

Billy, hearing their exchange, had already slipped out of his crevice and was stalking New York with the shotgun.

***

I heard Hodi moving on the gravel. He was just below me again. I readied the pistol. His head bounced once above the opening. He must have slipped because I heard a sliding sound.

"Damn!" he said.

But then he was up again. I heard his foot land on rock. It must have been the same small ledge I used to boost myself. And in a moment there he was. I lurched back a little under the fold. I could see the top of his head again, this time steady. He must have been adjusting the flashlight in his hand because its beam bounced all over the crevice.

Then he shoved himself forward and up, until his flashlight and my pistol met. The beam was blinding for a moment, so I turned my head slightly away and switched my flashlight on, pointing it toward his face. My eyes adjusted. His were closed, whether to avoid my light or because he couldn't believe what he was seeing.

I don't know why I didn't fire, but he seemed to be as afraid as I was, and so I hesitated. He didn't have a weapon. He must have left it below so he get up the rock more easily. He opened his eyes again, and he looked at me. I looked back at him.

The standoff only lasted a few seconds, but it seemed like minutes. Then something about him changed. He seemed to relax. He didn't say a word. He didn't have to. Somehow I knew he wasn't going to give me away. And he didn't. He just slid back down the canyon wall. I turned my flashlight off and breathed a sigh of relief.

Before I could even think again about New York finding the others, I heard yelling and somebody running on the rocks from the back of the cave. It was New York. Billy, who was right behind him, also heard the yell. And seeing the Minion turn suddenly and run, he dove to the ground on one side of the cave, ready to shoot as he approached, but the frantic New York ran right past him.

"Hodi, there're a ton of giant spiders back there!"

"What?" said Hodi.

172

"Giant spiders!" By this time, New York was already upon Hodi and added, "Dude, get your rifle and let's get the Hell out of here!"

"Yeah, let's get the Hell out of here!" said Hodi.

***

I went to the Hall of Knowledge to look up Hodi and find out why he didn't give me away. It turns out he'd seen something in my eyes that reminded him of himself. He could see I was scared and didn't want to hurt him or anything. And that pretty much summed up Hodi's experience with the New World Order and the Minions. Hodi, a peace-loving Muslim much of his life, had had enough of killing and being afraid. A week later, he deserted. Unfortunately, the Mark of the Beast made him easy to track, and within a few days, he was caught and executed. When one of his captors asked him where the Hell he thought he was going with the traceable 666 implant, he responded with one word: "Exactly."

But there was something else; something I didn't understand. I discovered that Hodi was here in the New Kingdom. I didn't understand it because it was written in the Book of Revelation that anyone carrying the Mark of the Beast was doomed. It must have been a mistake, I thought, but it wasn't, because a few weeks later, I actually looked him up and thanked him. So I went back to the Hall of Knowledge to find out about the discrepancy. What did I find out? It was so simple and so beautiful it brought me to tears. It was this: God can change his mind.

17

We walked out of the darkness into the light of the afternoon. Nobody said a word. Our eyes adjusted as we took in the mountain air and felt the sun that was still ours, at least for a time.

***

The Minions had given up the search and were already miles from our mountain. I thought about Hodi and what he had done. I thought about the sudden presence of so many tarantulas. All the times we'd rehearsed, I hadn't seen even one, yet when Billy and I went back to give the all clear, there were at least two-dozen of the giant spiders spread out across the ledges, just below the crevices where the others hid. The large spiders remained perfectly still as we approached, unflinching and unafraid, standing guard like British sentries at Buckingham Palace. It was impressive—enough to send New York running.

Hodi and the spiders had been little miracles. I looked up at the full moon, and for a moment, imagined it a great eyeball winking back at me. The hand of God was with us.

***

That night, cautious of Minion activity, we celebrated our close call beside a fireless pit. Billy broke out a couple bottles of wine from his most recent raid. Ironically, it was that particular theft that had prompted the Minions to search the mountain in the first place. The bottles came from the ranch house of a local big shot. The rancher had used his political clout to instigate the unusually large-scale search.

Even the sisters, who hadn't had a drink since they left Las Vegas, partook that night, probably to quell the anxiety that still lingered, fueled by the nerve-racking events of the day.

Together, we toasted our survival and the good Lord for seeing us through. We drank to the Minion, Hodi, for his moment of compassion. We drank to Roger for first spotting the Minions, even though we had to pull it out of him. And we drank to our eight-legged guards.

***

There were Christians on the old Earth who would have frowned on our celebration. Some believed it to be the "devil's juice," a sinful concoction with no useful purpose except to further the debauchery of man. Other Christians found it acceptable to drink moderately or on special occasions. And there were those like the Catholics, who involved alcohol in their weekly masses, and with a reputation for putting a few down outside the church—some with a certain unabashed pride.

The Bible itself did little to solve the debate, offering seemingly opposing viewpoints: "...Be not drunk with wine," "Wine is a mocker and beer a brawler...," "In the end it (wine) bites like a snake and poisons like a viper," "Jesus turned the water into wine," "Every man sets out the good wine first... ," "I will not drink again of the fruit of the vine until the kingdom of God comes," and on and on....

Why couldn't God make up His mind? Should I drink? Should I not drink? Was it acceptable to drink a little bit? Could I drink a little in church? Could I get drunk at a wedding? How about at a bar mitzvah? Jesus drank; why shouldn't I? Why had God created a fermentation process in nature if he didn't want people drinking alcohol? Was it all right I got hammered after losing my job? What about after my wife left me, even if it was my fault? How about after losing my little girl?

***

And while Christians argued, Bible skeptics and critics on the old Earth pointed to the debate as another example of Biblical

175

contradiction, just another example of why the Bible, God, and Christianity were full of baloney. They laughed at our silly quandary, our inner turmoil, our inconsistency, our hypocrisy, our weakness, our Christian guilt.

***

Well, was drinking ok? Was alcohol good or bad? What about other substances that caused impairment? And why were there so many inconsistencies on the subject, and lots of other subjects in the Bible for that matter?

***

I never considered myself an alcoholic on the old Earth. I often went weeks and months without it. Don't get me wrong; I drank plenty. I just never had the craving alcoholics describe, like I had to have drink. No, my problem with drinking was that once I had a few, all bets were off. I craved a party, and it was alcohol that usually got me there. More often than not, I'd end up doing something stupid like getting in a fight, getting behind the wheel, doing drugs, hitting a strip club or casino, and who knew what else.

Was there good in any of it? Of course not. But I got to thinking. I began to pour over those sad days and nights, and the sadder adventures that followed. I remembered the trouble and the depravity, and I winced at my pathetic lack of control. But there were other times.

***

My brother Geoff and I were close growing up, at least until we hit our early teens, when the year separating us seemed insurmountable as I became the little brother he didn't want tagging around. Then he joined the Marines, leaving home when I was seventeen. After that, he got married and moved to North Carolina. During those years, I saw him maybe three times. We talked sporadically on the phone, but it was always awkward. Eventually, we gave up on even that, and I didn't see him for about eight years.

He was a different person when he finally showed up at my door with his wife and two boys. Now a family man and a full-blown Southerner, he had come out to see my mom and take the kids to Disneyland. Sophie played with her cousins while Renee and my sister-in-law chatted away in the living room like old friends.

Then there were Geoff and I, nodding and grunting, trying to avoid each other by interjecting ourselves into the wives' conversation. Until they decided to take the kids to the mall, and we both went into a panic, offering to go with them, a suggestion met with surprise and quickly denied because neither of us had ever offered to go to a mall except maybe at Christmas.

So there we were—brothers, who had once spent long effortless hours at play, now sitting as complete strangers in brutal silence. At least until I had this thought: *Let's go to a bar.*

You might laugh at us, and you probably should. But I call it a small miracle, for two strangers walked into a bar and two friends emerged; two brothers, drunk, yes, but having become closer nevertheless.

Now our wives were none too happy when they picked us up, but that only brought us closer—as did our shared hangovers. From then on, we were brothers again because of the drink. I took my family for visits and we talked often after that. Could it have happened without alcohol? I don't know and I don't care. I got to know my brother again before he disappeared.

***

The point of my boring story is this: amongst the madness and stupidity, alcohol had served a purpose. And it wasn't the only time. A few glasses of wine broke the awkwardness of my first date with Renee and brought us closer that night. It inspired a dull audience at my sister's wedding, turning it into a celebration to be remembered. Alcohol numbed the pain of my father's death. It helped me through the aftermath of the Rapture, the first months of Sophie being gone, and the fear and horror of the Tribulation.

***

Alcohol and other natural, mind-altering substances were used and manipulated by man for both good and evil purposes. A good example is the drug morphine—derived from the opium flower—given as a painkiller on battlefields as far back as the American Civil War. Soldiers who had to endure all manner of horrific wounds, including broken bones, stab wounds, bullet wounds, burns, head and face wounds, torn and severed limbs, and blown-out eyeballs were given at least some respite from the pain by its use. It also saved lives by preventing wounded soldiers from going into shock. On the other hand, the street drug heroin, also derived from opium—basically super-charged morphine—was highly addictive, wrecking lives and causing death. Opium could both save and destroy.

***

Like nature, the Bible is filled with such contradictions. This is because they were both created to accommodate free will. Free will is about choice, and choice is, obviously, by *its* nature, full of contradictions.

The Bible doesn't state that alcohol is evil because it isn't. Its use is suspect but not forbidden. The Bible is a book of reason and possibility, not a book of rigid impossibility. Religious fanatics on the old Earth would comb the Bible for so-called rules, while often ignoring everything else related to a particular subject, especially if it interfered with one of their agendas. All this did was serve to alienate many intelligent people who weren't willing to live with the crushing guilt of such hypocrisy.

I'm not saying any of this to excuse my bad habits. But what religious fanatics failed to notice was the overwhelming yet subtle beauty of contradiction, alive and well, shifting about the rules, wherein lies the essence and greatness of the Book. The Bible is not a book of rules, not because there are no rules, but because the rules are useless without self-discovery.

There *are* absolutes in the Bible, clear rights and wrongs, but this doesn't mean that God is an absolutist. If He were, He would have stuck to the laws of the Old Testament, and He wouldn't have bothered sending His son to pay the price for our sins.

***

Drunk on wine or stone sober—my fondest memories of our days on the mountain are of sitting around the fire with my friends, laughing and talking, singing, fighting, or deep in prayer. Because it was there with them that I could forget, if only for a moment, what I was and the things I had done. And it was there that the pain of missing Sophie would subside just long enough to feel hopeful about seeing her again.

***

And it was there that I got to know Danny, got to know her toughness and keen intelligence, admiring her beauty while convincing myself I was falling for her.

I especially looked forward to the Bible studies because Danny usually led them, and I could watch her without being obvious. At times I would bait her with arguments, taking an opposing stance even if I wasn't sure of it, just to engage her in conversation.

***

Besides the Bible, the most important book in my possession was a book on California's edible plants. This book, more than guns, traps, or pilfered food, kept us alive, as it provided an immediate and relatively simple means for nourishment no matter the circumstance.

Danny, once a practicing vegetarian, was especially interested in the book and would eventually become our expert in the area. But it was I who first introduced her to the handful of plants I had been grazing on in the vicinity of the cave, and it was during these horticultural outings that I became smitten.

***

Despite our predicament and the accompanying grime, tedium and hardship, we couldn't help at times but to be in awe of our surroundings. And, on a clear, early summer morning, Danny and I, out gathering plant food, were treated to a particularly inspiring view.

We had reached a clearing in the woods, where the trail ended and the terrain grew rockier, until we were standing on a great boulder overlooking a valley. The sun threw a stretch of light, wide and straight like a highway, between the shadows of the mountains, intersecting the river below.

"Look—God is amazing," said Danny.

"It's pretty nice," I said.

"No, see the cross; it's a sign."

The rail of sunlight did pass the river at the exact middle of the valley and was absorbed by the shadows, so it was shorter above the river, as in the shape of a crucifix. "You think?" I said.

"Don't *you* think?" she said.

"I don't know; I'm not big on signs."

"What are you talking about, George? This whole thing is about signs: the star before the Rapture, the quakes, the wars, the Mark of the Beast."

"I mean personal signs."

"What's the difference? They're all personal. And what about all you went through with your old partner and your old student at the checkpoint sparing you? And how 'bout those spiders…and Hodi? Come on," she said.

***

In the previous weeks I had positioned myself to be wherever she was, again trying not to make it too obvious. But she knew what was up, and I didn't care because we had gotten to know each other. She told me about her life, and I told her a version of mine.

***

"Well, what does it mean then?" I said.

She held my hand. She did nice stuff like that all the time and it killed me. I never knew how to take her, but that was all my own baggage. She was just doing the things truly kind people do. "It means…we are going to be all right," she said.

"We have very little food, game is getting scarce, we could be captured and tortured at any time, and we've both read what happens next. I'd say things are just peachy."

She laughed. She always laughed at my stupid, pessimistic remarks. And I loved the way she opened her mouth wide, scrunching her nose and closing her eyes when she did.

I turned from the view and stared at her for a moment. Her face was dirty, and the day before, she had hacked at her hair with a knife till it was uneven and in places shorn nearly to the scalp. Still, it only set off her amazing features, and I couldn't help myself when I pulled her in and tried to kiss her.

She pulled back, but she didn't make me feel bad or awkward like some women in that situation might have. No, instead of moving away, she placed her hand on my cheek, looked me dead in the eyes, and said: "I love you for that."

I didn't know what to say, but somehow her words put me at ease. "I'm embarrassed," I said.

"Don't be."

"Why not?" I said. "We're clearly on different pages."

"Maybe…but we're both human. You might just be tougher than I am."

"Hardly."

"With all of this happening, you're able to remain human. I'm too afraid," she said.

"I'm afraid, too—believe me. Maybe I'm just too foolish to consider my priorities. I'm sorry."

"Don't be sorry—it was fine. I'm sure in other circumstances...."

"Why are you so nice?"

"I didn't used to be."

"I can't picture that," I said.

"The stories I could tell you...."

"I'd like to hear them."

***

This was the end of my attempts at romance and the beginning of our friendship. Though secretly I couldn't help but continue to be enamored with her. And I was good with that, probably because of what she had done for me. Even though it was all wrong—the time, the place, the two of us—she wouldn't let me feel bad about it. She sold me on that spectacular morning. That's what good people do: they sell kindness. A great salesman has to believe in what he sells. Danny believed in it wholeheartedly. Her kindness was complete.

18

The seven-year period of chaos, devastation, mayhem, and horror known to Christians as the Tribulation began immediately after the Rapture, but the really awful phases were fairly in their infancy as I settled into a routine with my new companions. Because we witnessed those world-shattering events from the skewed perspective of our mountain hideout, the following narrative is pieced together from what I remember and what I later learned at the Hall of Knowledge.

***

The Apostle John witnessed the events of the Tribulation while in exile on the island of Patmos for spreading the Gospel of Christ. John was given the vision by Jesus himself and was told to write down everything he had seen.

Many on the old Earth looked at the Book of Revelation as previously transpired events, a metaphorical teaching, somebody's wild dream, acid trip, or other such nonsense. What they didn't understand was that John was describing future events from the viewpoint of a man who had never seen technology, modern armies, mechanized and advanced weaponry, or weapons capable of mass destruction. He was trying to describe these unfathomable and horrifying visions in the context of his own experiences and with the only words he knew:

"…And the stars of the sky fell to the earth…And the sky was split apart like a scroll when it is rolled up; and every mountain and island were moved out of their places…the sun became black…and the whole moon became like blood…a

great star burning like a torch...."

Among the other horrors of the Tribulation, John had seen and done his best to describe a nuclear strike and its aftermath.

***

John wasn't the first prophet to glimpse the horrors of atomic war. The prophet Zechariah was treated to an up-close look at its effects:

...Their flesh will rot while they stand on their feet, and their eyes will rot in their sockets, and their tongues will rot in their mouths.

If anyone on the old Earth didn't believe this was an exact description of the effects on a human being during a nuclear strike, they had only to read the eyewitness and forensic accounts of Hiroshima.

***

America had little choice but to develop the atomic bombs dropped on Hiroshima and Nagasaki. But the world never forgave us for it. Critics argued that the development of the weapons and the destruction of those cities were unnecessary. The truth about the whole thing is at the Hall of Knowledge.

Although the Germans were never all that close to building a nuclear bomb, the Allies had no idea at the time, so they had no choice but to proceed at all cost.

Hitler was already living side by side with a demon who was feeding him all kinds of birdbrain ideas. The demon told old Adolf to push his scientists into creating the weapon, so he could have it dropped on London. Other demons tried to help the German scientists' efforts by whispering in their ears. The problem with those demons was their huge egos. Each of them thought they knew the best way to proceed, but the demons arguing in their heads only confused the scientists, delaying the whole process long enough for the Allies to take Berlin.

Meanwhile, the American scientists working on the Manhattan Project were getting a little help of their own. God had some of His best angels working with those scientists developing the bomb for the Allies. The demon interference had prompted Him to intervene on their behalf.

But why would God want to help create something so destructive that would eventually cause the deaths of millions of people? Answer:

He didn't want to, but He had little choice. Nuclear weapons would have been developed with or without God's help. Had the Germans, or the Japanese, or even the Russians, or any number of maniacal, totalitarian regimes possessed atomic weapons before the United States, they would have used them against other nations, unfettered and without remorse. Only America and some of its allies, founded on Christian or at least Judaic principles, could be trusted with such weapons, as would eventually be proven.

As far as Hiroshima and Nagasaki were concerned, President Harry Truman authorized the dropping of those bombs to save the lives of hundreds of thousands of American soldiers who would have died trying to take down the Japanese Empire island by island.

Well, why didn't he just invite the Japanese leaders to a demonstration or drop one in the ocean nearby? And why didn't he stop with Hiroshima? Answer: some people just didn't respond to subtlety.

***

Although we missed nuclear annihilation, as well as the brunt of the Tribulation Judgments, while hiding in our mountain enclave, it was of little consequence to most of the others who would perish anyway under violent and sometimes gruesome circumstances.

***

Joe Mellon was the first to die. Joe wasn't as quick on the draw as he once was, but he was a still a heck of a shot with a pistol. So, with ammunition being a diminishing commodity, it was he and I who did most of the hunting. Not that I was any great marksman, but I did own the other firearms, and I knew the area better than the others.

***

Although he was unpredictable, even dangerous at times, anyone who went anywhere usually dragged Roger along to give everyone a break from and endeavor to mollify his maddening hyperactivity. So it was on a cold April morning when the three of us set out on another quest to find and kill the scarce game that might feed our hungry group.

***

Three hours into the hunt, we had only managed to bag a squirrel

184

and a plump bird. We had planned on staying out another couple hours, but as usual, Roger's constant whining about not being allowed to shoot or even hold a weapon was driving Joe and me nuts, so we decided to head back, figuring we would be just as likely to run across game in the direction of the cave.

***

Roger wasn't forbidden from holding or using firearms because of his low IQ, or even for being a psychopath and devil worshiper. It was because the first time he got hold of a rifle, he became so excited that for no apparent reason, and not realizing it was loaded, he jumped onto a flat rock, swung the weapon around, and blew the tip of Speckle's ear off. (He would take more than a bit of ear from poor Speckle later.) When we asked him what the heck he was thinking, he replied, "I wasn't." It was a rare moment of honesty on his part.

***

The trail back to our cave took us close to the highway, which could be seen in short stretches woven through the trees and hills for quite some distance. Since the massive search several months before, when the Minions cornered us in the cave, we always had someone with a walkie-talkie watching the highway for their black SUVs. Billy had stolen the prized communication devices. Anyone venturing away from the hideout also carried one, so they could be warned of any possible Minion activity, especially if they were hunting, as not to discharge any weapons the Minions might hear. So far, our warning system had been very effective, allowing us time to leave the area during the Minions' infrequent searches.

***

But our luck had run out. For the first time, the Minions came our way with only one vehicle, and Ida, who was on lookout that morning, became distracted when a rabbit ventured near a trap she had set by the overlook. She kept looking back and forth between the highway and the trap, and in one of those moments, a single SUV slipped past the visible highway, remaining concealed by the heavily wooded environment as it made its way up the mountain. The small party pulled off the highway, well outside Ida's range of view, and on to a dirt road that ended near the trail we hunters followed that day.

***

Joe led this time, while I held the rear, with Roger between us where he could be looked after. The trail was narrow, curving wildly through the thick forest, and Roger, with his sizable build, also blocked much of my view, so I couldn't see that his constant dawdling and frequent stops to complain or comment on nothing had allowed Joe to unknowingly venture some distance ahead of us.

I was only alerted when I heard a short burst of fire that I knew immediately hadn't come from Joe's police revolver but from an automatic weapon.

Roger, too, heard the shot, but he assumed Joe was shooting at an animal and began to speed up, skipping happily down the trail like some deranged clown.

I figured Joe for a goner and sprinted after Roger to stop him from having his brains blown out, or worse yet, from capture, because I promised his mother I'd look after the big galoot. As soon as I caught up with him, I put my hands on his shoulders and pulled him backwards, driving him off his feet and onto his back. I jumped on top of him, covering his mouth and gesturing him to stay quiet and follow me into the foliage.

I must have given him quite a frightening look because he did exactly what I wanted for a change, quickly and without complaint. We barely managed to reach a safe enough distance from the trail and to conceal ourselves by lying low behind the trees when the Minions passed by us at a clip. Luckily, their urgency and the cold hard ground prevented them from noticing any foot prints that would have given our path away, but I figured it was only a matter of time before the light prints on the trail were discovered, turning them around. We needed to get back to warn the others.

***

I was hesitant to bring Roger past Joe's body because I wasn't sure how he'd react. Joe was like a father to the young man. Under his tutelage, Roger seemed to be thriving somewhat. Joe had even made some headway regarding the knucklehead's satanic views. Roger would be crushed. But there was little choice. The trail was the quickest way back to the camp, and there would be much to do to get everyone off the mountain.

***

Two hundred yards up the trail we found Joe blocking the path. He was lying on his back staring at nothing. He must have surprised the Minions (one of whom managed a fairly tight circle of fire to Joe's forehead, killing him instantly) because they always preferred capture. The Minions were probably disappointed, blowing an opportunity to beat and torture someone else to death.

No, the Minions didn't have their fun that day—Joe's death was a painless few bullets to the head. And he was already with Jesus; that much I knew. It was the only thing that made all the death bearable. In fact, much of our group, at one time or another, wished death upon themselves.

***

There was always talk of martyrdom, of the glory and certain finality of heading down the mountain with Bible in hand, to spread the Word to anyone who would listen. But it was I who always talked them out of it, sold them if you will on God's preference for our survival, sold them on the sanctity of life, even though none of it was true, not anymore. The good Lord needed all the soldiers He could get, spreading His Word before it was too late, and I was only getting in the way.

Why did I stop them? Because I was afraid to be alone and because, for all the faith I might have claimed, I was still way too much of a coward to die for it.

***

Ahead of Roger, I grabbed his arm to guide him around the body, but he pulled away from me to kneel beside his lifeless mentor. He did not cry, only stared at the small bloody holes in Joe's head. I gave him barely a moment. "We have to go," I said.

He didn't move at all.

"We have to get back. There is no time. Joe is with God now, Roger. We have to save the others. We have to save your mother." I tried to pull him up on his feet, but he was dead weight and resisting. It was the first time I realized how big and strong the kid actually was. Driving him to the ground from behind was one thing, but it was pointless trying to lift him. I would have to talk him into leaving or go without him. "Please Roger, we don't have any time—think about your mother."

Roger still didn't budge, and I almost left him there. I would have, too, but I knew I couldn't face his mother without him. "Get up, you big dummy…I'm not leaving without you!" I said, and I hit him on the shoulder, not gently, with the butt of my rifle.

He didn't react for a moment. But when Roger finally stood, the look he gave scared the crap out of me. He was about two inches taller, and he hovered over me with a blank stare that reminded me of the hazed, Private Leonard 'Gomer Pyle' Lawrence, in the movie *Full Metal Jacket*, right before Pyle cut down his drill sergeant with an M1 rifle in the latrine.

***

Neither of us said another word. Roger slid past me, heading up the trail. I watched him for a moment, realizing he had probably saved both our lives with his lagging, and so I followed him. He was never the same after that.

***

We all loved and missed Joe, but all of us, except Roger, smiled at the thought of Joe floating on a cloud, far removed from the daily grind, grime, hunger, and fear.

***

The Minions would comb the mountain for days, but we were already two valleys and a mountain away from our old hideout. The cave we eventually found was much smaller, and unstable, as we would soon find out, but for a short time it became our new home, until the Judgments of Revelation began to proliferate and turn our fleeting world upside down.

***

The rest of the world would experience the worst of it, death tolls that would make World War II and the genocidal purges of Hitler, Stalin, Mao, and Pol Pot look like the aftermath of a gang rumble. God had repressed Satan and his demonic legions for centuries to save as many souls as possible, but now that the end was so near, the wake-up calls would have to become louder to jolt the unrepentant.

Unfortunately, most of the survivors were too attached to the world and its trappings, too prideful or evil to listen, or too hungry or desperate to avoid the Mark.

***

Hitler got the press for being the biggest genocidal maniac on the old Earth, at least prior to the Antichrist's reign of terror, but it was really China's Mao Tse-tung who deserved the honor. Mao's death count totaled nearly eighty million, seven times that of the Nazi dictator. But Mao was never fully demonized for his nefarious works. Even the stubborn Russian government had eventually denounced Stalin for his crimes against humanity. Yet, there was Mao's big mug, hanging across East Asia from every available space up until the very end, like he was the Chinese Abraham Lincoln or something.

***

God did not release the full power of Satan and his cohorts all at once, otherwise the Tribulation couldn't have lasted more than a few months—not time to wake enough people up. Satan or Lucifer was the first to be released, however, and he immediately took full possession of Victor Talley, the world leader he had already been influencing for some time.

Talley was now the full-blown Antichrist, a willingly possessed soul capable of the most horrendous pursuits. Next, Lucifer's longtime fallen angel buddy, known in ancient times on the old Earth as the god Zeus, took possession of Peter, the last Pope in Rome.

Peter the Roman was the False Prophet from the Book of Revelation who would lead the remaining Catholics (those who missed the Rapture) and much of the rest of the world into the pagan religion of the New World Order. Together with the Antichrist and Satan, the three formed the unholy trinity.

***

In 1139, an Irish Bishop named Malachy travelled to Rome to give an accounting of his district, a tradition at the time. Malachy was blown away by the Italian City and was anxious to meet his fellow clergy working in the splendor of the Vatican. However, on his first day of appointments, he was suddenly stricken by waves of vertigo, which forced him to retire to his sleeping quarters. Once there, he began to

189

experience a series of visions regarding the future pontiffs of the Catholic Church. He began to write down these predictions concerning 112 imminent popes of Rome.

Malachy's predictions were buried in the archives of the Vatican for some 400 years before they were discovered and revealed to contain startlingly accurate descriptions of the previous reigning popes. As subsequent popes came to power, the predictions continued to align with uncanny precision. Malachy wrote that the last pope, number 112, would be known as Peter the Roman, and he would hold the office during a period of many tribulations and the total destruction of Rome. But Malachy, like other non-Biblical prophets and seers, viewed the future through murky lenses. He was off by one. The last pope would be 113.

***

The first order of business for this mendacious trio was to make sure everyone received the Mark of the Beast. To this end, they gained control of armies and police forces around the world. The ancient city of Babel was rebuilt in Iraq, and the New World Order solidified its power across the globe by brute force and vicious persecutions of the noncompliant. It was a time for men and women to search their souls, to choose between good and evil, between God and Satan.

***

Those who chose God were not left alone amid the ever-increasing power of Lucifer, his cohorts, and demons. Within the spiritual realm, the battle lines were forming. Free will worked both ways. The prayers of the remaining faithful had called in legions of God's angels to fight the onslaught of the Fallen Ones. And to help counter the unholy trinity, as predicted in Revelation, God sent two witnesses to spread the Good News of Christ for forty-two months.

***

These witnesses were actually the prophets Elijah and Enoch from the Old Testament, who hadn't yet died on the old Earth but were snatched up to Heaven thousands of years before. Now they were back, roaming the mountains and cites of Israel and spreading the truth to anyone who would listen.

The Antichrist sent the Minions to take them down, but as

predicted, they were indestructible for a time, spitting fire from their mouths and disintegrating anyone or any army that came at them.

I never got to watch them on the old Earth, but we heard some of the radio reports from the various pirate stations we were able to pick up. The announcers described wave after wave of attacks met with annihilation by the ferocious prophets. The Antichrist had not yet gained complete control over the media and the world was glued to their computers and televisions for a time to watch the Witnesses in action.

Millions turned away from the Antichrist to become martyrs over their miraculous feats, until the Antichrist realized he was losing thousands of potential followers by the second and wisely ordered the Witnesses to be left alone.

But the Antichrist would have his revenge. As was written, their Heavenly powers were eventually removed and the Antichrist pounced, laying waste to the Witnesses and leaving their bodies in the streets of Jerusalem for three and a half days, so the world could see them on television and renew their confidence in the dark leader.

***

Also on the side of good, 144,000 evangelists from the original Twelve Tribes of Israel, who had been dispersed across the globe, returned to their homeland during the last days. These were Jews who could no longer deny Christ as their long-awaited Messiah. They would make up for their blindness by preaching the gospel with a vengeance, until every one of the 144,000 had saved thousands and met their own martyrdoms.

***

For thousands of years, the Jewish people had been waiting for a messiah to rescue them from the constant persecution they had faced for their belief in God. The Old Testament prophets had left them hundreds of predictions so they could recognize this savior when He finally appeared. It was predicted He would be a descendant of Abraham and David, He would be born in Bethlehem, He would ride into Jerusalem on a donkey, make the blind see and the deaf hear, be betrayed by a friend for thirty pieces of silver, be beaten and spat upon, pierced in His hands and feet, given up to death by His own people, that He would return from the dead, and on and on.

191

And there was one other prediction in the Old Testament concerning the coming Messiah. It was predicted that the Jewish people would ignore all the predictions and miss Him altogether. And that's exactly what happened.

***

The Jewish people, like many of us, needed a baseball bat to the head to finally wake up. The two witnesses and 144,000 had converted many, but now they were dead, along with millions of martyrs. And most of the would-be martyrs were in hiding, often at the behest of cowards like me holding them back. But nothing could hold back the coming blows of the Tribulation, as we were about to discover.

19

The sisters were to die next. They had been the self-appointed mother hens of the tribe and were to be sorely missed. That motherly instinct would seal their fate. While everyone was outside fooling around, Ida and Eva were inside the cave cleaning and straightening, trying to maintain some semblance of a home.

***

That's when the earth began to shake violently, throwing us to the ground, where we rolled around helplessly. Had we managed to gain our footing, we might have tried to reach them and then perished ourselves. Instead, we could only watch in horror as the mountain collapsed on the good sisters, crushing them in an instant.

***

The birth pangs, increasing in their ferocity even before the Tribulation, mostly came our way in the form of natural disasters. We had already experienced raging wildfires that decimated the vegetation of surrounding mountains. Hurricane winds came through with such force they uprooted century-old redwoods. Floodwaters surged through the valleys below after the heavy rains. And earthquakes shook the mountains on a regular basis.

***

This quake was something special, though. I looked it up at the Hall of Knowledge. It was the largest ever experienced on the Earth. It measured a magnitude of 11.8, putting to shame the Great Los Angeles

Earthquake. It destroyed buildings in fourteen countries, caused three deadly tsunamis, and killed nearly three million people. And on a mountain far away from its epicenter, it took two of our good friends.

***

It was another tough loss. Billy, doted on by the sisters for his resemblance to Ida's raptured son, was crushed. And I was especially saddened because I had become quite close to Eva. But there was nothing much we could do except to mourn and pray for them, find ourselves another camp, and start over again.

***

Fortunately, the weather was fair and we'd slept outside the mouth of the cave the night before the quake hit, so we had inadvertently spared some crucial supplies. Regardless, most of our food was under the rubble in the cave. We packed what little was left and agreed to head toward the ocean where we might pilfer something to eat from one of the beach communities.

***

On our way across the mountains, the grumblings of martyrdom gained traction again. Billy, fresh off the deaths of his beloved sisters, led the chorus this time, but Danny and Howard were right there with him. Only Speckle, somewhere in his own world, and Roger, who wasn't paying attention, remained quiet, except to occasionally complain about the long hike.

"I say we just get it over with," said the distraught Billy.

"I don't know what we're waiting for," said Danny.

"Yeah—what are we waiting for?" Howard chimed.

"I don't know—maybe the avoidance of an excruciating and needless death," I said.

"Who cares? It's gonna happen sooner or later," said Billy.

"That's not necessarily true," I said. "Only God knows what's in store for us."

"Stop it, George! What's the point? We should be out there spreading the Gospel, not hiding in caves like cowards!" said Danny.

Danny was as angry as I'd ever known her to be, and this was the first time she sounded completely serious about martyrdom. It scared me, so I pulled out my only sure hand: "I'll stop, but who is going to take care of Roger?"

"Roger will come with us. He'll be better off," said Billy.

But it didn't matter what Billy said. I knew he was being emotional. His bravado would wane after he got some food and rest. And Howard, whom I'm pretty sure was secretly infatuated with Billy, would go along with him. My only worry was Danny, and when she didn't respond to my remark about Roger, I knew the martyrdom business would be dropped, at least for a time.

***

Martyrdom and Christianity had gone hand in hand since the beginning. All except two of the original apostles gave their lives to spread the Good News of Christ's sacrifice and teachings, and to share the miracles they had witnessed. Nonbelievers on the old Earth could not grasp the significance of this.

Christianity had not spread across the seven continents in a vacuum. The apostles didn't travel the known world, giving their lives to spout dogma. Such thinking should have been an absurdity to any reasonable man. Yet hundreds of thousands were martyred, and Christianity became the world's largest religion while many continued to view Jesus as some sort of philosopher.

***

The apostle Peter was crucified upside down by the Romans. They were going to do it the regular way, but he begged them to do something different because he felt unworthy of suffering the exact fate of Jesus.

Bartholomew was whipped mercilessly and skinned alive. Let me reiterate that: he was skinned alive. And yet, he did not deny the teachings of his "philosopher."

Andrew was also whipped, nearly to death. His tormentors stopped the beating because they didn't want him dying too quickly. He lived for two more days tied to an X-shaped cross. What did he do during those days on the cross? Did he beg to be let down? Did he deny his "philosopher"? No, he continued preaching the Good News.

James was sentenced to death for spreading his belief in Christ. While waiting for his execution, he witnessed to his Roman guard, who was so moved by James' faith that he asked to be martyred as well. James and the Roman guard were beheaded side by side.

Some local Jews tossed James the Younger off a cliff after he refused to deny Christ. He survived the fall, so they beat him and threw stones at him. When that failed to kill him, they bashed his head in with a club.

Thomas was stabbed with spears and burned alive. Matthew was done in by sword in Ethiopia. And so it went for these brave men. Even many of the later apostles, most notably Mark and Paul, who never knew Jesus, ended up martyred for their own great faith. Mark went to Alexandria to tell the Egyptians about Christ, the things he'd learned, and the miracles he'd witnessed. The Egyptians welcomed him by tying him to a couple of horses and dragging him down the street until he resembled a large cut of meat. And Paul, who was responsible for turning so many to Christ, was beaten, imprisoned, exiled, tortured, and finally beheaded by the Roman Emperor Nero.

***

These men were either insane or had seen things to bolster their faith to an extreme that could not be denied. Had they all been insane, it would have been some sort of strange, mass hysteria or hallucination, unshakable in so many even through the most cruel torture, unparalleled in the annals of psychiatry, science, or any other known history.

The idea is ridiculous. There was only one truth here. These men gave their lives because they witnessed and practiced miracles, speaking to God in the Spirit or after the return from the dead of their friend and teacher, Jesus, in the flesh. And it was a shame their deaths had to be ignored by even one man, let alone the billions of skeptics who questioned their sacrifices.

***

By the way, the two original apostles who didn't die spreading Christianity were Judas and John. Judas hung himself, unable to bear the guilt, after he betrayed Jesus for thirty pieces of silver, and John, the Revelation guy, was dropped in boiling oil for his faith, only he miraculously survived, and that's how he ended up exiled to the Island of Patmos where he received the visions.

***

Much later, some very confused individuals, referred to in their circles as Martyrs of Islam, would strap bombs to their chests, walk onto buses, into shops, or other crowded areas, shouting "Allahu Akbar," pull a cord and blow themselves up—along with many others, including women and children, who moments before had only been minding their own business. But this wasn't martyrdom in any sense of the word. This was known on the old Earth by another term: mass murder.

***

I had deterred any would-be martyrs in my own little circle, at least for a time, and we continued our journey toward the sea in silence.

***

Hours down the trail, we stumbled upon a rare doe feeding near our path. I pulled my rifle and promptly shot the creature before it could react. We dragged our kill another half-mile to a flat opening in the woods, made camp and settled in to eat and sleep.

Deer can sometimes smell humans a mile away. Even experienced hunters had difficulty tracking and killing these animals. Not to mention the shortage of any game in those sparse times. But these were the small miracles that happened when we needed them most. The good Lord was with us. Still, we were about to get some uninvited guests.

***

Between the loss of the sisters and the long hike, everyone was spent and quiet that evening, except for Roger, who had been acting stranger than usual ever since Joe's death and who began pacing and whispering to no one, it seemed, in one corner of the encampment. Danny went to him, and after some time, he seemed to settle down. A little later, I watched as he sat on his pack and began reading from what looked to be a well-worn book. Although he wasn't much of a reader, I didn't think much about it, mostly because I was too tired to care. I did notice Danny staring intently at him before I fell asleep, but that was the last thing I remembered before all Hell broke loose, literally.

20

With the best of us having been raptured and more being martyred every day, the spiritual battle between good and evil, raging in the Heavens and on the old Earth since the fall of angels and man, was finally coming to an end. God pulled back his forces and unleashed the last of the demon horde, held back for centuries to forestall the inevitable destruction that was to come.

***

The outside world was experiencing a deluge of supernatural phenomenon, unprecedented even by old world standards. Long ago, when men began to drift from the foundations and structures of the Old Testament teachings, and from their relationship with God, they found themselves at the mercy of demons, both spiritual and physical. In order to coexist, they made pacts with demons, setting up pagan religions, worshiping these fallen angels as gods, setting them up as chiefs and kings, practicing occult rituals to maintain their power long after they were dead.

In those days, the supernatural was natural. There was a prevalence of real magicians, soothsayers, clairvoyants, witches, warlocks, giants, ghosts, monsters, demons, and men possessed.

Cultures and nations had been built from pagan practices, but such evil could never be sustained, and those empires eventually failed. And once Christianity began to spread, the spiritual war took a turn for the good of man. Demons were cast out, their images, statues, and temples destroyed, their power and influences relegated to the shadows, to the dark spaces of the planet and the dark hearts of men.

***

But the battle was far from over. Just as in the days before the Great Flood, in the last years of the old Earth, there had come a resurgence of the occult, and the appearance of the Antichrist was the result. With each new pledge and recipient of the Mark, Victor Talley, now fully possessed by Satan, gained more and more power.

After solidifying this power across much of the world, establishing a one-world government and religion, and initiating peace in the Middle East, the Antichrist set his sights on the newly rebuilt Jewish Temple in the city of Jerusalem. He had all symbols and articles related to Jewish monotheism removed from the temple, replacing these with images and statues of himself, so *he* could be worshiped there as the one true deity. This was predicted by the prophet Daniel in the Old Testament and was known as the Abomination of Desolation.

The Abomination of Desolation was the beginning of the end of the Tribulation. God began unleashing the demons and along with them the worst Judgments of Revelation.

***

Far away from our mountain hideout, despite droughts and other natural disasters, in many cities and towns across the globe people were still out at the movies, markets, restaurants, bars, and pagan churches, waving their Marks to collect their tickets, burgers, booze, car washes, shoes, cakes and pies, and all manner of goods and services. Things were getting tougher, but all in all, there remained a decent quality of life for many of the worshipers of Satan.

God had been holding it all together, trying to give people an opportunity to repent, to come to the only reasonable conclusion that the material world was all for naught, that the Antichrist and his trappings were a big lie, a black hole of the death and destruction, and that all sins would have to be paid for, either by the blood of Jesus or by eternal separation from God.

***

But now the most virulent and loathsome demons were being unchained one by one, and the Judgments were to come like a hammer to wake the few whose hearts were not yet completely blackened by the bile of godlessness.

***

It began, much as it always had in days long past, with the voices of the dead. People would hear strange whispers, sounds that could not be traced to any specific location and sometimes seem to be coming from their own heads. The voices were mostly incoherent, but now and again a word or phrase of a vile and blasphemous nature could be understood.

Next came the manifestations—the feeling of a presence, the flash of a vaporous form, shadowy figures moving in the peripheral, the sudden appearance and disappearance of man or creature, real but not real.

Then the possessions—the vacant looks and odd behaviors of neighbors, friends and relatives; the cold staring and the fixated glares of malevolence; the guttural noises and vicious words carried by unfamiliar voices; the writhing bodies and fits of seizures; and the explosions of bloody violence and murder.

And finally, the onslaught—the familiar alien starships returning, but also joined by unfamiliar craft, filling the skies and doing battle with each over the rights to the last abductees; legions of the fallen angels, in hideous forms, roaming the land and skies, attacking and devouring humans with gleeful abandon; and the Antichrist backed by his armies, knowing his time was short, turning on his own masses, to rain on them a genocidal bloodbath, securing their places in the pit.

***

Before this, we had been hiding and praying and reading our Bibles, protected from the demons by our faith. But the good Lord had well begun his slow retreat from the evil of the old Earth, and that protection had been shrinking by the day.

***

And Roger, unbeknownst to us, had been doing his own bit of praying and reading, but from an altogether different book—a book he treasured and managed to hide for so long from the rest of us: LaVey's *Satanic Bible*. Shattered by the loss of Joe, his mentor and his last link to God and sanity, Roger decided the God of Moses was not providing enough comfort and protection, and began to fervently call

200

on the dark forces to fill the gap. He got his wish.

***

One of the last truly beautiful things I remember about the old Earth, before Christ's return, was the dream I had had that night. My daughter Sophie appeared to me in a great field of orangish grass. I ran to her and she ran to me. I lifted her and swung her around, while she laughed and laughed as she once had.

But that was the end of it. The laughter faded, and I heard the ominous whispers of something sinister grow loud, and I awoke that early morning to a horror show, and the beginning of a series of events that to this day I pray to forget.

***

It was still dark when I woke, but I could see because the moon was full, reflecting off a white mist floating in a single layer two feet off the ground. I heard Danny screaming from somewhere and strange voices shouting obscenities, which seemed to bounce off the trees in every direction.

***

Roger was standing in the middle of the camp, his knees just above the blanket of fog, staring again in Private Pyle mode. His shirt was off, blood on his chest, arms and hands, some around his mouth, as if he had wiped a bloody arm across his upper lip.

He was holding my axe in his right hand high above his shoulder. His left hand, dangling below his thigh, clutched a red mass of yarn, which I follow downward to where the yarn ended and became a thick pair of swaying eyeglasses. That's when I spotted the damaged ear and realized it was the severed head of the poor and gentle Speckle.

***

Now Howard was screaming, too. Between the voices of the demons, the screaming, and the grunting sound coming from somewhere deep inside Roger, the area sounded like a British madhouse.

The shadows of the trees began to shrink and move, dark figures, stalking, only visible from the corners of my eyes.

I heard Howard shout, "Stop him, George!" And I ran for my Bible because I figured Roger was possessed, that we were surrounded by demons, and our only chance would be the Word of God.

I opened the Book blindly, shouting out the first words I spotted on the page: "Behold, the Lamb of God!" Almost as soon as the words left my mouth, I was knocked to the ground. Roger had come for me, swinging the axe wildly at my head, but he missed, catching my shoulder with the dull, flat side of the blade.

He stood over me, preparing another swing, this one to split my skull. I still held the Bible. It was closed, so I could only use it as a shield, while I improvised from the many exorcism movies I'd seen. "Demon, leave him now!"

It didn't happen. Instead he swung hard, and I lifted the Bible to block the blow, which somehow caused the sharp blade to bounce sideways, putting Roger off-balance for a moment, giving me just enough time to roll over and slip away before his next attack.

***

By this time, Danny had stopped screaming and began to confront her crazed son. "Roger, stop it! Put that down!"

Howard took a thick branch from the fire pit, circling to the back of Roger. It was only then that I realized Billy was missing. I had no time to worry about him. I stayed to one side, continuing to spurt bad movie lines. "Name yourself, demon!"

***

This was actually the correct step to take in an official exorcism. Once demons state their names, they can be ordered out of a person's body much more easily. The problem was there was nothing really to compel them to give up their name in the first place. What I didn't do that Catholic exorcists did, was to keep hammering the possessing demons with scripture until their anger got the best of them, and the demons shouted out their names out of spite or a challenge to their egos, which were often quite inflated. Demons, for the most part, were highly intelligent, but were often at a loss when it came to controlling their anger and vanity.

***

But I was much too panicked to use psychology on Roger's demon, even if I'd known how. So I just kept repeating myself like an idiot,

"Name yourself, demon!"

Howard wasn't impressed. "What are you doing, George? Where the Hell are the guns?"

I hadn't thought about the guns, stuffed under my poncho twelve feet from where I was standing. It hadn't occurred to me to use them on Roger, and even after Howard asked about them, I hesitated.

"Nobody's getting any gun!" said Danny.

"Are you kidding me, Danny? He's got Speckle's head!" said Howard.

That's when I noticed Roger hadn't let go of Speckle's head. He had been swinging the axe one-handed the whole time, which was probably why I was still alive. Well, that and the Bible, which I had used to block some of the blows and might have been the thing holding him at bay because he just stood in the middle of the fire pit, groaning and swinging the axe wildly in the air.

"No guns!" said Danny.

"He killed Speckle!" said Howard.

"Where is Billy?" I said.

"He was already gone when that nut woke me up!" said Howard.

"I don't know either," said Danny, and she continued to plead with her son, "Roger, please stop. Put the axe down."

"Get the shotgun, George!" said Howard.

I knew Howard was right. No matter how I felt about Danny or Roger, he was going to kill someone else if I didn't do something. The cave-in, which crushed the sisters, left us with one rifle, a shotgun, a twenty-two caliber pistol, and not much ammunition, so feeling extra-protective over the weapons, I had collected them, rolled them in a poncho, and stuffed them under my blanket before I went to sleep.

Now I would probably have to use one of them to take down Roger. Howard was right—the shotgun would be most effective. I darted for the bundle, sliding and grabbing a loose corner of the poncho, but when I pulled it off, the shotgun and pistol were gone. I didn't have time to worry about it. I took the rifle and aimed it at the crazed young man's head. "Put the axe down, Roger, or I'll shoot you."

But this only seemed to excite the demon in Roger. He began cackling, a frightening, unconcerned laugh.

"Don't hurt him, George! Can't you see it's not him?" said Danny, and she moved closer to her son.

"Stay back, Danny!" I said.

"Shoot him, George!" urged Howard.

"Shut your mouth, Howard!" said Danny.

"Danielle, stay back!" I said.

***

The whole scene was a bit odd—Roger waving the axe, the demon in him laughing hysterically; Danny positioning for an opportunity to get the axe away from him, all the while shouting at me to put the gun away; Howard dancing around Roger, waving his branch around; and I, holding a rifle aimed at Roger's head, threatening to shoot him, the demon, or anyone else that might be residing in his body. And on it went for some time—we argued and circled and dodged, while the demon in Roger laughed and flailed the air with the axe. It might have been comical were it not for Speckle missing his head.

***

And with all the commotion, we were too distracted to detect Billy, who had been hiding in the trees, waiting for an opportunity to pounce on the unsuspecting Roger. Billy wasn't at all deterred by the axe. He'd grown up around gangs and had punched his way out of more than a few prison scrapes. It was Billy who had taken the shotgun and the pistol and could have easily taken Roger out, except he had no intention of killing him. He knew he could subdue the big lad even if Roger did have a nasty old demon in him.

***

One myth about exorcisms was that the priests had to tie the possessed individuals down because the demons gave them superhuman strength. This wasn't true at all. Demons had to work within the limits of the body they'd infiltrated. When little Linda Blair was smacking those priests around like a couple of balloons in the movie *The Exorcist,* it was all fiction. It was true the priests would often tie the victims down, but only so they wouldn't hurt themselves. Demons had no manners when it came to protecting their hosts; on the contrary, they loved to scratch, claw, hit, stab, gouge, and otherwise cause as much damage as possible to the bodies they occupied because they never planned on sticking around all that long anyway.

***

So, as soon as he saw his chance, Billy was upon him. He took Roger to the ground by hurling his body against the back of his knees, quickly rolling over, jumping to his feet and pouncing on the downed young man. It took us all by surprise. I thought he must have taken kung fu lessons or something, but when I asked him about it later, he told me he'd seen the move on some television show.

***

After Billy took him down, Howard and I jumped in to help. While Billy straddled his chest, Howard pinned his thrashing legs. I got hold of the axe, flinging it across the camp before prying Speckle's head from Roger's grip, sending that flying a good distance as well.

By this time, Danny was screaming again, not in horror, but at us—to leave her son alone. Meanwhile, Roger's demon continued his creepy laugh, so I started in again with the "name yourself" demon business and whatnot. Then Billy joined in, repeating everything I was saying. And all the while, Howard kept begging us to shoot him already.

***

That's when I heard it. It was a sound almost like helicopters in the distance, or a bee's nest, only much louder, like my head was stuck in a hive or something.

Danny stopped screaming at us. I looked over at her then. She was staring at the sky. Everyone got quiet—even the Roger-demon stopped his cackle. They were all looking at the sky. "My God," said Danny.

The buzzing was getting louder, and the light seemed to be fading when it should have been growing with daybreak. I hesitated because the looks on their faces frightened me, and when I did finally look up, I wished I hadn't.

***

They filled half the visible sky, these creatures—abominations, really, and so many they blocked most of the morning light. They did not resemble men with wings, or angels, even dark angels, by any

205

means, though they possessed a certain human quality about the head. They were much more insect-like than anything, having thin wings, bodies almost like a scorpion's, and stingers, not unlike that of a wasp, protruding menacingly from their sterns.

***

I think we all knew what we were seeing that morning, had read about them over and over again in Revelation, but the reality of those creatures was something else altogether, and nothing could have prepared us. If you had ever come across a potato bug, you'd have a reference point. Potato bugs are grotesque-looking things about thumb size, with roughly the body of a bumblebee and the head of a baby—so disgusting you wouldn't even step on one of them. Imagine that creature being the size of a large man, with great wings, and a sharp barb on its butt. Then imagine thousands of them buzzing over your head, and you might begin to appreciate what we saw.

***

Were we not too petrified to think straight, we might have remembered from our readings these fiendish beings could only sting those who had accepted the Mark of the Beast. But in our state, we had no doubt we were about to be slaughtered in some horrible fashion. And when a few dozen or so took notice of us, broke from the flock, and descended like pelicans to fish, we ran for cover, except for the Roger-demon, who remained flat where we had pinned him, frozen and staring up at his brethren.

I was already to the tree line when I saw Danny, from the corner of my eye, abruptly stop and turn back toward her possessed son. I dove behind a tree to watch. Standing a few feet in front of the Roger-demon, stone still, the terror gone from her face, Danny prepared to face the diving beasts.

206

21

Even before the scorpion-demons began their merciless stinging of the Mark-bearers, the good times for the followers of Satan were coming to an end. The last of the fallen angels had been released to wreak their havoc across the globe.

It had not rained in many places for quite some time, and the ensuing droughts and famines killed thousands by the day. The only creatures thriving in these environments were the flies, mosquitoes, ants, locusts, roaches, and all manner of insect, biting and swarming and infesting and multiplying. Animals, both wild and domestic, turned on humans in unprovoked and random attacks, leaving them bleeding, ravaged, or dead. When the clouds came back, they brought not rain, but giant hail that dented cars and crushed heads. A large meteor landed in the Baltic Sea, turning the sea red with the blood of sea creatures, and devastating the surrounding cities and villages with earthquakes, floods, and fires.

The Antichrist began losing his grip on the people. Riots and rebellions broke out in every major city. China and its league of Asian countries were posturing to attack the countries of the New World Order. Under those pressures, Victor Talley began gathering his forces to New Babel to prepare for the great battle in the Valley of Armageddon.

***

The Apostle John witnessed this battle in his vision. He saw an Eastern army of 200 million attacking the forces of the Antichrist in a valley near Jerusalem. At the time John penned Revelation, there were less than 200 million people on the whole planet, and John couldn't have been aware of even that population, let alone contemplating an army anywhere near that size. But in the 1960s, the world's population surpassed three billion, and China's Chairman Mao bragged he could produce an army of exactly 200 million men. And later, in the Valley of Armageddon, China would do just that. The battle would be so thoroughly destructive Christ would return early to avoid the annihilation of the entire planet's population.

***

But His return was still more than a year away, and though we had once remained relatively sheltered in the mountains of Northern California, we were of late experiencing our share of the nightmare. We had already faced persecution, hunger, fires, floods, earthquakes, and the deaths of our good friends—and now the demons were upon us. An unknown entity was in full possession of Roger, and a flock of hideous, flying bug-men were heading straight for Danny.

***

Where was I? Hiding behind a tree. All I could remember was the part in John's vision about the sting of these things causing the victims five months of serious pain, so horrible it made them wish they were dead. I had forgotten we were protected because we didn't have the Mark. But if I thought Danny was in danger, why wasn't I out there trying to save her? Well, it's pretty simple: I was scared to death.

And Billy and Howard must have forgotten, too, because they were also hiding in the trees.

***

I did manage to yell for her to run. Billy and Howard yelled, too. But she wasn't listening. She just continued her hard stare until the beasts were within thirty feet of where she stood.

The Roger-demon had gotten to his feet by then and was staring up at them, too, only his look was sort of idiotic, while Danny's remained fearless. Then she spoke. "Jesus, help," was all she said.

But as soon as she said it, the bug-men pulled up, hovering menacingly above the defiant woman and her possessed son. The Roger-demon opened his mouth, emitting a strange and deep groan.

Then, what looked to be black smoke shot out of Roger's mouth, forming a ball next to the hovering beasts. The ball expanded and reformed, until it became one of the bug-men. Roger fell to the ground, while the flock of demons departed, their new member buzzing beside them.

**

We came out from behind the trees to see if Roger was still breathing. Danny was already kneeling over her son. She looked up at me, but I was too ashamed to look her in the eye. It didn't matter— she wasn't judging anyone; she was well on her way to grace. "Please get some water," she said.

**

Roger, looking like he'd just wrestled a baboon, couldn't remember much, but seemed otherwise fine. Exhausted, and figuring the worst was over, we decided to stay put for the night. We gathered the head and body of Speckle, said some prayers, and buried another friend.

**

Still a bit shaken from the ordeal and fearful of more demons, we made a fire and dragged our blankets and sleeping bags together for the night. But before we retired, I had one bit of business to finish. "Where's that book, Roger?" I said.

He played dumb. "What book?" he said.

"How many books do you have, Roger?" I said.

"Get the book, Roger," said Danny.

Roger didn't bother to protest any longer. He shuffled over to his backpack to remove the foul literature, which he placed in my hand. He'd mentioned the book early on, but kept it hidden from us until the night before, and I didn't put it together till he went nuts. Danny must have figured it out, too. I showed it to the others and promptly tossed it in the fire. "Hey!" he said.

It was then I realized he hadn't asked about Speckle's death, and I wondered if he did remember something. "Do you even know how Speckle died? You didn't ask," I said.

"Don't!" said Danny.

I backed off. After what she had done in the face of those demons,

209

I wasn't about to give her any grief.

Billy wasn't saying anything either, but Howard jumped all over it. "Yeah, what happened to Speckle, Roger?"

"Please, Howard," said Danny.

"He got his head cut off," said Roger.

"Well, how do you think that happened…he bumped into the axe?" said Howard.

"Please, Howard!" said Danny again.

"This punk's been worshiping the devil. How do we know he won't kill us in our sleep?" said Howard.

"What are you talking about?" said Roger.

"Nothing," said Danny.

"You killed Speckle, you idiot, and you called in those demons, who almost took us all out," said Howard.

It was out now, and Danny couldn't do anything about it. She sat on her sleeping bag sobbing.

"Is that true, Mom?" But she didn't answer. "Is it, Mom? Please tell me, Mom! Tell me…is it true?"

"Yes…but it wasn't you. A demon got in you."

"What? No, Mom…it's not true…take it back, Mom, take it back!"

"It was the demon in you, Roger," said Danny.

"No, Mom," and Roger began to cry.

Danny pulled him into her, cradled and hugged her son while he sobbed.

That's when I realized, once again, he wasn't a man—just a lost, imbecilic and somewhat deranged kid, who was sorry and didn't know what he was doing half the time. I put my hand on his shoulder. "Roger, it's bad everywhere. These things are evil—they take advantage. I know you were upset about Joe. It's not all your fault. And it could have happened to any of us."

Danny looked at me gratefully, but Howard wasn't having it. "What are you talking about, George? He was praying with that book."

"Just leave it," I said.

"No, he needs to go."

That's when Billy finally spoke up. "He's right," he said.

"Nobody is going anywhere," I said. "He won't hurt anybody."

"How do you know?" said Billy.

"What don't you people understand? He chopped off Speckle's head!" said Howard.

"It was the demon, for the last time already, and Speckle's with God!" I said, but it was no use. This wasn't going anywhere, so I thought I'd help by using a tried and true sales technique: when the conversation is moving away from the close, change the subject. To accomplish this, I decided to turn the focus on Billy, who needed to explain a few things himself. What I couldn't know at the time was that the question I was about to ask would get Roger killed. "Billy, where the Hell did you go this morning with the weapons?"

It was just enough to turn Howard's attention away from his attack on the sobbing boy. "Yeah, what happened to you?" he said.

***

Billy told us he couldn't sleep. He kept beating himself up over the sisters and being a coward for not spreading the Word and becoming a martyr. That's when he decided to do something about it. He took his Bible and started down the mountain looking for the nearest town. But after a few hundred feet, he began shaking nervously. He was afraid, he said, and rightly so.

We still had about a half bottle of whiskey we carried for first-aid purposes. Billy decided he needed a few swigs to control the shaking, he said, so he went back for it. Billy had always been a bit of a lightweight when it came to hard alcohol, and in the thin mountain air the effects were even more substantial. In his drunken state, he began to formulate a new plan, he told us, a more aggressive one.

Alcohol had been the catalyst for most of Billy's legal problems. It fueled the rages that festered from his disturbing childhood, costing him years of his life. And now he pointed that rage at the Minions, so he snuck up to where I was sleeping, took the shotgun, stuffed the pistol in his waist, and headed down to foster a violent demise.

About halfway, however, the long trip down the mountain had taken its toll on his inebriation, and Billy began to see the vindictiveness of his plan. He didn't want to kill anyone. He decided then, with the little alcoholic courage he had left, to put down the weapons and continue toward martyrdom unarmed. But after a few hundred yards, he realized some things: he was tired, he was afraid again, he didn't have his Bible with him, and he would be leaving us without the extra weapons. It was an easy decision then. And that's how he ended up back in the camp to take down the Roger-demon.

***

After Billy's explanation, Howard forgot or didn't have the energy to continue hammering Roger about his devil worshiping. We went to sleep under the countless stars of the mountain sky, now empty of the demon flock, which had long passed to fulfill its mission of torment on the Mark-bearers of the world.

***

While the rest of us slept, the wheels in Roger's limited brain continued turning. He had listened intently to Billy's story, but actually didn't hear much of it. Roger fixated on the words and phrases in conversations that excited his feeble mind, usually ignoring any substance, meaning, even reality. And like a child at a dinner buffet, unable to ignore the desert table, Roger reached only for the cakes and pies of Billy's tale. He could be redeemed, a hero in the groups eyes even. He imagined the shotgun in his hot hands, stalking the city streets, picking off the Minions of the Antichrist like so many human avatars in one of the violent video games he once mastered. And lying there, unable to sleep, he could almost feel the weight of the weapon, hear the blasts, and see the bodies tossed backwards from the impact, the wide holes blown through their chests, the blood flying in every direction. It was all too much for a dimwitted psychopath to ignore.

22

I probably wouldn't have blamed myself for Roger's death just for prompting Billy into telling his story in front of everyone, but I had ignored Roger's almost gleeful reactions to it, and I did one other stupid thing to make his death possible. In all the madness, I completely forgot to secure the shotgun and pistol Billy left lying in the tree line.

***

Danny woke me the next morning frantic. "I can't find Roger!" she said.

"You know how he is. He's probably off taking a leak or torturing some animals or something."

She punched me in the shoulder. "I'm serious, George, something is wrong."

***

In those days I learned not to question Danny's sixth sense, which was uncanny at times. She would often alert us to danger or point us toward food and water. One day, on the run from the Minions, ready to drop because we were dying of thirst, she insisted we move in the opposite direction—a direction the rest of us were sure would lead us back into the net of our pursuers. Lo and behold, she led us right to a stream. After we had hung around awhile, drinking, filling our bottles and canteens, and resting, she told us to be quiet. She stood on the bank of the stream, wide-eyed and listening intently. We all looked at her like she was crazy. She ignored us, and a moment later, she spoke. "We have to get out of here."

The way she said it, with this certain intensity, and her finding the stream and everything, made us listen without complaint. We let her lead us up the hillside surrounding the stream. After we'd climbed about halfway up, we heard a loud roaring sound from somewhere upstream. Seconds later, a torrent of water came rushing into the valley, wiping out the area we had left just moments before. Danny had saved our lives again.

***

No, as soon as she said something was wrong, I stopped clowning. "Let me get my boots on and look for him." After I said it, I remembered about the weapons, and my heart sank. I didn't want to alarm Danny, so I asked her to fill some canteens for the search.

I ran over to where Billy slept, waking him to show me where he'd placed the shotgun and the pistol. We spotted the pistol quickly, but the shotgun was nowhere to be found. Billy insisted he'd left them in the same spot, and when we found the pack Howard always carried with the excess ammunition spilled open near the trailhead, we knew with little discussion that Roger had taken the shotgun and was probably mimicking Billy's failed mission.

Danny wanted to come along, but I convinced her to stay behind in case her son came back. I woke Howard to apprise him of the situation, passed out the canteens, gave Billy the pistol, gathered the rifle for myself, and the three of us sprinted down the trail to find him.

***

Some distance down the mountain, we heard the gunfire, except we were still too far away to see anything, so I had to read about it later at the Hall of Knowledge. I could have guessed. It happened pretty much as I'd imagined it while sprinting, desperately trying to reach him—not so much out of concern for Roger, but because I thought Danny wouldn't forgive me if we didn't get to him in time.

***

Roger wasn't afraid or anything; in fact, he was ecstatic, clearer and more determined than he had ever been. In his mind, he was being a hero, avenging Joe and saving us all from the Minions of the Antichrist.

He had become the invincible character of one of his video games, coming to life to wipe out all targets and reach a level of acceptance from us he believed had only been mitigated by his satanic activities. This, he figured, would mean redemption and fun at same time.

***

The trip down the mountain was longer than he'd expected, and Roger was exhausted by the time he reached the outskirts of the seaside town of Crescent City, California. He rested behind a low fence, watching the morning activities of the city's occupants on Main Street, his thoughts like wringing hands, impatient over the coming carnage he was about to impose.

Roger's original intention was to take out only the black-suited soldiers of the Antichrist, but he wasn't exactly the most focused individual. He did spot a checkpoint at the end of the busy thoroughfare manned by a half-dozen armed Minions, but the route to them was fairly crowded with civilians, so he simply designated them as bonus targets.

***

In 1999, two other deranged video game fanatics went on a similar, if much less well-intentioned, shooting spree. Dylan Klebold and Eric Harris loaded their car with twenty-pound propane bombs, stuffed their packs with Molotov cocktails and ammunition, gathered shotguns and automatic weapons, and set out for their high school in Littleton, Colorado.

The plan was to place the large bombs, set with timers, in the cafeteria, and to gun down the panicked students as they ran from the mayhem of the explosions.

The timers failed. Disappointed, the two killers moved through the campus picking out random student targets as they happened upon them. After killing a seventeen-year-old girl and wounding several others, they entered the school library, where they found dozens of students hiding under tables, and a massacre ensued.

By the time it was over, twelve students and a teacher were dead, and many more wounded in the ugly venture. The pair then committed suicide. Why did they do it? Were they bullied? Was it revenge? Was it demons? Nope. They did it because they wanted to be famous. In a way, they succeeded. Klebold and Harris are quite well known among the damned as two of the stupidest people who ever lived.

***

Before Roger's visit, the inhabitants of Crescent City had been relatively lucky regarding the events of the Tribulation. Their population had been small enough that the massive flock of bug-men barely took notice as their horde flew over the tiny village on their way to bigger fish. And though the seaside town had lost a few hundred of its occupants to various natural disasters, diseases, and Minion activity, their food supply held up, and the tidal wave and flooding, which had wreaked havoc on other California coastal cities, completely missed their quaint village, tucked away as it was above a discreet little bay.

Their fortunes were about to change, however—all our fortunes really, for better or worse. And though Roger's short reign of terror would only be a side note, it would mark a beginning of sorts, as the Great Tribulation was about to kick into high gear. The end of the old Earth was upon us, and only a handful would survive the last Judgments.

***

Roger smiled when he stood—the shotgun in both hands, bands of ammunition strewn wildly about his torso like some sloppy bandito—to begin his violent stroll down Main Street.

***

He probably wouldn't have been smiling so much, except Roger had failed to take into consideration a few minor details involving his attack plan. First, the shotgun only held five rounds. Next, he was a horrible shot, even with the shotgun's wide field of fire. Also, it had taken him five minutes to figure out how to properly load the shells he'd placed in the chamber just before the attack while away from the heat of battle. Finally, the Minions on the other end of the street carried automatic weapons, with which they were quite proficient.

***

The people on the sidewalk closest to Roger immediately stopped to stare at the dirty, bearded man in the middle of the street. They saw he carried a weapon, but they were more puzzled than afraid, as they

216

had always been well insulated and protected by the Minions from any criminal elements in their fair city. They didn't know what to make of Roger, until he turned and fired at them.

The first shot was aimed at a young couple who had just walked out of a Starbuck's coffee shop loaded down with overpriced coffee and muffins. Luckily, the center of the blast came between the two, and the pellets sprayed and ripped through an arm each, causing only minimal injury and spilled lattes.

With that first inaccurate shot, a woman screamed, and the people on the sidewalks dispersed like a kicked anthill. Roger's targets moved so rapidly, he began to panic, firing his next four shots wildly and in quick succession. He managed to maim a beautician on her way to work by shooting out most of her hip, and to remove the foot of a fleeing bicyclist as he pedaled around a corner, but the rest of his ammo exploded harmlessly into the air.

The Minions heard the shots and screams but took a moment to react because nothing much ever happened at their sleepy post. By that time, Roger was fumbling with the reloading of the shotgun, and they looked at the unlikely attacker with more amusement than fear.

Somehow, though, Roger managed to load all the shells, and by then he was within fifty yards of the guard post, so he was now in a good position to cause some damage to the bunched-up Minions, even if he was a horrible shot.

And before they quite realized the danger they were in, Roger fired and struck their captain in the chest. He flew back, knocking over the two Minions standing behind him. As one of them tried to get up, Roger, without aiming, managed to blow off the top of his head.

The remaining Minions finally raised their rifles, and Roger was only able to pull the trigger one more time, mortally wounding one of the shooters in the throat, before the others finished him. The Minions continued unloading their weapons into Danny's son long after he was dead.

***

By the time we reached the edge of the city, Roger's bullet-riddled body was hanging from a lamppost. It was a warning to any would-be rebels. Devil worshiper or not, I felt bad for Roger—we all did. And, of course, Danny would be devastated. This, I knew, would push her over the edge. He had been the only thing stopping her from martyrdom. I would have to tell her Roger was dead, and I was sure I would lose her for it.

***

Still, I wasn't going to let her see him like this, torn and bloody, hanging in the street. Knowing Danny as I did, I figured she was already on her way down to look for him, so I gathered Billy and Howard, and we hurried back up the mountain to intercept her.

But as it turned out, I wouldn't have to tell her about her son at all. Within a few minutes, I would be unconscious, Danny would be badly injured, and Billy and Howard, along with a third of Earth's remaining population, would be dead.

23

In his vision, John said it looked like *"a mountain burning with fire,"* and I can't describe it any better, except that I might have been closer to the object. What I had seen seemed bigger than a mountain, the size of a small planet, filling up a great chunk of the sky, descending rapidly.

***

Actually, Billy saw it first. We were heading up the trail, our backs to the ocean, trying to cut off Danny before she could reach her dead son. I was out in front, running as fast as I could, when I heard Billy say my name. But it was the way he said my name, like the last question of a dying man, which stopped me in my tracks.

Then Howard asked me what it was. I didn't take the time to answer him. I wasn't sure exactly what it was anyway, but I figured it must be a meteor of some kind, and we were all done unless we could get over the next ridge, still a hundred yards away, and quickly. "Move!" I said, and I waved them past me.

Before they passed, I looked back at it again. All I could see was a blinding light, and when I turned to run, I couldn't see the trail any longer. I dropped the rifle and took off anyway, scraping against the brush, bouncing off trees, until my vision cleared, and I found myself running through the middle of the forest, my companions nowhere to be found.

***

I don't remember much after that. I remember trying to get over the ridge and shouting for Billy and Howard. I remember a loud swooshing sound, a blast of wind that seemed to come from the ground, and what felt like the whole forest being sucked upward. And I remember flying through a valley of yellow light.

***

It was actually an asteroid—I read about it at the Hall of Knowledge—the third largest ever to hit the Earth. It landed in the Pacific Ocean, extinguishing much of the sea life there, shaking the entire Earth for nearly ten minutes, causing tidal waves across the globe, including a tsunami that sunk the Hawaiian Islands. The impact threw dust and debris into the atmosphere, triggering a nuclear-like reaction, which caused parts of the planet to heat up like an oven, igniting thousands of acres of forest all at once, and creating a great firestorm that wiped out thousands more.

***

In the city of Babel, the New World Order general in charge of Wormwood, the secret nuclear missile the Antichrist had kept hidden during the alien disarmament program, panicked when he heard the explosion and saw the great flash of light. The general was sure the Chinese had fired their own hidden missile. So he pressed the button. Fortunately, the general's missile missed the intended target—the city of Beijing—landing one hundred miles to the north at the Guanting Reservoir, an area with relatively sparse pockets of civilians. Still, millions were killed, and the Chinese began to plot their revenge at the Battle of Armageddon.

***

Between the asteroid and Wormwood, another two billion were dead, and thousands more would die from the fallout and the fires and the flooding and the toxic food and the poisoned waters and the disease and the demons and the persecutions and the fighting and the crime and on and on. And they would continue to die, thousands each day, Minions and Mark-bearers, good people, bad people, and Christians alike, right up until the end.

***

By the time I regained consciousness, it was nearly dark, so I assumed I had been unconscious for several hours. As it turned out, it hadn't been all that long. It was still midday. The smoke and dust had blocked out much of the sun, turning the early afternoon into twilight.

I lay sprawled in a ravine, on a tiny patch of meadow, a refuge protected by the only three remaining trees in sight. Everywhere around me, as far as I could see, the land had been laid bare, an apocalyptic wasteland of charred stumps and torched earth.

***

Beyond a raging headache and the sting in my eyes, I wasn't injured. I stood but hesitated to leave my sanctuary for some time, such was the devastation of my surroundings.

I thought there might be a slim chance Danny had survived, but I was pretty sure Howard and Billy had not. Even so, I climbed out of the ravine to the ridge where I lost them.

If I had had any hope for them, it was shattered as soon as I reached the top. Looking down, the destruction was even more complete on the other side. Nothing existed as far as I could see on that black and barren mountainside. And Crescent City, Roger's resting place, was no more. A giant wave had dragged it into the sea.

I cried then. I missed my friends, and I didn't want to be alone again. I prayed for them. I was now certain Howard and Billy were dead, but I asked God to spare them anyway. And I prayed to find Danny alive. I slid back down the ravine and began the steep hike back to our last camp.

***

We never found their bodies. I found out later that Billy died instantly when the impact of the asteroid launched him headfirst into a tree. And Howard didn't feel much either. He went up in flames very quickly with the forest.

***

There was little point trying to find the trail in that desert of scorched earth, so I took my best guess and headed in the general direction of our last camp. The going was difficult. My canteen lost, mouth dry, eyes burning from smoke and dust, I stumbled along. Exhausted after fifty yards, I took too deep a breath, my lungs filled with soot. It took some time to cough it out, and even with shallow

221

breaths, I had to stop every few minutes to clear my lungs. I kept at it, though, knowing there was once a stream below the camp I would eventually have to cross. If it still existed, I felt I could make it there within the hour, and there I would rest, drink, and rinse my eyes.

***

But I had sorely underestimated the distance, or the pace, or both. Two hours later, I was tackling a third ridge, practically crawling, black and mostly blind, choking up blood and dust and soot, nearly dead from dehydration, my strength gone, losing more hope with each step. I prayed silently for water or a quick death; either would do. I was almost to the top, but I knew if I didn't see the stream below I would be finished.

Once at the top, I lifted my ragged and bleeding body high enough to peer into the ravine. My heart sank. I had reached the stream, but now it was merely a river of black dirt and soot, a mocking and dry oasis of death. I was too tired and thirsty to be afraid. I asked God to forgive me for my sins again, and happily laid my worn-out body down to die.

***

Many had visions in those last days because of the demons being unleashed and the spiritual battle between the forces of good and evil raging to capture the hearts and minds and souls of the people. Some were sent from God; some from demons. Because I bore no mark, I drew the attention of demons. And though I would never have opened myself up to them to the extent Roger had, because I was not deeply rooted in prayer and the Word of God, I was quite vulnerable to their attacks. Eagerly lying down to die was apparently not part of God's plan for me, and so in that moment I became a particular target of the dark side.

***

God expected more out of me. Perhaps that was why I was still alive. I had taken the easy way out all my life, and now God wanted me to fight, to live, so I could spread the Good News of Christ, even go down as a martyr. But I was too much of a coward. And over and over, I had convinced the others not to martyr themselves, and now most of them were dead. God would forgive me, but He wasn't going to let me off the hook so easily.

***

As soon as I closed my eyes to die, it seemed, they were open again. I was standing next to Danny on the mountain where we first met. I was clean, uninjured, wearing a long white robe. Danny held my hand. Only she was much younger and somehow different, too beautiful perhaps.

I looked at her, and she smiled like she always did, but I had this odd feeling she had changed her mind, that she was in love with me. Then she said it; she said she was in love with me. I told her I loved her, too.

She asked me to follow her, leading me up a path to an overlook where we could see the valley below. It was greener than I remembered, with a great big lake and a wide river I had never seen before. "We made it, George."

And when she said it, a magnificent white city appeared from nowhere, and a golden road began to form and wind its way up the mountain until it reached our sandaled feet. "Are you ready?"

"We're in Heaven?" I asked.

She laughed. "Come on," she said, and she stepped on the golden road pulling my arm.

But I hesitated. I was confused. "Is this Heaven?" I asked her again.

"We'll be married, George…come on, hurry!"

"But you don't love me like that…you told me."

"It's different now."

"But why, Danny?"

"We're here."

Something felt wrong. "I know, but why is it different?" I said.

She stopped smiling. "Well, just forget it then. I won't marry you!"

She sounded like a spoiled little girl, not at all the Danny I knew. "What's wrong with you?"

"Nothing is wrong with me! You don't want me now—is that it?" she said.

"It's not that—it's just something isn't right."

"It's all ours—this is our paradise if we want it. You and I forever—

223

don't you want that?"

"I do want that, Danny," I said, and I did. "But what about everyone else? Where is my daughter?"

"We'll make our own children."

"That doesn't make sense. I want to see my daughter."

"You don't love me!"

"This isn't like you…what's going on, Danny?"

It was then that her face began to change. Her features contorted and her body twisted. In another instant, Danny had turned into a man. He had pleasant enough appearance and looked to be in his sixties. Like a caricature of a devil from some movie, he wore an immaculate white suit, his hair slicked back like an 80s Wall Street player.

I wasn't as surprised as I should have been, I suppose. I calmly asked him who he was and what he had done with Danny.

"She's waiting for you, and I am a friend," he said.

"I don't know you, sir. Who are you?"

"It's not important."

"I insist."

"I have many names. The Greeks knew me as Hades, and the Romans as Pluto, but you can call me Richard now," he said.

***

Hades or Pluto lived on the old Earth long before the Greeks and the Romans wrote down his myth. Both cultures knew him as the keeper of the underworld. Hades actually was in charge of the pit, but only when Satan wasn't around. He was particularly sadistic, known for wandering the pit with a two-pronged spear, poking doomed humans for fun. Satan was actually upset with him over this because he liked to think he operated with some finesse, and it was this activity that was responsible for the whole devil pitchfork stereotype. Every time Satan came across a picture of a red, horn-headed devil holding a pronged spear he'd wince and curse his old pal.

***

Now I faced a seemingly friendly, human version of the fiend. "You're a demon, then," I said.

"I don't much care for that designation, but I won't hide behind semantics."

"Have you harmed Danny?"

"I have not. But she is well and not well. We make our own realities here."

"What do you want with me, *Dick*?"

He ignored the jab. "I want to give you a gift."

"I don't want anything from you," I said.

"Ah...but you haven't seen the gift." And then I was inside the white city, in a great manor, sprawled on a throne of pillows, spread before me every dish and drink imaginable. And the demon, Richard, was there, too, lying next to me. "This is paradise," he said.

Then Danny appeared again. "That isn't her," I said, and with that, she disappeared.

"Perhaps you'd like a variety," he said, and a bevy of some of the most beautiful women I'd ever seen paraded across the floor in from of me, my very own Miss Universe pageant.

I won't lie and tell you it wasn't tough. I can't deny it. At that moment, I wanted those women, every one of them. And when he placed a tray of fine white powder in front of me, I was nearly done.

***

Except—I wasn't done. I mean, I thought about it. And I think part of me wanted to suck up a fatty and throw myself at those women like the fool I once was, but I couldn't do it. I wasn't exactly the same man. Events had changed me. The mountain had changed me. My new friends had changed me. God had changed me. Tempting as it was, I knew it was ugly, depraved, meaningless, and if I partook, I would never see Sophie again. For once in my pathetic, miserable life I chose her. I chose my daughter.

***

Richard didn't try anymore after that. He knew it was hopeless just by the look on my face. And with that I was back on the ridge above the black river, thirsty, filthy, bleeding, mostly blind, and utterly exhausted.

At the time I thought it could have been a dream, but it felt too real, and I found out later that it was both real and not real, a true vision. I had been visited by the demon spirit of the false god Hades, manifested as a man calling himself Richard.

***

I felt broken, ready to leave the Earth, but the experience had moved me, enough that I decided to give up my will to die. "Lord," I said. "I will stand and keep moving. Do with me what you will." I shuffled along the ridge for a few feet, to the rim of the burnt canyon wall and slid down into the ravine. Then I picked myself up and slowly crossed the soot-filled gap where the stream once flowed.

The other side was steep, unclimbable in my state. I continued moving upstream. There didn't seem to be a way up the ravine. Still, I walked, feebly, painfully, sliding foot to foot really, until I thought I would collapse again. I swayed for a moment, ready to fall, when I heard a faint sound, causing me to stiffen, and instead of dropping, I stood firm to listen.

It was slight but unmistakable. I even managed a smile and a pained laugh. It was a sound like a powered-up speaker, void of any music. Except it was music to my ears. It was the magnificent deep whistle of flowing water somewhere in the distance.

***

I stayed there for some time, stretched out across a spotless yellow boulder, cleansed as it was by the falling water, and large enough to pierce the black surroundings. Step by painful step, the sound of rushing water had led me to a single oasis.

***

My inclination had been to quickly drink, rinse, and set out to find Danny before she might succumb to any injuries, if the demon had not lied and she was still alive. But, as exhausted as I was, I was coherent enough to realize I wouldn't be able to make it at all if I didn't rest and quench my body sufficiently.

And there was something else to it. I didn't know what it was at first, but it came to me as the water poured over me. I was at peace for the first time in months. And I somehow knew I would find Danny and she would be all right.

***

It only took me two hours to reach the camp. But even having rested, I wouldn't have made it except for another huge factor. The aliens were at it again with their giant vacuum cleaners, ridding the atmosphere of smoke, dust, radiation, and the deadly nuclear particles. I couldn't see the spaceships above the debris and the clouds, but they were there. I could hear the familiar humming. The smoke and dust would have finished me without them. In that respect I had been rescued by demons.

But the demons hadn't sent the aliens to help me. They hadn't sent them to help anyone. They wanted the skies cleared for a fresh start, another go at destruction. The demons, the Illuminati, the Antichrist, the New World Order, all worked an ironic program of salvage and ruin, a dichotomy of self-interest: butchery and mayhem, liberation and indoctrination; torture and murder, rescue and reprogramming. All intended for one purpose: to garner more souls for the pit.

***

The area of the camp was devastated, but not as completely as the lower mountains. I was able to find the water containers, the first-aid kit, food, and other supplies. I could even make out the trail slightly. I filled a small pack and headed once again down the mountain, this time to find Danny.

***

I found her within an hour. The land was so barren, I could see clearly in front of me for some distance. When I crossed the second ridge, two lone trees stood against the horizon. She lay smack in the middle of those trees. The good Lord had provided Danny with a slight yet sufficient refuge of her own.

***

Danny was in pretty bad shape, unconscious and badly burned on her exposed arms and face. I wetted her mouth and tongue with a soaked cloth, tended to her burns as best I could, prayed over her until I couldn't keep my eyes open and fell asleep beside her.

***

I was dreaming about the strange orange grass again when she woke me. Danny was smiling, her white teeth shining out from her charred and scalded face. Perhaps it was just my happiness over seeing her alive

227

again, or my desperate joy over not being alone any longer, but she looked more beautiful than ever. And there was something else, something different about her, something I couldn't explain.

"You're here, George. You're alive."

It took me a moment to take her in, and then I began to cry.

"Don't cry," she said.

"I can't help it. I'm so happy you're alive."

She laughed a little then. "I'm happy you're alive."

But then I thought about Roger and the others, and I turned my head from her.

"I must be a sight."

I turned back and touched the side of her face. "It's not that, not that at all...you're so, so beautiful."

"You're crazy, George. I can feel my face."

"It's true," I said.

"What's wrong then, George? We're together. We're alive."

I turned away again.

"Is it the others? Is it Roger?"

I looked at her and I began to cry again, even harder. "I'm sorry, Danny. I couldn't get to him in time."

Her expression didn't change. In fact, if anything, she seemed happier. She even laughed again. Something was wrong with her. "You're not getting it, Danny. They're dead. Roger is dead—they're all dead."

She shook her head at me and smiled, wider than before. "I know that, George."

"You do?"

"Yes, George. I saw them in a dream. They're all there, George! Her joy was palpable. She was practically glowing. "And Roger, George! Roger made it, too!"

"How do you know?" I was skeptical, especially after the lies in my own vision.

"I just know," she said.

I was smiling then, and I began laughing, laughing hysterically for no reason. Roger made it? You're freaking kidding me? Now we were both cracking up, and she rolled on top of me. "Your son Roger is in Heaven? Are we talking about the same Roger? The same Roger who cut off Speckle's head with an axe?

"Stop it, George," she said, and she laughed harder.

"Axe murderer, Roger? Roger, the devil worshiper?" I couldn't help myself.

"Yes, Roger, you nut," she could barely spit it out she was laughing so hard.

***

We stayed like that for some time, laughing and rolling around on the ground until I insisted we stop. It wasn't helping her injuries, or mine for that matter. But we were exhausted anyway, so we ate and cuddled to stay warm, falling asleep that way, until the cold woke us, and we made our way back to the camp to build a fire and look for something more to eat.

***

We moved further inland, as far away from the asteroid's impact as we could without reaching civilization, to a smaller mountain, where the forest was green again and the wildlife relatively unharmed. And we made a camp for ourselves, in a small meadow, surrounded by a thicket of trees and brush.

For days we rested, talked and reminisced about Roger and our good friends. She told me about her dream and the paradise she'd seen. I told her about my dreams, and when I mentioned the orange grass she remembered the same detail in her dream, and we knew, if we already didn't, that we had seen the same place.

I also told her about the vision I'd thought I'd had. She agreed it was a vision, but the demon was real, she said, and she was sure it had been a test. She brought up the temptation Jesus had faced after his forty days and nights in the desert, when the devil offered him all the kingdoms and treasures of the world.

We talked about so many things, about what paradise would be like, about demons, and sin, and religion, and Christ. We were growing close, but I was the only one enamored. She was with me, but part of her was somewhere else.

***

I read the Bible for a little bit each morning and prayed before I went to bed; she read and prayed much of the day and often well into the night. Her faith was getting stronger while mine remained stagnant.

Some nights, I would hear her speaking a language I couldn't understand. I knew her, so I knew it wasn't evil. I figured she must be speaking in tongues, though I never asked her about it for some reason.

***

The gift of speaking in tongues was given to the very devout while deep in prayer. The Holy Spirit of God would speak through the individual in the language of the angels, strengthening and solidifying their faith and relationship to God.

***

Whatever it was, something odd was happening to Danny. The burns on her face, which should have left deep scars, began to heal at a rapid pace. Within a week of my hearing her speak the strange language, her wounds had completely healed. And we didn't have to spend a lot of time hunting or gathering food because, even in the relative wasteland left by the asteroid, she would lead us right to it with stunning precision. And then one day she pretty much stopped talking to me.

***

At first, I wasn't too concerned. I figured she was deep in thought with everything going on. I mean I wasn't that big of a talker myself. I once appreciated a little silence on the old Earth, what with so many people you didn't even know relaying to you every moment of their lives from birth to their last trip to the cleaners, when you had only asked them to pass you the ketchup or something. Still, we had grown so much closer, especially in the last few weeks, so I began to feel awkward around her, and hurt.

This went on for about a week, until out of the blue she told me she wanted to talk. She sat me on the ground facing her. "I know you think I'm ignoring you," she said.

"I guess."

She smiled. "Don't pretend. We're friends, right?"

"Yeah...of course we are," I said.

230

"I just don't know what to say anymore."

"Okay."

She could tell I was sour. "Don't be mad."

I didn't say anything. "Don't be mad," she said again, and she got right in my face, smiling with eyes wide, demanding I smile, too.

I looked at her and forced a smile. "I can't believe how you've healed," I said.

It's a miracle, George," and the way she spoke, with a soft yet careless joy that reminded me of a hippie I once saw being interviewed at Woodstock.

"I know it is," I said.

"You do and you don't, George," she said. "It's not that I don't have anything to say to you. I could talk to you all day long. But I'm done with small talk. And we've talked over and over again about God and faith and what we need to do. You know what we should do. You have to let go of this world. And after everything that's happened, after your vision, after the demons, what more do we need to know? Let's go. Let's try to save a few if we can. What do we have to lose?"

"How do you even know anyone is left?" I said, but I knew her answer before I finished asking.

"Stop, George. Come on. You know the Book of Revelation just as much as I do...probably more...that's all you ever read, practically."

I was stuck. I couldn't move, and I didn't have any other arguments. She knew my public stance on martyrdom, but she also knew the truth. Plain and simple: I was a coward.

She sat there awhile looking at me, not in any judgmental way, just smiling. She stood, pulling me up with her, and hugged me for a long time.

"Please don't go." I was crying and heartbroken and disgusted with myself.

"I love you, George. Goodbye."

***

Although I had somehow managed to pass the test with the demon, my objections toward martyrdom, my reluctance to embrace God—to quit hiding, to go down the mountain to spread the Gospel, facilitating my own death, were symptoms not only of cowardice, but of an incomplete faith.

Like most things, I did faith half-assed on the old Earth. I didn't go to church when I could have, I read the Bible sparingly even in the caves, I prayed mostly when I needed something, I worshiped with at least one foot firmly planted in the world, and I failed to build a relationship with God.

The Bible referred to people like me as "lukewarm". It was easy to go through the motions of church, Bible study, and even prayer. It was a hard thing to let go of the things of the Earth and to truly give it all up to God, a long process of sacrifice and unwavering faith that most danced around because it was too difficult, especially in the beginning when the faith was still weak against the resistance and outright ostracism of relatives, friends, coworkers, and people who didn't even know you.

But the reward was happiness, a certain perfect bliss, a contentment that could never be shaken, and there were relatively few people on the old Earth who had experienced that deep relationship with God. Danny got there after Roger's death. What did it look like? In her it looked divine. She glowed and smiled, and she looked peaceful and sounded joyful when she went down the mountain to die.

***

People on the old Earth would often mock that joy, the look of serenity, the excitement in the voices of the truly faithful speaking about their relationship to God. They would call these enthusiastic Christians phonies, nut-jobs, right-wing fanatics, Jesus freaks, or all of the above, rolling their eyes at the very sight or mention of their jubilance. Or they would shake their heads and feel sorry for "that poor Jane" or someone or other having "gone off the deep-end."

What they couldn't understand, and what I didn't understand until it was too late, was that these Christians' relationships with God were more real than anything the old Earth had to offer, and the faithful couldn't help but glow over and express that magnificent bond to anyone who would listen. The mocking and the pity affected them not one bit—it was they who had been sorry for us.

***

So I continued to beat her up about it even though it was pointless.

God was with Danny, and she had given herself completely to Him. Nobody could talk her out of her fate. She took her Bible, waved goodbye, and stepped lightly into the woods.

24

Except for regular visits to my daughter's big house and frequent trips to the Hall of Knowledge, I rarely ventured farther than a few blocks from my neighborhood in paradise, till one day, and I'm not sure exactly why, I decided to visit New Jerusalem.

***

Built in the blink of an eye, the city, five times the size of Manhattan, was rumored to be magnificent, but mostly by those who had never been there. Because most of those, like my daughter, who *had* been to New Jerusalem, simply would not talk about it. For them it was like a Christmas present, the surprise of which would be spoiled by even the slightest hint. Of course, like any impatient child, I pleaded with Sophie to tell me its secrets. It didn't work. She is much more disciplined than I.

***

Until recently, very few people from my neck of the woods had visited New Jerusalem. Maybe we were afraid we'd run into Jesus or Moses or someone and have to explain ourselves. Before I left, I got to thinking about Danny and the others, how I had kept them on the mountain because of my cowardice, and the awful thing I had done after she went to face martyrdom. Maybe it wasn't Jesus I was afraid to bump into, but Danny. In any case, I couldn't much stand myself, so I figured what the heck and took off walking toward the distant glow that was the city.

***

It would be a long journey, and I could have taken a bus, taxi, train, or any manner of vehicle, but my daughter had insisted I walk the first time. It was the way it was done, she said, like a vision quest or pilgrimage. Besides, I had lots of time, and the new bodies never tired.

***

Vehicles in the New Kingdom looked pretty much like vehicles on the old Earth, except they didn't have wheels and rode about three feet off the ground most of the time. They were also noiseless, needing no gasoline, diesel, or any other smelly, polluting, combustible liquid.

***

What amazed me about the old Earth was how technological progress had mysteriously left behind the automobile. I mean everybody walked around with their tiny cell phones, chatting away into space like they were on *Star Trek* or something—and this from smoke signals in less than 200 years. Technology had progressed rapidly, even miraculously, in most areas, yet, right up to the end, we were all driving the same basic clunker of an automobile invented near the turn of the previous century.

I found out at the Hall of Knowledge that the genius, Nicola Tesla, had invented a noiseless, fuel-less vehicle way back in 1923. He also invented free electricity. He tried to tell everyone about his great inventions, which could have gone a long way toward building a more utopian and peaceful society on the old Earth. But the powers that be didn't want to listen to anything sensible, especially if it had the word free in it, squashing any innovation that might limit the sale of gas or electricity.

People hardly complained, continuing to ride around in the same stinky, dirty, gas-guzzling dinosaurs for more than a hundred years, amid all the sleek, smooth, and ever-changing technology, like a bunch of hobos at a dinner party with one eye on the silverware.

So what did Nicolai get for his genius, innovation, generosity, and hard work? He was ridiculed, ruined, and eventually suffocated in his New York apartment by goons of the Illuminati, who then stole all the papers detailing his brilliant inventions. What a world it was.

***

Strolling along the gold highway of the New Kingdom toward New Jerusalem, I passed the factories and farms where people toiled joyfully at their labors. Unlike the old Earth, where many people avoided work, especially menial labor, people in the New Kingdom love work more than most anything, and the harder they work, the better they feel.

I have a pretty good job loading trucks at one of the big warehouses where food is distributed to grocery stores across the New Kingdom. All the great jobs like farming and construction had already been taken.

But we don't work for money. There isn't any money in the New Kingdom, no currency whatsoever. The stores are filled with food and clothes and all manner of necessity, there for the taking. There is abundance in the New Kingdom.

There was abundance on the old Earth, too, enough to go around for everyone a thousand times over. But people just didn't share enough. Men were jealous and selfish and greedy and power hungry. They would collect as much food or cash or jewelry or cars or boats or women as they could, storing them someplace where no one else could get to them. There was even a bumper sticker which read:

He who dies with the most toys wins.

Congratulations!

***

Why do the people here love hard work so much? Because hard work breeds humility, and humility is bliss.

***

Instead of rewarding people for hard work on the old Earth, the Illuminati came up with the idea of rewarding people for not working. The idea was to make it easy for everyone to participate in well-meaning programs like welfare, food stamps, free health care, free tuition, farm and energy subsidies, bailouts, and on and on; until enough people became like babies, coddled in the arms of the state, unmotivated and unproductive and completely dependent on their huge, out-of-control governments.

***

I, too, would avoid work whenever I could on the old Earth,

preferring to sit at home watching the History Channel, or reruns of a cartoon about a family with a diabolical two-year-old and a talking dog, or a reality show about a group of people fighting to survive on a deserted island in front of a film crew and a catering truck, or sometimes the boring, rehashed news loaded with Illuminati propaganda and acts of senseless violence.

***

I came to a fork on the golden road. I couldn't tell which way to go because the glow of the city in the distance filled much of the horizon. I spotted a gentleman 200 yards away, harnessed to a plow in a great field. I hollered and waved to get his attention, so I could ask him for directions. He immediately ran over to assist.

***

That's just how it is in the New Kingdom. If you waved to a stranger on the old Earth, they'd often as not pretend they didn't hear you or ignore you altogether. People were too busy, too lazy, too selfish, or perhaps too afraid to help each other, being that you could be a serial killer or just your average, run-of-the-mill nutcase.

***

The gentleman farmer moved gracefully and speedily in his new body, which was "maxed out" like mine. Maxed out was the term we used for those who had reached or been granted the perfect body age of thirty-three. I would have thought the perfect body age to be somewhere in the mid-twenties before I came here, but that's because I was already a slouch by the time I turned thirty on the old Earth.

***

I tried to guess when he lived on the old Earth. He was wearing a pair of overalls popular in the early 20th century, only that didn't mean much. You could find outfits from any period in history, and people didn't necessarily choose from their own time. I mean you didn't see a lot of people running around in sheepskin or 15th century tights. Once people saw others wearing more practical clothing, they changed styles rather quickly. Besides he *was* farming.

You could sometimes tell if a person was really old in the New Kingdom by their eyes, which could hold the great wisdom of

237

someone who had been around centuries. I guessed that this man had existed at least two or three hundred years. But it was just a guess, and quite incorrect as it turned out—as the saying went: *Some men are wise beyond their years.*

***

When he was close enough he smiled. "You want to know which road to take to New Jerusalem? I get that all the time."

"Well, yes," I said. "It looks like both roads might get me there?"

"'Two roads converged in a wood, and I—I took the one less travelled by,'" he offered, with not a little drama.

I remembered it from some long forgotten English course. "Robert Frost, right?" I said proudly.

"Good, young man!" said the stranger. "What is your name, sir?"

"George," I said. "And you?"

"Millard Tobias Sinclair," he said, wiping the nonexistent sweat from his face out of habit with an embroidered handkerchief he pulled from a back pocket.

"I see the initials," I said, pointing to the neatly woven letters on his handkerchief. "That's a fine cloth. You don't see many like it these days."

"I had a bunch recreated to look like the ones I carried when I was a young man on the old Earth," said Millard.

Since he had referenced Robert Frost, I realized he was much younger than I had first assumed. "When was that?"

He chuckled to himself and began to speak with pride and melancholy. "I saw the first two World Wars, my friend. I saw a dozen or more presidents come and go. I watched the world slide into debauchery and mayhem until I couldn't take it anymore."

"Debauchery and mayhem—you were around near the end, then?" I asked, but immediately realized it would have been impossible.

"No," Millard said. "I died of a heart attack in 1971."

***

The mayhem and debauchery he'd been referring to had happened during the 1960s, when, for him, all Hell did break loose. All Hell didn't really break loose then. That would come later. No, this was simply the decade known for the hippie movement. Some well-meaning college students, weary of corrupt politicians and war and parents and suits and short hair, decided it would be good to stage a few protests. But what might have been an opportunity for real change became an excuse to quit school, quit work, riot, get loaded, fornicate all over kingdom come in the name of free love, and to destroy the family while they were at it.

All this fun ended around the same time a loveable vagabond named Charles Manson talked some of his hippie "family" into massacring a pregnant actress and her houseguests in 1969.

Manson's family consisted mostly of runaway young girls and other gullible types. They all lived together in a drug-fueled haze on an old western movie set where they practiced their "free love." One day, Manson became bored with all the orgies and drug taking and whatnot, and decided he would start a race war by butchering white people so it would be blamed on black people.

***

Free love was an expression used during the hippie movement as a euphemism for premarital sex, extramarital sex, sex with multiple partners, sex with the same gender, sex on alcohol, sex on drugs, group sex, and casual sex. It wasn't free and it wasn't love.

***

Manson sent his right-hand man, the cowardly Tex Watson, and some of his "girls" over to the actress Sharon Tate's home in the Hollywood Hills to begin his idiotic and horrific plan. One of the houseguests saw Tex coming up the driveway and asked him who he was and what he was doing there. Old Tex replied, "I am the devil, and I'm here to do the devil's business." He was only half right.

Tate, pleading for her baby's life, was answered with three bullets and forty-one stab wounds.

The next night, Manson, Tex and some of the other family members drove over to the home of Leno and Mary LaBianca. Manson tied the innocent couple up, ordered Tex and company to make a mess of them, and fled the scene.

Before Tex and the girls left, they scribbled the words "Helter Skelter" in blood on the door of the LaBiancas' refrigerator. That was a line from a Beatles song Manson stole as the title to his race war.

Tex and the girls involved were tried and convicted of first-degree murder and sentenced to death. All through the trial, they snickered and laughed, continuing to follow Manson, believing in his race war and other nonsense.

Manson never cared about any race war. He was a lifelong criminal, con artist and control freak, seeking infamy and revenge for his failed life, preying on the gullibility of Tex and the young girls.

After several years, the harsh reality of prison life and the looming specter of their own executions set in for Tex and the girls. They finally came to the conclusion they had been hoodwinked by a madman and began to feel the weight of their ugliness.

But later, they were granted a reprieve after California outlawed the death penalty. So, every seven years, the victims' families had to relive the details of their loved ones' suffering in front of the parole boards, so they could remind everyone of the viciousness of the crimes and keep the animals locked up. Still, the killers would show up, pleading their cases of youth, naivety, and sorrow.

It didn't work. Some things can't be taken back once done. They would have to look to a higher power for some sort of absolution. But only one of them ever came to the realization that ultimately they had made their own decisions to butcher those poor people.

Manson would never come to that conclusion, nor would he ever admit any wrongdoing. He would continue playing the victim through his mad rantings and die in prison after so many years, welcoming the whispers of the demons that were to guide him into Hell.

***

Millard Sinclair and I spoke for over an hour. Millard told me about the World Wars he had seen; I told him what I knew of the last wars. He told me about his experiences on the front lines of World War I and II; I told him about hanging around the barracks during the Gulf War, laying low through World War III, and hiding in a hole while millions perished at the Battle of Armageddon.

He told me he was sitting in a trench with his best friend, William Corduroy, drinking bad coffee, when a mustard gas shell exploded nearby. A moment later he heard screams as shrapnel rained down on the trenches.

***

Bad coffee was the God-given right of every U.S. service member. The United States Armed forces could develop a missile capable of hitting a squirrel between the eyes after being launched from an airplane 30,000 feet in the air, but they couldn't make a decent cup of joe.

***

Millard told me he had only turned his head for a second after hearing the explosion. When he turned back, Big Bill, as his friend was known, was bleeding all over from a spray of shrapnel. The mustard gas clinging to the shrapnel lodged in his face quickly worked its magic, causing much of it to melt away while he choked on the fumes—in another instant he was dead.

***

Before World War I, chemical warfare was considered uncivilized. That's when some French military leaders grew tired of staring at their toy soldier brigades lined neatly on the painted trench lines of their battlefield maps day after day without much movement of any kind, so they decided to stir things up by adding some gas to the game.

It worked better than expected. With everyone running from the gas, the generals could finally do something. Toy soldiers and real soldiers were finally moving all over the place.

Well, the Germans weren't about to let the French have all the fun, so they decided to take chemical warfare to new levels and developed the first deadly gases for the battlefield.

***

After World War I, several of the most proficient German chemical companies involved in the development of deadly gases merged to form I.G. Farben. During World War II, the owners were asked by the Nazis to develop a gas that could be used effectively to exterminate large groups of people quickly. I.G. Farben didn't have to look very far, as they were already producing a pesticide that, with a little bit of tweaking, could be quite effective on humans. They named it Zyklon B.

The Nazis, quite pleased with I.G. Farben and their special gas, ordered lots more. Farben and its owners made gobs of money. And even after the war, the bad press over the holocaust didn't slow the company down one bit. They simply changed their name and began producing volleyballs and children's aspirin, which made them even more gobs of money.

***

Millard had known Big Bill since they were little kids, playing war with sticks in the woods near their Connecticut homes. All the boys came out to play war with their stick guns. They would run around shouting, "Bang, bang...you're dead!" That was when they still thought war was fun. They would pretend to be fighting the Civil War because that was the last big war for America at the time. About half the boys would pretend they were fighting for the Union Army, and the other half for the Confederate side. They would spend a lot of time arguing about who would fight for which side. All the boys wanted to be on the Union side because they all knew the Union side had won. No American boy wanted to be on the losing side.

***

Americans hated losing at anything, especially wars, because they were so used to winning. For nearly 200 years, Americans won war after war. We beat the French, we beat the British, the Spanish, the Mexicans, the Germans, the Japanese, and the Germans again. And though we should have had a wake-up after the North Korean stalemate, we shrugged it off as some sort of fluke, continuing to believe in our winning streak, our invincibility, our victorious and God-given destiny.

Then the Vietnam War came along and kicked America's butt. We were so ashamed of losing that we were too embarrassed to commit to any of the wars that followed. American politicians and journalists were the most embarrassed. They shamed the military into fighting wars with politically correct policies and regulations that tied the hands of soldiers in battle, so they would continually second-guess themselves, as if war were some kind of sporting event or debating match, causing the unnecessary death of even more brave soldiers. They decided they would rather let their boys and girls be butchered than be embarrassed again by a war.

***

242

Millard didn't quite know how, but he survived World War I after being wounded four different times. He received quite a few medals for bravery, and some, he told me, just for standing around. He, like many soldiers before him, once believed that standing around was the worst part of being in the Army. But that was before he saw so many friends blown to pieces.

***

We did a lot of standing around when I was in the Army. We'd wake up in the middle of the night, splash water on our faces, dress in our fatigues, throw on our boots, run outside the barracks, jump in a truck, drive to some training area, jump out of the truck, line up in formation, answer to roll call, break up, and then stand around for two or three hours drinking the crappy coffee.

While standing around, we'd moan and groan about not only the coffee, but the lack of sleep, the regulations, our commanding officers, and anything else we could come up with. Soldiers in just such a situation coined the expression, "hurry up and wait." We also complained about missing the war by a few months, losing the opportunity to fight for our country, and missing all the action. We were as dumb as could be.

***

Besides giving him all kinds of medals, the U.S. government further rewarded Millard by drafting him back into the Army just in time for World War II. He was already past forty with a wife and four daughters and a bad taste for war in his mouth, but he went willingly and without complaint. There were very few draft dodgers in those days on the old Earth.

***

During the Vietnam War, there were all kinds of draft dodgers and war protesters. Some were simply men of peace and some were afraid. The reality was that men would always wage war, some justifiable and some not. Regardless of reason or legitimacy, men would have to fight and men would have to die. Some men could not let someone else take their place in line for death and some men could.

After the men who bravely and willingly took their place in line for death, who had lost their friends and brothers and witnessed all

243

manner of bloodshed and horror, came home from Vietnam, they were ridiculed and spat upon by many of the same men who stepped out of line. Later, some of those men became the politicians and journalists who continued spitting on soldiers with their absurd, defeatist, and politically correct agendas. Why did they spit on them? Answer: they were ashamed of themselves.

***

Because of his World War I experience and medals, Millard was given the rank of captain and command of a bunch of boys chosen to storm Omaha beach during the invasion of France. This was arguably the most dangerous mission of the Second World War. The German defenses above that beach on the cliffs of Normandy were so thorough and formidable Millard lost every one of his boys within eight minutes of the landing. The impervious Millard, on the other hand, didn't receive a single scratch that day, or for the rest of the war for that matter. Millard never could understand why he survived another war, while so many good young men perished.

***

People on the old Earth often said such and such a death was God's will or meant to be. It made them feel better, I suppose, to think their lost loved one had taken part in some big plan that was somehow more meaningful than someone else's demise. So why did Millard and other good men survive when so many died? Answer: mostly dumb luck.

***

We talked awhile longer about the wars, about life on the old Earth, about his daughters and other things. I asked him lots of questions, saying little about myself. He sensed my avoidance and didn't pry. He was an interesting and wise man, and I promised to visit him someday. By then it was close to noon, the sun directly over our heads. "I've got a long walk ahead. I should get going," I said.

"Yes, I should get back to work myself," he said.

I hesitated. "I never did anything important like that with my life. I had a chance once, but I failed everyone."

"We all have regrets...your daughter loves you," he said.

I wasn't sure why he said it. I had only briefly mentioned Sophie. "I better go." I started toward the fork, then turned back. "I'm sorry so many of your friends died for my American Dream. I'm sorry I wasted it. I've done some terrible things."

"We all have to answer for what we've done...but you're here, George, because you've been given a second chance," he said.

"It was good talking with you, Millard...so long."

25

few hours down the road, I flopped in a meadow to take a nap in the short blue grass. I awoke to a full-grown lion licking my ear. This was not uncommon here in the New Kingdom, where animal and man not only lived together in perfect peace, but communicated on a nearly psychic level. The former king of the jungle was simply telling me hello. I sat up. "Hello," I replied. "What are you doing, Lion? Do you want to walk with me a bit?"

He seemed to say yes, and I asked him to lead me to water, so I could splash some on my face. The new bodies didn't get dirty or anything, but old habits die hard, so most people showered and scrubbed and brushed their sparkling white teeth just the same.

We walked a short distance through some woods to a lake, the color of purple Gatorade. A small herd of cattle grazed near the shoreline. The lion did not bother the cattle, nor would he ever eat cattle or any other meat again. He joined them, grazing alongside as if one of the herd.

***

People are the only meat eaters in the New Kingdom. We don't need to eat meat, or anything for that matter, but most of us still enjoy it. The markets are full of fresh beef, chicken, lamb, goat, venison, fish, and even dinosaur—every meat imaginable. Yet no animal had ever been slaughtered in the New Kingdom. The markets are stocked from warehouses that never empty, much like the bottomless baskets of fish and bread passed out by Jesus on the Sea of Galilee.

***

Some people on the old Earth despised the killing of animals for food or sport. They especially hated the use of animals in medical experiments. They would complain and curse, throw fake blood and even bombs, anything to stop the torture and killing of animals. The other side would argue that these "bleeding hearts" would rather see humans die than animals. And some of them would, but as with most things on the old Earth the answers were somewhere in between.

Just as there were people on the old Earth who valued animal life over human life, there were despicable human beings who outright tortured animals or allowed for cruel means of wholesale slaughter to save a buck. Animal rights activists did great work to protect animals, improving living conditions, preventing animal torture and unnecessary slaughter.

But some of these people would get carried away. Some of them would rather see people starve than eat meat, or take in a dozen homeless cats before they'd feed and house an orphaned child, or blow up a laboratory and kill a few security guards to protect a monkey.

It wasn't wrong to eat meat, wear fur to stay warm, or even experiment under humane conditions. God created animals for many purposes: food, clothing, protection, transportation, work, medicine, and companionship.

And God initiated animal sacrifice not because He didn't value animals, but because He did value animals, as most men did, especially before Christ became the sacrifice. When those men had to kill an animal because of their sins, it meant something. They treasured and loved their animals. It sure as heck made them think twice about sinning again.

As for the animals, as much as they loved being squeezed to death by lonely old ladies, they'd have just as soon been on their way to Heaven already.

***

After I completed my washing ritual, I sat by the side of the lake enjoying the play of the many species now gathering at the water's edge. Any animal that had lived with man on the old Earth at one time or another could be found in the New Kingdom. I thought about my dogs and how they would have enjoyed this scene. Wiley was with

247

STOCKWELL

Sophie, but the two dogs I had grown up with and taken care of were waiting for me when I arrived. If you had been good to your pets on the old Earth, they were waiting for you. Because of the shooting of his beloved dog when he was just a boy, my father never wanted any pets around, and he certainly would never pay good money for a dog that could be gotten from the city pound. But my mom was able to convince him, anyway, to let us keep a couple of strays that wandered into our lives. My siblings liked them well enough, but for some reason it fell on me to walk and otherwise look after them, maybe because I was the only one willing.

***

Missing but not missed in the New Kingdom are all the reptiles and insects, the "crawling things," perfectly content dwelling down in the pit with Satan and the rest, as if they didn't have enough problems with the heat and the stench and the teeth gnashing and such.

The reason there are no reptiles or insects in the New Kingdom was simple: unlike other creatures, they are soulless. They have no way to temper their violently ravenous natures. So they are literally killing machines. But they had been created for specific purposes, mainly as food for smaller animals and to keep the plant cycles going and whatnot. Only, once Satan worked his magic, he made sure they continued proliferating to hazardous and maddeningly annoying levels. He and his Illuminati cohorts even genetically engineered their own super hideous and vicious versions. Man had an awful time keeping their verminous masses under control. But justice would prevail. Right now, old Lucifer was getting a taste of his own insect management polices down in the pit.

***

Dinosaurs were spared the pit, being that they are only part reptile, having bird and mammal DNA in them as well. So God decided to give some of them souls. But it wasn't enough to allow them to roam freely round the New Kingdom because the reptile in them made them uncomfortable living around humans and other animals. In other words, a dinosaur might just forget where he was and attempt to take a bite out of someone. Not that he could hurt the new bodies, but it would be kind of awkward for everyone, so it was best keeping them at a distance.

248

Dinosaurs now live in a place called Dinosaur Planet—it is like a super Jurassic Park, but without all the attractions and such. People will be able to visit there one day, but there will be plenty of time for that. I plan on going there with Sophie; she once loved all things dinosaur.

***

That dinosaurs even lived on the old Earth was always held up by non-believers as some sort of proof the Bible was full of baloney. They would thumb their scholarly noses at the so-called Bible version of history, specifically its timeline for the creation of the earth and the genealogy of man, calculated at about 6000 years because of the seven day creation story and the lineages that follow. They would point to scientific data proving the existence of dinosaurs some sixty million years before the existence of man as part of their ammunition.

The truth was that they didn't understand the Bible or time. Even those big-brained old Earth scientists, who had discovered and developed theories in quantum physics, were only skimming the surface of creation, time, and space. God had laid out the Biblical timeline and creation of the Earth in terms the earliest man might grasp, using the language of days in a week to overcome the still incomprehensible reality of eternity, folded time, and something so complex created from what man could only perceive as nothingness.

One of those scientists, Albert Einstein, was the first to advance reasonable theories of space and time. He surmised that both time and space were relative to the motion or experience of the observer. He was right. And God had the best seat in the house.

The Earth was both eons and seconds old at the same time. It was all there at the Hall of Knowledge. But, like most everyone else, I was a long way from understanding all of it. Even in paradise, with our enhanced cognizance, we still used but a fraction of our brains. The understanding would come, and we would have eternity to figure it all out.

Before Einstein died, he came to the conclusion that there had to be a creator of some kind. This irritated a lot of scientists, especially those who held up Darwinism as some sort of religion. But even Darwin understood the gaps in his own theory. Still, most scientists and teachers continued pushing it as definitive truth.

Even after the discovery of DNA revealed a genetic imprint, encoded with precise and specific instructions, too incredibly detailed to even suggest randomness, many of these stubborn brainiacs continued to ignore the mathematical impossibility of accidental life, which was more than sufficient proof based on the principles of their own   god   of   science.

As quantum physics suggested, what was possible was astounding, but it shouldn't have been news to man. The Bible had already informed us that we could do anything, that we could move mountains were we so inclined. Jesus walked on water, turned water into wine, raised the dead, and on and on.

Children were doing the impossible here already. It was all tied to their innocence, their inclination toward belief as opposed to skepticism, their unwavering faith. I'd seen children running and playing on lakes like they were concrete. I'd seen them move boulders without touching them. And I would see my own daughter fly.

***

I took off my clothes and dove in the water, which I knew would feel perfect no matter what time of year it was. Had I been a child, I could have willed my body to feel the water, or air, at whatever temperature I chose. I would like to do that someday, to feel the sting of a freezing wind or even the burn of scalding water. Sometimes things could be too perfect. How foolishly greedy I am, still.

Floating on my back, I stared at the stars and planets, easily seen even in daylight. The Earth had moved closer toward the Heavens, and the skies had been wiped clean of the foul air and other debris that once tainted our view on the old Earth. I could see the craters on the moon and the rings of Jupiter as if they were features of the Earth's landscape somewhere in the distance. But this was only the beginning. We would be able to see it all one day, to move through time and space, to will our bodies to any destination in the blink of an eye. I was ecstatic over the thought, filled with the joy of endless possibility.

But the joy was short-lived. As always, my thoughts turned to what was once my life, and what was once my family, to my guilt and regret, and to the coming judgment. The new bodies were free of pain, but our souls could still carry the pain of our old lives, as long as we held on to it.

And I still had no idea how to let go.

***

I continued on the road to New Jerusalem, which ran close to the sea. People were sailing on wooden vessels near the shore, where others frolicked in the waves and sand, swimming and playing with dolphins and seals.

A beautiful woman passed me on a bicycle and smiled. All the women here were beautiful and all the men handsome in the New Kingdom, and yet their basic features had not changed one iota since the old Earth.

Moreover, all the hours of plastic surgery were gone; all the tucks, lifts, and add-ons were history. True, the blemishes, scars, excess fat, and even most of the wrinkles were gone, but the permanent features—the huge noses, the buck teeth, the pointy chins, the giant foreheads, the small eyes, and whatever else was considered ugly or at least less than desirable by the shallow standards of our little minds—were now perceived for their true and unique beauty, as if a veil of stupidity had finally been removed.

Beauty had been an obsession of people on the old Earth. Some people would do almost anything to possess a version of it. They would have their skin poisoned, their faces stretched, their noses broken, their chests cut open, their stomachs stapled, their fat vacuumed, and on and on. By the time most of these people were done, their skin was unusually tight and their features unnaturally sharp or bulbous, so they didn't look pretty or young even by old Earth standards—go figure.

***

The road curved and I spied a couple with a young boy packing up their vehicle. The boy looked to be about eight or nine and must have been a baby when he was raptured or died. What bliss, to never know the pain of the old Earth, to live here without shame or guilt.

I assumed the two were once married on the old Earth, unless the boy was a relative or something. Although there were no new marriages in the New Kingdom, families with children would remain together, at least until the child was of age, and afterwards, if they decided. That is, if they made it into the New Kingdom intact. If not, they would live with one parent, close relatives, or foster parents of some sort.

Marriage had been a necessity on the old Earth, where children, especially—but men and women, too—needed structure and protection from the disorder and vindictiveness of the world. Man's sinful nature had created a barrier to God's light and love, which the love and faith of family served to overcome. And while not ideal, even the love of a secular family offered hope to a child. After all, all love was of God.

***

There was no sex in the New Kingdom either, and nobody missed it. It was looked back upon like a bad habit, like nose picking and such.

***

Ignoring Sophie's insistence that I walk the whole way, I decided it was time to speed up my journey to the city, if only to get out of my own head for a bit, and asked them for a lift. It was just a formality. I knew they would say yes. People were once afraid to pick up hitchhikers on the old Earth, what with so many thieves and psychopaths roaming about. But there was nothing to fear in the New Kingdom, and people were glad for the company of strangers.

I sat next to the young boy as we glided down the road. The sky was mostly clear with thin wisps of purple, yellow, and red toned clouds. We joked and laughed and talked. They had been a tight little family, living a quiet and simple life in Indiana, when the Rapture took them. The father asked me if I had children.

"I have a little girl…not so little, twenty-one now," I answered.

"Are you still living together?" the mother asked.

"She's with her mother."

"Your marriage didn't last on the old Earth, then?"

"No…I messed that up."

"I'm sorry," she said. "That must be hard."

"It is," I said.

"What happened?" asked the father.

***

Such straightforward questions were unusual, and mostly unheard of among strangers on the old Earth, where people were afraid of discussing things real or important, unless they were spoken about behind somebody's back. No, people would rather discuss hot weather, motorbikes, football, television shows, and all manner of nonsense. They were afraid somebody might say something challenging or uncomfortable. People on the old Earth would go to great lengths to avoid awkwardness, even if it meant ignoring people, leaving them alone with their problems, helpless and without hope.

***

"I was a fool," I said.

The boy laughed.

"Sorry…it's not funny," said the father.

I smiled at the boy. "No…it's fine. It might be funny, if it weren't so pathetic."

"Still, he knows better," said the father.

"Do you see them?" said the mother.

"Just my daughter, mostly…her mom already gave it all she had."

"Well, you have that," said the mother.

"Yes, I have that."

***

We drove in silence for a while, not an awkward silence. There was too much truth for that. Silence in the New Kingdom was reflection and love, pure and simple.

Finally, the boy spoke. "Have you been to New Jerusalem before?"

"No. This will be the first time," I said.

"Oh, you're going to love it!" said the boy. "I've been twice already. I won't tell you about it because I don't want to spoil it."

"Thank you," I said.

But he was a child and couldn't hold it in, so a moment later, he began spilling the beans about the "weird-curvy" architecture, a pyramid "big as a mountain," and great museums filled with "old stuff that used to be dust." He told me of a building, "high as the sky," "streets shining like diamonds," and shops "filled with toys and cakes and candy." And he told of a movie theater "with a thousand screens, where you could watch yourself, and cowboys and monsters and

253

stuff."

I already knew about the Theater of History. I read all about it at the Hall of Knowledge, but I kept quiet. I didn't want to spoil the boy's fun.

"Let the man be a little surprised," said his father.

"Sorry," said the boy.

"Sounds wonderful," I said, and I winked and smiled at the boy.

He smiled back.

***

I had to admit I was excited. But I was also nervous and afraid. I felt like Pinocchio, eager to venture to the Land of Play, only to be turned into a donkey.

***

When we came to a long driveway off the side of the road, they stopped the vehicle to let me out. I could see a dozen or more large houses perched along the cliffs. I picked a house, pictured their happy life there, and smiled to myself. "Thank you," I said.

The boy hugged my legs and the woman held my hand. "Don't give up," she said.

***

It was good to see a family together, and it made my heart glad. They drove up the driveway, and I waved and watched them for a moment before I continued my trek toward the city.

***

It grew dark, but I kept walking. I walked most of the night, thinking about the years on the old Earth when Sophie was small, and Renee and I were happy. How I had failed to cherish and hold on to the beauty of those days was my deepest regret. So I let the memories slip into self-loathing, until I grew tired of thinking and slept to clear my mind.

***

The new bodies didn't require sleep. Sleep was a choice. People here still slept at night out of habit, or to clear their thoughts. It was the thing I needed, a break from my troubled mind, a sure respite from the pain and the memories. There was no such thing as a nightmare in paradise, or so I thought.

26

I'm not sure how long I slept, but it had mostly done the trick. My self-loathing had waned to an acceptable degree, and I continued my journey with renewed vigor.

***

After a few miles, I saw floating in the distance what appeared to be a huge white quilt spanning the entire length of a vast plain, surrounded by a thick barrier of woodlands. As I got closer, I began to make out individual structures, and I knew what I had seen moving from a distance were the cloth tops of Tent City.

It was the reason I had chosen this route. I didn't know exactly why I needed to go to Tent City, but something was drawing me to this enclave of the nearly damned. Perhaps I felt a special kinship toward them. Still, I became fearful as I approached, slowing my pace until I reached the woods surrounding the tents, then stopping completely.

Just past the tree line were two large storehouses. Men loaded carts with supplies, and I immediately recognized the distant look in their eyes because I had seen it in the mirror so often, and so at once felt at ease.

They finished loading, and I followed them as they pulled the carts through the woods and into the city. What struck me most about Tent City was the heavy silence. There must have been thousands of men and women milling around, yet no one talked beyond a few whispers here and there. Some worked, but most sat or stood staring at the ground as if in contemplation of something monumental.

***

I wondered what was on their minds. Was it the family they destroyed? Was it the wrongs they committed toward their fellow man? Were they bitter about their lot in paradise?

Nothing confined them to Tent City. Sure, they were brought here to settle in the beginning, but they were free to move around like anybody else. Still, people from Tent City, I read, didn't often travel. Perhaps they were afraid their patch of paradise wouldn't be there when they returned.

***

The few people that did look up from their meditations and did happen to notice me, I could tell, knew instinctively that I wasn't one of them. According to what I read, the people of Tent City were the fringe of the fringe. If I made it into paradise by a spider hair, they made it by the hair of a flea. I couldn't see much of a difference, but it was written there at the Hall of Knowledge in black and white. And the sad part was that some of these people wouldn't make it.

At the end of the thousand years, the pit would be opened and Satan would lead the whole pit crew in one last foolish battle with God, offering kingdoms to anyone in paradise who would join. And though they could have easily looked up the suicidal outcome of that battle, just as I did, hundreds from Tent City and more from other parts of paradise would follow Satan in his quest for eternal damnation anyway. I am a stupid man, but this takes the stupid cake.

***

There were fires everywhere. I smelled something cooking, so I felt like eating. I saw a man and women dressed in garb from the middle ages, stirring a large pot hanging over a wood fire like a scene from some medieval postcard. I stood on the path in front of them knowing they would offer me something to eat.

***

William and Althea Stout were their names, and they gave me food and their story in low whispers. They were married and lived their lives in 16th century England, a particularly harsh period of history. They died of disease while in their mid-fifties. They didn't deserve to be in paradise, they told me. True, they had been Christians, part of the

257

Church of England, but times were tough, so they begged and stole and even killed a man once out of revenge during their quest to preserve a slice of the survival pie.

It happened when they were very young. Through no fault of their own, they had been thrown off of the estate where they had lived and worked all of their lives. The work the Stouts did on the estate was a kind of slavery. They were part of a system known as serfdom. And like slavery, serfdom was another Illuminati invention—slavery disguised to look like something else. The Stouts were thrown off the estate after the owner, a Lord Peckham, made advances on the innocent Althea and was soundly rejected.

***

Men of stature throughout history often assumed it was their right to accost women of lower economic standing. The king at that time, Henry VIII, decided it was his right to take as many mistresses and wives as he wanted. Since the church frowned upon divorce without good reason, Henry made up terrible stuff about his wives so he could have the marriages annulled, even having a couple of these poor ladies beheaded to make it look good and because he didn't want them moving on to other men.

The only thing Henry liked as much as women was eating. Portraits of the king show a pretty hefty dude posing in all his finery. I quoted earlier from the Bible that it would be easier for a camel to pass through the eye of a needle than for a rich man to get into Heaven. Well, it's even harder for a wealthy and gluttonous man, especially one who murders women in order to sleep around.

***

To his small credit, Lord Peckham could have simply taken or raped Althea anyway. And he might have, had he thought about it right away. But he was so embarrassed by Althea's rejection that his first reaction was to get rid of the evidence by having his guards remove the Stouts from his property.

People on the old Earth, especially people of power, hated being embarrassed. Some of them would go to great lengths to avoid embarrassing situations. They would lie and steal and hide, and even commit murder if it meant saving face. What a world it was.

***

Starving and on the road, the Stouts fell in with a group of mendicants, quickly learning the lower arts of survival—mostly how to steal without getting caught, conning their fellow man out of goods and coins, and the most effective methods of garnering sympathy for handouts like feigning injury, holding "borrowed" babies, self-mutilation, and other tricks of the trade.

Eventually, they made their way to the city of London. At the time, London was seeing a population explosion while it became the center for European commerce and culture. The Stouts were just one couple out of thousands of desperate people pouring into the city to make a living. Soon after they arrived, they split from their fellow vagabonds and set up on a busy corner to beg and steal on their own.

The problem was that the corner they picked had already been claimed by a ruthless, criminal entrepreneur, known as Hans the German because he hailed from Frankfurt. Hans would slit his mother's throat for a half a schilling, and when he saw the couple plying their trade on his corner, the much larger German pummeled poor William nearly unconscious and then ripped the dress off the screaming Althea just for fun.

***

William and Althea had had enough of being pushed around. They had been taking crap all their lives, and the big German was the final straw. Jesus would have told them to turn the other cheek. Had they listened, they would have avoided much of the guilt and misery that followed them the rest of their lives.

Instead, they plotted their revenge. Each day they watched Hans the German from the shadows, monitoring his crafty comings and goings, until they caught him unawares in one of his many sleeping spots, spread out in various corners, crevices, and cubbyholes throughout London.

With a dull knife, a rock, and a broken piece of iron-gate, they pounced on Hans with a viciousness summoned from Hell and a lifetime of frustration. They continued stabbing, pounding kicking, and gouging the German long after he was dead.

Many who kill gain a taste for blood or at least an apathetic view toward killing. The Stouts never killed or hurt anybody again. They

259

never even raised their voices in anger, nor did they steal again. They spent the rest of their miserable lives working any job they could find to scratch out a living, trying to forget about what they had done to the German. But they couldn't. They never talked about it, but it had been eating at both of them, and at one time or another they silently confessed and asked God's forgiveness. It worked.

***

Some on the old Earth hated the concept of confession, or at least they complained about it. Especially the idea that someone could drink and whore around, committing all manner of sin on Friday and Saturday, only to ask for forgiveness on Sunday, was for them the ultimate in hypocrisy.

What these nonbelievers didn't understand was that we were all sinners on the old Earth. The sin wasn't as important as what was in a man's heart. Some who confessed were forgiven; some who confessed were not. Only God can see into a man's heart. Forgiveness is gained by self-awareness and understanding, not by some earthly absolution.

The greater hypocrisy was that nonbelievers loved to point a finger at someone calling themselves a Christian for any little error, while at the same time bending over backwards to defend child molesters, murderers, rapists, baby killers, homicidal Islamic terrorists, and genocidal dictators, and on and on. This was because they had an unreasonable and supernatural hatred toward Christians. Under the gentle prodding of Satan and his Illuminati, they set out to destroy all things "God" on the old Earth. The Illuminati exploited their guilt to this end by feeding them a sense that Christians were judging them all the time.

And this was true to an extent. Many so-called Christians and believers could be extremely judgmental and just as hypocritical, if not more so, than nonbelievers. It was Jesus who first called out the religious leaders (Pharisees) of his day for this very thing. It was Jesus who said, "Let he who is without sin cast the first stone" and "Before you can remove the splinter in your neighbor's eye, remove the branch from your own."

I would often hear coming out of various religions this person or that person wouldn't make it into Heaven. The Baptists would say the Catholics wouldn't make it, the Catholics would say the Protestants wouldn't make it, the Protestants would say the Jews wouldn't make it, the Jews would say the Muslims wouldn't make it, the Muslims would say the infidels wouldn't make it, they'd all say this or that sinner wouldn't make it, and on and on. The truth was that no one but God knew the names written in the Book of Life, and no one but God would sit in judgment.

***

The Stouts were gracious, and after we ate they invited me to spend the night by the fire. I accepted, but it was still early, so I told them I wanted to take off for a bit to explore the city.

I didn't know exactly who or what I was looking for, but I'd heard there were a lot of famous people in Tent City, so I thought I might find somebody I recognized from history or television or the movies or whatever. I guess it was kind of silly searching for celebrities in paradise, but I'm a silly man.

There were a lot of people out, but it was hard to tell who anybody was because most of them had their heads down. There was a lot of contemplating going on in Tent City. Besides, a thick bank of clouds had drifted in, blocking the moonlight, making my shallow hunt even more difficult.

I had just about given up when I spotted Calvin Harper, of all people, the slick reverend whom I'd seen many times on television back on the old Earth. Even in his new body, I had little trouble recognizing the smooth-talking Harper. Now I would have preferred George Washington or even George Carlin for that matter, but Harper was an interesting character and pretty well known in my time.

Good old Cal would show up anytime there an issue concerning black people, especially if he felt his people had been slighted in any way, or if there was any chance he might get on television. Harper came along at the tail end of the Civil Rights Movement. An effective speaker, he was able to shine a light on some of the injustices his people were facing. However, he got so good at defending the rights of black people that he could defend them even when they didn't need defending.

Bigotry and prejudice didn't go away after the Civil Rights era, and things moved much too slowly in that department for a long time. Still, things moved. After all, the first black president had been elected, which did take a white majority vote. If you were to ask people of different races how they were getting along in the years before the Rapture, they would tell you better than ever. But every time Harper got on the television with that fast talk of his, he seemed to get everybody riled up over stuff that had nothing to do with race or bigotry or prejudice, whatsoever, and by the time he was done, everyone was on different sides again. I guess he had become so used to his shtick he couldn't help himself anymore.

***

Anyway, I had nothing against the man; I had nothing against any man—I just thought it was kind of neat to be meeting someone so well known on the old Earth. "Mr. Harper, right?"

He seemed surprised. "Yes."

"I recognized you from television. I just wanted to say hello," I said.

"You're not from around here, are you, son?" he asked. "People don't talk to one another much around here." Gone were most traces of the slick, speed talking Harper I'd remembered from television.

"No, I live in a shack a few days from here. We don't talk much there either," I answered. "I'm heading to New Jerusalem."

"Looking for something, are you?" he said.

"Yeah, I guess I am," I said.

"Have a seat." He pointed to a shaved log on the other side of his fire pit. "I don't have any food; I don't eat much."

"That's okay—I ate," I said and sat down. "I figured you for the suburbs, at least, Mr. Harper."

He laughed. "Yeah, I guess I got a little carried away." Another great thing about the New Kingdom was that nobody defended their actions from the old Earth.

"No one ever had to guess what side of an issue you'd end up on," I said. "But hey, you were consistent anyway."

"I could have really made a difference....I missed the boat.... Heck, I missed the dang ocean."

"At least you tried to do something good with your life...all I ever did was fool around," I said.

He smiled. "You fooled around and I played the fool."

I chuckled.

"I'm lucky to be here," he went on. "I don't even remember when it stopped being about helping people and started being about helping myself. As people came together, there was less of a need for my services. My job was derision based on division. I pushed for integration and equality, but I never let anyone embrace it fully—not on my watch. I kept pushing and pushing. If we got equality in some area, I took it and demanded more. If we got respect, I wanted retribution. If we got love, I wanted their guilt. If they came with color blindness, I made them see again."

✳✳✳

He stood during his monologue, and for a moment I pictured him in front of the cameras again, a few pounds heavier, gesturing to dramatize the hyperbolic plights he once championed, but there was none of that. And his voice carried not indignant rhetoric, but reflection, humility, and the great sadness of lost opportunity.

"I do remember looking in the mirror one morning," he continued, "and I knew what I'd become, but I turned away in an instant and never looked back."

We sat together in silence a long while. Finally, I offered, "You know what I'm doing out here?"

"What are you doing, young man?"

"I'm stalking famous people."

He laughed at that. "Well, you shouldn't have any trouble...you got half of Hollywood living here, and President Nixon's tent is just down the road."

✳✳✳

Richard Milhous Nixon had to resign his presidency after being linked to the burglary of the Democratic Committee Headquarters at the Watergate Hotel in Washington. He had rubber-stamped the plan by some of his cabinet henchmen, who were after information helpful to his reelection campaign. Only the henchmen's burglars were caught, and the whole thing was traced back to the White House.

There had always been political corruption in the U.S, government, but outright criminal theft condoned by a sitting president was a new low. The Office of the Presidency was never seen in the same light again, trust between the American people and its government forever tainted.

Why did Nixon do it? He believed in his own greatness, his superiority, the righteousness of his vision at all cost, and he lost control of his senses. Of course, the demons didn't help. Power was the last gratifying vice of the wealthy, and it was there the demons most flourished, for at a certain pinnacle of supremacy, muted by self-aggrandizement, the conscience goes silent.

How did Nixon make it into paradise? He learned to laugh at himself. It didn't happen overnight. After his public disgrace, he defended his actions to anyone who would listen, believing his superiority somehow made it all right. He attempted to rebuild his reputation by becoming a respected elder statesman. To some degree he succeeded, but the stain of Watergate was too great.

Still, he held to the belief he would be vindicated. This was because the demons kept right on telling him how great he was. They encouraged him to write books, imparting his wisdom to an inferior world in need of his great insight.

One of these books was to be a further testament of his greatest achievement. Nixon was the first U.S. president to visit communist China, opening vital relations with that ardent Cold War enemy.

While doing research for the book, he decided to get in touch with his main liaison, Zhang Wei, an affable Chinese government worker who worked closely with Nixon and his interpreter during the 1972 visit. It was a difficult task, but after months of failed attempts, one of Nixon's assistants managed to get the illusive Zhang Wei on the telephone with the aging former president:

Nixon: Is this Mr. Yang?

Zhang Wei: Yes…Zhang Wei…Zhang Wei…Mr. President Man.

Nixon: You're a tough man to find, Yang.

Zhang Wei: No…they not let me answer phone for long time, Mr. President Man.

Nixon: You remember me, don't you, Mr. Yang?

Zhang Wei: Of course, Mr. President Man, I show you China. You were very big deal.

Nixon: Well, all right, Yang…I just wanted to get some information. I'm writing a book about my trip there…and…ah…there are a few details I've forgotten. I thought you might be able to help.

Zhang Wei: I thought you dead, Mr. President Man.

Nixon: Oh no…I'm not dead…not yet, anyway.

Zhang Wei: Not yet…ha-ha-ha-ha-ha-ha…you do bad, Mr. President Man, very bad…I thought they kill you…ha-ha-ha-ha-ha-ha.

Nixon: No, Yang…I just resigned…that's all.

Zhang Wei: You resign…ha-ha-ha-ha-ha…no one resign here…ha ha-ha-ha.

Nixon: No…ah…I'm just fine, Yang…anyway…I wanted to ask you a few…

Zhang Wei: Just fine…ha-ha-ha-ha-ha…just fine…ha-ha-ha.

Nixon: Yes, yes, Yang…I just need to ask you…

Zhang Wei: You very bad…ha-ha-ha-ha-ha…President Man…very bad…ha-ha-ha.

Nixon: Please, Yang…I need to ask you some….

Zhang Wei: I going now…you bad man…ha-ha-ha-ha-ha…I cannot talk long…bad man…ha-ha-ha-ha.

(Click.)

Nixon was a little stunned. He sat awhile, contemplating Zhang Wei and his silly laugh. He walked over to a mirror. Zhang's laughter and words, still ringing in his head, moved to his lips. "Bad man…ha…ha…ha-ha-ha-ha," he cackled again and again, staring at his long upturned nose and close-set eyes, the pronounced features, the easy highlight of so many political cartoons, of which he was now reminded….

Those cartoons used to make him angry, but now, for some reason, he laughed. It was the first time he had taken a hard look himself. *What an idiot I've been.* The thought made him laugh harder. The demons began to flee. This kind of laughter burned their ears. This was the laughter of revelation, of self-deprecation, the birth of humility, of enlightenment.

People close to Nixon noticed a change. He was more relaxed. He was kinder. He had made his peace with God. He scrapped his current book projects and began writing not for himself and his image, but to help others, to help the country.

***

I said my goodbyes to Calvin Harper. Tent City became darker as the clouds thickened in the night sky. It wasn't a good night to hunt for celebrities. I didn't feel like it anymore anyway. I thought about Harper and the Stouts, the people of Tent City, and still had no idea why I lived in a shack and they lived here. So, why had I come to Tent City? I could only think of one reason: to feel better about myself.

***

The Stouts were sleeping when I returned, but they left a blanket for me by the fire, so I lay there awhile, staring at the faint glow of New Jerusalem in the distance and thinking about the great city. I wondered what the following day would hold for me. I had been drawn to Tent City, but my experiences here weren't anything earth-shattering. Maybe this journey to New Jerusalem was just giving me bits and pieces of what I needed, and it would take years or centuries or eons to find what I was looking for. Who was I kidding? I knew what I wanted—probably what most people wanted—something they could never have: a chance to give back what they stole.

27

Yelling woke me up. It was raining and the Stouts were shouting for me to come into their tent. I thought about it for a second, thanked them for the offer and their hospitality, and declined. I shouted back that I wanted to get an early start toward the city, and I would come back and visit. They said they understood and that I would be welcome anytime. I waved goodbye.

***

The high-waisted trousers and long sleeved white cotton shirt, soaked and hanging from my body, were more popular in the 1930s than in my time on the old Earth. William had been impressed and couldn't wait to discard his woolen garb for a similar change of clothes. I chose them because I remembered the style from films I'd seen of the Great Depression years. I appreciated the conservative look of that era, and the way everyone seemed to be dressed up even in the worst of circumstances. These clothes, often worn with necktie, suit-coat, and dress shoes, remained fashionable for the next three decades, until the late sixties, when from there began a mostly hideous parade of apparel that should never have been repeated: leisure suits, bell-bottoms, platform shoes, pajama-pants, stone washed jeans, backwards baseball caps away from the ball field, and anything made by Ed Hardy. Still, similar styles could be found here in paradise anyway. Unfortunately, Godliness didn't account for poor taste.

***

Even drenched, I wasn't uncomfortable. The new bodies wouldn't allow it. My wet clothes did, however, prevent me from hitching another ride. I didn't want to mess up anybody's vehicle or anything. So I walked again, only slightly disappointed I wouldn't arrive in the great city until after dark.

***

The rain was left to a soft drizzle as I meandered down the gold highway. The road curved, and I hugged the side of a hill to avoid being run over by one of the many vehicles in the increasing traffic gliding toward the city. It wouldn't have mattered much if I did get hit, as the car would have bounced harmlessly off of my new body. Even so, it would have been a disturbing sight to the many people who were so close to the time on the old Earth when hideous car wrecks were commonplace.

***

The thing of it was—cars on the old Earth could have easily been made out of more pliant materials. But just as the oil industry suppressed innovation in engine manufacturing, the steel industry wouldn't let those friendlier materials anywhere near an automobile. Instead, everyone raced around in their iron battering rams without a care in the world. By the 1980s, about 80,000 people were being mangled in automobiles every year. Still, it didn't seem to bother people. They continued speeding down the road, eating their cheeseburgers, shaving, plucking their eyebrows, texting away on their phones, smacking their kids, and who knew what else.

***

The rain stopped, and my clothes were nearly dry by the time I began to pass some of the other pedestrians gathering in number as we moved closer to New Jerusalem. Moving beside a small cluster of these fellow travelers, I heard someone call out my name. I turned to see a tall man walking with a boy. He caught up with me.

"You're Somerset, right?" said the man.

"Excuse me?" I said.

"Private First Class Somerset, right?" he said.

I didn't recognize him, so I stopped to find out who he was.

"It's me, Vince, remember? I was your roomie at Fort Sill for a

268

while."

I still didn't recognize him. As I mentioned, I was twenty-three and living on my friend's couch when the Gulf War broke out. Since I wasn't doing anything else, I thought it might be fun to go over to the Middle East and play army. I was an old man compared to the other recruits, mostly in their late teens. I was like some loser high school graduate, hanging around campus to be popular. It worked. The young recruits looked up to me by default, and I had no shortage of friends and acquaintances, so it was no wonder I couldn't place him.

"Fat Kid...don't you remember, Somerset?" If you didn't have a nickname, peers in the Army called you by your last name. "I'm Fat Kid. You gave me that name!" He seemed excited about that.

"Fat Kid!" Now *I* was excited. This strikingly handsome man with the boy was one of my Army roommates, the roly-poly kid who used to bug the crap out of me with his whining, snoring, nose picking, and potato chip chomping in bed. "I'm sorry; it's Rosario, isn't it? Private Vincent Rosario? I can't believe it! Man, you look different. How have you been? Is this your son?"

"I'm good, I'm good. This is Vince Junior," he said.

I looked at the boy and back at his father. "I'm sorry. I didn't mean to call you that again. I'm sorry I made up that stupid nickname."

Vince Junior laughed and pushed his father a little. Rosario rubbed his son's head. "He knows all about it. I was a slob. I never even tried to take care of myself, at least not then. And I didn't mind it, really," said Vincent.

"Well, I'm sorry, anyway."

"No, the other guys knew me because of it, and it made me laugh."

I remembered he took all the teasing really well. Still, this man wasn't anything like the boy I remembered. That boy was a pain in the behind—not a jerk or anything, just a real pain in the behind. This man was cool and confident. He didn't have food on his chin or anything.

I looked at the boy, who was about nine, a small version of his New Kingdom father. "Nice to meet you, young man," I said.

"Good to meet you, too, sir," said Vince Junior.

"You look just like your father," I said. I gave Vincent a long look. "Wow, Vincent! It's so good to see you!"

"It's good to see you, too."

"Daddy, can I go climb those rocks?" said Vince Junior.

"Yeah, go ahead," said Vince.

***

The rocks the boy was referring to were actually a couple of huge boulders that no parent would have allowed a nine-year-old anywhere near on the old Earth. But this wasn't the old Earth. In one huge leap, Vince Junior was straddling the larger of the boulders, a good twenty feet off the ground. From there, the child Evil Knievel jumped back and forth between the two, a gap of six feet, as casually as if he were playing hopscotch. Vincent never even glanced at the boy.

***

"I don't think I was very nice to you, Vincent. I'm sorry about that," I said.

"Stop it, already." Vincent looked me in the eye. "Do you think it matters one tiny, tiny bit in the grand scheme of things? You teased me a little, but you paid attention to me, and you helped me get through."

"I just remember giving you a bad time."

"No, man—you helped me with inspections, and cleaning my rifle, and my sloppy uniform. Don't you remember? You got me squared away all the time."

"I don't remember all that, but I was probably covering my own behind somehow."

"No, Somerset, you were all right."

"Well, it's nice to hear you say it, anyway. Wow…Private Rosario…I can't get over the change in you. Is there a wife in the picture?"

Vincent finally looked up at his boy, still jumping back and forth across the boulders. "She left us a long time ago. She said I was getting too fat. Do you believe it?" He laughed after that, just for a second. "I wish she could see me now, but she didn't make it."

"She'd be proud of you, Vincent," I said, "Maybe she makes it out." I was hopeful but not optimistic.

He looked sideways at his son. "Maybe."

"My wife left me, too, but it was all my doing," I offered.

"No, she didn't…not you, Somerset!"

"Yeah, she did. What a couple of schmucks, huh?" I said.

"Yeah, a couple of schmucks," he said.

***

Thicker crowds hurried past us along the highway. Many were still hitching rides, hopeful to catch some daylight in the great city, but it was already too late in the day and even the vehicles wouldn't make it before nightfall.

"Will you walk with us?" asked Vincent.

"I'd like that," I said.

Vincent gathered his son, who skipped ahead while we walked together for a few miles, talking and laughing about the old Earth, the Army, the guys we knew. We remembered PFC Rocklin, who needed a place to stay after his discharge and made us padlock him in a vacant room with a big cup so he'd have somewhere to pee. This, so he wouldn't be discovered when they cleared the barrack rooms for morning assembly. And Private Ryder, a tall blond kid, who robbed houses in Philadelphia before joining and was blamed every time something turned up missing. There was Private First Class Reed, whose feet stunk like cat food, so bad nobody would bunk with him. And Sergeant Kyle from Oregon, with his huge head and torso, and skinny, skinny legs, wanting to fight with everybody all the time because he was some kind of All-American wrestler in high school or something. Then there was Private Lowe, slyly unbuckling his belt and unbuttoning his trouser fatigues while he stood conversing, uncomfortably close. He'd work his pants and boxer shorts below his knees, until his Johnson was hanging out an inch from your own crotch. He'd continue to tell story after story just to see how long it took you to notice. When you finally did, and reacted by jumping back a few feet, screaming at him, or smacking the son of a gun, old Lowe would fall over laughing for about a half hour.

They were good guys, all of them. None of us ever made it out of Fort Sill. The Gulf War was over before we even finished training. We all thought we wanted to go, but instead we spent two years training and hanging round the fort. That's when I gave up on real soldiering and became the older frat brother in a platoon full of teenagers.

***

271

The Gulf War started after Saddam Hussein, the Iraqi dictator, decided he didn't have enough people in his own country to torture, rape, and murder, so he decided to invade his neighbor Kuwait. George Bush, the president at the time, gathered a coalition of other nations to help liberate the tiny country and to drive Saddam and his army back to Bagdad. Playing politics, Bush and the other leaders allowed Saddam to remain in power and to continue his reign of terror against his own countrymen.

Later, his son, George W. Bush, would also become president of the United States, sending an army himself into Iraq. He told the American people that Saddam was hiding weapons of mass destruction and needed to be taken out. He was mistaken. By the time U.S. troops pulled out, a half million people were dead.

Why did he do it? Critics said the president wanted the oil in Iraq. They also believed his vice president, Dick Cheney, put him up to it to make a fortune off military contracts for the companies he was in bed with. Others said he wanted to finish what his father started. And some said he simply hated Saddam and wanted to take out the fiend.

What was the answer? Demons told him it was a good idea. They were messing around again.

***

We reached a clearing along the road where a herd of deer frolicked on the other side of a stream. Vince Junior asked his father if he could play with them. Vincent looked toward the sun, which was getting pretty low on the horizon. "Might as well," he said. "I don't think we can make it before dark anyway."

"Thanks, Dad." The boy ran through the clearing and right over the stream without creating so much as a ripple. The deer looked up, and for a moment, I thought they might run, but they began a dance of excitement, circling the boy and playing happily.

"It's beautiful; he's beautiful," I told Vincent.

"Yeah," he said, and he paused. "He never knew his mother. He was just a baby when she left. She hated me. She never wanted to get pregnant. She got mixed up with some bad people, druggies and the like. A lot of it was my fault. We used to party all the time. But I wanted to quit after he was born. She kept it up. It was hard after she left, but it changed me. I stopped being a slug. I took care of myself. More importantly, I picked up a Bible and began going to church again. I used to go when I was a kid. I don't know why I stopped. It was so amazing coming back. Most people didn't understand what it could do. I gave it all up to Him—all the worry, all the fear, all the ugliness I had in me…all the weight. I let it go, but I couldn't have done it without my boy." He looked at his son running freely with the herd. "That's why I'm here, because of him."

"I'm proud of you, Vincent. I'm not sure I ever gave it all up to Him," I said.

"You must have," he said.

"I don't know. You ever think you don't deserve to be here?"

"Every day," he said.

"Yeah."

***

We sat down near the edge of the clearing and talked some more about our Army days. After a while, Vincent decided to play with his son. He asked me to join them. It would be dark in a half hour, I surmised, and I told him to go ahead, I would be leaving soon anyway.

"Well, goodbye, Somerset."

"Goodbye, Rosario."

He saluted and turned, sprinting after his son like an Olympian. I remembered yelling at him during PT one day because he had cost everybody an extra mile on the morning run for being so slow. I was a jerk. Seeing him now brought shame and joy to my heart at the same time.

***

I watched them play awhile longer. It made me smile and think of Sophie. I didn't like being so far from her. And even though I didn't get to see her all the time, now that she was an adult, living together with my ex-wife like sisters, living her own life, the years of separation during the Tribulation had taken their toll on my psyche, and I needed her close. I had asked her to come with me, but she told me I needed to go alone the first time. She was right.

Sophie was always right. Sophie was a smart girl on the old Earth, but here she was some sort of ethereal genius. She had already spent nearly eight years in Heaven. Still thirteen when I first saw her again,

273

still my little girl, but different. She reminded me of the angels I'd met, brighter and more loving than most humans, childlike but fiercely and beautifully moral. She knew things instinctively—even back when I first saw her again—things of a spiritual nature, things about Heaven and the universe, about God and people, things I would've had to dig up at the Hall of Knowledge. One night, a few months after I'd arrived, we were lying on the grass in front of her house looking up at the stars, and I asked her what it was like after the Rapture. She didn't describe it as I expected, as any thirteen-year-old might; she said this:

"*I was weightless, Daddy, removed from the pain and the darkness I felt on the old Earth. It was all there. I could see it, but it meant nothing. There was light coming out of me, so much light, Daddy—much more than now. All the people had so much light and the angels did, too. I could see the light, but it wasn't that. It was that I could feel the light. There was so much of it. It was in me and around me, Daddy, and I thought it was all the beauty that could possibly be. How tiny, how meaningless, my old Earth troubles, a dark ball I could hold in my hand or toss into oblivion. But I didn't. I watched it from afar because I wasn't quite ready to let it go. But I could have, Daddy…I could have let it go.*"

She was teaching me. My dark ball was a great big boulder I carried on my back that I needed to drop before it crushed me. That much I knew; I just didn't know how. I should have asked her. I had become the child in our relationship. Perhaps I always was. And though it was shameful, I felt only pride for her. Still, I couldn't bring myself to ask.

***

I left Vincent and his young son to continue my journey. As darkness fell, the glow of New Jerusalem grew brighter with each mile, until it felt so close I couldn't contain my excitement, and I began running as fast as my new body would let me. I suppose I could have run all the way from my shack, but there was a time to run and a time to walk. This was a time to run.

Up and down the low hills I ran. I soon left the highway to follow the glow, darting through yet another valley of orange grass, this one circling a shiny silver lake. I ran beside the lake until I reached the base of a long ridge, which looked to be mostly flat on top. I spotted the trailhead, which led to a series of switchbacks, and I slowed to a fast walk to savor the anticipation now building frantically with every step.

Looking up, all I could see was an intense and massive light that would have blinded an old Earth pair of eyes. I don't know how long it took me to reach the top, though it wasn't long considering the number of switchbacks I'd traversed. But even having climbed so high, I couldn't see the city because it was below the far edge of the massive ridge.

Not that it made a difference—I was immersed in such a glaring light I could only see my feet now, shuffling carefully toward the other edge. But instead of reaching the edge, I stumbled into a maze of boulders not visible from the bottom. The boulders gave me a break from the light, and my eyes quickly adjusted to the night sky.

Weaving my way through the huge rocks, I began to hear strange sounds. I knew they came from the city, but it wasn't the clanging, honking, yelling, screaming, screeching, frantic noise of an old Earth metropolis. This sound was low and smooth, calm and beautiful—more beautiful as I moved closer. It was music, a chorus of angels welcoming the new arrivals.

***

Rays of light pierced the surrounding rocks, and I knew I had reached the last boulder. I paused for just a moment, turned a corner, and beheld the great city for the first time.

28

Nothing could have prepared me for New Jerusalem. It was more spectacular than any had described or I could possibly have imagined. Spread across the great valley below, which must have stretched fifty square miles, the city seemed to reach the horizon on three sides. The center of the valley, a slight plateau, cradled the giant pyramid, glazed in gold and glass. Its base covered at least five square miles of the plateau, and its peak reached another mile into the sky. Its surface was impossibly smooth, as if somehow lifted from a mold in one piece.

As tall as the giant pyramid was, directly behind it, but a great distance away, a silver skyscraper was stretched so high I couldn't see even its middle and top at the same time.

Surrounding the pyramid were hundreds of smaller buildings of every shape and size, made from gold, platinum, silver, bright copper, and other metals I could not name, each magnificent in its own right.

A street of gold brick circled the pyramid, more streets jutting from it like spokes in a wheel. Thousands of people milled and moved about, and vehicles of all kinds went to and fro, gliding high and low. Brilliant light came from everywhere, yet no fixture, lamp, or bulb could be seen.

***

I stared in awe for close to an hour, and I could have stood on that ridge for days, but I was also anxious to see what the city had to offer, so finally I looked for a way down.

There were many to choose from. Now I noticed others along the ridge choosing their routes. To my left were elevators, moving at great speeds; just below me, a wide staircase; to my right, large platforms where bus-like transports picked up scores of waiting passengers; and beside those, smaller platforms, scattered hundreds of feet apart, where children leaped like frogs in quick succession down to the valley floor.

Jumping with the children was not an option, and the buses and staircase were extremely crowded, so I went to the elevator and waited my turn. Once inside, I barely had time to blink, when suddenly the elevator came to a halt, and the door slid open at the bottom of the ridge. Now I was nearly eye level with the great city, and it seemed to absorb me just as I absorbed it.

***

All streets seemed to lead to the giant pyramid, like sun rays in reverse. I moved as one with the masses, carried in the current of a slow but determined river of light. The shops and stores lining the streets were mostly empty because the crowd had one intention, to reach the pyramid, now a mere block away, before it closed for the evening.

***

As I mentioned before, the Great Pyramid of Giza was built by demons posing as gods. New Jerusalem was a replica of the City of Heaven from where the fallen angels had been exiled hundreds of thousands of years before. Giza was their attempt at recreating part of that city. And though they managed to build an amazing structure, they failed miserably. Theirs was but a child's clay model in comparison to the monolithic brilliance of the Great Pyramid. The demons knew they had fallen short with Giza, but it was their way of thumbing their noses at God, letting Him know the Earth was their kingdom. And in a way it was, for a while anyway.

***

But now it belonged solely to God, and it was glorious. I was humbled again, and I felt my smallness, and felt blessed, so blessed to be there—as I knew most of those around me were, because I felt their joy.

***

Yet there were a few—I sensed them—a tiny, unbelievable few, like those from Tent City, who were feeling a twinge, a slight, nearly imperceptible sliver of jealousy. I looked around and I became sad. I began weeping then, weeping for those poor fools. And I saw that others were also weeping. But the few did not notice, and they marched toward the pyramid with their germ intact.

***

Vehicles circled to view the Great Pyramid, stopping occasionally to drop passengers. I continued moving toward it. Crowds from every direction converged on pillars marking the entrance. Like some opulent and eclectic Halloween party, the crowd wore clothing from every period of the old Earth. I reached the steps below the pillars and continued with the flow of glowing bodies, moving past pillars and under an enormous gold archway engraved in ancient Aramaic. It was John 3-16: *For God so loved the world that He gave His only begotten Son, that whosoever believeth in Him should not perish, but have everlasting life.*

***

I could read it because I could read, speak, and understand all languages. I could read, write, and speak fluent Hebrew, Greek, Latin, Spanish, German, French, and Russian as well. I was also fluent in Chinese, Japanese, Korean, Vietnamese, Arabic, Nepali, Somali, Romanian, Wu, Xiang, Fula, and hundreds more. I wasn't extra smart or special or anything. Everyone here could do it—an added bonus of our new bodies.

***

Once inside, we passed through a long tunnel leading to the center of the pyramid, a vast open space. On the opposite wall there hung a crucifix carved in gold and measuring nearly four stories. On either side, only slightly smaller and carved out of multi-hued marble slabs, were hung the Stations of the Cross. Looking up, I could not see the ceiling, only elevators speeding into blackness.

Nobody in our group went directly to the elevators, but like me, they studied in awe the magnificent carvings: Jesus is condemned, Jesus carries His cross, Jesus falls, Jesus meets His mother... These carvings were like nothing seen on the old Earth, not in any cathedral, not in the Vatican itself. They seemed to breathe, to speak somehow, and the intense detail brought most, including myself, to tears, and I cried for the second time that evening.

I didn't know exactly what the others were feeling, but I knew it must have been something like I felt. It was like my own daughter was going through Christ's ordeal, and I couldn't bear it. I was overwhelmed, and along with many others, collapsed to my knees with heartache.

***

There were hundreds of wooden benches set back in small vestibules where people sat collecting their thoughts. Other groups headed toward the elevators. More came through the entrance and the tears continued.

I stayed, crouched on the floor, for some time. I thought I knew pain. I thought I knew sacrifice. I knew nothing.

***

Not everyone was hysterical. Some had been here before and some had seen their own children suffer and die; their bodies knew well the pain, and they comforted the others. A kind woman put her arm around my shoulder and led me to one of the benches. I immediately felt better.

Her name was Umut; I knew it meant hope. Umut told me she was from Turkey, that two of her children were murdered in front of her. She said she cursed God and tried to kill herself by cutting her own throat. Some nuns found her and patched her up. Umut woke up in the back of a church. She told me she hated God. And for a long time, she still wanted to kill herself. She couldn't handle the pain. But the nuns prayed for her and told her to pray for peace and understanding. She resisted at first, but they were insistent. They told her that time was a gift from God, that time would ease her pain. They were right. As the pain subsided, Umut prayed more and more, until she came to an understanding. It was the only understanding she needed. It was this: her children were with God and they were happy.

***

Nuns were always doing great stuff like that on the old Earth. They were the rock of Catholicism, which had seen more than its share of scandal and controversy. This cardinal was taking bribes, that pope was

279

in bed with a dictator; this priest molested children, that bishop covered it up, and on and on. By the time of the Antichrist, Satan was deeply entrenched within the hierarchy of the Vatican, paving the way for the last pope, the False Prophet, who would promote a counterfeit Catholicism, a blasphemous religion devoted to his satanic master.

Don't get me wrong. There were great priests, and great bishops, even great cardinals and popes, who had done wonderful work, but the whole of it had become corrupt, a big infected corporate and political animal that could not be saved even by the saints.

***

Her words lifted my sadness. Then I heard the singing I'd heard from the cliffs. It seemed to be coming from the walls. I hugged and thanked Umut. I left the vestibule, passing back through the great hall where many still recovered and comforted one another below the Stations of the Cross.

I looked up. I was directly below the Twelfth Station. His eyes closed, his head tilted, blood dripping from his wounds—Jesus dead on the cross. I closed my eyes and pictured another lifeless body, a female, a friend, battered and bloody, and I would have wept again, but the music filled me, and I couldn't push back the joy.

***

The music lifted everyone in the room. I moved toward the elevators. There were signs posted for hundreds of different offices and meetings and seminars located on the many floors. The most popular, I'd heard, were the seminars led by the different apostles. The times were posted next to the names of the speakers. It was late; most of the lectures and classes of the evening had already begun. But, to my surprise, Paul would be speaking in a few minutes.

Of all the apostles, his story and letters in the Bible most carried me and kept up my hope through the Tribulation. He would be speaking on the seventy-seventh floor.

***

Almost as soon as the elevator door closed, it seemed, it opened again. We exited onto a long balcony that lined the inner edge of the pyramid. Looking down, I could barely make out the people milling around the Stations of the Cross. I moved with the crowd, all heading the same direction, until we reached a staircase leading to a large auditorium that must have been somewhere near the tip of the pyramid. I entered with the crowd and scattered to find an open seat.

The room filled quickly, and we waited in silence for the great man to appear. A moment later, a man stood from a seat in the front row and approached the podium. He was short, mostly bald. His new body was the same as ours except it glowed brighter and more intensely. I knew it was him, though I had no idea what he looked like.

"Peace and love and blessings in the name of Christ our Savior," he said in Greek, in a voice so calm and confident and eloquent it sent shivers through my body. "I am glad you are here, good people, but I am sad listening to your hearts. And what I tell to you now may have little meaning, I'm afraid, for some of you are not ready, but I say it anyway because it will plant a seed that will help your light grow."

He paced for a few moments. "It's true you are sinners," he continued, "and you are full of the guilt of those sins, for they have been laid out before you, and you are devastated, for you have been in contemplation of those sins."

His voice became louder, filled the room from every direction, and without a microphone or a single speaker. "I was a sinner. I was greedy and full of pride. I was self-righteous and jealous and hateful, a killer of men. I stoned a man to death. I smiled as he fell, and while he took a long time to die. I killed him because I thought I was better than him."

"Stand up, my friend!" he shouted and smiled, pointing a short finger toward the audience. Another man sitting in the front row, whose light was even brighter than Paul's, stood up. "Do you see his light?" he continued. "This is Stephen. I condemned this great man of God. I bore witness against him. I watched with satisfaction as the crowd flung stones at his naked body. I tortured and killed this man as surely as if I'd thrown each and every stone." Paul was crying then. But as the tears poured over his face, he began to smile, until the tears and the smile became the same joy. Then he shouted out: "And Stephen forgave me! God forgave me! Christ forgave me!"

Stephen stepped up to the podium and hugged Paul. Their embrace lasted a long time. "You forgave yourself," Stephen said.

Paul nodded and Stephen sat down. "I *have* forgiven myself; I have accepted the pardon," he continued. "I was on the road to Damascus...." He paused and the crowd roared. And Paul smiled more. "You know the story?" he laughed. "I was on the road to Damascus when Jesus came to me and brought me home...."

***

We all knew well the story of Paul—his amazing conversion, his relentless and dangerous mission of spreading the Good News, and of his martyrdom, from the Bible and other historical accounts—but I learned even more about him at the Hall of Knowledge.

He wasn't always Paul. He was once Saul of Tarsus, by ancestry and religion a Jew, by birth and upbringing Greek, and by citizenship Roman. He received a formal education in a strict, rabbinical school, which fostered hatred toward Christ and his followers. Saul took his hatred and joined the Sanhedrin (the Jewish religious court) in the condemnation and persecution of Christians.

After Stephen's murder, he was on the road to the city of Damascus, where he was going to speak on behalf of the Sanhedrin against Christians being held prisoner by the Romans. About halfway there, a blinding light stopped him in his tracks, filling the sky and the road. He heard a thunderclap and a voice called his name.

"Saul, Saul," said the voice.

"Who is there? I cannot see!" said Saul.

"Why do you persecute me?" said the voice.

"Please...who are you? The light...I cannot see!"

"I am the one you persecute...I am the one crucified. I live."

"Let me see you!"

"Go to the city and a man will tell you what to do."

At that moment, the light grew more intense, until his eyes began to burn. Paul pleaded for the pain to end, yet no one answered. Still, the pain began to wane and the light to fade, but, when it was over, he could not see.

A traveler returning home took pity on him, and upon Paul's insistence, took him to Damascus. He wasn't there more than an hour when Ananias, a disciple of Jesus, found him resting at the traveler's home. He told Paul that Jesus had sent him to heal him and to give him a message. Ananias placed his hands over Paul's eyes, and when he lifted them he could see again.

Paul was astounded, but even more astounded by Ananias' message. It was this: "You have been chosen as a vessel of the Lord Jesus Christ. You will bear his name to the Gentiles, to kings, and to the children of Israel. And you will suffer greatly for it."

Paul's first response to Ananias wasn't noted in the Bible. Paul answered him with one word. He said this: "What?"

But Paul was filled with the Holy Spirit that day and would eventually spread the gospel to every known corner of the world. For this he was hunted, imprisoned, beaten, tortured, and finally murdered. The persecutor had become the persecuted— such change in a man could only be possible by the truth and greatness of God. And without Paul, Christianity could not have spread as it did. So many, here in the New Kingdom, owed their eternal life to him.

***

Paul continued, "you are here because Jesus has come to you. He has seen your hearts, and He wants to bring you home. Which one of you has tortured and killed a man? Yet, it is I standing at the podium; it is I who knows redemption. You were given a pardon. Your sins have been paid for. Accept your redemption. You still have mountains to climb and perils to overcome. But they are not of Satan anymore. The destroyer has no influence here. The perils come from within, and they dim your light. Accept the pardon. Forgive yourselves, good people. Peace and love in Christ our Lord and Savior."

***

The crowd gave him a lengthy standing ovation. Paul disappeared behind the podium. When the applause finally let up, the room became a mixture of laughter and tears. The collective light emanating from the bodies in the room seemed to have intensified. People hugged and shook hands. As I turned to leave, I noticed a very bright light coming from the back of auditorium behind the podium. I thought at first Paul had reemerged, but then I realized it was a woman.

She walked out into the audience to greet and comfort some of those who were still milling around. She seemed taller than I remembered and her hair flowed, and she was clean, of course, and even more beautiful, but it was her. It was Danny. I closed my eyes, but there was Danny still, until I shook away the image of her battered and lifeless body and opened my eyes again.

29

I was in a panic. I needed to get out of there; I wasn't ready to face her, at least not yet. Still, for some reason I couldn't move. I felt she knew, without looking at me, that I was in the room. And as she hugged and held hands and stroked the people, she seemed to be circling toward me, and soon we would be face to face.

***

My stomach hurt again like it did when I first met her. It had to be my anxiety. It couldn't be yearning of the romantic kind. There was no such thing. Still, I was torn. I wanted to be near her as much as I wanted to turn and run from my shame. Those thoughts paralyzed me, but as she moved closer, a worse kind of panic set in, and I was able to lift one heavy foot, which was just enough to urge the other and get me moving toward the doors. Once there, like Lot's wife, I looked back before I bolted. It wasn't enough to turn me to salt, but close. Unmistakably, Danny had seen me. She wasn't looking in my direction any longer, but she'd seen me. I could tell by that look of hers—that slight smile, not quite a smirk, and the way her eyes seemed set to roll but would not. I could almost hear her: *George, quit being so silly...come talk to me.* She carried no anger, no pity; I knew that, too. And still, I ran for it.

***

Sodom, that ancient cesspool where Lot and his wife once made their home, had been condemned by God for its unapologetic wickedness. But Abraham had made a bargain with the Lord: *If there were even ten righteous men left in the doomed city, He would spare the whole place.* So God sent two angels disguised as men to have a look. Abraham's nephew, Lot, met them at the gate, but so depraved had things become that by the time they reached his home, a mob had already formed, eager to have relations with the visitors.

Lot managed to get the angels inside, but the crowd was growing and threatening to break in and kill everyone if Lot didn't send out his new guests. Lot refused, even offering his virginal daughters in their place. But the angels weren't about to let that happen. They had seen enough. They went outside and blinded every one of the fools. Then they took Lot and his family out of the city before it could be destroyed by hot sulfur sent from the Lord.

As they were leaving, the angels told everyone to cover their eyes and not to look back at the burning city, lest they turn into pillars of salt. But Lot's wife was the curious sort and couldn't help herself.

Some people said it was mean what God had done to the poor woman, just for looking back at the doomed city, turning her to salt and all. And what was the big deal about looking back anyway?

The Lord was making a point that people would remember. The point was that no earthly ties, no pleasures, no material goods, no memories, were worth taking your eyes off Heaven even for a moment. The heart was either with God or with the trappings of the old Earth. Besides, Lot's wife didn't feel a thing, and she was much better off in Heaven.

But why turn her into a pillar of salt? Why couldn't he just snatch her up or strike her down? He did it for effect. No one would have remembered the story otherwise. God did all kinds of things for effect—storms and floods, bringing people back from the dead, parting seas, talking bushes, and all kinds of neat junk. The drama of the event had served a purpose, one that was especially tough to forget. You ask almost anyone: *Yep, Lot's wife looked back. Yep, she turned to salt. I know that story well.* I knew the story myself, backwards practically; even as a child I knew it. But what did I do anyway? I kept looking back, of course.

***

Through the doors, down the stairs, to the elevator I ran. To the bottom floor as fast as I'd ascended, then across the lobby, through the entrance, down the steps, past the crowds, up one golden street, down another, beneath the floating traffic, I ran some more. I ran longer and harder than I had ever run before. I ran to forget.

The mind of my old Earth body would have been sufficiently clouded with fatigue, the body itself near collapse miles before. But this body would not tire, would not produce a drop of sweat, would not let me forget. It was pointless.

I slowed to a fast walk. Never once did I notice the grandeur of the city surrounding me. Instead, flashing images of Danny, wonderful and violent, passed back and forth like so many bartered visions in the marketplace of my mind's eye. The more I tried shaking them off, the faster they came, until I thought I might go mad. I fell to my knees crying out, "Only me, God! Only George Somerset could go mad in paradise! Yes, I admit it. I'm a dang fool, Lord. I'm a dang fool!"

I looked to the sky to face the addressee of my rant. Except I could not see the sky, only a glowing white sign on a gigantic square building. Three words, at least 300 feet across; sixteen letters, each 25 feet tall—which read: *THEATER OF HISTORY.*

***

I was distracted as soon as I saw it. Most people had come to New Jerusalem wishing to meet one of the apostles, or Mary, or perhaps Jesus Himself. I, on the other hand, being a pathetic and unapologetic couch potato, was most excited for this place—paradise's version of the History Channel.

I smiled—a nod to God for landing me there—climbed the wide marble steps and entered the massive theater through one of the many double doors. Just inside, perched on stools behind the glass of a long booth, dozens of brightly uniformed workers handed tickets to lines of waiting theatergoers.

***

That's what was so neat about the New Kingdom, everything done like it once was on the old Earth during the best of times—doormen, ticket takers, ushers, and everybody in fancy uniforms and such. And even though there wasn't any money in the New Kingdom, they passed out tickets for everything anyway, so we didn't have to walk in everywhere like a bunch of hobos. God was a good guy like that, making things like they used to be, familiar and all, just because he knew we liked it that way. Who would do that? That cracked me up.

***

I said thank you to the girl in the booth and collected my ticket. Behind the booth the theater lobby was filled with concessions stands where uniformed concessioners passed out all manner of food and drink. There was popcorn, candies, fruit, breads, meats, juices, milk, and so much more, too many to name, and some I had never seen before, but none of it junk food like you'd get at a theater on the old Earth, with fake butter and the red and yellow dye and all. It was all fresh and made from scratch, and the whole place smelled like a bakery I once visited on a trip to my dad's hometown in Nebraska when I was a boy.

Regardless of the appetizing odor, I wasn't in the mood to eat. I wasn't thirsty, either, but I ordered a bottle of water, if for no other reason than to have something in my hand like my fellow patrons, to be the same in some small way, for I believed them, at least, to be content.

I headed down a long hallway toward lighted doorways marking the entrances to the many individual theaters. The doorways glowed *vacant* or *occupied*. Choosing an empty theater, I entered through the swinging door.

Inside, though fairly dark, I could easily make out the large screen hanging on the wall behind four rows of six plush seats, like a home theater in some rich guy's house on the old Earth. Each seat had a keypad and a small screen reading: *Touch Here.* I picked the middle seat in the middle row, just like I would have at any theater on the old Earth.

I pressed the screen. Immediately the little screen and the big screen turned a bright blue with thin moving clouds upon them. Then a loud clear voice filled the small theater from all directions. *"Welcome to the Theater of History,"* said the voice. That cracked me up, too. It sounded like Darth Vader or somebody with authority like that. That was God being a good guy again.

"Almost everything that happened on the old Earth is here," the voice continued. *"Type an approximate date and place or a brief description of the*

event, or all of the above. The event will appear exactly as it was then on the large screen in front of you. You may press the fast-forward or rewind button to reach the exact portion of the event you are looking for. Don't worry; the screenings are fine-tuned to each audience, so nothing inappropriate or traumatic to any specific audience member will be shown at any time. You may begin."

My heart just about ran out of my chest, frantic at the thought of viewing anything from my past. What was I thinking coming in here? I never did die on the old Earth, so my life never passed before me or anything like that. I knew everything would be revealed about my life in the final judgment, but that was a long way away, and I didn't feel ready just yet to see myself pulling all the crap I did on the old Earth.

Besides, I still couldn't shake the incessant thoughts and images of Danny and the horrible thing I had done to her, and it certainly wouldn't help to view any of it on the big screen. No, the only way to shake them would be to look at other people's crap. And it needed to be extra crappy. I typed: *1-9-4-5, H-i-t-l-e-r, b-u-n-k-e-r, s-u-i-c-i-d-e.*

***

The funny thing was, as I was typing, I realized something: I don't know why, but I'd always felt kind of sorry for the man at that moment in his life. I mean I know he did all this horrific stuff to everybody, and I hated him for that and all, but still, I just couldn't help but feel bad for him, for anybody so doomed in the moment. There were probably only about a half-dozen people in the whole history of the old Earth who were as crappy to other people as he was. I imagined he must have been scared and full of regrets, but was it just for his fate, or did he have any actual remorse? I always wondered about stupid stuff like that.

***

Abruptly, the lights dimmed further and there on the big screen, sitting on a couch and hunched over a Luger lying on a small coffee table, was good old Adolf in living color, looking pretty sick and tired and everything. He was saying something I couldn't understand, not because it was in German, but because he was mumbling in a barely audible voice.

Then a woman appeared that must have been Eva Braun, though I didn't recognize her, except for the blonde hair, because she was looking pretty sick and tired herself. Hitler became angry and began

288

ranting at the poor woman. "It's time; it's time," he said.

She was crying hysterically and grabbed his hands. "No, I won't be alone," she said. "We go together."

"Nonsense, Eva," said Hitler, pulling away. "You have to be sure I'm gone."

"Aren't you afraid?" asked Eva. She sat next to him, grimacing and tugging at her hair with two fingers.

"For what, Eva?" he yelled. "I tried to make Germany great, but they betrayed me. History will prove my greatness." His voice was shrill, unconfident.

"I'm afraid," said Eva.

"We should be proud of what…" But he stopped in mid- sentence. The room he was sitting in looked to have darkened a moment before, almost imperceptibly. Hitler seemed to notice, too, and he looked nervously about the room. His face changed. It was either madness or fear or both—I could not be sure. I pressed the rewind button. He began the sentence again, and I caught a shadowy mass move above his head. I thought it must be a demon.

"Enough talk," he said, "get your pill." He reached for the Luger and checked the chamber.

I had seen enough. As terrible a person as he was, I didn't want to see his brains flying out all over the place or anything, and I didn't want to see that poor miserable women die either. My desire to watch another man's misery had only made things worse.

***

I pushed the red button on the keyboard, and the screen went all blue and cloudy again. I typed: *D-a-l-l-a-s, P-i-t-t, S-u-p-e-r-B-o-w-l-X*, something, anything to lighten my mood. It was the first Super Bowl I'd ever seen. I heard the roar of the crowd, and the screen lit up with the stadium on its feet and the players lining up. It was the fourth quarter. The Cowboys were behind, but from the shotgun the great Roger Staubach moved the team steadily down the field. Inside the forty, he took the snap, rolled to his left and threw a thirty-four yard strike to wide receiver Percy Howard for a touchdown.

It wasn't enough. They lost the game by four points, but they had fought hard, and I remembered becoming a diehard Cowboy fan because of that game. If Pittsburgh had lost, I would have become a Steeler fan that day. I'd always preferred the underdog.

***

The football game was just the thing I needed to get me out of my head. I was again ready, I thought, for some heavier history. My favorite documentaries on the History Channel were about World War II. Perhaps because it was the last American war with a defined purpose and an altruistic goal that hadn't been clouded or hampered by political correctness or questionable motives. I must have seen every documentary of that war two or three times. I had also watched the movie *Saving Private Ryan* and the scenes at Normandy Beach with all the blood and flying body parts and whatnot, acclaimed for their realism, at least a dozen times. It was probably my favorite movie. None of it could have prepared me.

The screen lit up again. I had typed the word blitzkrieg. It was a German word meaning *lightning war*. The term was first coined after the German Army's rapid onslaught of Poland, an invasion that took merely four weeks. I lasted three and a half minutes. This was no movie. I might just as well have been in the middle of the battle myself, screaming and covered in blood. The scenes were indescribable—the violent clarity, the intense awful noise, the agonizingly vivid color of death—horrors all too much even for me, a tired veteran of film gore and witness to horrors of the Tribulation.

I needed to get away from it. I would have turned it off after the first deadly explosion, except I was in shock. I should have left the theater, but I didn't want to leave with those images still fresh. I began to punch frantically on the keyboard, places and dates, anywhere, anytime, any way to escape. But it was no use. Every place I searched, more violence and mayhem: beatings, hangings, shootings, stabbings, clubbings, fighting, kidnappings, thieving, rape, war and murder—a slide show of our ugliness, old Earth's very own home movie. I shut it off.

***

I sat for a while in the leftover haze of that overwhelmingly dark imagery. Then a thought came: *I wasn't thinking about Danny any longer.* I forced a slow and broken laugh from the bottom of my throat at the irony. It was enough to break the spell, which gave me a chance to

290

form another thought: *I need to go to a safe and familiar place.* It was a bad idea that would prove neither safe nor familiar.

I typed two simple words into the keyboard: *M-e; B-a-b-y.* The screen lit up for a third time. The blue sky faded, and there was my mom with her big weird glasses being helped out of our station wagon by my father. My brother Gerry was standing on the porch with my aunt, who was holding Geoff, all waiting for their little brother to come home. My mom's smile was huge; my father's even bigger.

***

I didn't remember that part from the old grainy home movies, him smiling so wide. I'd heard he didn't want the name George for me. My father had a childhood nemesis by that name, but my mom insisted. I always thought he hated me; I thought I knew it after I heard that. It must have been one of the few times she'd gotten what she'd asked for.

I mostly remembered him mad at me or my mom or somebody or other all the time, but especially me. I was afraid of him. He was big and he could yell like nobody's business. When he yelled, I couldn't speak. Then he'd interrogate me. I couldn't answer with him yelling and all, so I'd just cry. This made him even angrier, and he'd yell some more. If I didn't say the right thing, I'd often as not get a whipping.

***

I fast-forwarded a little. My father held me and tickled my chin. I kept going. I was a toddler, walking precariously while he urged me toward him, arms outstretched. Then he was playing with all of us, chasing us around the backyard. Gina was there, and he caught her and pulled her gently to the ground with him. We boys began to pile on, and he rolled over to protect her as we wrestled around on his back.

Forward through time, finger on the button: Dad throwing soft pitches, Dad driving us to Boy Scouts, Dad singing in the car, Dad cooking his stew, Dad with a cold wash-rag on my forehead, Dad with me on his lap watching an old Western, and on and on.

Further in time: Dad pacing around a waiting room while a doctor set my broken arm, Dad arguing with my teacher about my grade being unfair, Dad siding with me after I quit my first job, Dad telling my mother he was worried about me, Dad, close to death, asking my

291

mother to take care of the credit card mess I had gotten myself into, Dad telling me he loved me...

Who was this man? Where was all that anger, the constant yelling, the whippings, the put-downs, that hatred towards me I so cherished with my angst? This wasn't my childhood. Or was it? What had I done with it? I had kept all the bad memories, taken my anger and erased the good in him, brushed it off my memory with the back of my hand, rewritten my own version, carried it with me like some schoolboy's note to excuse my reckless behavior.

Who was my father? What right did I have to disparage his life? Who was George Somerset? Did I even know? What did my daughter take from our life together? What did I give her to take? Could I even remember all the things I'd done to her? Did I know what I had done to Renee? To everyone I knew? I knew I lied to people's faces. How much did I lie to myself? How could I be truly sorry for things I refused to think about? How could I be forgiven? Why was I even here? How did God see me? It was time to introduce George Somerset to himself. And so I watched.

***

I watched my brothers getting whipped for my lie about the donut. I watched as I stole money off the dresser of my hardworking father. I watched as I picked a fight with a kid named Donald just because I knew I could beat him up. I watched as I ditched church. I watched as I read a Bible one morning and smoked weed the same afternoon. I watched as I cheated on practically every girlfriend I ever had.

I saw my drunkenness, my boasting, my gluttony, my lust. I saw my perversions disintegrate every bit of morality I possessed. I heard the profanity and the blasphemies spewing from my mouth on a daily basis. I watched the promises I made to God while suffering go broken as soon as I felt better. I saw my wife curled on the floor in pain at the news of my infidelity. I saw my little girl hiding under the covers while Renee and I screamed at each other over and over again.

***

I watched it all. And when I couldn't remember any more specifics, I just typed in *"the rest of George's sins,"* and there it played: one long, awful movie about a pathetic creep who destroys everything good around him.

292

There goes George driving drunk and smashing into the side-rail of a freeway exit, causing his friend a permanent limp. There goes George running a stolen credit card and taking the cash out of the register of the gas station he works at for fuel he never pumped. Now George is at a whorehouse in Mexico, wasted on tequila, spending money he doesn't have.

See George push his girlfriend into getting an abortion. See George snorting cocaine until all hours of the morning. See George pick another fight at a bar. See George give out another bad loan. See George the vandal. See George the liar. See George the thief. See George the pervert. See George the hypocrite, and on and on and on.

***

Now see George in his house. There he is fighting with his wife. There's his little girl crying in her bedroom. There goes George packing his bag. There goes George slapping his wife. There's his little girl standing outside her room screaming. There goes George walking toward the door. There's his little girl holding on to his leg. There goes George pushing her away. There's his little girl begging and sobbing: *"Daddy, Daddy, Daddy, Daddy…"* There goes George.

Then I heard a loud voice, and a shiver went through my core. But it only said this: *"The Theater of History will be closing for the evening in five minutes."*

30

I exited the Theater of History to find the streets of New Jerusalem fairly empty, the light of the great city dimmed. Dark clouds had moved in, shielding the night sky. There began a heavy snow.

I walked in a stupor of self-loathing, drained and miserable. I had succeeded in one way by pushing Danny to the back of mind, only to trade it for images of my hysterical little girl and the rest of my shameful life. I found a hotel and tried to sleep. It was useless.

***

I could not check the ugly images, or the racing questions they provoked: *How could I do all those things? How could I live with it? Why didn't I make things right? Why didn't I change? Why was I here? Why, when so many were in the pit?*

The pitiful truth of my life was a parade of sin and debauchery completely unworthy of even the tiny shack in paradise I'd been gifted. How could I stomach my existence here while others burned? I jumped out of bed and fell to my knees. "Lord," I prayed aloud, "trade me for someone in the pit."

I felt the heat immediately, even before I heard the screams and the moans and the cursing. It was a thick, intense heat that hung in the air like clear soot from some great, invisible chimney, and left me gasping for breath. Then I felt the anguish, a feeling of unimaginable loneliness and despair—a feeling like coming off a cocaine binge, multiplied a thousandfold, an emptiness so excruciating I begged to get out of there even before I opened my eyes.

***

When I did finally open them, I was sorry. I saw a scene like an insane asylum in one of the horror films I once dragged poor little Sophie to. I'd landed in a dark and cavernous room, pocked with darker tunnels in every direction, swarming with all manner of flying insect. People, if you want to call them that, were wandering aimlessly, pulling at their hair, picking their skin, grinding their teeth, spitting and cursing, and exhibiting other signs of madness. They were naked, covered in boils and open sores, their eyes wide as half dollars, darting and vacant, as if they were searching for something they knew they could never find.

I became frantic, my begging turned to a scream. The people around me laughed. I screamed louder; they laughed louder. I began sobbing hysterically; a group of hellions surrounded me. I put my hands to my face, and that's when I felt the worn hands of an old man and realized I was back in my old Earth body.

Then those miserable creatures were upon me. They scratched and clawed and punched and kicked and pulled at my naked flesh. The pain was excruciating, and all I could do was beg them to finish me off, but just as soon as they tore a chunk of flesh out of me, it would heal into a puss-filled boil, and I realized there was no death here either. "Please, Jesus!" I cried. "Help me! Please, help…" My heroic sacrifice had lasted exactly twelve seconds.

***

Even before I finished begging, the unbearable heat diminished, and the boils on my skin began to retract. The flesh-tearing Hell zombies suddenly stopped their violent attack, recoiling with fear as they backed away. I was glowing again, and within a few moments, I had my new body back.

Gone was the anguish and pain. I was still in the pit but back in my new body, protected and actually feeling a bit of joy, or was it simply relief?

But this lasted only a moment. I was still in that horrible place, nervous and frightened, and the misery before me tore at my heart. I wanted out, but I took account of the situation. I could function in my new body down there, and I somehow knew I could leave at any time. And although I had been foolish to think I could trade my life in the

295

New Kingdom for even five minutes of anyone's miserable existence in that wretched place, I knew I needed to stay for some reason. And it came to me in an instant. I had to try and do something for at least one poor soul down there.

***

And I had one name in mind. It was Justin Lister, my old friend and partner in business and other crimes. He helped me get out of the city when I needed him. He saved my life. I had to find him. Justin could talk anyone into anything, but he couldn't talk himself out of this place.

It was a futile venture, I supposed. There were reasons nobody came out of this place, but I had to try. I launched my new body into a frantic search. I picked a tunnel and moved as quickly as I could to find him. I didn't want to be down there any longer than I had to.

Around every corner, always, in the distance, I could see the orange glow of what I thought must be a great fire, and instinctively avoided the direction from which it seeped because I somehow knew going there would lead me to Lucifer himself.

Aside from this avoidance, I had no clue of what direction I should travel, and it didn't take long before I realized I needed help in this seemingly endless maze of tunnels and lost souls. So I prayed, "Help me find him, Lord." And just like that, I knew where I was headed, unconsciously taking lefts and rights like I was heading to the corner store in one of my old neighborhoods.

I must have passed fifty thousand people in every manner of dysfunction before I came to the opening of a larger cavern. It was fairly dark inside, most of the light coming from the glow of my own body, but I could make out a figure sitting on the ground, legs spread, chin on chest, back up against the cavern wall.

"He told me you'd be coming." I heard his voice, now only a dull, scratchy, deeper version of the clear and excited voice I listened to for so many hours on the old Earth.

"Who told you?" I said. I was close enough to see him now. He was barely recognizable, thin and wretched, his skin yellow and full of sores. His face was worn like it had been dragged across gravel and healed under a hot lamp. His lips were bloody and cracked, his eyes red as lipstick.

"You think you're the only one with supernatural friends," he snarled.

"What are you doing, old friend?"

"Waiting for you," he offered through the grinding of his teeth.

"With your life, Justin, your life!"

He laughed then, and it was genuine laughter—the only genuine laughter I heard since I'd been down there.

"You still have choices," I said.

"Look at you and your fancy body. I have choices? A thousand years I have to be in this hole. What do you know?"

"I know what's going to happen," I said.

"You know everything up there, don't you?" said Justin. "Well, we got a little surprise for you!"

"You can't win. You saw what happened on the old Earth. And how do you think you got down here anyway?"

He stood up, pointed a long, bony finger at me and began shouting. "You piece of shiny garbage! You're trying to sell me...I do the selling around here, remember! You wannabe saints up there think you got it all figured out! You're just puppets to Him! Free will my ass! When the real man takes over—then we'll have some free will, baby!"

"Listen to yourself, Justin, this isn't you. He's already got you. You're miserable down here. You've already ground half your teeth away. Look at your skin; you look like a leper, man. Please, Justin. Think for a minute. You were a conniving son of a gun, but you always had a big heart. Why do you think I stuck around? You never talked like this."

His shoulders slumped, and he seemed, for a moment, to be taking it all in. Lifting his head, he fixed his eyes at me. They were just as vacant as before but somehow meaner, and he began a string of vile cursing so twisted and overblown, it would have been comical had it not been so tragic. I knew then it was futile. He was lost. I gave him a pitiful look, and he came toward to me, fists flying and feet kicking. I stood my ground, while the new body easily absorbed the blows.

"This is what you'll be facing up there, my friend. Please, Justin, think for a moment...." But he kept punching and kicking, until he fell to the ground from exhaustion.

"You think you're some kind of superman! You don't know his power. Wait till you meet *my* king...." He couldn't finish his rant. He was hissing and spitting and out of breath.

I turned from him, demoralized and full of heartache. Still, I had to try. Crying, I turned back and rushed him, grabbing him in a bear hug. "Stop, Justin...please, Justin, think about it!"

He struggled. "Get away from me!"

I held tight for a while longer, but it was no use. The curses continued long after I let him go.

***

I walked slowly back to the mouth of the cavern. I had seen more than enough of this place. "Jesus, take me back," I prayed. Immediately, I felt a rush of cold air. My eyes were open, but it was too bright to see anything. After a long minute, the hotel room came into view, and I fell to the bed to forget.

***

It was still snowing when I left the hotel the next day. There were children everywhere, laughing and playing in the fine white powder. I thought about Justin and all he would miss. I was still quite shaken and sad about it, but I knew something now—it was his choice; it had always been his choice. He had been making bad choices ever since I knew him. I always told him he had a big heart; I used to think it was true. I would tell my wife that, every time she asked me to stay away from him. Now I knew it wasn't true. It had never been true. There were moments, sure, but it was always about him in the end, and so he would always make the easiest choice, the one that was the most self-gratifying in the moment, no matter who got hurt.

Faced as he was with 900 plus years down there, he would please his new master to make things easier for himself. And so he was doomed. Still, I vowed to give it one more shot when they came up for the last battle. Maybe the fresh air up here would knock some sense into him. I was still full of stupid ideas, even in paradise.

I thought, too, about what self-serving and wishful thinking it had been to have asked to take someone's place down there. Even if it were possible, I didn't have the courage to go through with any of it. Everywhere I turned, someone had been telling me to stop dwelling

298

on the past, to move forward, to accept my redemption, to forgive myself. I still wasn't sure how, but I was determined to make it happen.

I'd always run from my problems on the old Earth. I'd wander frantically like the rat I was, pacing in my giant cage of self-denial, searching for a way out…anything to make me feel better without acknowledging the real and confining issue.

Even this trip to New Jerusalem had been just another attempted escape. Had anything really changed in me? After all I'd been through, after all I had witnessed? What was I running from now? The future? The coming judgment? God?

And why wouldn't I face Danny? Face the horrible thing I had done? We both knew I was a coward. So what was I afraid of? Danny would forgive me. She always did. So what was it? Was I kidding myself that she didn't already know what had happened after she left me on the mountain? She could have looked it up. Heck, she could have watched it over and over again at the Theater of History. And so what? Danny was Danny—she would forgive no matter what. Still, I couldn't go to her. I needed to, but I couldn't. Why?

***

I found a bench where I could watch the kids playing in the snow. Normally, I would have joined them. Sophie and I would play with the children in her neighborhood for hours and hours when I visited, chasing them through the orange grass, playing hide and seek in the bright green woods. I never felt like an adult playing with children in the New Kingdom. I was one of them, completely, while we played.

Where was the child in me now, innocent and free? That child came and went like old Earth memories playing hide and seek in my head. I didn't want to face Danny because I would have to come to her as a child, real and shamelessly exposed, ready for her open arms. And she would provide them. But I was too ashamed. My pride wouldn't let me go to her.

Still, I had already told everyone else who would listen that I was a coward, that I was a creep and a liar on the old Earth, that I was a bad parent, a loser. She already knew. So why not face her? Why not get it over with?

***

299

A little girl packed a snowball and threw it at an older boy. He laughed, packed his own, firing it her way. It missed her and hit me smack between the eyes, exploding harmlessly like feathers in a pillow fight. I laughed.

"Sorry, sir!" said the boy.

"No worries," I said.

"Do you want to play?" he asked.

"Oh, thank you, but no—perhaps some other time."

He packed and threw another snowball toward a group of his mates. I watched. All the kids joined, snowballs flying in every direction. The game was on. And I thought: *Same old George, still playing games, except nobody to play with anymore.*

I laughed again, this time at myself. I laughed hard and hysterically. I laughed so long the kids even stopped their friendly battle to look at me. Then they began to laugh, so I laughed even harder.

***

My dad told me once: *"Never trust a man who can't laugh at himself."* I had forgotten about that. I had forgotten so much. I needed to see him again. The last time had been so formal, as if two strangers were meeting for the first time. I needed to talk to him, to tell him I was sorry, to tell him I appreciated the things he had done for me.

***

Then, watching the children, it came to me. I stopped laughing. The children's laughter died out as they went back to their game, but they were still smiling. Except their smiles were somehow different—they seemed to know I had learned something, some great truth about myself, perhaps, and this made them happy.

All this time, I had been paying lip service to my sins, my faults, my cowardice, as if by the very telling of them, by my vacant admonitions, they'd belonged outside my body, to that other George who lived and bore the blame far away from any truth. I could not accept redemption because I could not accept my ugliness. I pretended to, but I could not.

The reason I couldn't face Danny was the same reason I couldn't face Sophie, my father, my mother, my brothers, my sister, or even Renee. I had seen them, but I had never really faced them, come to them as a child. The reason was simple. I had yet to face myself, to

300

look into the mirror other than to check my teeth, my hair, or my skin. These were no acquaintances to be fooled for a time. They were my family, my friends, my loves, my very life. I chose them as my mirror, but I refused to stare into that mirror, to see what they already knew.

I was ashamed of myself, but I wouldn't let myself feel that shame, even before I knew what it felt like. I suspected enough to avoid that feeling on the old Earth at all cost—to lie, run, drown myself in immorality—but I had no idea how horrible that shame was. Not until my last day on the old Earth—the day He came, after Danny was gone. I was hiding in a hole, nearly dead. And He came and He showed me.

***

In the Valley of Armageddon, the Armies of the New World Order waited. Over the horizon, a black mass of unfathomable proportions moved toward the valley. The mass consisted of horses, tanks, artillery, trucks, jeeps, all manner of military vehicle and heavy weaponry. It carried and dragged with it an arsenal of small arms and ammunition of every size and kind.

The black mass swept into the valley like an ocean. As it drew closer, the mass began to take shape in the eyes of the soldiers who waited. It soon became clear to them that the bulk of the mass was made up of men. The men were an army from the east. The rumors were true. The army was the largest ever amassed. The great army numbered two hundred million.

***

The armies of the New World Order, gathered from every corner of the Western world, were just as formidable. What they lacked in manpower, they made up for in weaponry. Besides, backed by Satan and his legions of powerful demons, they had a supernatural advantage. Also, on their side, unbeknownst to the Eastern army commanders, waiting above the thick clouds, thousands of alien spacecraft hovered. Only Satan wasn't ready to turn them loose. He held them back, biding his time, waiting for the right moment, waiting to give yet another army time to arrive.

***

Still, when the Army of the East got too close, the Antichrist gave the order, and his artillery batteries began to fire at the great mass of men. The barrages, though obviously devastating to the soldiers blown to pieces, barely made a dent in their numbers. The Army of the East continued toward the center of Armageddon relatively unperturbed.

And when the armies were close, both sides began to fire their weaponry at will. Explosions ripped through the valley, while the screams of the torn and battered soldiers filled the air with one horrible hymn of pain and death. Before even one vehicle or soldier reached the other army, hundreds of thousands of men were dead. And when the armies finally did clash, a bloodbath ensued that would make Antietam Creek, the Somme, and Stalingrad seem like cage matches.

***

The carnage continued throughout the day in the Valley of Armageddon. Millions were dead and dying on the battlefield. The bodies began to stack up, the blood soaked the ground until it could take no more, pooling at the feet of the fighters and the bodies of the fallen.

The fighting grew close. Heavy weapons became useless at such ranges. Unable to stabilize because of atmospheric and gravitational conditions caused by the asteroid strike, all manmade aircraft had long been grounded. Without air support or heavy ground weapons, the battle raged soldier-to-soldier, old school, violent, brutal, unforgiving.

One million, two million, five million, twenty million, fifty million—the body count mounted. The blood became a river, and as John had foreseen, it filled the valley until it flowed neck deep amid the bodies, while the men continued to thrash one another like sharks in a crimson sea.

***

God had seen enough. It was time. The gift of light and love, millions of years of creation, life, history, purpose, truth, coming to a head. So much time gone by, so many lives lived, yet a moment in the scheme of things—so important, but still a moment. And without interference, without His army of angels, without one final battle, the armies of the Earth would massacre each other until not a one—not one soldier, not one soul was spared.

***

The clouds began to part. Satan, sitting comfortably behind the battle lines in the body of the Antichrist, smiled to himself. He called for twelve of his favorite demons to possess the generals of the Army of the East. He ordered every soldier and every weapon in the valley redirected toward the sky. He called down the alien ships to hover above the valley floor and to point their powerful weapons toward the parting clouds. He called up his demon cohort, ordering them to strategic positions.

Impressed by the armies he'd amassed, he felt confident. He had waited so long for this moment. This was his time, he thought. Finally, he would take his rightful place as supreme ruler of the universe.

***

It was over in less than five minutes. And Satan knew he was finished as soon as the clouds parted and Jesus appeared, surrounded by the Archangels and legions more of the great winged creatures following. It was an overwhelming spectacle of force, even for the battle-hardened Prince of Darkness. And for the first time since his creation, he was afraid.

***

The aliens and their ships, the mass of ground weapons, many more soldiers, the throngs of demons, Satan himself—all went down before any of them could fire a single round, like so many cans on a fence. And only those soldiers who threw down their arms were spared. The Battle of Armageddon was finished.

***

The Second Coming was upon us. I was nearly dead by then and wishing I were. Curled up in a hole I'd dug under a rock, I hid from the heat and the Minions, and from my guilt.

It was silly to be afraid of the Minions. Most were away preparing for the Battle of Armageddon. Supply chains had been cutoff and rerouted to the front lines. The few left behind to keep order had to fend for themselves, and searching for strays was no longer a priority. But the sun was real, hot and penetrating, exacerbating an already dreadful thirst. I hadn't eaten, either, in so many days I'd lost count. When I could have hunted or trapped something to eat, I was too depressed to be hungry. By the time I came around, it was too late. I had sealed my fate. I couldn't have gone down as a martyr then even if I'd wanted to. I was too weak. No, I would starve to death or die of thirst in the grave I'd dug for myself.

The heat of the day was brutal, the cold at night unbearable. Except when passing out from exhaustion for an hour here or there, I didn't sleep. I prayed for death for the second time in so many months, only this time I wouldn't be treated with a visit from any demon. They were busy.

***

I'm not sure how long I was in the hole, but I was dying. That much I knew. I was a skeleton, licking rocks for moisture, my breaths few and shallow. I wanted to go; I begged to go, and yet I held on. One more day, then two, then a third—it wasn't possible. Then one morning I heard a great sound, a huge explosion of sorts, but this was no bomb. I was familiar with that sound. This sound was quite different. This sound was everywhere and nowhere at the same time. No, it wasn't a weapon, more like a great thunder or blast from a trumpet of unfathomable proportions.

***

I was in fear of it. But not like I'd feared the Minions. This was a strange and unfamiliar feeling, a feeling of nakedness that made me curl up even tighter. My eyes were buried in my hands, my head pressed beneath the rock above my hole, yet I was seeing a white light, and it seemed to be growing brighter.

Puzzled, I parted my hands to reveal my hole awash in the thick white light. As bright as the light was, it didn't blind me. My eyes absorbed it—my whole body absorbed it. And the fear increased.

But the fear was not simply fear, but something else, something worse. It was the shame I'd been afraid of all my life, and I knew then why I had feared it. The shame was all-consuming, a relentless, unbearable feeling of guilt and remorse that pummeled me from within and crushed me from without. And when I could take no more, when I thought I might go mad from the pressure and weight of my shame, the light began to change and it was over—except for the memory of it, which I would take with me into paradise.

***

As my shame subsided, the light became brighter, and it filled me with something joyful, something extraordinarily good, and something I vaguely recognized. I had known slivers of it at times in my old life, microscopic compared to this, but I had known it—known it when I held Sophie for the first time, known it when she begged me not to leave our home. This was love, big and pure. It was everywhere. My scrawny body quivered and shook until it seemed I could no longer breathe.

***

Then I saw a figure coming toward me in the light, and I could breathe again, though I was still afraid and ashamed and crying even more.

"Who are you?" I said.

"Don't be afraid," said a voice.

At the words, I wasn't afraid anymore, but suddenly calm and completely at peace. Now I could make the figure out. He was sort of like He was pictured in the paintings with the long hair and beard and all, except his skin and hair were darker.

"Forgive me, Lord Jesus," was all I could say.

He walked toward me and placed His hand on my shoulder. I saw the nail wound in His hand as he moved to touch me. And when he touched me, I began to shake again until I couldn't take it and blacked out.

***

Then I was conscious again, standing in a great valley staring at my arms and hands. They were sticking out of a white robe and glowing. I was fixated on them for a moment, until I realized there were people standing next to me, beautiful glowing people in white robes like mine. They were everywhere, thousands of glowing people as far as I could see.

There were men and women and children. The people next to me looked as surprised as I was, except they were all grinning at each other like a bunch of dorks. Then I realized I had a big dorky grin on my face, too. And I began laughing, and many other people were laughing, too. It was wonderful; I felt wonderful.

My body was my body, but it was new. I wasn't beat up anymore. I wasn't emaciated. I wasn't hungry or thirsty either. Neither was I afraid.

I felt strong, eager. It seemed I was young again, perhaps in my twenties, I thought, and I had this weird light in me that came through my skin and made my body glow. I thought for a moment it must be a dream, but it was too real and it didn't end.

***

Then there was that sound again, that great thunder that filled the air throughout the valley and into the sky. Everybody looked up, and I looked up, too. There were clouds rolling and parting and reforming in all directions. The sky between the clouds was a color of blue I didn't recognize. I glanced downward slightly, toward the mountains, and I realized their colors were odd, too. There were browns and greens in weird tones on those mountains, and strange vegetation with oranges, purples, and reds that were beautiful, but not like any nature I had ever known.

***

Another blast of sound like a trumpet startled me from my sightseeing, and I looked back to the sky to a giant patch of clouds rolling apart like a scroll. Two winged men, much brighter than any of the people, appeared on either side as if they had pulled the clouds apart. These could only be angels of God, their great wings flapping behind them. Such beautiful creatures, in human form but larger and more magnificent. They wore short tunics, baring animal-like muscles on every visible appendage. They moved like animals, too, with such ease and grace.

Through the parting clouds, more appeared, legions of winged angels soaring down upon us with speed and finesse, hovering and landing among us. They smiled at our excitement and looked back toward the sky.

This next part did seem like a dream (and does to this day) but when the last angel touched ground, another trumpet sounded and from the opening in the clouds, the Lord God Himself appeared.

***

We walked for a long time, the masses and I, down the gold highway, past cities and villages, past orchards and farms. We moved in shocked silence, in awe, not of the wondrous New Kingdom, but of having seen the face of God.

***

Our masses diminished slightly with each forgotten step as people broke from the pack on smaller roads and trails, across open fields and over hills and mountains. To our new dwellings we traveled, without map or compass, guided by an unseen navigator, like birds returning home.

31

I stayed on the bench long after the children had quit their games. A certain peace settled over me. My shame was upon me, but it wasn't as heavy as before, buried as it had been under so many pounds of denial. I had lent easy names to my sinful nature—liar, cheater, thief, gambler, coward, and on and on—but I had failed to own up to the facts. So, in that sense, I had admitted nothing. There was an expression on the old Earth: *The devil is in the details.* I had to see Danny. It was time for her to meet the devil in me.

***

I headed toward the Great Pyramid to see if I could find her again. It was a huge place, and I didn't know her job title or anything, but I figured someone must know her there. And perhaps, since she seemed to be working with the Apostle Paul, she would be easy to find.

***

As I walked, I thought about how I would tell her about that day. The old George was already back to work editorializing. I shook my head. I just needed to lay it out for her, exactly as it occurred. And so I began to let myself remember. I continued toward the pyramid, flinching as the images of that awful day played in my head.

***

I cursed Danny after she went down the mountain to die. I was terrified for her, but mostly for myself, so I masked the fear with anger. I paced around the camp, wringing my hands, the expectant father of indecision. I'm not sure how long I waited, just long enough, I suppose, to remain noncommittal, if need be. Then, when it was too late, I ran down the mountain to find her.

***

The nearest town was about five miles away. We didn't even know the name of it. Danny and I had done some reconnoitering in the hills above the town soon after our departure from the wasteland left in the wake of the asteroid. We decided to leave it alone because there was at least a platoon of Minions stationed there, and the town was so small that any pilfering would have been quickly discovered and met with another Minion search party. We couldn't chance it. We didn't have any caves to hide in, and besides, Danny, with her uncanny intuitions, was keeping us fairly well fed.

***

I heard the commotion as soon as I reached the edge of the town. I sidled up against an old tire shop and peered around the corner. I couldn't see where the commotion was coming from, but what I did see shocked me. It wasn't at all the same well-oiled New World Order city we had seen from the hills only months before, the clean and pressed Mark-bearers going about their business with rosy cheeks and nary a care in the world, protected as they were by equally content and polished Minions.

No, the town before me now was like a scene from the film *Mad Max,* about a cop shooting his way through an apocalyptic and nightmarish landscape. There were cars everywhere, some with their hoods up, most with their gas doors open. Between the cars, the streets were full of garbage: empty cans and broken bottles, plastic containers and empty boxes, cleaned bones and rotting animals. And then there were the people.

The people were a mess. I came out from behind the building. I no longer feared discovery. I fit right in with them—a few haggard young women, but mostly older folks, unkempt and unshaven, their marks hidden beneath layers of grime, their clothes spent and hanging, their faces gaunt, their eyes vacant as if their minds existed in another place.

***

309

Their leader had failed them, the promised utopia of the New World Order now a distant dream, as faint and despicable as the Third Reich. Like Hitler, the Antichrist had ultimately stripped his kingdom, drafting anyone who could fight, leaving the cities and towns mostly to their own devices, gathering almost every resource for his last hopeless battle.

***

The people moved slowly but with purpose. They were headed toward the commotion. I eased into their staggered flow as they turned a corner. There was already a crowd in the middle of the street. They were watching something, shouting obscenities and threats, waving their weak fists with halfhearted excitement and a reluctant bloodlust, like fallen Roman citizens in a crumbling coliseum.

I knew it was Danny behind the crowd, but I pushed through to be sure. Any heroic thought I might have had while coming down the mountain was quashed the minute I saw her.

Kneeling and broken, yet somehow clutching her Bible, she was unrecognizable, but for one tiny corner at the tail of her blue flannel shirt not yet covered in blood. Her head and face, black, blue, and dark red, were spotted with swollen lumps like some forbidden alien planet. Three Minions in faded jumpsuits stood over her holding heavy wooden batons.

"Denounce your God!" ordered one of the Minions, his voice firm yet somehow panicked at the same time.

"Forgive...please forgive...Jesus...." she mumbled.

Any real man would have jumped to her defense, would have protected her, would have thrown his body over hers to block the blows. At the very least, he would have said something.

I was too afraid even to blink. Everything I already knew about myself was true. I couldn't move. I couldn't speak. I was a coward. The brave Danny, through torn lips and broken teeth, managed to forgive them, while George Somerset stood frozen, protecting himself, as always, until a last blow struck her dead.

***

Slinking from the crowd, tears pouring down my face, I moved quickly, staring at the ground, as much to avoid discovery as to cover

310

my deep shame. Still, a woman noticed and grabbed hold of my shoulder. I looked up at her.

"You knew her?" she said.

"No," and I immediately thought of the Apostle Peter; I could almost hear a cock crow.

"Why are you crying? She's an enemy of the New World Order!" she said, and took my grimy wrist, turning it over to examine.

I tore it from her grip, moving away from her as fast as I could walk. When I looked back, she was conversing with some men in the crowd. I took off running.

**

At the Last Supper, Jesus took Peter aside, informing His disciple he would betray Him before the morning cock crowed. Peter protested, proclaiming his unwavering loyalty to his Messiah, even if it meant certain death. That very evening, Peter denied even knowing Jesus—not once, but three times.

Peter would be given other opportunities to prove his loyalty. He would go on to build the Christian church, face death on many occasions, and ultimately martyr himself. Redemption was always on the table. God was a good guy like that.

**

I had been given at least one more opportunity at redemption myself. I could have done something right. I could have gone for my Bible. I could have brought it back to that miserable town to scream my faith. I could have demanded a proper burial for my friend. I could have at least gone back to say a small prayer over Danny's broken body. What did I do? I crawled into a hole, curled up, and waited for the end of the old world.

**

I was in front of the Great Pyramid much sooner than I expected, more likely sooner than I wished. My feet felt heavy moving up the long staircase. By the time I reached the top, a measure of shame had returned. I kept on. *It had to be today.*

**

As soon as I saw the first station of the cross, I was moved again,

311

but this time I felt not overwhelming sadness, but a flash of hope, so I kept going.

I spotted the information desk where a smiling woman attended a short line of tourists. I waited until it was my turn.

"I'm looking for somebody," I said.

"A particular apostle? A saint, perhaps?" she said.

"A woman…I think she works here."

"Her name?" she said.

"Her name?" I said.

"Yes, her name?"

I stumbled. I hadn't said her name out loud for so long that I wasn't sure I could. "Danny…Danielle…Danielle Knowles," I finally managed.

Her smile grew wider. "You know Danielle?"

"Yes…I do…well, I did…from before."

"Isn't she great?"

"Yes, she is…. She is great."

"She's not here."

"Oh…"

"She's off today."

"Do you know where I might find her?"

"I don't know…maybe at home."

"Where's that?"

She paused, but only for a moment, as if still vaguely aware of old Earth customs regarding privacy and confidentiality. "The Tower," she said.

"The Tower?" I asked.

"You can't miss it…it's only the tallest building on the planet," she said. There was still a tiny bit of sarcasm to be had, even in paradise.

"Thank you."

**

I ran for her, ran like I should have down the mountain to join her that day. I thought if I didn't run, I might just change my mind, go away sulking for a few more years, try again later. After all, I had eternity.

I didn't stop running until I was in front of the Tower. When I had pictured Danny before, it was on an estate, something similar to my daughter's place, with wild horses and great fields of orange grass. But I should have known. Danny was a city girl at heart. After she left the fields of her home in Iowa, beyond her forced sojourn in the mountains, she would have little to do with the country. And now, looking up, I pictured her lounging on a velvet couch in a silk bathrobe, in a spectacular top floor penthouse with 360-degree views, and believed it silly to imagine her anywhere else.

***

I found her name on the directory and pressed the buzzer. She didn't say hello. She didn't ask who I was. Only this came out of the speaker: *It's about time, George, come on up!*

***

I nearly cursed the lightning-fast elevator that carried me the 200 floors for not giving me time even to digest her flippant greeting. The elevator stopped, not quite at the top, but pretty close. I must be right about the views though, I thought; hers was the only penthouse on the floor. I stepped into the large foyer, filled with a large selection of indoor plants. She wasn't ignoring nature altogether. I spotted the door, approaching it to rap the silver handle, but it was open before I could take two steps, and we were face to face again.

***

"George Somerset, as I live and breathe!" She moved to embrace me. She was way too happy to see me, and it only made me feel worse. I tried to step back into the elevator, but the door had already closed. Then her arms were around me and she held me tight.

I tried to move away. She held on. "No, Danielle, I'm a coward…a Judas," I said.

She giggled. "Always so dramatic, George." She held my face. "Look at me. I love you George—and you saved our lives…."

"You don't know, Danielle."

"Would you quit calling me Danielle—you're my friend. You found the cave. You took us in. We were lost, thirsty and starving…you knew how to survive. You fed us, you taught us…you saved my son…."

I felt only shame; I began to sob.

313

"No, George, will you stop?" She led me inside and sat me on her couch.

"You don't know. I was there...I didn't stop it." I looked up. She wore a plaid dress with an oversized knitted sweater. Her hair was tied carelessly, but I could see her neck, and it reminded me of our days on the mountain. I closed my eyes and the tears came harder. When I opened them, she was smiling. I didn't understand. "You were murdered, right in front of me. They were hurting you so bad...I didn't do a thing..."

She sat next me, rubbing my shoulder. She didn't say anything for a long time. Then she spoke: "I knew you were there. I was sad for you to have to see it, but I felt you and it gave me strength."

"Sad for me? I'm a coward."

"I made the choice. It wasn't for you to jump in and stop it. You're not a coward. You're just normal. I didn't think it through. If I had...If I'd known what was coming, I wouldn't have been able to go down there. You were the practical one. That's what kept us alive for so long."

"A lot of good it did everyone."

"Every minute of life is precious. More than anyone...you believed that. Of course you're not perfect. You have to stop beating yourself up. That's an old Earth mistake...that's what kept people from becoming closer to God...kept them on the same path...kept them sinning. Look at you now, George—you might be the most miserable person in paradise. You still haven't let go. You thought you could stop sinning, you thought they were your sins to beat; you never could and they never were. Accept it—they are His to bear—this is the only freedom there is."

"That's what I came here to do. I came to come clean—to tell you everything."

"I know...and it means everything that you came. I don't want the details. Close your eyes. Give it to God."

***

I sat praying for a long time, praying and crying until my tears were spent. I felt lighter. I sat back on the couch and opened my eyes. It was first time I noticed the view. The window encompassed an entire wall of the living room, one flawless pane of lightly tinted glass, beyond it

314

the shining beauty of New Jerusalem, beyond that, the magnificently odd colors of paradise stretching for miles to the sea. "Wow!" was all I could get out.

She elbowed me and smiled her infectious, self-pleasing grin. "Pretty sweet pad, huh?" she said.

I finally managed to smile. "Not bad."

"Not bad? Worth a few little smacks from the Minions I'd say—don't you think?" she laughed. I frowned. "C'mon…will you stop already? What, did you want me to listen to every gruesome detail? It was bad enough the first time."

"No, I guess not."

She mussed up my hair like she often did on the old Earth. "You look good, George. Not like that old man I knew on the mountain."

"*You* look amazing."

"Thanks," she said.

I put my head down, thinking about that day again. I couldn't help myself.

"It's okay, George; this isn't going to happen overnight. You're making progress. Your light is a little brighter than it was the other day."

"I *knew* you saw me at the lecture," I said.

"I did. So what?"

"I couldn't face you. See—I am a coward."

"No…just a big wimp," she said and laughed at me.

"Yes…that's exactly what I need…you to quit being nice to me—to give me the grief I deserve. Please…keep going," I said.

"That's not what you need, George. But I know what you do need." She took my hand. "Follow me."

32

She held my hand as we walked the golden streets. The snow had mostly melted. It was a bright and glorious day. "Where are you taking me?" I said.

"It's a surprise."

"I don't know if I can take any more surprises here. I've had a few already."

"All the visitors do, George."

"They do?"

"They all have their reasons for coming."

"And what was my reason?"

"You came to see *me*, of course," she said, grinning.

***

We walked beside the Great Pyramid. "So you work here?" I said.

"Yes."

"Amazing place... What do you do exactly?"

"I guess I'm a counselor of sorts. After one of the apostles speaks, I talk to people."

"I should have guessed. You're perfect for that. I suppose I'm your client today."

"You're my friend," she said, and she gave me a rap on the head with her knuckle. "But you do need help up here."

"I won't argue," I said.

"A lot of people come here for help—most don't wait so long the first time."

"I had a lot on my mind."

She smiled. "Seriously, though, George—eight years!"

"I know...huh."

"And in all that time, you didn't visit any of the others."

"You know everything, don't you? How *is* Roger?"

"He's really good. He's so different, so smart. You wouldn't believe it. He lives in Tent City." She was beaming.

"I was there...I could have seen him...I'm sorry."

"And you should meet Speckle. Well, actually, his name is Albert. He's so nice...so happy. You have to meet him," she said.

"I know."

"It's silly. They're your friends, George. They miss you. They say only good things about you."

"Maybe that's what I'm afraid of...."

***

It was almost noon and the streets filled as more visitors poured into the city. We crossed the street behind the Great Pyramid. Things became familiar. I'd been down these streets before. We were near my hotel. I felt uneasy.

"Promise me you'll go see them."

"I said I would. Will you go with me?"

"Yes," she groaned, "I'll go with you, little child."

I grinned. "Thanks."

***

We walked further, turned a few corners. I knew where we were headed even before I saw it. I shivered when I did. We were in the shadow of the Theater of History. I stopped.

"You're taking me *here?*" I said.

"Yes, George," she said.

"I've already been here, Danny."

"I know that."

"You're like the New Jerusalem secret police or something. Did you bug my hotel room yet?"

She just laughed and pulled me along with her. "Come on, George!"

"I didn't exactly have the best experience the last time."

"This will be different."

"It was pretty awful."

She kept her smile, all the while dragging me toward the theater. "The truth can be painful," she said.

"I'll say. Are you sure about this?" I said.

"This will be a different kind of truth."

***

We took our tickets and moved past the concession stands. "Popcorn?" she joked.

"No, thanks."

The place was busy. We had to go all the way to the far end of the building to find an empty theater. Once inside, my apprehension intensified. "Relax," she said, "it will be just fine."

"If you say so," I said.

"Trust me."

I looked at her. Even in the darkness, she looked radiant, her glow reflecting off her lovely smile. It put me at peace, and I was even happy for a moment.

She didn't fumble with the keyboard and the little screen as I had. She just spoke, and as she did her words came across the large screen: *In the beginning was the Word, and the Word was with God, and the Word was God.*

***

Nobody on the old Earth could understand the beginning; understand how something came from nothing. Scientists with their Big Bang Theory as the starting point always made me cringe because many of them would avoid stepping backwards to ask where the material came from to create the Big Bang in the first place. Not to do that, not to ask that, went against every tenet of science; and yet, volumes were filled with so-called proofs by important scientists on the Big Bang and the forming of the universe and creation of earth and evolution while ignoring the question any first grader would have

318

asked: *"Well, where did that stuff come from?"*

Why couldn't these scientists just admit some things went beyond human understanding? Admit there was such a thing as a miracle? This was reason lost once again on the old Earth—Satan was able to blind many intellectuals because of their pride.

***

As the little light left in the theater grew dimmer, I took one last look at Danny. "Trust me," she said.

I turned back toward the screen. So engrained was I in old Earth creation documentaries, I half expected the screen to light up with footage from one of my grade school science classes—stars exploding, volcanoes erupting and whatnot. Instead, the screen seemed only to be getting darker.

I became fixated on the blackness. The screen *was* getting darker, blacker and blacker by the second, so black it began to absorb every last bit of light in the room. All of my light, even the bright light of Danny, was no more. It frightened me, the pitch black, a feeling like drifting gradually down some endless hole. She squeezed my hand. If she hadn't been there I would have bolted.

The screen was no longer distinguishable from the rest of theater, which was just as black, and quiet as death—this was the blackest black and the deepest silence I had ever known. Danny squeezed harder and broke the silence. "Trust me," she said again.

I was only slightly calmer. Then something—I felt something or heard something or saw something—I couldn't tell which. The something was there and it wasn't, but it grew until, nearly imperceptibly, it was... And that something became a kind of warmth, or a whisper, or a tiny, tiny speck of white light; I don't know what came first, the whisper, the light, or the warmth, maybe all of it.

Danny let go of my hand, and the warmth began to take hold of me, the speck of white light began to glow, and the whisper began to form a sound I couldn't exactly hear and didn't understand. Then I thought I heard the sound, and I thought I understood for a moment. Except the sound wasn't really a sound. It was more like a warming thing than a sound. And I felt the warmth was a kind of joy. That's the only way I can explain it, and that the light was the energy feeding the warmth and the joy.

But it didn't become hot, though, or even warmer, if that makes sense. But the joy that was the warmth seemed to grow. The joy was alive; it had life. It *was* life, I somehow knew. It began to expand. And the whisper became louder, but only slightly. The whisper became a word, and the word and the life were the same.

I can't explain it any more than that, but the word was becoming clearer, whispered to me now over and over again, rushing through me, just as the warmth and joy and life rushed through me, and the light came through us and from the screen and around us. It filled the room, and it filled us, until we were full and lighter than ever before.

And the warmth and the joy were the same as the light, the same as the word, whispered it seemed, but also inside of me. The word was the joy and the light. The word was both goodness and hope. The word was everything—everything important, everything necessary, everything good. The word was God. And it was so much more. The word was love.

***

Outside the theater, in the sunlight, the two of us stood, Danny smiling like she almost always did, but with me smiling just as wide for a change. I was calmer and happier than I'd ever been.

"I told you so," she said.

"You've been waiting eight years to say that," I said. "Do you take everyone there?"

"Only the real desperate cases," she said, and she laughed.

"Thanks…I mean that…really, thanks."

"Look at you, George…you're brighter, even in the sunlight."

"I am?"

"Yes…a little brighter. You see what can come from nothing, from blackness. Nothing is enough. And you've always had light in you. Just think how far you can go—and all of us, George, together. Stop looking backward all the time. We need you with us. I want you with me."

"You do?" I was practically gushing.

"Yeah—you're one of the good guys."

"Me—I'm a good guy?"

"Yes…you are."

320

"It's easy to be good here."

"Good is good. It's exactly the same as it was on the old Earth."

"I don't know about that."

"Go look it up. You're always at that library anyway."

I gave her a push. "You *have* been spying on me."

"Someone you know came to visit."

"Sophie?"

"She's a sweetheart."

"Man, I should have known. You two sneaks. She kept insisting I come here."

Danny just smiled.

I shook my head and looked at her for a long time without saying anything. "You know I still have a crush on you?" I finally said.

"Yeah, I know that," she said, and she mussed up my hair again.

We walked away from the Theater of History, down the streets of paradise, two lovers, light and pure and innocent.

***

The next day, I took a high-speed floating train back to my shack. I greeted, wrestled and rolled around with my dogs for a bit, changed clothes, apologized to them for my brief return, and ran all the way to my daughter's house.

***

I couldn't wait to tell Sophie about my trip, and I pounded on the door a little too hard. I heard Wiley bark. It was Renee who answered. Wiley jumped at my legs.

"Take it easy, George," she said.

"Sorry," I said, and I rubbed Wiley's head. "Good boy. Hi, Renee. Where is she?"

"Hello, George. It's good to see you, too," she said.

"I'm sorry—how are you?"

"I'm good, thank you. She's in the fields playing with the children. She's teaching them how to fly."

"She's flying?"

"Yeah—for a couple weeks now. It's pretty neat."

"Flying? No kidding—she's amazing."

"Yeah—I did all right, didn't I?" she laughed.

"You did Renee—you really did," I said, and I meant it.

"Thanks."

"It's nice seeing you," I said. Renee was always good to me—despite everything I put her through. We always chatted awhile when I came to visit Sophie, but I had been away too long and missed our daughter terribly. "Well, I better go find her."

"Wait a second, George. What's going on with you?"

"What do you mean?"

"I don't know. You're not sulking for a change."

"I sulk?" I asked, even though I knew it was true. I just wasn't sure Renee had noticed.

"Yeah, George, you sulk. It's pretty obvious. You're the only one I know who sulks around paradise. And something else, George—you're brighter or something."

"I might be," I said, and I smiled.

"You went to New Jerusalem! Didn't you, George?"

"You can tell?"

"About time," she said.

"Yeah—I should have done it years ago."

She looked at me for a long moment. "Yes—you should have. What made you go, finally?"

"I don't know. Sophie's been asking me for a while. One day, I just woke up and decided to go."

"Just like that?"

"Just like that."

"Well, you look happy, George," she said, and she smiled at me like she hadn't since a lifetime ago on the old Earth. "You'll have to tell me about it sometime.

"I will, Renee. I will."

***

I found her sitting by herself in the tall orange grass. The sun was half gone below the mountains, the children already on their way home. I tried to sneak up on her, but when I got close, she suddenly turned and screamed. I jumped.

"Got me," I said.

"You know you can't sneak up on me anymore," Sophie said.

"I know—you're a ninja with super powers. How are you, sweetheart?"

"Good…I missed you, Dad," she said, and she stood and gave me a hug.

"I missed you."

She looked at me for a moment. "You went—didn't you?"

"I did."

"Why didn't you tell me you were going?"

"I wanted to surprise you."

***

Lying on our backs, we admired the Heavens while I told her about my trip. I told her about Millard and meeting my old Army roommate. I told her about Tent City and my visit to the Great Pyramid, about seeing Danny and my experiences at the Theater of History. I even told her about Justin. She listened wide-eyed like she couldn't believe any of it.

"Boy Dad—I guess if you were going to go, you were going to go big."

"That's not the average trip to New Jerusalem then?"

She laughed.

"You didn't tell me you and Danny were in cahoots."

"Must have slipped my mind," she said and smiled like a busted seven-year-old.

"Slipped your mind," I said. "It's a good thing you're cute."

"She's nice. I like her," she said.

"Yeah, she's all right."

***

I stood, pulling her up to her feet with me. "Your mom said you're flying now; I want to see you fly."

"Dad, I did it a couple times. I can't do it all the time."

"She said you were teaching the kids."

"Just to jump higher is all—they'll fly when they're ready."

"Give it a try, then. I want to see it," I said.

"I'm tired."

"Don't give me that. Fly, will you!"

"It's gonna be dark soon."

"You owe me for that Danny business."

"Dad."

"Fly, girl!"

"Okay, already." And with that she took three quick steps and leapt a good fifty feet into the air like it was nothing, landing a hundred yards or so in the distance.

"That looks like flying to me!" I shouted.

She walked back toward me, blushing and looking at the ground. "Anybody can do that."

"You're holding back—I bet you can go even higher."

"Maybe a little," she said when she reached me.

"Let me see—it's exciting!"

She shook her head.

"Please."

"Okay, okay—one more," she said, and she took off running. When she reached the edge of a low hill, she hurled herself upward, one hundred feet in the air, spread her arms and soared like an angel for at least 200 yards. Then she began to glide, taking three quick, downward spirals, tilting backwards until her feet were under her, landing softly in the orange grass.

"Incredible!" I shouted. I was astonished. I ran to her. "I can't believe it, Sophie!" When I reached her, I scooped her up in a hug and twirled her around a few times before letting her go. "My gosh!" I said. "That was the most amazing thing!"

She laughed and blushed. "Stop, Dad! It's not a big deal—you could do it."

"No way," I said.

"Yes, you can."

"I really doubt it."

She grabbed my hand and led me to the bottom of another low hill.

"Look, just relax—empty that weird head of yours. Clear all those wacky thoughts. Take a deep breath. Picture yourself touching a cloud or something. Take a few quick steps up the hill and jump."

"All right, here goes." I did what she said and managed to get about four feet off the ground. "That's about what I could do in high school," I said.

"Maybe if you were Kobe Bryant," said Sophie. "Come on—clear that head."

I laughed and tried again. This time I jumped about eight feet high, landing twenty feet or so in the distance. It shocked me.

"Nice! See, Dad?"

"Wow—that was pretty cool." I took another few steps, this time I made it about twelve feet off the ground, landing maybe thirty feet away. I leaped again, this time even higher. I kept leaping, higher and farther—over and over again—ever further, leaping and laughing in amazement. Until, glancing over my shoulder, I spotted Sophie, just a blur in the distance.

I stopped and ran back toward her as fast as I could. When I could see her clearly, I shouted: "That was incredible!"

"That was great, Dad!"

It did feel wonderful. "I'm going to keep going. Do you want to come along?" I shouted.

"No, Dad. You go ahead!"

"Come on, honey!"

"You go!"

"I won't be long!"

"All right, Dad!"

"Wait for me!"

"I will!"

"I'll be back!"

"Okay!"

"You sure?"

"Yes, Daddy!"

But I didn't move. I stood there for a long while, looking at her, admiring her. The shadows of dusk isolated a pale stretch of light across her face. She was lovely, a young woman now, but always my little girl. I jumped straight up—ten or twelve feet off the ground. She looked up at me and smiled. I landed.

Still my little Sophie, I thought, and in my heart, she would always be looking up to me for something; something I never gave her. Sure, this was paradise, but I said it before—some things can't be taken back once done. And I know I told you there was no such thing as romantic love. But there was heartbreak. I didn't have to look that one up. I turned away from my little girl, faced the dying sun, and took another leap forward.

Dear Reader:

You would be doing me a great favor by writing an honest review on Amazon. If you click on the link below, it will take you directly to the review page. Either way, thank you so much for taking the time to read the novel. I hope you enjoyed it.

Sincerely,

Todd Stockwell

To write a review—go to:

https://www.amazon.com/review/create-review/?ie=UTF8&channel=glance-detail&asin=B00MG14B1U

Or go to amazon.com, look up the book, and click on the review section.

Give the gift of prophecy. If you enjoyed the book, please share your enjoyment and the message with a beautifully printed copy for friends and family, or just to have for your own library. Available now at a special price.

Go to:

http://www.amazon.com/dp/B00MG14B1U

Or go to amazon.com and type in What the Hand

ACKNOWLEDGEMENTS

I want to first thank my beautiful wife Ana for her love and support all these years.

I would like to thank my editor Cheryl Redman, godsend and rescuer of this book.

I would like to thank my first readers/editors: Karen Lacey, for her fine editing on the first draft. My brother Tracy Stockwell, who meticulously read and edited the first several chapters. My mother and sister, Sharon Stockwell and Teresa Montgomery (love you sis) for letting me know I was getting away from the story too much. Jessica Aouati for her blunt editing advice. Ana for her keen eye. Finally, Sylvia Redman Allen, Andy Meisenheimer, and Charlie Emery for their invaluable editing and critiques.

I thank Jarrod Leitch, "the greatest salesman I've ever met," for his expertise with certain sections of the novel.

Also, my brother, Timothy (Bobo) Stockwell, for coming back from the dead.

Thanks to Mike Ashmore for technical support and editing.

And Jeff Boe for technical support.

To David Lorenz, a great man of God and a real life "Charlie," who took the high road so long ago…

Thanks to my Mom, again, this time for being the most compassionate and generous person I've ever known. I love you.

To the researchers, writers, guests, and hosts, who fuel Coast to Coast AM, for their tireless pursuit of the truth.

To the godfather of modern eschatology, Hal Lindsey.

Forgive me Jesus and please get everyone through.

About the Author

Todd Stockwell was born in Torrance, California. He lives and writes in Southern California. He is a U.S. Army Veteran and has worked as a cab driver, clerk, banker, accountant, psychotherapist, business owner, and traveling salesman among other things. He is also a former high school teacher with an MA in Psychology and a passion for eschatology. Mr. Stockwell can be reached through:

ZFS publishing
40891 Sonata Court
Palm Desert, CA 92260

Or by email:
todd.zfs@gmail.com

www.ingramcontent.com/pod-product-compliance
Lightning Source LLC
Chambersburg PA
CBHW071523260626
47170CB00002B/479